A CRY FROM EGYPT

"Hope Auer's book, *A Cry From Egypt*, succeeds on multiple levels. There are shining examples of young people wrestling with doubts and trying to understand what God is doing. There are delightful examples of healthy families, under difficult circumstances, doing what families do – caring for each other, teasing each other, loving each other. There is romance - young people thinking about marriage and seeking wise counsel – facing the eternal struggles of the course of true love. **As a historian, I particularly admired her portrayal of ancient Egypt in the time of Moses.** We pass too lightly through the list of the ten plagues. We know how the story ends. For those who lived it, it must have been terrifying. They had no idea what would come next, or how the story would end. Miss Auer has done an admirable job of showing us the impact that the dramatic events of the Exodus must have had on ordinary families in Egypt. *A Cry From Egypt* is a great read for young adults from upper middle to high school (and adults could profit by reading it too!)

– Rob Shearer,
Publisher, Greenleaf Press and Director, Schaeffer Study Center

"I seriously have no words that can properly explain everything awesome about this book.** The author, Hope Auer, is a young Christian woman who has an overwhelmingly amazing writing talent! *A Cry From Egypt* is a story like no other I have read."

– Dawn Winters, "Guiding Light Homeschool"

"I have worked as a writing teacher and editor for my entire adult life. I have read more stories from young authors than I can count, but **Hope's work is the first to make me think of JRR Tolkien, CS Lewis, and Frank Peretti when I read it.**"

– Patsy Brekke, "Mrs. B's Bonnet" at WritingFoundations.com

"Hope Auer... achieved the seemingly impossible; in *A Cry From Egypt*, she's written historically (and Biblically) accurate Christian fiction that leaps off the page and captivates the imagination as well as any secular tale... **This is exactly the type of writing that the Christian fiction genre needs.** Not fiction that is preachy, not fiction that is blatant and obvious, not fiction that has a few token things thrown in to make it "seem" Christian – but **fiction that has a Christian heart and soul.**"

– Shawna Bradley, "Tenacity Divine"

"In addition to accurate historical content, I enjoyed knowing that Hope had begun this book when she was a child herself. Reading a book about what children would have experienced from a child's point of view is enlightening. I hope that even more than learning about history, that **it has made my children think about their own faith, about the identity of the God we worship, and about their place in His plan.**"

– Debra Haagen, "Note-able Scraps"

"*A Cry from Egypt* is **one of the best Christian historical fiction novels I have ever read.** I am not exaggerating one bit."

– Hope Jackson, "Homeschooling 3"

"I **highly recommend it for all families** — families that enjoy engaging read-alouds, students wanting to take a closer look at the story of the Israelites' redemption from Egyptian bondage, or homeschoolers looking to add a greater depth of understanding to their Biblical history studies."

– Cristi Schwamb, "Through the Calm and Through the Storm"

"I've said it before and I must say it again. This is my heart's desire to see my children draw near to our Heavenly Father. **I want them to knew the power of GOD and feel His love for them. A Cry From Egypt helps us do just that.**"

– Lynn McInnis, "This Day Has Great Potential"

"My youngest and I read *A Cry From Egypt* and both enjoyed the story. It was **a book that neither of us could put down easily.** Not only does it follow the Biblical account accurately but it adds another dimension to the account making us think more about what happened during that time in history."

– Barbara Campbell, "Alive in Spirit"

"Throughout the story we experience what it was like to actually be there when the plagues were sent. Seeing Aaron and Moses, hearing them tell Pharaoh to "Let the people go". **I cannot describe the feeling that came over me while reading this book. You must get this book and read it with your children.** They will be talking about this for days to come."

– Jan Brandes, "Reflections in the Window"

"**The story really brings the events of Exodus alive!** Jarah's struggle with her faith in the midst of her people's captivity is realistic, and the relation of each plague to a particular Egyptian god is deftly woven into the story and dialogue."

– Kara Haschke, "Home With Purpose"

"*A Cry from Egypt* brought new perspective to my reading of the Exodus account in Scripture. **Good fiction is not just entertaining but enlightening, too. This book met that expectation.** It just seemed to add flesh to the bones of the story. Moses is seen from a distance, but the true focus is on Jarah's family and the struggles of slavery. You know, I've read the story from Exodus many times. I never stopped and imagined just what it was like for the Israelite families. Perspective is everything."

– Laura Lane, "Harvest Lane Cottage"

Route to Sinai

Succoth

Trade Route with Midian

Dry River

Pi-hahiroth

Marah

The Red Sea

Rephidim

Mt. Sinai

A Stand At Sinai

A Stand At Sinai

Book Two of The Promised Land

BY
Hope Auer

ILLUSTRATED BY
Mike Slaton

GREAT WATERS PRESS
MAKING BIBLICAL FAMILY LIFE PRACTICAL

A Stand At Sinai

Scripture quotations taken from the New American Standard Bible® Copyright © 1960, 1962, 1963, 1968, 1971, 1972, 1973, 1975, 1977, 1995 by The Lockman Foundation. Used by permission. (www.Lockman.org)

Text copyright © 2014 Hope Auer. Art, illustrations, and design copyright © 2014 Great Waters Press. All rights reserved.

Publisher's Cataloging-in-Publication Data
Auer, Hope, 1992.
    A Stand At Sinai./ Hope Auer
    p. cm.
    ISBN-10: 1-938554-06-X (trade paperback)
    ISBN-13: 978-1-938554-06-3 (trade paperback)
Egypt – History – To 332 B.C. – Fiction .... 2. Illustrated by Mike Slaton. II. Title.
PZ7. A94 AC 2014 [Fic]

DEDICATED TO MY
ACCOUNTABILITY PARTNERS,
LINDY MEEKER, NAOMI HINDS,
AND ELLIE FAGGION

THANK YOU FOR BEING MY AMISSA AND
MY REIA, MY AARON AND MY HUR,
AND HOLDING UP MY ARMS AND SUPPORT-
ING ME AND LOVING ME AND COMFORT-
ING ME NO MATTER WHAT. GOD GAVE
ME SOME OF THE GREATEST TREASURES IN
THE WORLD WHEN HE GAVE YOU TO ME
AS FRIENDS, CONFIDANTS, AND FELLOW
SISTERS IN CHRIST TO CONSTANTLY POINT
ME TOWARDS CHRIST-LIKENESS. I LOVE
YOU ALL SO MUCH, AND I AM SO
THANKFUL TO HAVE YOU IN MY LIFE!

CONTENTS

CHARACTER LIST & PRONUNCIATION GUIDE
(in order of appearance)

Jarah (JAY rah): The heroine, a young Israelite woman who is traveling with her family towards the Promised Land after the Exodus from Egypt.

Tirzah (TEAR zah): Jarah's little eight-year-old sister, lovable but also a little annoying at times.

Eitan (EE tan): Jarah's older brother at eighteen. He's very mature, kind, and responsible, and is also engaged to Ada.

Ada (A dah): Jarah's sixteen-year-old friend, older sister to Ezra and Amissa, and Eitan's fiance. She used to be a servant to the queen in Egypt.

Asher (ASH er): Jarah's father and their family leader, a firm believer in Yahweh.

Mariel (MAR ee el): Jarah's pregnant mother. She believes in the Egyptian gods and is having a very hard time leaving Egypt.

Lemuel (Lem U el): Jarah's fourteen-year-old brother, her confidant and one of her best friends, and her fearless protector.

Raphael (RAF ee el): Jarah's five-year-old brother, a little mischief-maker.

Yanni (YAN nee): Jarah's two-year-old brother, an adorable and loving little boy.

Manni (MAN nee): One of Ada's seven-year-old twin brothers.

Manuel (MAN u el): Ada's brother and Manni's twin.

Amissa (Ah MEE sah): Jarah's best friend and Ada's younger sister.

Shayna (SHAY nah): Jarah's very pretty, but also proud, older sister.

Ezra (EZ rah): Ada's little brother, and one of Jarah and Lemuel's best friends.

Moses (MOE sus): God's appointed leader of the Israelite nation.

Aaron (AIR ron): Moses' brother.

Joshua (JOSH u ah): Moses' helper and one of the commanders of the army.

Emmitt (EM it): A kind Israelite father who offers to take in Ezra and Jarah when they are lost.

Acenith (Ah SEE nith): Jarah's Egyptian friend who left Egypt and is staying with the Israelites.

Yachne (Yah KEEN): Emmitt's wife and a mother-figure to Acenith and Jarah.

Hava (HA vuh): Emmitt's little daughter.

Yael (YAY el): Emmitt's sickly son, around ten years old.

Adriel (A dree el): Emmitt's fifteen-year-old son, and a good friend to Ezra and Jarah.

The Widow: A sweet elderly lady who gives comfort and good news to Jarah and Ezra.

Chaz: One of the widow's sons.

Sethur (SETH ur): Jarah's grandfather, Asher's father, and one of the elders of the tribe of Asher.

Marnee (MAR nee): Jarah's grandmother and Sethur's wife. A very sweet woman known for her story-telling.

Zuriel (ZUR ee el): Mariel's cousin and only living relative. Her family was taken away from Goshen several years before.

Daton (DAY tohn): Zuriel's husband.

Rishon (REE shon): Daton and Zuriel's seventeen-year-old son, a very reserved but strong young man who is skilled in metal work. He and Shayna were arranged to be married when they were younger.

Jaden (JAY den): Ada and Ezra's father.

Sanne (SANE): Jaden's wife and mother of Ada, Ezra, and Amissa

Joleen (JOE leen): Zuriel and Daton's energetic daughter.

Chanah (CHAY nah): Zuriel and Daton's younger child at six-years-old.

Reia (REE uh): Zuriel and Daton's beautiful thirteen-year-old daughter, sweet and loving, but very shy.

Miriam (MAR ee um): Moses and Aaron's sister.

Hur (her): Miriam's husband and Moses and Aaron's brother-in-law.

Pagiel (PEG ee el): The leader of the tribe of Asher and a friend of Sethur's.

Ennis (EN niss): A friend that Asher meets while traveling.

Cham (CHA am): A man who accuses Asher of stealing.

Uri (UR ee): Hur's son. He takes on Rishon as an apprentice and is very skilled in metal work.

Bezalel (Bez ah LEL): Uri's son and Rishon's co-worker. He's also very skilled in metal work.

Ximena (Zih MEEN uh): Jarah's baby sister, born very sickly and premature.

Mayer (MAY ur): A flirtatious boy and one of Shayna's friends.

Yaphet (YAF ett): A boy in Mayer's little gang of good-for-nothing youths.

Zephon (ZEF on): Another boy in Mayer's little gang of good-for-nothing youths.

Gershom (GER shum): One of Moses's sons.

LIST OF FAMILIES
(ages given at time of the Exodus)

ASHER'S FAMILY:
Asher (father)
Mariel (mother)
Eitan (18)
Shayna (15)
Lemuel (14)
Jarah (almost 13)
Tirzah (8)
Raphael (5)
Yanni (2)

JADEN'S FAMILY:
Jaden (father)
Sanne (mother)
Ada (16)
Ezra (14)
Amissa (12)
Manni and Manuel (7)

EMMITT'S FAMILY:
Emmitt (father)
Yachne (mother)
Adriel (15)
Yael (10)
Hava (4)
Acenith (adopted daughter, 12)

SETHUR'S FAMILY:
Sethur (Jarah's grandfather)
Marnee (Jarah's grandmother)

DATON'S FAMILY:
Daton (father)
Zuriel (mother)
Rishon (17)
Reia (13)
Joleen (9)
Chanah (6)

PREFACE

This book was very hard to write. I don't say that because I didn't enjoy or that I didn't have fun writing it or that I don't believe in the story. Sections of this book came easier than anything I've ever written before! But a few months away from finishing the writing of this book, I actually thought that I might not be able to complete it in the way that I wanted. You see, the lessons that the characters learn in this book are very hard to grasp—lessons I struggle with every day. I realized that I needed to learn these lessons before I could teach them to my characters. And that was hard. Really hard. It was especially difficult to write about facing trials in a time period in which the New Testament of the Bible hadn't been written yet! I hope and I pray that I have really learned these lessons and taken them to heart, and that you will be encouraged and inspired and strengthened in your faith through reading this book.

A Stand at Sinai is the second book in The Promised Land Series and picks up where *A Cry From Egypt* left off, with the Israelites traveling towards the Promised Land. We once again follow Jarah in her quest to learn more about Yahweh and find a new home in the Promised Land. We see the struggles of her family and her friends, watch the Israelites blindly follow the cloud that is Yahweh's presence, and go with them as they experience their first battle.

The lessons that Jarah, Ezra, Amissa, Eitan, Lemuel, and many others learn in the pages of the book is to always trust Yahweh and His plan for their lives, even when it hurts and it doesn't make sense and it doesn't seem like Yahweh is really there or that He really cares about them. The fact is, Yahweh never left them, and He will never leave us. We worship the same God that the Israelites worshipped thousands of years ago! He is just, merciful, loving, kind, compassionate, caring, and a God that is so jealous for our love and a close relationship with Him that He'll even sacrifice His own Son to bring

xvii

us to Himself. Many times we learn that the hard way, but that doesn't mean that God isn't there or that He's left us alone to figure out life by ourselves.

While I once again stayed as true to the Biblical account as I could, it was exciting for me to research the Israelites' path and the most likely place for the Red Sea crossing, then fill in details of the trip from the passages from Deuteronomy which illustrate their travels. You'll find all of my research and Bible verses and references in the research section in the back of this book. There are some things which are not described in the Biblical account but are derived from Jewish legends; I have also explained these in the research section.

I have again tried to keep Moses, Aaron, and Joshua (one of our new leaders) as distant parts of the story so that I don't add anything to their characters or personalities that God didn't put into the Biblical account. I hope that through this you will learn a lot about the Israelites and their journey and that it will bring the Bible to life for you in many ways.

The hardest part of writing this book was portraying the older generation as it slowly started to reject Yahweh and slip away from Him. The Biblical fact is that, because of the faithlessness of the people, only two persons over twenty years of age at that time lived to enter the Promised Land. The older generation died off along the way, so almost all of the parents and grandparents of the current generation at the time of this book eventually leave the faith and turn from following their God. But in this tragedy, you see the younger generation rising up and embracing the earlier faith of their fathers.

In many ways, this is what I see happening in the world today. Many strong Christians went before us, but their children seem to be falling away. Even now, though, there are little pin-points of light shining through the darkness all over the world, just like what happens among the Israelites in this book.

My prayer is that A Stand At Sinai will encourage all readers, young and old, to stand firm in their faith, resist the temptations of the world, and constantly strive towards Christ. May you be blessed, uplifted, challenged, and inspired through these pages as you follow the Israelites towards the Promised Land.

THE CLIFFS

It was dark. Jarah lay on her mat in the sandy soil, feeling little grains of dirt press against her cheek. A chilling desert wind blew the tent flap frantically back and forth, making a loud cracking noise, but Jarah didn't even hear it. She was mesmerized by what she saw beyond the tent flap. It was a gigantic pillar of fire, reaching from the ground to the sky. It was so bright that the glow from the fire dimly lit the tent, even though it was miles away. She could even make out the distant roar that came from the pillar. The fire, swirling and dancing, looked so vibrant and alive. It was hard to think that the one true God, Yahweh, had His presence in the pillar of fire that led the Israelites by night and the pillar of cloud that led them by day. It was scary and difficult for Jarah's twelve-year-old mind to grasp that Yahweh was actually living in the midst of over one million traveling

1

Israelites. She had really just begun to trust Him and follow Him as her God and she wasn't quite sure what to think of His awesome pillar.

She watched, awestruck, as the sun finally peeked over the distant mountains, making the white sand sparkle. The pillar of fire constricted, started to spin, and slowly grew darker and darker, changing into a pillar of cloud. Jarah groaned softly as she saw the cloud start to lift and heard a long trumpet blast. That was Yahweh's signal to pack up camp and get ready to move on.

Jarah slowly rose from the ground, her body aching and sore. She needed to wake up the other eight members of her family and get everything packed up into the wagon.

They had left Succoth in Egypt over a month ago and had been traveling day and night ever since. Following Yahweh wasn't easy, but it was what they had to do to get to the Promised Land, which would be their new home.

Home... Jarah thought, smiling to herself. *We'll finally have a home.*

א

It was still early in the morning, and Jarah and her little sister, Tirzah, were riding on their donkey, following the long line of traveling Israelites. Jarah wiped the sweat from her forehead. It was already scorching hot. The people usually traveled in the morning, stopped for the unbearable afternoon hours, and then traveled on for several hours in the evening and often late into the night. Jarah could hear Tirzah mumbling something from behind, but she couldn't hear what her little sister was saying. Between the treading of millions of feet, thousands upon thousands of people's voices, the braying of countless animals, and the creaking and swaying of wagons and goods, there was always a loud, constant, bothersome hum of noise. Jarah sighed. There was never silence, and no privacy anywhere. Traveling was getting monotonous, at least to Jarah.

"What did you say, Tirzah?" Jarah called over her shoulder.

"When will we stop for the day?" Tirzah whined.

"We just got started, Tirzah!" Jarah replied, annoyed.

"But it's so hot already," she grumbled.

"Then get down off the donkey and get some water from the wagon," Jarah ordered.

Tirzah sighed, jumped from the donkey, and weaved her way through the trudging Israelites. Jarah looked up ahead. Something seemed to be different on the horizon. She craned her neck and struggled to see through the mass of wagons and animals. Looming up ahead of them were gigantic red cliffs.

At last! Maybe we can walk right by those cliffs and be in the shade, she thought in relief.

"I'm back," Tirzah announced. "Stop the donkey so I can get up."

Jarah directed the donkey towards the side of the road and helped Tirzah clamber up. Jarah's oldest brother, Eitan, drove their wagon ahead, grinning as he and his fiancé, Ada, passed them. Jarah maneuvered the donkey behind the oxen and cart and followed her big brother.

The minutes felt like hours as the throng of people crawled past the cliffs. Eitan suddenly stood up slightly as if to look at what was happening. He sank down again, whispered something to Ada, then called to their father.

"Father, the pillar seems to be leading us off the path and going back to the cliffs. Do you know why?"

Father, sitting on a donkey, struggled to see where Eitan was pointing. "I don't know, son. But Yahweh does."

Eitan nodded and goaded the oxen forward, his face grim.

"What's happening?" Tirzah questioned.

Jarah shrugged. "I don't know." She squinted her eyes and tried hard to focus on the pillar. It did seem to be going backwards and taking them towards the cliffs. "I guess we'll just have to wait and see," she finished.

It wasn't long before Jarah was urging her donkey into a deep canyon. Tirzah, sitting behind her, tightened her arms around Jarah's waist.

"It's amazing," she breathed. Jarah could only nod. She had never seen anything like this. She'd only seen mountains from a distance. Almost the entire crowd fell silent, observing the massive rocks in awe. They towered hundreds of feet into the air, and their craggy barrenness of any vegetation made them foreboding.

Hours crawled by as Jarah guided her donkey through a maze of canyons. Jarah was dizzy and almost anxious. It felt like the cliffs were closing in on her. It was getting darker in the gorge, and the cliffs were getting higher. But suddenly, they came over a small rise and were out in the open. Mid-afternoon sunlight struck Jarah's face. They were on a wide beach, right in front of the Red Sea. Jarah and Tirzah both drew in their breath sharply. The glistening, shimmering sea stretched out in front of them for miles and miles. Distant, enormous brown mountains stood up out of the other side of the sea. A fresh, salty wind blew into Jarah's face, making her thick brown hair whip out behind her. She inhaled deeply of the wonderful scent.

"Jarah? Come on! Keep up!" her mother ordered from where she sat curled up in the back of the wagon. "We're going to set up camp."

"Mariel, don't be so cross with the children," Father scolded, sounding annoyed. "They're doing the best they can."

"Well, you don't want them to get lost, do you?" Mother retorted.

"They're fine, Mariel. They're old enough to handle themselves." Father glanced back at Jarah and rolled his eyes in exasperation. Jarah tried to grin back at him, but she felt uneasy. Ever since they had left Goshen over a month ago, things had not been right between her parents. True, there had been problems with them getting along when they lived in Egypt. Her father believed in Yahweh, and her mother believed in the Egyptian gods. But they had at least been able to tolerate each other. Now it seemed that they were always arguing, always at each other's throats. It wasn't making the trip very enjoyable.

It worried Jarah. Her father had always been so kind, so loving, and so strong in his beliefs. Why was he seeming to snap now? Eitan had told her that things were different now and would be a lot harder on Father. Before, Father would be out of the house most of the day and so there was less conflict between him and Mother. Now, they were forced to be together all the time, and there really wasn't a way to get any personal space when you were traveling with over a million other people.

4

I just wish that they'd get along, Jarah thought, sighing a little. She made the donkey trot over the sand after her parents. Tents were already dotting the beach. Jarah glanced over her shoulder at the pillar of cloud, standing still at the edge of the sea. Father led the family towards the south side of the beach and away from the main crowd. In a few minutes, Father, Eitan, and her fourteen-year-old brother Lemuel were assembling the tent. Mother was lying down in the wagon, listless. Jarah heard shrieks and squeals. Her little brothers, Raphael and Yanni, were running around and making a ruckus with their friends, Manni and Manuel. Jarah winced as Mother rose to her elbow. She knew what her mother was going to say.

"Jarah!" she barked. "Get your brothers this instant. And tell your friend Amissa to get her brothers, too. I'm great with child and I need my rest!"

Jarah sighed, handed the blankets she had been carrying to her beautiful older sister, Shayna, and then chased down the little boys.

"Raphael, Yanni, be quiet," Jarah ordered, catching each little boy by an arm.

"But we want to play with Manni and Manuel," Raphael pleaded, trying to wrench away from Jarah's grasp.

"You can if we find someone to help me watch all four of you. Mother wants us to go play somewhere else so she can rest. Remember, she's pregnant and tired. Manni? Where's your sister?"

Manni shrugged. "I don't know."

Someone spoke at Jarah's shoulder. "Is something wrong?" It was Ezra, Ada and Amissa's brother.

"I'm trying to find Amissa. Mother wants me to take the boys somewhere away from the tents, but I can't watch all—" Jarah was interrupted by Raphael finally managing to escape her grasp and dart away towards the ocean. "...All of them..." Jarah finished, sighing helplessly.

Ezra chuckled a little and gave her a grin. "I'll find my sister for you."

"Thanks," Jarah exhaled in relief. Ezra's dark eyes twinkled at her before he left to find Amissa. *He's so handsome,* Jarah found herself thinking. She gasped a little, realizing what she had just thought. *Don't think that,* she rebuked herself.

"Jah-Jah, come!" Yanni cried, dragging her towards the water. Jarah shook her head to clear her thoughts as she ran with Yanni to catch up to the other boys.

As the boys played in the waves with many other Israelite children, Jarah sat with her back against a boulder, enjoying the luscious wind and the sprays of mist that hit her face. She closed her eyes blissfully until she felt Amissa sit down next to her.

"Shalom," Amissa said softly.

"Shalom," Jarah replied. Then she whispered dreamily, "Amissa, I could stay on this beach forever. The wind, the water... it's quiet and private."

"It's lovely. But I feel it would get boring after a while," Amissa responded. There was a moment's pause as Jarah closed her eyes again, breathing in deeply.

"Jarah, why do you think Yahweh led us here, so far off the road?"

Jarah slowly opened her eyes. The shadow of the rock she was leaning against stretched out before her. It was getting late. Jarah shrugged.

"I don't know. Perhaps He wanted to give us a rest. We've only rested a few days since we left Succoth after our time of slavery in Egypt. The animals definitely need a rest."

"I suppose so..." Amissa's voice trailed off. Jarah looked into her face. Amissa's dark blue eyes were focused on her finger, drawing designs in the sand. She was worried.

"What's wrong?" Jarah ventured to ask.

"I just—I just have a weird feeling. I don't know. Maybe it's nothing. I feel that something's going to happen, but I don't know what." Amissa took a deep breath and tried to smile. "I suppose it's nothing."

Jarah tried to smile back. She was starting to feel uneasy, too. She gazed into the pillar of cloud which stood in the center of camp, a few miles away. People were beginning to set up their tents closer and closer to the water. A low hubbub of noise reached them as more and more children were splashing and screaming in the waves.

Everyone looks so peaceful. Surely everything will be all right.

Raphael ran up to Jarah. His clothing was soaked and his thick black hair was sprinkled with water.

"Jarah, we're tired of playing in the water. Can we go climb the cliffs? Please, please, please?"

"Yes! Pwease, pwease, pwease?" Yanni entreated, jumping onto Jarah's lap.

"Yanni, get off! You're dripping wet!"

"Sowwy." Yanni penitently flopped onto the sand, his big brown eyes gazing into hers, begging.

"Please?" Manni asked, directing his pleading query towards Amissa.

Jarah rose. "I see no reason why not."

Amissa grabbed her hand. "It might be dangerous," Amissa fretted.

"Oh, we'll be careful. Very careful," Manuel asserted. He tugged on Amissa's other hand. "Come on!"

"Oh… all right," Amissa consented.

The boys yelled in delight and took off racing away from camp towards the cliffs, hundreds of yards away and to their left. The girls followed; by the time they caught up, the boys were already attempting to climb the cliffs.

"Don't go too high," Amissa warned.

Jarah was about to sit down on a rock when a noise from over her head startled her. Looking up, she saw three little lambs skipping up a tiny path on the cliff.

"Look at those lambs. I wonder if we should tell someone that they're here," Amissa said.

Jarah glanced about. No tents were set up within one hundred yards of the cliffs, though more and more Israelites were pouring onto the beach every moment. *They must have wandered off a good ways…* Jarah thought. She looked up at the lambs and then gasped and said, "Amissa, those are our lambs! They must've strayed away."

"What? Are you sure?" Amissa exclaimed.

Jarah nodded vigorously. "Yes. Lemuel tied those ropes around their necks so that we knew which animals were ours." She jumped to her feet. "I've got to get them. They're going higher and I'm afraid they'll fall!"

"Jarah, you can't!" Amissa cried, clutching her arm. "You'll get hurt!"

"I'll be fine. Go back and get Lemuel. I'll need his help. Take the boys with you."

"Can I help, Jarah?" Raphael asked, eagerly.

"No. Go with Amissa and find Lemuel," Jarah commanded. She ran towards the cliff and noticed a small path etched into its side. *That must be how the lambs had gotten onto the cliff*, she thought. Jarah clambered up after them.

"Come on little lambs. Come on down," Jarah soothed as she approached them, but the lambs continued to frolic on like they were playing a game.

"No! Come back!" Jarah exclaimed. The path was getting steeper, when suddenly a lamb slipped and lost its balance. Jarah's heart stopped as the lamb slid downward, but it quickly regained its footing and chased after the others. "Not higher!" Jarah exclaimed.

Soon the path became quite narrow. There was barely room for Jarah to walk. Then, she looked down.

Jarah's heart leapt into her throat. She could feel blood pounding in her ears. She flattened herself against the cliff, trembling so much she could hardly stand. The bottom was far away, over a hundred feet down. Jarah was frozen to the spot in fear. She hadn't realized that she was up so high. She couldn't go on. She was panic-stricken, but the lambs—without them their family would lose some of their precious food.

Father would want me to get them. Yahweh, give me courage, Jarah prayed, breathing hard. She tried to moisten her dry lips but found her tongue felt like wool in her mouth.

She was just getting up the courage to continue when she heard a voice calling her name.

"Jarah? Jarah?"

"Lemuel!" Jarah called out weakly. Utter relief washed over her like a wave, making her feel faint. Her brother was coming to help her.

"Where are you?"

"Up here!"

In a moment, Lemuel came into view, climbing the steep path with the aid of his staff. Ezra was right behind him. Lemuel soon reached her.

"You shouldn't have come up here," he told her. His tone was a mixture of rebuke and worry.

"I'm sorry. I was just trying to help," Jarah apologized.

"It's fine. You might still be able to help. We need to get those lambs."

But the lambs were more nimble than the humans and continued to travel even higher up the cliffs, soon reaching the top. Jarah gulped, trying hard not to look down. By now they must be hundreds of feet in the air.

The path, which had been switching back and forth along the face of the cliff, suddenly veered steeply upwards and widened slightly. Jarah drew in her breath. She could see the lambs on top of the cliff, but making the final assent looked very dangerous. Lemuel sighed, gently moved Jarah back against the cliff, and motioned for Ezra to go around them as he talked.

"Stay here, Jarah. This is too dangerous. Ezra and I will get the lambs and then come back for you." Lemuel glanced up at Ezra who was slowly scaling the path. Lemuel's face was grim. "Do you understand?" Jarah nodded in agreement and Lemuel hurried after his best friend.

"Look out!" Ezra shouted abruptly. A large rock had come loose and was now rolling and bouncing down the path towards Lemuel. A scream caught in Jarah's throat as she clung to the cliff. Lemuel tried to jump out of the way, but it was too late. His legs were knocked out from under him and he was sliding down the hill, coming closer and closer to the edge of the cliff. He was flailing about, trying to stop his fall.

"Lemuel!" Jarah shrieked.

Everything happened so fast. Before Jarah could force her limbs into action Lemuel was shooting over the edge. He tried to grab at something—anything. His hand grasped the edge of the cliff, breaking his fall. But Lemuel's grip was not firm. His fingers were slipping. Jarah couldn't breathe. She felt frozen.

Out of the corner of her eye, Jarah saw something dash past her. The next instant Ezra was at the edge of the cliff. He fell to his knees and reached out for Lemuel, just as his friend lost his grip. Their hands locked and Lemuel was saved, but the ledge on which Ezra was kneeling began to crumble from their weight, and Ezra didn't have the strength to pull Lemuel to safety.

"Hang on, Lemuel. We'll get you up somehow," Ezra encouraged.

Jarah forced her shaking limbs forward. She was right next to Ezra now. She had to help them.

"Jarah, get back! You'll fall, too!" Lemuel commanded. Jarah shrank back.

"Ezra, what should we do?" she cried.

"Just let me think!" Ezra shouted back.

"Ezra, I'm—I'm slipping! I can't hold on much longer!"

"You have to, Lemuel! Just a little longer. You can do it!"

"I can't!"

"Yes, you can!"

"Ezra!" Jarah screamed as a large piece of the ledge gave away.

"Jarah, get back!" Ezra yelled.

Jarah slowly stepped backwards, pressing herself against the cliff. Her whole body was trembling. She saw the determination on Ezra's face, but there was no hope left in Lemuel's eyes, and Ezra's hands were losing their grip.

"Ezra, just let me go! The ledge is crumbling and I don't want you to fall, too."

"No, Ezra! Please, get him up!" Jarah pleaded.

"Ezra, it's the right thing," Lemuel urged.

"I... I..." Ezra looked back at Jarah, fear and indecision in his eyes. Jarah's mind went blank. She didn't know how to get them out of this. Ezra didn't know how to get them out of this. They were doomed.

Please, Yahweh, Jarah prayed urgently, *help Ezra. I don't want either of them to die. Please, give Ezra strength.*

בּ

"Eitan?"

"Over here, Ada!"

Ada circled a large rock and found Eitan sitting in its shade with a staff in his hand. He was watching the herd of sheep and goats which were happily resting on the clean sand. Looking up at her, Eitan smiled and motioned for her to take a seat by his side.

"I'm sorry to be looking like this," Ada apologized, blushing a little. She was wearing a plain brown dress that was patched and ragged. "Mother's washing the clothes in the sea, so…"

Eitan gently lifted her chin and looked tenderly into her calm brown eyes. "Ada, nothing you wear could take away from the beauty in your heart that has always drawn me to you."

Ada smiled with pleasure, her eyes glowing. They both sat in silence for a moment, just enjoying the relative peace and stillness out with the flocks.

"Eitan, Father wanted me to ask you… I know it's a little soon to talk about it, but… When do you think we should plan for the betrothal ceremony?"

"That's what I've been thinking about," Eitan said, letting out a long sigh as his eyes wandered over the flock. "I thought that it might be best to wait until we got to the Promised Land. But Yahweh isn't leading us the most direct way. It's already taken more time than any of us had expected. Perhaps when we camp for a few days and have time to rest and plan… I don't know. It might be better to wait, even though I don't really want to wait…" His voice trailed off, wistfully.

"I can wait," Ada murmured. She looked confidently into Eitan's eyes and whispered, "I trust your judgment."

Eitan smiled broadly. Gently, he squeezed her hand. "Well then, we'll trust in Yahweh and His perfect timing."

LOST

"Jarah, come here," Ezra commanded.

Jarah obeyed with trepidation, coming as close to the edge as she dared. Her head was spinning.

"Now listen carefully," Ezra began, talking fast, "I'm going to pull as hard as I can to get Lemuel up here. Lemuel, once I pull you up a little higher, reach out your other hand and Jarah, you grab it. I think we can both get him up. If he's pulling too much on you or the ledge cracks again, just drop his hand and get back. *Do you understand?*"

Jarah nodded and swallowed hard.

"Everyone ready?" Ezra looked from one to the other. "All right. One... two... *three!*"

Ezra pulled with all his might. Lemuel's head came over the ledge. His hand shot out towards Jarah and she grabbed it, squeezed it tightly and pulled as hard as she could.

"I found a foothold!" Lemuel cried out.

"Good—use it," Ezra grunted, straining with all his might.

A sudden cry from Lemuel made Jarah's heart stop. The ledge was cracking.

"Pull, Jarah!" Ezra commanded.

With every ounce of strength left in their bodies, Jarah and Ezra yanked Lemuel over the edge. He was safe.

"Look out! The ledge is breaking!" Ezra shouted. Lemuel grabbed Jarah and pinned her up against the cliff. The ledge completely broke away. They watched helplessly as more and more rocks fell down the cliff, breaking the path and separating them from the trail they had just climbed.

As the dust and dirt settled Ezra asked, "Are you both all right?"

"I'm fine," Lemuel replied. His voice was tremulous. Jarah's whole body was shaking. She felt like bursting into tears. She was barely able to nod her head in answer to Ezra's questioning look.

There was a long silence before Lemuel breathed, "Thank you both." Ezra nodded modestly. Jarah laid her head on Lemuel's shoulder. Silent tears streamed down her cheeks. Lemuel put his arm around her and drew her into a comforting hug. There was a pause as each of them thought how close they had come to death.

Jarah was soon able to brush back the tears and whispered, "What are we going to do now?"

"There's probably another way down somewhere," Ezra said, thoughtfully. "Let's climb up to the top and see if we can't find another trail."

"And if there's not another trail?" Jarah questioned nervously.

Ezra gave her a grin. "Yahweh's watching out for us. I don't think He's going to leave us stranded up here."

"I hope not," Jarah murmured.

They slowly and cautiously climbed up the hill without saying another word. Jarah struggled up behind Lemuel, using the footholds he had used. Lemuel pulled himself up the cliff, then reached down and lifted Jarah over the edge, and then assisted Ezra.

"There are the lambs," Lemuel said.

14

The lambs were standing a few feet away, looking scared and tired. Each picked up a lamb, then Jarah exclaimed breathlessly, "Look!"

"Unbelievable," Lemuel said in awe.

From the cliffs, they could see in all directions for miles upon miles. Looking forward, they could see the mountains on the other side of the Red Sea. Behind them and to their left they could see the maze of barren river beds they had come through earlier that day. To their right they could see miles and miles of cliffs and desert and the Red Sea, reaching beyond eyesight. The sun was setting behind them over the great desert.

The greatness and grandeur took their breath away. Lemuel stepped up next to Jarah, looking at the Israelite camp spread out on the beach below them. Jarah peered down at the camp, too. As she did so, Jarah noticed a long, deep gash on Lemuel's shin.

"Lemuel, you're bleeding," Jarah gasped.

"I'll be fine," Lemuel said, trying to shake the look of pain from his face.

"That's a bad cut," Ezra stated, looking worried. "We'll need to get Shayna to look at it soon, before you lose too much blood. Here." Ezra put his lamb down, untied his sash, and bound it tightly around Lemuel's leg to stop the bleeding. "Come on. Let's try and find another way," he urged.

The boys began searching for another trail. Jarah started to help them, but then she noticed a large cloud of dust in the dry river beds. She stared into it, hard.

"What's that over there?" she asked.

"Probably just a sand storm," Lemuel answered, barely glancing in the direction Jarah pointed.

"No. It seems like there's something moving in it," Jarah persisted.

Ezra and Lemuel shaded their eyes with their hands.

"She's right," Ezra agreed. "There's something moving in the cloud. Shiny things."

Through a break in the cliffs, Jarah caught a glimpse of what was stirring up the dust. Dozens and dozens of chariots were racing forwards, their wheels shining gold. The horses were galloping at an alarming rate, and the charioteers had swords at their sides.

"Soldiers!" Jarah screamed. "They're Egyptian soldiers. They've followed us!"

"We've got to tell Moses before they get to the camp," Lemuel shouted.

Ezra was peering over the edge of the cliff. "Look, here's another path. Let's get down, quickly!"

Carefully but hurriedly, they slipped and slid down the steep path. Thankfully this way was a little wider, but Jarah noticed that it wasn't broad or smooth enough for a small cart or even an ox. Since Pharaoh's army was coming down the dry river bed, they were trapped by the cliffs on either side, the sea before them, and soldiers in their rear. The beach was a trap, a prison. The thought terrified Jarah.

"Lemuel, what're we going to do? How can we get away? There's no way out!"

"We've just got to tell Moses," Lemuel huffed, climbing over a boulder.

At last they reached the bottom. No Egyptians were in sight—yet.

"There you are!" Amissa and the younger boys came running towards them. "Where have you been?" Amissa cried. "We were so worried." She noticed Lemuel's bloody, bandaged leg and her face turned pale.

"There's no time to explain," Ezra blurted quickly. He shoved his lamb into Amissa's arms. "Get these lambs and the boys back to camp immediately. And tell our fathers to pack up everything. The Egyptians are coming!"

"The Egyptians?" Amissa shrieked. The little boys' eyes grew wide with horror.

"Yes. Now hurry! I'll go find Moses."

"Do you know where Moses is?" Jarah asked, hastily.

"Well, no," Ezra admitted. "Lemuel?"

Lemuel shook his head. "I don't know, either."

"Why don't we all go and split up? We can cover more ground that way," Ezra suggested.

"But Ezra, Lemuel's bleeding," Amissa fretted.

Lemuel shrugged, but his face was pale and Jarah saw him grimace.

16

"I'm fine," he insisted. "We've got to find Moses. The three of us are the only ones who saw the Egyptians and know what's happening."

"Let's go!" Ezra commanded, taking off at a run. Jarah and Lemuel followed him. Jarah glanced behind her and saw Amissa herding the younger boys and the lambs towards camp.

They were soon in the midst of the tents. Even though Jarah was fast, she was struggling to keep up with Ezra and Lemuel's speed.

"Split up," Ezra yelled. "I'll go this way." He disappeared into the crowd. Lemuel veered off to Jarah's right, and Jarah ran straight ahead, dodging people, tents, and wagons.

"Excuse me, pardon me! I'm sorry," she huffed out as she ran through campsites and through groups of playing children. Her heart was pounding like a hammer in her chest, but she couldn't slow down. She had to find Moses and Aaron. Perhaps they could do something to stop the Egyptians. But there were so many people and there were miles and miles of beach. How would she find the leaders in time?

Jarah kept running, her legs and lungs aching. How much further would she have to go? It was getting harder and harder for her to breathe.

Suddenly, Jarah saw a large tent by the edge of the Red Sea. It was larger than any of the other tents she had seen and she quickly ran towards it. She broke through a ring of people surrounding the tent and saw three men sitting at its entrance. She recognized two of them as Moses and Aaron and stumbled forward to tell them her news. Moses' eyes fell on her and he looked upon her kindly.

"Is there something you wish to ask of me, my child?" he asked, compassionately.

"Sir, there—there's a force of Egyptians coming—here!" Jarah panted out. Exclamations of terror and surprise came from the Israelites surrounding her.

"What?" the third man exclaimed. "Are you sure of this?"

"Yes... yes sir," Jarah continued to gasp for air. "I saw them myself, with—with a friend and my brother."

"Moses, what shall we do? The pharaoh is after us, and none of the men are trained in warfare!" the third man exclaimed.

But Moses' eyes were full of peace as he answered, "Yahweh is with us. He will fight for us, Joshua."

Joshua was about to say something else when abruptly screams and yells burst out from all over the camp. Looking towards the mouth of the dry river bed, they could see a long line of Egyptian chariots charging down upon them. Instantly the camp was in utter confusion. Men were running around looking for their families. Women were scooping up their infants. Children were dashing into tents, and the animals were charging to and fro wildly. Jarah was knocked to the ground as the people around Moses dispersed and fled.

Above all the other screams and shrieks and chaos, Jarah heard a loud noise, like the roar of a rushing wind. Looking up, she saw the pillar of cloud lift and place itself between the Israelites and the Egyptians. Everyone watched in wonder, but they all knew their troubles were far from over. Soon the Egyptian army would penetrate the cloud and fall upon them. The crowd turned on Moses, yelling at him in fury.

"Is it because there were no graves in Egypt that you have taken us away to die in the wilderness?" a man yelled out from among the crowd gathered around Moses' tent.

"Why have you dealt with us in this way, bringing us out of Egypt?" a woman shouted.

"Isn't this what we spoke to you in Egypt, saying, 'Leave us alone that we may serve the Egyptians'? It would have been better for us to serve the Egyptians than to die in the wilderness!" another man bellowed.

Cries of anger and hatred filled the air. Jarah rose to her feet and backed away from the throng of people, disoriented and trembling with fear and exhaustion.

"Do not fear!" Moses called out, "Stand by and see the salvation of the Lord which He will accomplish for you today; for the Egyptians whom you have seen today, you will never see them again. The Lord will fight for you while you keep silent."

The people's shouts subsided and guilty looks rested on many faces.

He's right, Jarah thought. *Yahweh fought for us in Egypt. He freed us. He's going to free us from this, too. He has to. He promised to take us to the Promised Land, and He will. He must! Please, Yahweh, please keep Your promise.*

Slowly, the crowd began to melt away. The sun had set, dusk was falling, and with it came billowing, dark clouds. Jarah heard someone run up behind her and turned to see Ezra, winded and out of breath.

"What's he doing?" Ezra asked Jarah in a whisper. Moses was staring up towards heaven, but he wasn't doing or saying anything.

"I don't know," Jarah whispered back.

Moses stood there for a long time. Then he shook his head and took up his staff. With darkness coming on, he stretched out his staff towards the Red Sea. Instantly, a strong wind came up from the west. It was bitterly cold and very strong; so strong that Jarah had to grab Ezra's arm so she wouldn't fall over.

"Let's head back to our tents," Ezra shouted to Jarah above the wind. "There's nothing else we can do here." Jarah gladly followed him further into the camp as they tried to find their way back home.

The cloud had now turned into a pillar of fire, giving them some light. But the clouds above them were dark, making it difficult to see, and Jarah's directions began to get mixed up. She thought that their tents were on the other side of the beach, but she couldn't make out where the cliffs were or where the beach ended and began. The gusts tore at her clothing. She hugged herself and leaned into the wind. The tents beside her shook back and forth violently. A bucket went flying pass Jarah's ear. Jarah desperately hoped her family's tents were staked down well.

The wind was rocking wagons and flinging anything unsecured into the sea. Animals huddled together, trying to stay warm in the stinging chill of the wind. It was so cold it hurt to breathe. Jarah found that tears were forming in her eyes.

Why is it so windy and cold? she vaguely wondered. She fought to keep up with Ezra, but he almost seemed to be wandering around aimlessly. Jarah was beginning to chatter from the extreme chill. Her body ached from pushing herself against the wind.

"Let's stop for a minute. We need a break," Ezra yelled, plopping down in the shelter of a large rock. The rock blocked most of the wind and Jarah gratefully sank to the ground and curled up into a ball, conserving all her energy and strength. Ezra wrapped his cloak more tightly around himself.

"Are you all right?" he asked.

"Oh, yes. Just… cold," Jarah answered. She was nodding off. She was so tired. But Ezra's hands were on her shoulders. He was shaking her.

"Jarah, don't go to sleep. It's too cold to go to sleep. Stay awake."

Jarah heard concern in his voice. She forced her eyelids to stay open.

"Come on. Sit up," Ezra persisted. Wearily, Jarah rose to a sitting position. "Rub your arms and legs. Try to stay warm. We'll be moving in a few minutes." Jarah obeyed as best as she could. It seemed like only a few seconds before Ezra stood up and offered her his hand.

"We've got to get moving. We need to get back to our tents and to warmth and shelter."

"Yes," Jarah murmured. Ezra helped her to her feet and they plowed ahead, heads bowed, walking into the fierce wind again.

They wandered on and on for what seemed like hours, pushing forward against the extreme, biting wind and taking frequent stops to regain their energy. Jarah's fingers were so numb from the cold that she could barely feel them, and her feet felt like blocks of ice. *Where are we? Where's my family?* were the only thoughts circling through her mind.

Ezra finally stopped and stood still. He sighed and turned to her, shouting above the roar of the wind, "Jarah, we're lost. I'm sorry, but I can't seem to find our families. There are too many tents and not enough light to find our way back."

Jarah barely heard what he said. She was so tired and frozen that nothing seemed to matter any more. She just wanted to get warm. Jarah stuttered between her chattering teeth, "It, it's all right, Ezra. I, I, un… understand wh…why we're lost."

"Let's try to find some shelter," Ezra yelled. Jarah felt his arm go around her shoulders. Through a blur she saw an over-turned wagon in front of them. Her head was spinning and her ears were ringing. She barely heard Ezra exclaim, "Jarah, you're freezing!"

Everything seemed to be swirling around Jarah. She felt something coarse and heavy thrown on her. It was warm. Then she heard a deep voice in the distance.

"Young man, is something wrong?"

Ezra yelled back, "We're just trying to get to a place of shelter. We can't find our way back to our tents."

"Then come in here," the voice shouted back. "We have plenty of room, and you're going to freeze to death on a night like this."

Jarah felt an icy hand grasp her arm and she was pulled along. She didn't know where they were going, but she found herself being pulled into a tent. There was a small fire inside of it and Jarah felt a warm, tingling sensation creep over her.

"Please make yourselves at home," the voice boomed.

Jarah staggered to the fire and sat down, holding her hands out to its warmth as Ezra said, "Thank you, sir, for your kindness. I don't know what we would have done if you hadn't asked us into your tent."

"It's no trouble," the man responded. "We're not a big family ourselves, and would gladly help any fellow Israelites. You and your sister may stay here until the morning when you should be able to find your family."

"Oh, Jarah's not my sister," Ezra hastened to explain.

"She's not?" the man questioned in obvious surprise, glancing first at Jarah, then at Ezra. Jarah could feel her cheeks burning.

"No, sir. We're just friends," Ezra replied, awkwardly. "We're both from the tribe of Asher. My name's Ezra."

"We're also from the tribe of Asher," the man stated. "My name's Emmitt." He grasped Ezra's hand warmly.

A quiet voice by Jarah's side asked, "Jarah?" The voice sounded so familiar... Turning around, Jarah saw the speaker and gasped.

"Acenith?" It was her beautiful Egyptian friend from Rameses. The girls both gave a little scream of delight and embraced each other warmly.

"What are you doing here?" Acenith questioned. She looked shocked but also very pleased.

"We got lost in the storm. What are *you* doing here?"

"It's a long story," Acenith said with a slight smile. "Why don't I tell you after you have a nice meal."

"You know each other?" Emmitt inquired.

"Yes, sir. We met each other in Egypt," Acenith replied. She squeezed Jarah's hand and gave her a big smile.

"Yachne, do we have any food for our guests?" Emmitt asked.

"Of course," a warm, motherly voice responded. Jarah found herself looking into the face of a woman with a darker complexion and a gentle, kind face with large brown eyes and a graceful smile. Her very air was dignity and grace, and she looked tenderly at Jarah and asked, "Would you like some bread?"

"Yes please, ma'am," Jarah replied, taking the warm loaf that was held out to her.

"This is my daughter, Hava," Emmitt continued.

Hava peeked out from behind her mother's full skirts. She looked to be about four years of age. Hava had honey-colored curls, a chubby face, and the same big brown eyes as her mother. She let go of her mother's skirt and came and sat down next to Jarah, looking at her. It almost seemed as if she was searching Jarah's heart to determine whether or not to trust her. Jarah smiled down at the little face and Hava smiled back, a satisfied look resting on her countenance.

"Then there's Yael." Yael was small, dark, and thin. He smiled at her, a weak, thin smile. His eyes seemed empty and lonely. "He's often very sickly," Emmitt continued, sadly, "and this trip has taken a heavy toll on him."

"I'm learning to persevere, Father says. And if I don't make it to the Promised Land, I'll be with Yahweh," Yael said, confidently.

"That's right, my son. That's right," said Emmitt, laying a hand gently on his son's head, a tear rolling down his cheek before he went on.

"And this is Adriel, our oldest. He's fifteen years old."

Adriel was tall and strong, with curly copper hair and a warm grin. He looked a lot like his father, had a broad build, and he seemed kind and friendly. His eyes were very dark, almost black, and they seemed to be boring right through Jarah. She squirmed uncomfortably, but in a moment the eyes relaxed and only held a welcoming glow.

"It's a pleasure to meet you all, and we thank you for sharing your tent with us," Ezra said. Jarah nodded in assent.

"It's our pleasure, Ezra," Yachne said, hospitably.

"Now, Ezra," Emmitt began as he and Ezra sat down by the fire, eating the bread that was provided for them, "how is it that you and your friend were wandering about the camp?"

Ezra told the story of how they had seen the Egyptians on the cliffs—modestly cutting out the part where he had saved Lemuel—and how they had tried to warn Moses.

"You actually saw the Egyptian army?" Adriel asked. Ezra nodded and Adriel questioned, "How large a force do they have?"

"I'm not sure. We only saw a cloud of dust and a few chariots at the front. I can't tell you exactly how many there were, but I'm sure there's enough to put up a good fight."

"I hope the pharaoh has underestimated our abilities," Adriel said. "I'm sure we can defeat him."

"With Yahweh's help we can," Ezra agreed, pointedly.

Ezra and Adriel continued to talk about the Egyptians and how to prepare for the inevitable attack. Hava sat on Jarah's lap, not saying much at all. Acenith darted around the tent, setting out blankets for Jarah and Ezra, giving them food, and packing up the dinner dishes. Finally, she was able to sit down next to Jarah and talk.

"I'm sure you're surprised to see me," Acenith began, smiling again, but sadly this time.

"When the last plague came, Bes was taken." A big tear rolled down her cheek and she stared hard at the ground. "My father was enraged and drunk. He never liked me. Bes was his pride and joy—his treasure. I was his servant, good for nothing more. When the plague came and Father realized that Bes was dead, he... he... attacked me." Acenith absentmindedly rubbed her arm. Jarah's eyes grew wide as she saw several long, deep scars down Acenith's bare arm.

"I ran for my life," she continued, "but I didn't have anywhere to go. I had no friends, besides you. So I ran to Goshen. I wandered around until dawn, trying to find any sign of you. Of course, I didn't. So I just slumped into a corner and wept. Yachne saw me and took me to her house. She bandaged me up, listened to my story, and offered for me to come with them. She was so good to me, and I didn't have anywhere else to go. So, I came here. I didn't want to go back to those horrible priests or gods, and that's the only life I've ever known."

23

"Acenith, I'm so sorry. I wish I had known. We would've gladly taken you in. But it's wonderful that you're here and that you trust Yahweh now," Jarah said, excitedly.

"Oh, I *don't* trust Yahweh," Acenith corrected, hurriedly.

Jarah's jaw dropped. "You... you don't?" she asked in wonder.

"No. I—I don't. I can't," Acenith murmured, staring at her hands which were folded in her lap.

"But why not?" Jarah asked, almost in shock.

"Because He took my brother. He devastated our nation. I'm glad I'm here and out of Egypt, but I can't love your God after all He's done to me." Acenith's voice was quivering as if she was about to cry.

"But Yahweh has done a lot to me and I still trust Him," Jarah asserted.

"But Jarah, He didn't kill *your* family members or destroy *your* nation. You may've been beaten a couple times, but you haven't had anything truly bad happen to you. Yahweh helped you and your nation. He didn't help me. I can't trust Him. I can't." Acenith finished with a long sigh.

"Then, who or what *do* you trust?" Jarah ventured to ask.

"I... I don't know. I know that your God is real. I just... don't think that He's my god."

Jarah didn't know what to say. What Acenith said was true about Bes and the Egyptian nation. So, what did it mean to her? Wasn't Yahweh everyone's God? Not just the God of the Israelites?

Or, was He really just for Israelites and didn't care about anyone else? But that didn't make sense, because there had been Yahweh-fearing Egyptians. Jarah's head swam with contradicting thoughts.

"Time for bed, everyone," Yachne called softly. "We need to be ready for whatever happens tomorrow morning."

"Don't you have a tunic?" Adriel asked Ezra as everyone prepared to go to bed.

"I have one, but I gave it to Jarah."

Jarah glanced down and noticed for the first time that she was wearing Ezra's tunic. Ezra had given her his tunic so that she would stay warm. *That was very kind of him,* Jarah thought, a slight blush coloring her cheeks. Out loud she said, "I'm warm enough now, Ezra. You can take it back. Thanks."

"You're welcome," he responded, taking the tunic from her outstretched hand. As he turned away Jarah was struck by a thought.

"Ezra," Jarah suddenly blurted. "Do—do you think Lemuel got back to our families?"

Ezra's face became white and he just stared at her for a long time. Jarah could see doubt in his eyes. She could picture the look of pain on Lemuel's face and how much he had been bleeding. What if Lemuel hadn't gotten back to their tents? For a moment it looked like Ezra wanted to go out and look for him. But then he shook his head and smiled at her.

"I'm sure he's safe, Jarah. If he didn't find a way back, he probably found another family to stay with," Ezra assured her, but he was obviously forcing himself to appear unconcerned.

"Who's Lemuel?" Adriel asked.

"My older brother," Jarah murmured sorrowfully, looking down at her feet so as not to show her worried countenance to Ezra.

Jarah snuggled down in the blankets between Acenith and Hava and tried to go to sleep. She heard Ezra and Adriel talking in hushed voices. She could hear Emmitt's heavy breathing and Yachne's feet softly thumping the sand as she cleaned up the extra rugs and blankets. Hava's warm breath fell gently on the back of her neck.

Jarah kept her eyes closed, trying to go to sleep. Slowly, Adriel and Ezra's whispers drifted away and Yachne soon lay down on her own blankets. The only sounds now were of the wind outside, howling furiously around them, and the crackling from the dying fire.

Jarah could not rest. She tossed and turned, but she could not get comfortable and she could not stop thinking about Lemuel. *He might be out there, huddled in the cold, dying*, she thought. If only she could find him or at least know that he was all right.

Please, Yahweh, keep him safe, Jarah begged. Against her will, she felt tears falling from her eyes and silent sobs began to shake her body. She turned to her left side once again but it was no use. She could not get comfortable or stop the tears. Jarah quietly sat up and hugged her legs, burying her head in her knees and letting herself cry silently.

She sat like this for a long time until she felt eyes staring at her. Jarah started and wiped away the tears as she turned to see who was looking at her. She expected it to be Ezra, but instead her eyes locked with Adriel's piercing stare. She was embarrassed that he should see her crying and began to pull the blankets over herself, but they felt cold and coarse. She could not get comfortable. What made it worse was that she could feel Adriel's eyes still resting on her. In a few minutes, he got up and came noiselessly over to her.

"Is something wrong?" he asked, softly.

"I'll be all right," Jarah said, hoping he would take the hint and leave her alone.

"We have some more blankets if you're cold." He paused. Jarah wasn't quite sure what to say. "Would you like another blanket?"

"Yes, please," Jarah replied, sitting back up.

Adriel found another blanket for her and then asked gently, "Is there something troubling you?"

Jarah could see from the look in his eyes that Adriel really cared. Before she could catch herself Jarah told him, "I'm worried about my brother. I couldn't imagine my life without him. He's always been there, teaching and helping me. I'm just worried that he's hurt, or..." Jarah could not bring herself to say the dreaded word. She sighed. Adriel's mysterious gaze never left Jarah's face.

"I'm sorry," she ventured. "I guess I just worry too much."

"I understand. I'm quite the worrier myself," Adriel said kindly, a slight smile on his lips. "You see, Acenith and I can relate to each other in at least one way. We've both lost siblings. One day I'll tell you my older sister's story, but right now I don't think it would be appropriate with what you're going through."

Jarah shook her head, fighting back tears. Hearing that two siblings had died... Was Yahweh trying to prepare her for Lemuel's death?

"You have to trust Yahweh, Jarah. Everything is for a reason. Everything. Even the bad things. Worrying won't help you at all. It'll only take your eyes off Yahweh and what He's doing for you and turn your focus on yourself. You'll start pitying yourself, and it makes everything worse. When we keep our eyes focused on Yahweh, He will make the path straight before you and lead you."

Jarah swallowed hard and nodded, blinking back tears.

"Does that make sense? Can you do that?" Adriel persisted.

Jarah gulped.

"I will... try," she murmured. "I will try very hard. But I don't know if I can do it."

"But that's just it, Jarah. You can't do it," Adriel whispered fervently. "Father told me that I was trying too hard. Yes, we have to try, but we also have to surrender and let Yahweh work through us. You can't conquer your fear and anxiety in your own strength. We both saw how powerful Yahweh is during the plagues. But it's hard for us to realize that He cares about us and wants to help us." Adriel's voice faded away.

"Yes, but it's hard to let Him completely take over, too," Jarah admitted, hanging her head. Adriel grabbed her arm and she looked up into his face.

"Just let Him in, Jarah." Adriel's eyes were intense. Jarah moistened her lips and tried to smile.

"I will, if He wants to help me," she said softly, doubtfully. Another tear spilled from her eye.

Adriel let out a deep breath. He smiled warmly and said, "He'll help you. I can tell you have great strength and a love for Yahweh. Never lose sight of that."

"Thank you, Adriel." Jarah felt better inside. She knew what she had to do.

"Do you need anything else?" Adriel asked, quietly.

"No. Thank you," Jarah replied.

Adriel went back to his bed and Jarah lay down, wrapping the extra blanket around her to keep away the cold.

"Dear Yahweh, please, I want to give You my love for Lemuel," she whispered. "Help me not lose sight of You and Your purpose. If You want—" She choked, gathered up her resolve, and then continued.

"If You want to take him, please, help me and my family bear it, and remember that You do everything for a reason. Help me learn how to surrender everything and use Your strength, not my strength. I... I don't know how to do that, but I know that if You care about me, You'll teach me. Thank You." Tears were flowing down Jarah's cheeks, but she felt almost peaceful now. In a few minutes, she was sound asleep.

THE RED SEA

"Jarah, wake up."

Jarah's eyes flew open. Someone was shaking her and calling her name. She found herself looking up into Ezra's face. Pale morning light shone in through the tent flap, but the wind still howled around the tent and it looked as if the morning was stormy and cold.

"What's going on?" Jarah shook herself and groggily tried to get up.

Ezra smiled and said, "Go outside and see for yourself."

Jarah rubbed her eyes, rose from her blanket, and stumbled out of the tent. She was completely unprepared for what she saw. Directly in front of her was the Red Sea. But there in the midst were two walls of water, shooting up into the air like a long fountain, and between the walls of water a pathway going right through the sea to the distant opposite shore. The beach was already half-deserted, with a stream of Israelites going from one end of the Red Sea to the other. The people who weren't crossing yet were hurriedly breaking camp.

"Hava, please sit still. I need to finish packing. Why don't you finish eating your breakfast? Acenith? Please bring me that basket," Yachne's voice, still gentle but with a note of stress, came from inside the tent. Jarah pulled herself away from the magnificent sight and stepped back into the tent to help Yachne and Acenith pack up to leave the beach.

The next few minutes were chaos. Jarah and Acenith ran back and forth from the tent to the wagon, bringing bundles of food, clothing, and blankets for Ezra and Emmitt to pack. The wind was still blowing, almost as strongly as last night. Adriel frantically tried to contain their sheep and goats who were crazed with fright amid the confusion. The tent was emptied of belongings in just a few minutes, and Ezra, Emmitt, and Yachne struggled to get the tent down without it blowing away. Acenith and Jarah collected the tent pegs and helped Yael into the cart. Hava was clinging to Jarah's arm, thumb in her mouth, her eyes wide with fright.

With difficulty they lifted the tent into the wagon. Emmitt and Yachne climbed up onto the wagon box and urged the donkeys forward. Acenith followed, leading their other donkey loaded with barrels and clay pitchers full of water. Jarah and Hava ran behind the wagon as it turned towards the Red Sea.

Soon there was damp sand under her feet. Jarah's heart was pounding as she saw the walls of water rushing upward into the sky. Her nose tickled as she smelled the tangy, salty scent and felt the moist air against her face. The wind kept whipping her hair out before her eyes. She squeezed Hava's hand tightly and tried to see what was happening. They were literally walking into the sea. Jarah's knees were knocking together. *What if the water falls down? What if we all drown? And what about Lemuel and my family?* Jarah looked back over her shoulder into the howling wind. Tears sprang to her eyes. Maybe her family was still on the beach. What if they were separated forever? What if her brother was dead?

Yahweh will take care of us. The thought suddenly flashed through Jarah's mind and began to calm her heart. *Just follow Moses. Follow Yahweh. He'll make the way straight for me.*

Jarah slowly realized that it wasn't muddy or rocky. They were walking on cool, damp sand. A greenish blue light sparkled around them as the walls of water quivered and rolled. Jarah hurried along, trying to keep away from the herd of animals that Ezra and Adriel were pushing forwards. Hurrying people jostled her to and fro. Animals ran about in confusion, threatening to trample little Hava. Twice Jarah almost lost Hava in the crowd, but Hava clung to her hand and they remained together.

Acenith was ahead of Jarah, struggling to get the overloaded donkey through the mass of people. Miraculously, the ground did not slope steeply nor give them many problems. It was as if Yahweh had prepared the sea floor just for the Israelites to pass through. Jarah was still dumb-founded that they were walking on the bottom of the sea.

The hours slowly dragged by, but the wonder of what they were doing and how Yahweh had prepared an escape for them rested upon Jarah. Then, as they were about four miles into the Red Sea, Jarah saw the pillar of cloud rising up and moving back to the front of the Israelite line.

What about the Egyptians? Jarah thought fearfully, turning back to see if they were still there. To her amazement and horror, tiny black specks were moving towards them. The Egyptian army was following them into the Red Sea!

"The Egyptians are following us!" Jarah cried. Instantly people turned to see if what she said was true; in moments, panic struck. They were running and trying to get out of the way.

We have to get out of here. If the Egyptians catch up to us now then why did we ever leave in the first place? Oh Yahweh, please, oh please, get us out of this! Jarah prayed as she hoisted Hava onto her back and raced to keep up with the others. Her feet pounded against the sand. Her heart leapt in her chest. She ran as fast as she could, not daring to stop.

But fatigue began to overtake her. Her legs felt heavy, but she pushed on. Already she could hear the distant shouts of the Egyptians and the clatter of the chariots.

Jarah stopped for a moment to catch her breath, glancing back over her shoulder. To her astonishment she saw the charioteers were having problems. The wheels were falling off their chariots; horses

31

were screaming, rearing, trying to free themselves from the broken chariots as they swerved and fell.

"Ezra, Acenith, look!" Jarah gasped, and they both turned to stare.

"Yahweh's fighting against them," Ezra said. "He's truly doing what He said He would do—fighting against them while we keep silent."

The Israelites were still moving along at a very fast pace, but the Egyptians were slowly gaining on them. The distance between them continued to close and Jarah's fear gave her strength to keep running. She could now see the Egyptians unsheathing their swords and fitting arrows on their bowstrings.

"Go faster, faster," she urged herself.

The ground began gently sloping upwards and she saw that the wall of water ended just a few hundred feet ahead. The sight gave her the energy needed to climb up the hill. Adriel and Ezra were already out of the sea and onto the beach. Acenith and the donkey and the wagon were right behind the boys. A few more wagons and people lagged behind Jarah, but the Egyptians were coming up to them quickly.

"Come on, Jarah! Hurry!" Acenith urged.

Jarah staggered onto the beach, completely spent. Adriel took his little sister from Jarah's shaking arms.

"Get away from the water," Ezra ordered, helping Adriel herd the animals up the hill. Acenith and Jarah grabbed the donkey's halter and urged it forward.

Jarah looked over her shoulder and saw the last wagons coming onto the beach. Incredibly, at that very moment, the wind suddenly stopped blowing. The wall of water stood for a moment, then collapsed onto the entire Egyptian army. Momentary screams and yells were heard from the soldiers, but there was nothing they could do. Millions and millions of gallons of water came crashing down, crushing and drowning them.

In just a few moments, the sea had returned to its normal state. Waves gently lapped against the shore and silence reigned amongst the Israelites. All were awed by what had just happened. Not one of the soldiers had survived. The pharaoh and all his army had been utterly destroyed.

None of the Israelites moved. All Jarah heard were a few murmuring voices saying, "Praise Yahweh." Soon, dead bodies of the Egyptians and their horses began to wash up onto the beach. The people began to move on, but even then they were unbelievably quiet. From somewhere in the midst of the throng of Israelites, a lone woman's voice started singing a song of praise, deliverance, and thanksgiving. Slowly, one by one, the other Israelites joined in. And then it suddenly hit them. There was nothing for them to worry about now. They were completely free! People started to cry with joy. Some were laughing. All were dancing and praising. The rising chorus of celebration grew steadily louder.

Cheers and laughter surrounded Jarah as the Israelites exultantly continued into the mountains. Tears of joy and relief flowed freely down her cheeks. She could scarcely believe what had just happened. She pinched herself to make sure she wasn't sleeping. She was laughing, singing, and crying all at the same time. It was like a beautiful and glorious dream. They were free—really and truly free.

Slowly, the people around Jarah grew quiet. A sense of awe and wonder settled on them, as everyone felt great amazement at the power and awesomeness of their God.

At first, Jarah could think of nothing else. Then a rush of thoughts came into her mind.

Where's my family? Did they make it off the beach? We had camped close to the cliffs. And what about Lemuel? Is he alive?

"WHAT HAPPENED TO LEMUEL?"

For the rest of the afternoon, Ezra and Jarah stayed close to Emmitt and Yachne's wagon, asking everybody they met on the road if they had seen their families. The other Israelites seemed preoccupied with what had just happened and offered very little helpful information.

"I think I saw a family like that on the beach yesterday," one man suggested.

"Thank you, sir," Jarah replied, trying to smile. Her heart was sinking. No one had clearly identified her family or Lemuel. No one had even offered a real clue that would help her find them.

The pillar of cloud stopped moving at dusk. Camp was set up after a whole day of traveling. Once Emmitt chose a place for his tent, Ezra and Jarah spread out, asking family after family if they had seen their fathers. Again, no success.

As it became too dark to see, Jarah made her way despondently back to Emmitt's fire. She plopped down on the sand next to a warm bowl of stew that Yachne set out for her. Acenith looked at her sympathetically. Jarah could tell that Acenith knew she was discouraged.

"Thank you, Yachne," Jarah said gratefully as she ate her stew.

The kind lady nodded. "You're welcome."

"Jarah, did you find your family?" Hava asked eagerly, bounding out of the tent.

"Hava." Acenith gave the little girl a rebuking look. "We'd better not talk about it."

"No, it's fine," Jarah said, trying her best to appear joyful. Turning to Hava, she continued, "No, Hava. We haven't found them yet. Perhaps tomorrow." But Jarah's tone was rather sorrowful.

Hava came up to Jarah and laid a tiny hand on her knee. "I think you'll find them. I've been praying for you."

"Thank you." Jarah smiled half-heartedly at the little upturned face.

Emmitt rose and stretched. "We should be getting to bed quickly," Emmitt suggested. "It's already quite late and we may have another long day tomorrow." Everyone agreed. Jarah's eyes met Ezra's as she rose from the ground. He looked at her cheerfully, but Jarah could see that he was weary, too.

Though Jarah's mind was still spinning with questions and thoughts, her body was utterly exhausted. Tonight she fell asleep almost instantly, curled up in between Acenith and Hava.

א

"Excuse me sir, I'm looking for my family. My father's name is Asher, of the tribe of Asher. He's about your height, with brown hair and a long beard. My mother's name is Mariel. She's pregnant and has long curly black hair. I have six other siblings, and my family is traveling in a large wagon. Have you seen them?"

"A lot of families look alike. I can't really think of anyone that particularly stood out. I'm sorry," the man apologized.

Jarah sighed and her eyes clouded with moisture. All day, she and Ezra had been looking through the lines of traveling people. Everyone

36

Jarah had asked said the same thing. "Sorry, I haven't seen them." What had happened to her family? And what about Lemuel? She plodded along, surrounded by hundreds and thousands of Israelites, but feeling very, very alone.

"Did you find anything?" Ezra asked hopefully, coming up behind her.

"No. Nothing." Jarah struggled to keep back tears of frustration as she maneuvered around a stopped wagon.

"Don't worry," Ezra said, optimistically. "We've only been looking for two days. We'll find them."

"But Ezra," Jarah pleaded, on the verge of tears, "what if they stayed behind because they were worried about us? What if they never made it into the Red Sea and were—" she stopped abruptly. She couldn't say the word.

"Killed?"

She nodded.

"Jarah," Ezra sighed, "I don't think that's what happened. I'm sure they're here somewhere. There are millions of people out here, and we're trying to find fourteen."

"Maybe only thirteen," Jarah muttered, staring into the last rays of the setting sun to hide her emotion.

Ezra was silent, seemingly searching for the right words. He stopped walking, put a reassuring hand on Jarah's shoulder and said, "Jarah, I'm still holding onto hope that Lemuel is alive. Perhaps he found help with a different family, like we've found with Emmitt. And if Lemuel has died, Yahweh has a reason, even though we may not understand it."

Jarah slowly bobbed her head up and down. This was starting to sound like her conversation with Adriel. Was Yahweh trying to tell her that there was a reason for Jarah to be separated from her family?

"So far Yahweh has faithfully looked out for us. I believe that He has looked out for Lemuel, too," Ezra finished with hope in his voice.

"How can you have such faith?" Jarah asked, stifling a sob.

Ezra smiled softly. "I have to trust Yahweh because there's no one else to trust. He's never failed me yet, and I have faith that He won't fail me this time, either. We'll find our families. I know it."

Jarah brushed away a tear. "I'll try to do what you say."

"That's all you need to do," Ezra said, a teasing grin spreading over his face again. He started to walk away, but turned back. "And Jarah... I know you can do it."

Jarah's eyes followed him. "I don't know if I can do it, Ezra," she whispered, "but I can certainly ask Yahweh for the strength to try."

ב

It was pitch black when Jarah finished spreading out her blanket next to Acenith's and stepped outside where the family was singing praise songs. Adriel's small harp accompanied them. Adriel and Emmitt were teaching Ezra a song that they had composed. Ezra's high tenor voice blended well with Adriel's baritone and Emmitt's deep tenor, and Jarah found herself humming along. The song talked about Yahweh's deliverance and protection. It made her feel peaceful about what had happened to them in Egypt and what was happening to them now. Hava fell asleep on Jarah's lap and Jarah soon felt herself nodding off. She gazed at the pillar of fire, blazing in the distance.

Yahweh's still with us, she told herself. *I must have faith in Him and remember what He's done for us. There's nothing to worry about. He'll protect us and lead us to His Promised Land.*

Acenith sat down next to Jarah and squeezed her hand. She smiled and whispered, "Hava really likes you. She doesn't fall asleep on just anybody's lap."

Jarah grinned. "She's really sweet. She reminds me of Tirzah when she was little..." Jarah's voice drifted off as she again wondered what had happened to her family.

Acenith seemed to sense what Jarah was thinking. She squeezed Jarah's hand again.

"Let's do one more, then we'll have to go to bed," Emmitt's voice broke through her thoughts. "Adriel, how about the most recent song you wrote?"

Adriel nodded and raised his harp. He began to pluck the strings slowly in a minor key and began to sing:

"Through the desert now, I wander,
 Ov'r a path I cannot see.
 And though sometimes I lose my way,
 Yahweh, You're so close to me.

"Though I run the other way,
 And don't listen to what You say,
 You forgive, and You show me what's true.
 Lord You always see me through...
 The desert.

"Yahweh, help me to trust,
 In Your perfect plan.
 Keep me close in the shelter,
 The shelter of Your hand!

"Though I run the other way,
 And don't listen to what You say,
 You forgive, and You show me what's true.
 Lord You always see me through...
 The desert.
 I am in Your hands."

As Adriel sang the chorus again, Jarah joined in, harmonizing. Their voices floated up into the night air and echoed among the mountains. The last note swelled, then faded away. Emmitt, Ezra, and Acenith clapped in admiration and Adriel looked approvingly at Jarah.

"That was beautiful," Acenith encouraged.

"Yahweh has definitely blessed you both with the gift of music," Emmitt said emphatically. He stood up, stretched, and yawned. "Let's get some sleep and save the other songs for another night," he advised, picking up little Yael who had fallen asleep curled up by the fire.

Everyone murmured in agreement and slowly made their way into the tent and to their beds. Jarah gently laid Hava on the mat next to hers and then crawled under her soft, warm blanket. She quickly drifted off to sleep with the words of Adriel's song still playing in her mind.

ג

It was the third day. Jarah and Ezra still searched fruitlessly through the horde of traveling Israelites. There were so many people that once again Jarah began to despair. As she blinked back tears she looked towards Emmitt's wagon. Emmitt had strapped a flag to their wagon, and Ezra and Jarah always kept it in view so that they wouldn't get lost again.

It was getting dark and the pillar of cloud had stopped moving. *Emmitt will be setting up camp soon,* Jarah thought, wiping her sweaty brow. She was getting extremely thirsty. *Maybe we should head back.*

As if in answer to her thoughts, Ezra abruptly said, "We'll head back in just a few minutes. I need some water, and I'm sure you do, too."

"All right, and—" Suddenly, Jarah froze in mid-step. Ezra almost ran into her. A young boy darted across Jarah's path after a ball made of scrap cloth. His wavy black hair blew back in the wind and he laughed merrily—just like Raphael! Jarah ran after him, winding her way through the procession of wagons and animals.

"Jarah, where are you going?" Ezra called after her.

Jarah heard him as if in a daze as she continued to run after the little boy. She finally caught up to him and grabbed his arm, spinning him around. The boy turned inquisitively and Jarah started back. It wasn't Raphael.

"Oh, I'm sorry. I—I thought you were someone else," Jarah stammered.

The boy nodded and ran off, leaving Jarah standing in the middle of the path, Hebrews streaming pass her. She exhaled deeply, sorrowfully. Ezra came up behind her and placed a tender hand on her arm. "I'm sorry," he said compassionately. Jarah avoided his eyes and looked down at the sand, trying to hide her tears. "We'll find them. I know we will," Ezra assured her. But Jarah could hear that the normally confident tone in his voice was weak and unsure.

"Let's go back now. We don't want to get lost again," Ezra teased, trying to lighten her spirits.

Jarah consented, but wouldn't trust herself to speak. They had spent so much time searching, but to no avail. What had happened to her family? Even Ezra didn't have anything to say as they walked back towards Emmitt's wagon. Jarah glanced up at him to see what he was thinking. His face was pale and he appeared solemn and deep in thought. When Ezra saw that she was looking at him, he smiled a comfortless smile at her.

When they reached the wagon, Emmitt and Adriel were just dragging out the tent. Jarah ran to get a drink before helping set up camp.

"Jarah, please don't drink too much. We've been rationing the water all afternoon. We're getting low on supplies," Yachne said, gently but firmly.

"Of course, Yachne," Jarah assented. She lifted a water jug to place it to her lips. She realized with dread that it was very light. There wasn't much water in it at all. Ezra joined her, grabbing another pitcher.

"Not too much," she warned him. "Yachne said that they're rationing their water supply." Ezra nodded and took a few sips of water. He wiped his mouth with the back of his hand before running off to help Adriel stake down the tent. Jarah took a few mouthfuls of water. It didn't satisfy her thirst, but it was better than nothing. She helped Acenith bring the blankets and mats inside the tent.

"Do you think there will be enough water?" Jarah asked her friend.

Acenith shrugged. She looked worried. "I don't know. We need to find some soon." Jarah nodded, absently drawing designs in the sand. Ezra poked his head into the tent.

"Jarah, we have a little while before it gets dark. Let's go talk to a few more people."

"Very well," Jarah agreed slowly. She followed Ezra outside.

"I'll start over here. There's a family I know I didn't talk to yet," he said.

"I'll be over there," Jarah said, pointing to where a middle-aged widow was setting up a tent. She had three older sons who were helping her.

"Excuse me, ma'am." The lady looked up at her, politely. "I'm looking for my family. My father's name is Asher, of the tribe of Asher. Have you seen him?"

"Asher…" The woman looked doubtful, then a light of recognition flashed into her eyes and she gasped, "Oh yes, I met a young man who said he had a father by that name. His name was Lemuel."

"Lemuel? Did you say Lemuel?" Jarah asked breathlessly.

"Yes, I did." The lady raised an eyebrow curiously.

"Ezra!" Jarah almost shrieked. "Come here!"

Ezra saw Jarah's shining eyes and broad smile and dashed over to her, just in time to hear the next sentence.

"Where was he? Is he safe?"

"We first met Lemuel the night before we crossed the Red Sea. Chaz went outside to secure the animals when he saw someone lying on the ground, unconscious. He brought him in and we found that he was bleeding badly from a cut on his leg. He never really told us how he got it. Lemuel was very weak and it took us some time to bring him to consciousness. He stayed with us that night and rode in our wagon when we went through the Red Sea. He seemed to recover pretty quickly, especially considering the amount of blood that he lost. Anyways, we kept Lemuel with us for two nights until he was well enough to go on by himself. He left just this morning saying that he had to find his father, Asher. I suppose Lemuel is your brother? You look alike."

"Yes, he is," Jarah said. She was feeling mixed emotions. She couldn't believe that Lemuel had left this family just this morning. They had missed him by only a few hours. But he was alive! The overwhelming emotion of joy swept through Jarah like a wave. Lemuel was safe and well and was probably somewhere close by. She and Ezra would find him. They *had* to.

"Thank you, ma'am," Ezra said. "We haven't heard anything about Jarah's brother for three days."

"Oh, you aren't related?" the lady asked in surprise, looking at Jarah, then at Ezra.

"No ma'am. We're just friends," Ezra explained yet again. Jarah quickly nodded in assent, feeling her cheeks turn pink. "But our families are very close," Ezra hastened to say. "Jarah, Lemuel and I were separated from our families before we crossed the Red Sea. We've been trying to find Lemuel and our families ever since."

"I hope you find them very soon," the woman said with a tender smile.

"Thank you, ma'am. We hope so, too," Jarah replied.

"Jarah, Ezra, dinnertime," Acenith called.

"Coming," Ezra shouted.

"Thank you, and good-bye," Jarah said to the lady. The woman nodded pleasantly and Ezra and Jarah went back to Emmitt's tent.

"I told you he was fine," Ezra said, grinning.

Jarah laughed. "I guess you were right." Then she breathed quietly, "Thank you, Yahweh. Now, please help us to find everyone else quickly. They can't be too far away now..."

MARAH

The next morning dawned clear, bright, and calm. Jarah's hopes soared as they loaded everything into Emmitt's wagon. The constant murmur of noise was growing louder as the other Israelites were also packing up. The widow that Jarah had talked with last night noticed her and smiled a friendly greeting. Jarah waved back. *We'll find our families today,* she told herself. *I just know it.*

"Yachne, is this the only water we have?" Acenith asked, hoisting a clay pitcher into the wagon.

Yachne came up to the wagon, balancing Hava on her hip. For the first time this morning, Jarah realized that there was a worried furrow in Yachne's brow and she wasn't smiling. Laying a gentle hand on Acenith's shoulder she answered, "That's the last of the water, Acenith."

Jarah's jaw dropped open. She stared at Acenith. Acenith's eyes were very round. She gulped and then whispered, "I'll go get the rest of the food."

"Thank you, dear."

Jarah stepped up to Yachne. She felt horrible. She didn't realize that she and Ezra had made their water supply diminish so quickly.

"Yachne, I'm so sorry about the water. I didn't know. Ezra and I will move on right away. We've been so thankful for your hospitality and kindness, but for your family's sake—"

"Nonsense, Jarah!" Yachne interrupted. "It's not your fault. There hasn't been a well or a spring in days. But I know Yahweh will provide. He always does." Yachne smoothed Jarah's hair and tried to smile. Jarah nodded and blinked back tears. She felt miserable. Jarah turned her back to Yachne so that she wouldn't see her crying.

What can we do to help them? What if we can't find any water? Their children and animals are going to suffer because of us.

Emmitt goaded the donkey forward and it moved the wagon into the mass of people. Jarah plodded alongside the wagon, trying to hold back her emotions. Out of the corner of her eye, Jarah saw Ezra and Adriel approaching her.

"Are you ready for another day of searching?" Ezra asked her, grinning.

"Yes, I suppose so." She tried to return his playfulness, but Ezra instantly realized that Jarah had been crying. A look of concern crossed his face.

Adriel exchanged a look with Ezra that said, 'I can tell you two need to talk.' Out loud, he said, "I'll come help you all in a bit, but right now I have to take care of the animals. I'll see you soon."

"Thank you, Adriel." Ezra watched his new friend fall back in line, herding the animals. When Adriel was out of earshot he questioned, quietly, "What is it?"

Jarah glanced away from the wagon. "Let's move on and then we'll talk about it."

Ezra nodded and they distanced themselves from Emmitt's wagon. Ezra moved up to Jarah so that he could see her face and looked at her, searchingly. Sighing, Jarah said, "Ezra, Emmitt and Yachne barely have enough water for today." Ezra's eyes grew wide. "What are we going to do?" Jarah asked. "What if we can't find our families tonight? I don't want their children and animals to suffer because of us."

Ezra bit his lip, thinking hard. After a pause he said, "Keep your eyes open for any sign of water. If we need to move on to another family who has greater provisions, we will. Besides, we should find our families soon."

"And if we don't find them?" Jarah persisted.

Ezra shrugged. "You let me worry about that," he said, almost jokingly.

Jarah smiled to herself. She knew that Ezra would do everything in his power to help her, and Emmitt's family, too. With renewed vigor, Jarah searched for familiar faces.

א

The day wore on monotonously. Sadly, Jarah saw very few people she had not already talked with. The sun felt like it was scorching her. Wearily, Jarah headed back towards Emmitt's wagon for a drink of water. When she reached it, she discovered that there was no water left.

"I'm sorry," Yachne apologized, genuinely concerned.

"No, you don't have to apologize. It's fine, really," Jarah said, trying to sound careless. "I'll move ahead and look for some water." Acenith, holding a sleeping Hava on her lap, gave Jarah a cheerless grin. She looked worn out and listless.

Weaving in and out of the mass of moving Israelites, Jarah kept her eyes open for a well or spring beside the trail. She felt a tap on her shoulder. It was Ezra.

"Find out anything?" he asked hopefully.

"No, not yet."

"It's almost the middle of the afternoon. The cloud might stop soon. Let's go back and get some water," Ezra suggested, wiping his forehead.

"Ezra, there's no water left," Jarah told him.

"What?"

Jarah nodded. "It's all been used up. I told Yachne I'd be looking for a well or spring while I continued to search. But it's so dry out here. I don't think we'll be able to find anything."

Ezra's countenance was dark. "This isn't good," he muttered to himself. "If we don't find something soon people are going to suffer and die from thirst." He looked at Jarah and said, "Let's pray."

As they continued to walk, Ezra said a short but heartfelt prayer asking Yahweh to show them a water source soon. During the prayer, Jarah began to notice the whimpering cries of young children pleading for water. The animals' heads were drooping and no one seemed to be talking much. Jarah's throat felt swollen from dust and thirst.

"Amen," Ezra finished.

"Amen," Jarah breathed. She peered into the distance, looking for a sign of water. Everything was hot and shimmering and blurry. Jarah's eyes finally rested on the pillar of cloud.

Yahweh, You have to help us now.

Then she gasped. What were those green things? Were they trees, or was her mind playing tricks on her?

"An oasis!" the cry came from a man farther up the line. "We've reached an oasis, at last!"

At those words Jarah felt a cool refreshing peace flood over her, almost as if she had dumped water all over her head. Ezra's face lit up.

"Come on. Let's go to Emmitt's wagon and get some skins for water. The two of us can get through these people faster than their wagon can," Ezra urged.

Feeling new energy, Jarah ran after Ezra as he weaved in and out of people. They soon reached the wagon with the flying flag, told Emmitt and Yachne the situation, and took some water skins from the back of the wagon.

As Jarah neared the oasis she was jostled to and fro by the crowd. Everyone was fighting to get to the water first. Ezra cleared a path through the people and Jarah followed him, clinging to his arm so she wouldn't get separated. Suddenly, they found themselves by a large, clear spring. It was as wide as a big creek and flowed away into the distance. Small trees and bushes grew along its shallow, sandy banks. Instantly, Jarah and Ezra knelt by it and scooped up water in their cracked, dry hands. Ezra started coughing, almost as if he was choking, and Jarah quickly discovered why. She began to drink, but then spat out the water in disgust. The water was bitter! She could barely swallow it! How could they drink that? The other Israelites were finding out the same thing and there were cries of anguish and anger rising from everywhere.

"What shall we drink?" a man grumbled.

"We can't possibly drink this," another stated. "But if something doesn't happen soon, we're going to die out here!"

"Where's Moses? He'd better have an answer to this problem," a third man asked, upset. The Israelites peered around, trying to find Moses.

Jarah saw Moses emerge from the crowd. He came and knelt besides the wide brook. He squinted up towards heaven and stared into space for several minutes. Not a person moved; no one even dared to speak.

Finally Moses stood upright and walked through the people, soon disappearing from sight. The crowd murmured in annoyance and disappointment. Children's whining, plaintive cries once again filled the air. The animals stood still, looking ready to drop dead. The people and animals were covered in dust and sweat and everyone was too exhausted to move. Jarah glanced at Ezra. He was sitting silently, patiently, waiting for Moses to return.

There was a buzz of commotion. Moses reappeared, dragging with him a tree that was about twenty feet in height. He rolled the tree into the water. There was a large splash and sprinkles of cold water fell onto Jarah's face and arms. Her skin tingled and a refreshing coldness swept over her. *If only I could drink the water, too,* she groaned inwardly.

Then Moses bade the people to drink. No one stepped forward. What difference would a tree make? Surely the water was still bitter, wasn't it?

Jarah gazed into Moses' face. She saw frustration and weariness. But there was still that look of kindness and love in Moses' troubled eyes. *I'll just have to trust him,* Jarah told herself. The water was so tempting. Jarah couldn't resist trying to drink it one more time. She thrust her troubled thoughts aside and scooped up some water into her mouth. She found to her astonishment and disbelief that the water was sweet. It was deliciously cold and almost immediately quenched her thirst.

"It's sweet!" she proclaimed.

Instantly others tasted the water and realized the wonderful truth. Shouts of joy and wonder filled the congregation. Ecstatic with joy and relief, Ezra and Jarah drank to their heart's content. Moses raised his hand for silence.

"Yahweh says, 'If you will give earnest heed to the voice of the Lord your God, and do what is right in His sight, and give ear to His commandments, and keep all His statutes, I will put none of the diseases on you which I have put on the Egyptians; for I, the Lord, am your healer.' Now trust Him, and know that He will care for all your needs."

An awed stillness rested over the people as Moses finished his speech. Heads nodded and there were whispered assents. Then the animals were brought forward to have their fair share of water. Jarah and Ezra filled their skins with liquid and proceeded to push their way through the Israelites and back to Yachne and Emmitt.

That night the pillar of fire rested at the brook and the Israelites camped at the waters, which had been called Marah because of the bitterness. Since camp was set up earlier than usual, Jarah and Ezra had more time to look for their families and met many new people. But they didn't find Lemuel, nor did they receive any other clues about where their families might be.

"I thought we were so close," Jarah moaned as she crawled into bed that night. She lay in bed, thinking about what Ezra had said at dinner. 'We should find them tomorrow,' Ezra had assured her. But he had said that yesterday, and the day before yesterday. She could tell that his optimistic spirit was slowly fading and that he, too, was worried about whether their families had made it across the Red Sea in time. Where were they?

ב

Five more days passed of almost constant walking and unsuccessful searching. Then they reached Elim where there were twelve springs of pure, clear water, and seventy date palms. Emmitt pulled up the donkeys in the shade of a large boulder. Everybody sighed with contentment as they sat on the ground, resting for a few minutes before they unpacked and set up their tent for the night.

"I'll go get some more water for the animals," Jarah offered. "Then Ezra and I can continue our search."

"Thank you, Jarah. That would be a blessing," Yachne said gratefully. Yael and Hava had immediately fallen asleep and Yachne and Acenith could now focus on preparing dinner for the family.

Jarah threaded her way through the tents, animals, and people towards the nearest spring. There were only a few other women here, and Jarah felt herself relaxing in the relative privacy of the spring. Kneeling beside it, Jarah drank deeply of its water. She rocked back on her heels and began to fill up one of the skins. Sighing, a tear slowly slid down her cheek. Jarah missed her family terribly. She had never been away from them for more than one day, and now she hadn't seen them for nine. How would they ever find them? Ezra continued to assure her, 'We will find them Jarah. We will.' But even his comforting words seemed hollow to her poor, aching heart. Acenith had been so sweet and kind to her. She was a real and true friend. Ezra and Adriel, too, were being compassionate and caring. But Jarah could see that Ezra was struggling. Just last night Jarah had seen him creep out of the tent. Looking through the opening, she had seen Ezra kneeling on the sand, praying. His shoulders had been shaking with sobs and Jarah knew that Ezra missed his family, too. Adriel had soon joined Ezra. Though Jarah had not been able to hear the conversation, Adriel seemed to have encouraged Ezra to keep on praying and persevering.

How can Ezra pray? Jarah huffed inwardly. *I've been praying, but Yahweh doesn't seem to hear me or answer. Sometimes I almost feel like quitting…*

An overwhelming feeling of guilt stole into Jarah's heart. She gulped, rose to her feet and whispered very softly, "Yahweh, I'm so sorry. I must trust You. Like Ezra said, there's no one else to trust. Please help me to focus on You and surrender everything to You—my hopes, my fears, my worry, and my dreams. Please, give me that peace that You promise Your people."

There, that feels better, she thought, pausing to savor the relief and peace that began to trickle into her heart.

"Jarah!"

Jarah looked around. Who had called her name? Was it Ezra? No, it wasn't Ezra's voice. Could it possibly be…?

Suddenly, Jarah felt arms encircle her from behind and she was twirled in the air. She was set down and a voice exclaimed, "Thanks be to Yahweh I've found you!"

"Lemuel!" Jarah shrieked. She spun around and threw herself in her older brother's arms. They were both laughing and tears of joy streamed down their cheeks.

"Where have you been?" Jarah asked.

"Where have *you* been? We've looked everywhere for you and Ezra. You can't imagine how worried everyone is about both of you. Ezra is with you, isn't he?" Lemuel looked around in concern.

"Oh yes. I don't know what I would have done without him. We found another family that we've been staying with, and that's where he is now. But we've been worried about you, too. Are you well? How's your leg?" Jarah was stumbling over her words in her haste. The women by the creek looked on with curious faces, but Jarah was too excited to feel embarrassed.

"Much better. It still hurts some, but it'll be fine," Lemuel explained.

"Praise be to Yahweh," Jarah sighed. "Where are the tents?"

"Over there. Let's go get Ezra and then we'll all go back together."

Jarah agreed, leading the way back towards Emmitt's tent. "So where were you?" she asked. "Ezra and I have looked everywhere and asked everyone we met. We heard that you were all right from that widow you stayed with, but we never heard news of Mother and Father."

"It took me about a day to find them, too," Lemuel explained. "They were in the very front of the column. They were some of the first that went into the Red Sea. Father and Jaden were making just as many inquiries about you, and once we discovered you were nowhere to be found we starting working our ways backwards in the line. Now we've met each other right about in the middle."

"Well I'm so glad you did. There's Ezra. Ezra!" Jarah called, waving frantically at him. Ezra looked up from where he was nailing in tent pegs with Adriel and he jumped to his feet in shock. He stood as if frozen, his jaw open in disbelief. Then—when he realized he wasn't dreaming—Ezra ran forward and wrapped Lemuel in a brotherly hug. The two friends laughed with relief and thankfulness.

"Ezra," Emmitt began, walking up to the happy party, "who's your friend?"

"Emmitt, this is Lemuel, Jarah's brother."

Lemuel was warmly welcomed by Emmitt, Adriel, and the rest of the family.

After Lemuel told everyone the story of how he'd been found and met up with his family, he said, "We'd better go back. Mother and Father will worry about me if I'm gone too much longer."

Ezra nodded. "Yes, we should." Looking Emmitt in the eyes, Ezra said, "Emmitt, we can't thank you enough for all that you've done for us."

"It was nothing, Ezra. We would've done the same for any other Israelite. You feel like part of the family now. Please come and visit us again. But this time, visit us on purpose," Emmitt replied, jovially.

Everyone laughed. "We will," Ezra promised.

Quick good-byes were said with Ezra saying his last farewell to Adriel. "It was wonderful to meet you. I've really enjoyed our friendship. You feel like a brother to me now."

Adriel responded with that infectious smile that Jarah was now accustomed to. "It was wonderful to meet you both. I've been inspired by the ways you've served our family while you were here. I know we will all miss you terribly."

"Well, I pray that this is not a final goodbye. Since we are of the same tribe we'll hopefully see each other again soon," Ezra assured his friend.

"Perhaps so," Adriel murmured. "Perhaps so."

Jarah hugged Acenith long and hard. "Thank you for your kindness and help, Acenith. I love you and I'm going to miss you."

"I'll miss you, too," Acenith said, pulling away from Jarah. She was crying. "You're almost like my sister, Jarah. I almost wish I could go with you," she whispered, a pleading look on her face. Jarah shook her head.

"Emmitt's family will take care of you. My mother, well—" Jarah paused, carefully choosing her next words. "You wouldn't like my mother. She wouldn't be an encouragement to you like Yachne is. She's with child, too, so I don't think she'd want another person in the tent, even one as sweet and beautiful as you. You're better off here." Jarah forced a smile. "But don't worry, Acenith. I think we'll see each other again, and remember that Yahweh will be your Father and your family, too." Acenith stiffened visibly but Jarah continued, lowering her voice. "I hope you'll at least consider turning to Him, Acenith." Acenith nodded slowly, blinking back tears.

As Jarah left, she looked back over her shoulder to see Acenith and Adriel watching them go. The expression on Acenith's face was pitiful and heart-wrenching. It made her feel sorry to be leaving Acenith, but she knew that Yachne would be able to take better care of her than Jarah ever could. Yachne's love for Yahweh was evident, and it was obvious that she treated Acenith as if she were her own daughter.

Yes, she'll be better off with them, Jarah told herself, though the thought made her sad inside. She was going to miss Yachne and Acenith so much. They had both been so good to her.

On their way back to their families, Lemuel's eyes traveled over Jarah's beaming face and he mentioned to Ezra, "I see you've kept Jarah safe."

Ezra shrugged modestly. "I tried. She really took care of herself."

"Don't listen to him, Lem," Jarah retorted. "If he hadn't been with me I probably would've died the first night we were away. He's been very helpful, and encouraging."

"I see…" Lemuel nodded and stared into Ezra's face. Ezra's cheeks reddened slightly and his eyes averted Lemuel's gaze.

They had walked over a mile when Lemuel exclaimed, "Look, here we are."

They both looked where Lemuel was pointing. He was looking at a tent in the shade of a short scraggly tree. Jarah heard a delighted shriek.

"Jarah!"

Tirzah appeared out of nowhere and threw her arms around Jarah's waist, squeezing her so hard that she couldn't breathe.

"Tirzah!" Jarah hugged her sister back. Tears were dimming her eyes. She felt Raphael and Yanni clinging to her legs. They were asking so many questions that Jarah couldn't understand what they were saying. Jarah blinked back her tears and saw Ada and Amissa hugging Ezra. Her father was running towards her. Jarah stretched out her arms to him and he wrapped her in a warm embrace.

"My daughter, it's so good to have you back," Father whispered. His voice was hoarse, like he was about to cry.

Jarah heard her mother's voice at her shoulder. "It's about time you got back," she said a little gruffly. But there was a twinkle in Mother's eyes that made tears fall down Jarah's cheeks once again. She could tell that her mother really did love her and had missed her.

Ezra and Jarah repeated the story of getting lost, finding Emmitt's family, and trying to find their way back home. Then their family members caught them up on all their news. Everyone was talking at once.

"Jarah, I lost a tooth! See?" Raphael said, opening his mouth very wide.

"Ezra, we found your flute that was lost," Amissa was saying.

"Jah-Jah, we have a new baby goat!" Yanni exclaimed, jumping up and down.

Ada's arm crept lovingly around Jarah's shoulders. "It's so good to have you both back," she said with a sweet loving look into Jarah's eyes. Shayna's arm slid around her waist. Her big sister was smiling. A thrill of delight made Jarah's heart flutter.

Eitan stepped forward, grinning. "We're glad that you're safe."

"What did you eat? You look skinny, girl," Mother almost interrupted.

"Everyone! Everyone, calm down," Father yelled above the hubbub. "We're going to tire Jarah and Ezra with our excitement and questions. Let's finish preparing dinner and then we can all talk. It's already growing dark."

As her family moved away, Jarah saw two people that she didn't recognize. There was an elderly man and woman, standing on the outside of the circle and smiling on what was happening. Father took

Jarah's hand and said, "There are some people I would like you to meet, or meet again, rather." Father led her over to the couple.

"Jarah, this is your grandfather, Sethur. You probably don't remember him. You were only four or five when they were taken to another part of Egypt. Sethur is a well respected man in our tribe, one of our elders. I expect you to treat him with the same reverence and obedience as you give me," her father said, solemnly.

Sethur was tall, strong, and dignified, with a long gray beard, but Jarah could see a twinkle in his dark eyes as he asked, "So this is our long lost little granddaughter? Though I shouldn't be saying little anymore, since she's grown into quite a beautiful young lady, Asher."

Jarah giggled and said, "Thank you, sir."

"And this is your grandmother, Marnee," Father introduced.

Marnee gave Jarah a hug. "It's so good to have you back, dear. I'm sure you don't remember me, but I used to tell you stories as a girl. You were a very attentive listener."

An image flashed through Jarah's mind of a woman perched on a stool, telling stories in a sweet, low voice. She pictured herself sitting on the floor, her chin on her hands, listening. She nodded and smiled in remembrance.

"I do remember you, Grandmother. I'm so glad to see you again," she said.

"Now, come, let's eat," Father said.

After dinner that night, Jarah cuddled down next to Tirzah exhausted, but peaceful and happy.

"I've missed you a lot," Tirzah murmured softly, inching closer to her older sister.

"I've missed you, too. I hope I can introduce you to Hava. You'd love her. She's so sweet. And Acenith, too."

"How many children do they have again?" Tirzah asked.

"Three. Hava's the youngest, then Yael, the sickly one. He barely has the strength to move by himself. He loved my stories, just like you do. And then Adriel is the oldest."

"How old is he?"

"Do you ever stop asking questions?" Jarah asked with mock-severity.

Tirzah grinned from ear to ear. "No. Now, how old is he?"

"I think he just turned fifteen."

"Hmm… He's not much older than you, Jarah." Tirzah looked teasingly up at her older sister. She giggled as she continued, "Isn't it romantic that you were lost with Ezra?"

"No, it's not," Jarah replied, hotly.

"Yes it is," Tirzah said with a suppressed laugh. Jarah felt her cheeks growing hot.

"He—he's like a brother to me, Tirzah. Like another Lemuel." Jarah almost choked on her own words. She was beginning to think that the usual explanation that Ezra was a 'brother' was no longer true.

"Really?"

"Tirzah!"

"All right, all right," Tirzah muttered, slightly annoyed. Suddenly she started, "Oh Jarah, you came back so late that you didn't get a chance to see Aunt Zuriel's family!"

"What?" Jarah asked, surprised. Aunt Zuriel was Mother's cousin and Mother's only living relative. They hadn't seen Aunt Zuriel's family in six years. They had been made to work in a forge, far away down the Nile.

"Didn't you know?" Tirzah questioned, breaking into Jarah's thoughts. "Mother found Aunt Zuriel's family. It's been so much fun. Except that you weren't here, of course. But it's *so* romantic, Jarah, because Rishon and Shayna were going to be betrothed, but then they moved away. Now they're older and can get married very soon!"

"Does Rishon want to marry Shayna?" Jarah queried.

"Well, it's been pretty awkward. They're just getting to know each other again. We'll just have to wait, I suppose. But Rishon is *so* handsome, Jarah. And everyone thinks that they will be a good match."

"*Everyone?*" Jarah repeated, mimicking Tirzah's exaggeration.

"Yes. Everyone," Tirzah said, matter-of-factly.

"Well, we'd better go to sleep. Good-night, Tizzy," Jarah said, playfully.

"'Night, Jarah," Tirzah said, yawning. Tirzah's breathing soon became soft and rhythmic.

Jarah's thoughts drifted to her long-lost relatives. She remembered that Aunt Zuriel had been very sweet and motherly and had looked a lot like Mother. She remembered that her uncle, Daton, was a quiet, almost intimidating man. But their faces were vague in Jarah's mind. She wondered if they would be different now and if Aunt Zuriel had turned to the Egyptian gods, like Mother.

Next she thought about Rishon. From what she remembered of him he was a loving, playful young boy. He and Shayna had been very sweet on each other when they were young. But Shayna had also been much more considerate and kind than she was now. She vaguely remembered her parents talking about a formal betrothal between Shayna and Rishon. But then Rishon's family had been taken away and they'd never heard from them again. Would Rishon still consider Shayna as his intended? Would there really be a formal betrothal? She sighed, wistfully.

Will everyone be the same as I remember them?

ג

Ezra helped his father throw sand on the fire to put it out. As the fire sizzled and smoked, Ezra found that he was finally starting to relax. Ever since he and Jarah had been separated from their families, Ezra had felt a great weight on his shoulders to get them both back home. He was slowly feeling that weight slide away.

"It's so good to have you back, son," his father said, clasping Ezra's shoulder.

"It's good to be back," Ezra replied, smiling. He glanced up at his father and realized that his father wasn't looking at him. He appeared to be deep in thought and rather troubled.

"Is something wrong, Father? Was there trouble with anything while I was away? With any of the animals or anything?"

"No... No... Not that," his father said, absently.

"Can I help with something?" Ezra prodded.

"Not really, son."

Ezra waited to see if his father was going to tell him what was troubling him. He was about to head inside the tent when his father spoke.

"Ezra, it's Asher. Something's wrong with him."

"Jarah and Lemuel's father?" Ezra asked, somewhat alarmed. "What do you mean?"

"Ever since this trip began, something about him has been... different," his father said. "I know Mariel has been particularly complaining and irritable. But Asher loves her. I know he does. But he seems to be avoiding her. Eitan's had to help even more than usual with providing food and taking care of the animals. I can tell it's wearing on him. Ada's very concerned. And I'm concerned about Asher's attitude. He can't run away from his problems and from his family. He's got to be the leader and provider and not force that on his son. I just hope that he realizes his mistake and comes back soon."

"I hope so, too," Ezra said softly. His father was obviously burdened by this. Asher was one of his father's closest friends. "Are you going to talk to Asher, Father?"

"If Yahweh so leads, than yes. But right now I'm just praying for him. Please, be in prayer, too."

"Of course, Father," Ezra replied, nodding.

"Thanks, son. Now, let's get to bed. We need to be ready to move on whenever Yahweh leads."

CELEBRATIONS

Jarah moaned and stretched. Golden sunlight filtered through the tent flap. Jarah sat up abruptly. No one else was in the tent. Had she overslept? Hastily, Jarah grabbed a fresh dress and changed. She pulled a shawl over her thick, curly hair and put an over-tunic around her shoulders before exiting the tent. The glare of the sun against the white sand stung her eyes.

"Good morning, Jah-Jah!" Yanni exclaimed. He threw his chubby arms around Jarah's legs and looked up into her eyes with a merry laugh.

"Good morning to you too, Yanni." Jarah scooped up her little brother and held him on her hip. She noticed that Mother was cooking porridge that bubbled and boiled and smelled warm and inviting. It was early in the morning and the sand was still cold on Jarah's bare feet. Hearing peals of laughter, she saw Raphael romping with Manni and Manuel. Shayna was sitting in the shade of a date tree, watching them warily. Amissa emerged from her family's tent about twenty yards away. Jarah waved to her and Amissa smiled back, looking very happy.

"Jarah, you're just in time for breakfast," Tirzah proclaimed. "Our relatives will be here soon to join us. And Amissa's family is coming, too. And Ezra, of course." Tirzah's eyes danced and she looked knowingly at Jarah.

"Tirzah…" Jarah gave her sister that 'You'd better stop that right now' look. Tirzah shrugged her shoulders and rolled her eyes.

"Tirzah, go get the bowls from the tent," Mother snapped.

"Good morning, Mother," Jarah ventured.

"Good morning," Mother replied shortly.

She's not in a good mood, Jarah thought. A bit of sorrow stole into her heart as she suddenly realized that she felt more comfortable around Yachne than around her own mother. She would do anything to have such a wonderful relationship with Mother.

Once Tirzah returned to the fire pit with the bowls, Mother commanded, "Jarah, go get Eitan and Lemuel. They're tending to the animals."

"Yes, Mother," Jarah replied, trying to sound warm and friendly. Mother didn't even seem to notice. A small sigh escaped Jarah's lips as she put Yanni down and trudged towards a large, flat rock in the distance where her oldest brother and his fiancé were sitting. Sheep and goats lay sprawled out on the sand, resting for the day's journey ahead of them.

"Hello Jarah," Lemuel's head popped up from among their family's sheep. "I hope you slept well."

"Very well, thank you," Jarah answered, grinning. "Mother says it's time for breakfast," she added.

"Finally! I'm famished," Lemuel declared.

Jarah vainly tried to suppress her giggles. "You and your appetite. Will you ever stop eating?"

"I only eat three meals a day," Lemuel protested.

"That's one more than the rest of us," Jarah retorted.

Lemuel grinned. "Why don't you go get Eitan and Ada? I need to check on that old ewe before I eat." He pointed with his staff towards a gray sheep. "She's been pretty sick."

"All right," Jarah agreed.

62

As Jarah approached the rock, Ada was the first to notice her and greeted her with a warm smile.

"Jarah, good morning. I'm afraid I didn't get much of a chance to speak to you last night," Ada apologized.

"It's fine, Ada. I'm sure you were spending time with Ezra," Jarah assured her.

"Well, yes, I was," Ada said, appearing pleased. "He said that you were such an encouragement to him."

"I'm the one who should be thankful," Jarah told her. "The first night we were lost, I almost froze to death. Ezra gave me his cloak, and after that he was always looking out for me. He's been wonderful."

"Yes, I'm sure he has." A knowing smile tugged at the corners of Ada's mouth and she and Eitan exchanged a glance.

"Eitan, Mother says it's time for breakfast."

"We'll be right there." Eitan stepped down from the rock and offered his hand to Ada. He helped her down the steep side and then they followed Jarah back home.

As Jarah entered the camp, she heard Raphael shout, "Joleen, come play with us!" A little girl almost magically appeared. Her tangled black hair flew back in the wind as she raced towards Raphael and the other boys. Her knees sported several bruises.

"Asher, is this Jarah? My how you've grown." A woman who looked surprisingly like her mother came up to Jarah with a bright, beaming countenance.

"Yes, Zuriel," said Father. "This is Jarah. And yes, she's grown into quite the young lady. She'll be thirteen years of age in just a few days."

That's right, Jarah thought. *I was so busy trying to find my family I forgot about my birthday!*

"It's good to see you again, Jarah," the man standing next to Aunt Zuriel said.

He must be Uncle Daton, Jarah thought.

"Thank you, sir," she said respectfully. Her uncle was a quiet, almost stern-looking man, but he didn't seem mean.

Jarah now noticed a young man coming towards them. He was broad and muscular with a set jaw and dark, honest eyes. He seemed wise, mature, and quiet. Jarah knew at once that it was Rishon. She glanced sideways at Shayna and saw her older sister blushing and smoothing an imaginary wrinkle from her tunic. Jarah bit her lip to keep from grinning.

"Jarah, this is my new friend," Tirzah was dragging a petite and very pretty young girl towards her. "This is Chanah, our cousin."

"Are you Jarah?" Chanah asked, sweetly. "Tirzah has told me about you."

"Yes, I'm Jarah. It's nice to meet you. Are these all of your siblings? I can remember Rishon and another girl, but that's it."

"Well, there's Rishon." Chanah pointed out her family members as she talked. "Rishon's very old. He's a man now," Chanah explained with a very serious expression, nodding her head up and down. "Joleen is nine, then there's me. We love each other lots," she said earnestly, her brown eyes glistening. "Reia is here somewhere, but I don't know where."

Jarah suppressed a laugh at the girl's solemnity. "Thank you. We better get some breakfast. The cloud will be moving soon." Jarah turned to sit down, and that's when she saw her.

A gorgeous young lady emerged from behind Aunt Zuriel's shoulder. She was slender and small and had a very graceful, feminine build. The girl's scarlet colored dress off-set her smooth skin, rich, flowing black hair, and the softest, warmest brown eyes Jarah had ever seen. A tiny smile graced the girl's exquisite face. Jarah was enamored by her beauty and wished with all her heart that she could get to know this lovely girl.

"Oh, there's Reia!" Chanah announced. "She's really quiet. But you'll like her."

Several large blankets were spread out on the ground in the shade of a date tree. A few other Israelite families were already sitting there, but they ignored the newcomers, and soon all of their relatives and friends were seated on the sand, eating and talking. Jarah had been trying to find an opportunity to talk to Reia, but the girl seemed very timid and avoided her. Instead of sitting with the other young women and children, Reia was sitting next to her mother, listening intently to her parents' conversation. Somehow Shayna had managed to sit quite close to Rishon. Rishon, however, didn't seem to have any interest in her. He would reply to Shayna's questions and ask her a few, just to be polite. But otherwise he ignored her. Jarah wondered what would happen with that relationship. She thought that Shayna and Rishon would make a very handsome couple.

As Jarah turned back to her food, her eyes met Ezra's. She quickly averted her eyes but she felt her cheeks turn red.

"Have you talked much with Reia?" Jarah asked Amissa very softly so that Reia wouldn't overhear them.

Amissa shook her head. "No. She's very shy. I think it will take us a while to get to know her."

Jarah nodded. She snuck a look at Reia out of the corner of her eye and noticed that Reia was fingering a pewter pendant strung on a leather string around her neck.

"Oh Reia," Jarah breathed. "That's a beautiful necklace."

Reia started at the sudden exclamation from Jarah. "Thank you," she whispered modestly. "Rishon made it for me. He's a very skilled metal worker." There was an awkward pause. "Would you like to see it?" Reia finished, quietly.

"Yes, please," Jarah replied eagerly.

Reia unfastened the necklace and reached across the blanket to hand it to her, though she seemed reluctant to do so. The pendant was in the shape of a lily. It was intricately fashioned and showed incredible skill and workmanship.

"It's lovely. Rishon is certainly very talented," Jarah agreed as she handed the necklace back to Reia.

"Yes, he is," Reia responded and then she lapsed back into silence. Jarah didn't know what else to say to her. There was a long, awkward pause.

Amissa finally cleared her throat and said, "Uh… Jarah, I didn't really hear your side of the story last night."

Jarah turned her attention towards Amissa and after the meal was over, Reia disappeared. Jarah didn't get an opportunity to talk to Reia through the whole day. Whenever she and Amissa tried, Reia shied away. Jarah was sad. Would she ever be able to win her cousin's friendship? She was so lovely. Could Jarah get her to open up?

א

For the next six days, nothing much happened. The days became monotonous: Eating their morning meal, packing up, walking all day, setting up camp, eating dinner, and sleeping. All of the Israelites were beginning to grumble. The cloud was leading them through a bewildering maze of mountain passes and valleys. Surely this was not the way to the Promised Land. Where was Yahweh taking them?

Jarah was starting to get tired of the desert when the cloud finally came to a stop. Food was beginning to run short. Wearily, Jarah slid into bed that night cross, irritable, and hungry. But worse than her hunger was her thirst. The dry dust and the scorching sun seemed to sap all of the energy from her body. They had some goat's milk, but this did not completely satisfy. Though they had stopped at a place where there were a few springs and a few scrubby trees, it was nothing compared to the abundance of Elim.

The next morning Grandfather strode into camp. He looked a little relieved, but also annoyed and anxious.

"Moses seems to think that the cloud will stay here for a few days. Moses knows that our supply of food is diminishing but says that Yahweh will provide for us. How, I don't know. But Moses seems confident." Grandfather shrugged.

Jarah saw her father and Jaden, Ada's father, exchange a glance. They turned and looked at Eitan and Ada, sitting in the shade of a tree a couple of yards away.

"We've talked about holding a betrothal ceremony for Eitan and Ada as soon as we came to a resting place. Everything is in readiness with Ada. Should we hold it tomorrow afternoon?" Jaden suggested.

"I think so. Only, will there be enough food for the feast?" Father asked.

"As Moses said, Yahweh provides. I know our family has some food stored and some animals to kill and prepare. We'll help you," Jaden offered.

Jarah was grinning ear-to-ear as she ran to tell Mother, Shayna, and Eitan the news. She couldn't wait for tomorrow.

ב

The sun was beginning to sink in the bright, desert sky as Eitan and Ada's families hurried to prepare for the betrothal ceremony. Eitan was behind Jarah's tent, talking in low tones with their father and Ada's father. He looked a little nervous, but his eyes shone with a joy that Jarah had never seen before. She ran past him, grinning ear-to-ear as she chased Yanni, trying to get him washed up after a late lunch. She herded Yanni through the tent flap and then gasped in amazement and wonder.

"Ada," she exclaimed, dreamily, "you look beautiful!"

Ada, standing in the center of the tent, was adorned in a flowing white linen dress. A few yellow desert flowers were twined in her luxurious brown curls. Her eyes were sparkling with an inner love and beauty and she smiled a big, inviting smile that made Jarah's spine tingle with warmth.

"Thank you, Jarah," Ada murmured, too happy to speak anything more.

"Pwetty pwetty!" Yanni shouted. He ran towards Ada, arms out-stretched.

"Yanni no!" Jarah cried. "You're going to mess up Ada's dress."

"Oh, it's all right," Ada assured Jarah, folding the little toddler in her arms. She looked up, still beaming.

"Yanni, go outside now," Ada's mother Sanne said, laughing softly. "We must finish getting Ada ready."

"I'll get him cleaned up, Jarah," Mother said. "Go help Amissa with the other preparations while we finish getting Ada ready."

"Yes, Mother." Though her mother's tone was cold as usual, Jarah could tell by the twinkle in her eyes that her mother was very happy.

Jarah ran outside. Tirzah was stirring stew for the celebration meal.

"Smells good," Jarah called to her as she hurried by. Tirzah raised her head, her amber curls dripping with sweat, and grinned.

"Jarah, go help Amissa," Lemuel called. "She's trying to bring the fabric for the canopy." He and Ezra were setting up the canopy behind the tents and away from the sprawling Israelite camp and the thousands of people that surrounded them. Jarah hurried over to where Amissa was struggling with a pile of white fabric in the back of their wagon.

"Here Amissa, let me help," Jarah said, grabbing the fabric.

"Thanks, Jarah," Amissa huffed. "This is such a mess," she said, laughing a little.

"How does it feel to know that your older sister is getting betrothed?" Jarah asked, untying a knot in the fabric.

"I—I honestly don't know," Amissa said, shrugging. "I guess I just don't actually realize it's going to happen. But I'm so happy. And besides, she'll still be living with us until they're married. I actually think Ezra's the one having a hard time. He and Ada are so close because they're only two years apart—they're even closer than Ada and I are. I know he's been a little upset that Eitan's getting so much of Ada's attention. But he's starting to get over it, I think."

Jarah glanced over at Ezra. He was hammering the canopy into the sand. He lifted his head and saw Jarah looking at him. Ezra threw her a grin. *He's really handsome,* Jarah found herself thinking. She gasped a little and quickly looked away, shaking her head to clear her thoughts.

"There, I've got it," Amissa said, gracefully sliding out of the wagon. Jarah jumped down after her. She followed Amissa to the canopy and the girls started winding the cloth through the sticks and poles.

"Looks good, girls," Ezra said, brushing the damp hair from his forehead.

"Ezra," Lemuel said as he walked over, "we'd better go round up the boys and get them changed into something... presentable. We've all been working too long in this heat, I think."

"Oh, Lemuel?" Jarah hastily began, "Someone needs to find Shayna." Jarah tried to seem nonchalant and shared a knowing look with her brother. Shayna had been spending her time flirting with good-for-nothing boys she'd met, and the arrival of Rishon gave her a new boy to pursue.

Lemuel sighed a little. "I'll find her."

Jarah and Amissa quickly finished their work, and just in time. Eitan and the two fathers appeared to take their places under the canopy. Jarah and Amissa ran to the tent to tell Ada and the mothers that it was time.

Soon, the four families were standing and watching Ada slowly approach the canopy, radiant and expectant. Eitan's grin reached to his ears. His eyes were practically dancing. Jarah observed the two mothers' pride-filled faces. There were tears in Sanne's eyes. Tirzah watched in a dream-like state, sighing romantically. Jarah had to keep a close eye on Raphael, who was constantly poking one of Amissa's twin brothers and making disgusted faces. Jarah jabbed him in the ribs to make him behave, then looked up to see Jaden present Eitan to his daughter.

"Ada, I present this man to you as your future husband. From this time on you will treat him in every respect as you have treated me, but with even more love and reverence. You must act in all ways like he is your husband, except for the intimacy which is reserved for the day of your marriage. Do you consent and agree to enter into a betrothal with this man? Once you agree, there's no turning back."

Tears of joy were shining in Ada's eyes. With an unwavering voice she answered, "I consent. I will enter into a betrothal with this man."

"Eitan," Father began, "becoming a husband is no easy task. You must guard her and protect her with your life, showing more love and care than you have ever shown before, and lead her in the will of Yahweh. You must not abuse your authority, but treat your betrothed as your helper and your treasure. If you don't submit to Yahweh and His plans, it will be much harder for your betrothed to submit to you. This is a great responsibility and it is not to be taken lightly. Do you promise to protect and cherish this woman and to treat her with love and lead her as a man of Yahweh should?"

"Yes, I do," Eitan responded, his voice quiet but strong and resolute. He looked deeply into Ada's eyes for a moment. Jarah heard Tirzah sigh blissfully.

"Eitan, I present this cup to you as you become the head of this household. As both of you drink from this, you symbolize that you will now begin a new life together." Father offered a clay cup filled with wine to Eitan. Eitan drank from it and then passed it to Ada for her to drink.

Jaden and Father laid their hands on Eitan and Ada, praying Yahweh's blessings on them. Everyone bowed their heads in reverence, silently offering up prayers for the new couple.

Yahweh, please bless Eitan and Ada, Jarah prayed in her heart. *It's obvious from everything you did in Egypt that you meant them to be together. And please, I know that Eitan and Ada know You and love You. I've just come to really believe in You when we left Egypt. Can I have some of the peace and joy that You've given Eitan and Ada to keep them strong? Thank you. I pray—*

Jarah's prayer was interrupted by Jaden loudly announcing, "You are now betrothed!"

A chorus of shouts, cheers, applause, and well-wishes sounded from the family members. Eitan and Ada were instantly enveloped in warm embraces.

"Now, on to the celebration!" Father shouted above the hubbub. "Let's have a feast and give thanks to Yahweh for His mercy towards us and to this new couple!"

א

The feast lasted for several hours. They were still eating, singing, and presenting gifts to the new couple as dusk fell. Ada was given five blankets, a length of cloth, several bowls, and a couple of clay pitchers. Jarah and Amissa darted about, serving Grandfather and Grandmother and their cousins and younger siblings. As she cleaned up the younger children's plates, Jarah glanced over at Eitan and Ada. They were beaming. Jarah saw Eitan cautiously reach out and squeeze Ada's hand. Her smile was beautiful. Ezra was sitting close to Ada, playing a song on his reed flute.

"Jarah!" Ezra called, ending his song.

"Yes?"

"Go get Amissa. It's time for some dancing! I'll play for you."

70

"Oh, dancing!" Tirzah squealed. She grabbed Shayna's sleeve. "Come on!"

Shayna rolled her snapping hazel eyes and groaned, but she jumped up with Tirzah and adjusted her shawl to cover her hair. Jarah saw in annoyance that she cast a winning smile in Rishon's direction as she prepared to show off for him. Rishon responded with an emotionless grin and then moved to talk to Grandfather. Jarah shook her head and sighed a little as she rushed off to find Amissa. When would Shayna ever stop flirting?

Jarah quickly found her friend. Amissa was lighting torches so that they could continue the celebration into the evening hours.

"We're going to dance. Join us," she cried, pulling on Amissa's hand.

"Oh Jarah, I can't. I'm so tired," Amissa moaned.

"Yes, you can! Hurry up! Ezra's starting the music." Jarah spun around and saw Reia, sitting silently by herself in the corner.

"Reia, do you want to join us?" she asked, eagerly. Reia shrank back as if afraid of her.

"Oh, no. I don't know how," she protested.

"You don't know how?" Jarah exclaimed, incredulous.

Reia shook her head. "No. We never had time in our city."

"It's not hard. I can teach you," Jarah offered, holding out her hand to Reia.

"No, thank you. I'd much rather watch," Reia replied, a bit stiffly.

Jarah sighed sadly and dragged Amissa over to where Ezra was playing the music.

"Don't mind her, Jarah," Amissa whispered. "She's just shy. She'll warm up to you soon."

"I hope so," Jarah whispered back.

Shayna and Tirzah joined them and the girls formed a circle, dancing to the music. It was a lively dance of celebration and Jarah became dizzy as they spun around in circles. As the girls gracefully finished the dance, everyone cheered. Jarah and Amissa collapsed on the sand, panting and laughing.

"Thank you, Ezra," Jarah gasped out, still giggling. "That was fun."

"You're welcome." Ezra's teasing smile grew a bit more serious as he looked deeply into Jarah's eyes. Jarah caught her breath. Why did Ezra look at her like that? But it was only for a moment and he turned away to talk to Lemuel.

"Jarah, it's time to get the little ones to bed," Father said softly, coming up behind her.

"Yes, sir." Jarah hastened to obey.

As Jarah tucked Raphael and Yanni into bed, she looked through the tent flap towards the pillar of fire. Today had been a wonderful day of celebration, even if there hadn't been as much food as at a typical betrothal. But there had been enough. Jarah could only hope that they had enough for tomorrow... But Jarah knew that Yahweh would provide for them. She sighed happily and stood in the doorway for a few moments, staring at the swirling mass of the pillar of fire.

ד

The next morning Jarah lay lazily in bed. She didn't feel like getting up. She was tired from the night before, and very hungry. She knew there wasn't much food so she just lay there, blissfully resting. It was cooler in the tent and everyone else—besides Yanni—was up and about. Jarah could hear Raphael and Joleen's playful shouts outside.

Abruptly the tent flap was pulled aside. A bright beam of light struck Jarah in the face.

"Ouch. Lemuel," Jarah rebuked, covering her face with her hand.

"I'm sorry," Lemuel apologized, "but it's time for the young lady of the day to get up."

"What?" Jarah asked sleepily, stretching and yawning.

"Today is the eighteenth day of the second month after we left Egypt! Don't you know what that means?" Lemuel said slowly as if that would force the fact into her head.

Jarah sat up, shocked. "What? Today is my birthday?"

"You didn't know?" Lemuel asked in mock surprise. "We have a special birthday breakfast for you. So hurry up and get moving," he smiled.

"Thank you. I'll be out in just a few minutes," Jarah exclaimed. Excitement ran through her veins as she hurriedly dressed. Her birthday meant a day free from chores, a gathering together of friends for fellowship and encouragement, and a few small gifts to celebrate her entrance into womanhood.

"I'm thirteen," Jarah thought aloud. "I'm a woman now. I must remember to act like one."

Jarah stepped outside and her aunt called to her. "Good morning dear, and Yahweh's blessings on your special day! You're a young woman now. How does it feel?"

"I'm not quite sure yet," Jarah replied. "I feel so much older, but then I don't feel like I've changed."

Aunt Zuriel laughed merrily. "It seems to me that you've already been making the transition from girlhood to womanhood over the last few months. I don't think the adjustment will be a difficult one for you," she said as she handed a bowl of cooked eggs to Jarah.

"For me?" Jarah asked in wonder. "How could you spare them? We don't have much food left. I don't want you wasting food over me."

"Oh, it was nothing. Just a few eggs from our chickens. Now don't argue—go enjoy this special day," her aunt said, smiling tenderly and wrapping an arm around Jarah's shoulders.

"Happy birthday, Jarah!" Joleen, Raphael, Tirzah, and Chanah smothered her in hugs. Everyone seemed to have a kind word for her this morning and Jarah felt her spirits soar. Even Mother seemed to be happy.

Breakfast was wonderful. It was a nice change from the thick dry bread or porridge that they usually had.

After the meal had ended, Amissa pulled Jarah aside.

"Here, these are for your birthday." Amissa brought a bundle of cloth from behind her back and shoved it into Jarah's hands. "Look at it!" she exclaimed eagerly. It was two head coverings embroidered with colorful flowers.

"Amissa, did you embroider these yourself?" Jarah gasped. Amissa nodded, clearly pleased by Jarah's delight.

"They are beautiful! Thank you so much." Jarah wrapped her friend in a hug.

Amissa giggled. "You should thank Ezra, too. I had no idea what to make for you. He suggested the head coverings and I've been working on them for almost a week."

73

"I'll try to remember to do that," Jarah agreed, but the thought of talking to Ezra made her feel uncomfortable. Up until last week, when Tirzah had teased her again, it hadn't been a problem for her to talk to Ezra. What was wrong with her?

Jarah felt a touch on her shoulder. Her mother stood behind her, holding out something covered in a coarse sack.

"I want to give this to you. Open it," Mother urged.

Jarah eagerly pulled away the fabric to see what was inside. What she saw was more wonderful than she could have ever dreamed. It was a beautiful linen dress, pure white and trailing to the ground. Lavender linen with silver and gold cording decorated the garment.

"Mother, it's gorgeous," Jarah breathed. She was too shocked to say anything more.

"Go put it on. I want to see how well I measured it," Mother ordered with pride, motioning towards the tent. Jarah was only too happy to oblige.

ה

Jarah spun and twirled until she had seen every angle of the dress. It was obviously meant for a betrothal or wedding dress. The pure white dress fit closely around her neck. The sleeves were tight at the shoulders, but then widened and draped down to her wrists. The lavender and blue accent linen were sewn and twisted together into an over-tunic. A braided belt of gold and silver cording from Egypt tied around the waist. The three colors of linen trailed out behind her and cording graced the neck and sleeves of the dress. It was absolutely perfect. Jarah couldn't have longed for a lovelier garment. She had always wanted a dress just like this, and now she found it hard to believe that it was actually hers.

Jarah stepped outside to show her mother and Amissa. Mother looked on with pleasure as she fingered the garment. "I guessed perfectly," Mother quietly praised herself.

"You look charming, Jarah," Amissa said. "Though for your betrothal you should arrange your hair in waves down your back. That's the only thing that can make you any more enchanting."

"And perhaps this," a quiet voice said from Jarah's side. Jarah turned and saw Reia, standing in the shade of her tent. "This is for you," Reia continued shyly. She held something towards Jarah in her outstretched palm. Jarah took it gingerly. It was a beautiful necklace, much like Reia's, but it was engraved with a desert rose.

"It's the sweetest flower," Reia whispered. "Jarah means 'sweetness.' I thought it was fitting."

"It's perfect. Thank you," Jarah replied. She smiled and looked deeply into Reia's eyes. Reia relaxed and smiled back without fear for the first time. In that moment, Jarah knew that she had won Reia's friendship.

א

Jarah sat in the shade of a bush with Reia and Amissa. They were embroidering head coverings. Even though it was Jarah's birthday, she couldn't think of a better way to spend the day then by being with her friends and doing something productive.

"What are the boys doing?" Jarah suddenly asked. Eitan, Rishon, Lemuel, and Ezra were moving past the girls, out towards the desert. They were carrying armloads of swords, spears, shields, and other weapons.

"It looks like they're going to practice fighting," Amissa said, shading her eyes from the sun.

"Have they been doing that a lot?" Jarah watched as Eitan and Rishon gathered stones to put in their slings.

"Oh, yes. You didn't know? Oh, that's right—you haven't been here," Amissa said, giggling. "Though I would have thought that you would have seen them practicing by now." Amissa shrugged before continuing, "It's the boys' favorite pastime. In Egypt they weren't allowed to practice with weapons. They could have been killed for having a sling or a dagger. But now Joshua, the commander of the army, has said that everyone needs to be practicing with their weapons. We're no longer in Egypt and others could be hostile towards us, and we may have to fight," Amissa explained. "Sethur was in a small Israelite garrison that the Egyptians were training to go with them into battle. He's been teaching the boys and men what he knows."

Jarah saw Eitan send a rock flying towards a large stone. He hit it right in the center.

"Well done, Eitan!" Grandfather's voice boomed. He was coming out of the camp to watch the boys and instruct them. "Let's see you try, Rishon."

Rishon put a rock into his sling and swung it around and around until all Jarah could see was a blur of brown leather. He let go of a strand of leather and hurled the rock towards the target. It bounced off the upper portion of the rock.

"Very good, but make sure you release like this," Grandfather instructed, helping Rishon adjust his hold on the sling.

Jarah started as she heard the *clang, clang* of metal against metal. Lemuel and Ezra were fighting with swords. Grandfather, Eitan, and Rishon backed away from the fight and started cheering the boys on.

"Go Lemuel!" Jarah cried, laughing.

"Come on Ezra!" Amissa shouted. Reia just sat quietly, a smile spreading across her face.

"Block with your shield, Ezra," Grandfather yelled above the noise. "Good, Lemuel. Be quick on your feet. Now lunge!"

The boys circled round and round each other, their swords clashing and reflecting the sunlight. Lemuel's face was grim and determined. He was obviously the better swordsman, having had more practice. Ezra was grinning ear-to-ear, almost like it was a game. Though he swung his sword around awkwardly, he was holding his own very well.

"Ezra's doing well!" Amissa beamed. "He's only been practicing a few days, and Lemuel's been practicing for a couple of weeks."

As the fight went on, Ezra's smile faded and he looked very serious. He and Lemuel were really going at it now. Ezra's sword scratched Lemuel's arm. Lemuel leaped forward and brought his sword down —hard—on Ezra's shield. Ezra fell to the ground with a low cry. Amissa jumped to her feet.

"Ezra's hurt," she gasped.

Apparently, Lemuel seemed to think the same thing. He lowered his sword and took a step closer to his friend. Ezra was suddenly up again and with a quick movement he hit Lemuel's sword, twisting his own sword around at the same time. Lemuel was immediately disarmed and fell to the ground, stunned. Ezra leveled his sword and pointed it at Lemuel's neck. A grin was spreading over his face.

"Any last words?" he panted out, sweat glistening on his brow.

Lemuel stared up into Ezra's face, awestruck.

"How did you do that?" he murmured.

"Those are your last words?" Ezra insisted, grinning.

Lemuel couldn't help but laugh now. Ezra offered his hand to Lemuel and pulled him up from the ground. They both shook hands, smiling.

"Good fight," Lemuel said.

"You too." Ezra nodded his head in respect.

"You both have grown immensely in your skills," Grandfather said approvingly. "A little more time with the spear and the staff and I would say you both could be prepared for combat."

Lemuel and Ezra were beaming. Jarah felt her heart swell with pride for her brother and her friend.

"I'm going to get your fathers out here to practice with us and check on the other men in our garrison. Lemuel, have you seen your father?"

Lemuel's countenance clouded a little. "No, sir. I haven't."

Grandfather shrugged, then with a wave of his hand said, "Please, continue. I'll be right back." The boys picked up their staffs and started to practice their moves against each other.

"Do you know where your father is, Jarah?" Amissa asked.

"No. I didn't realize he wasn't around," Jarah replied.

"He's been wandering off a lot lately. I was beginning to wonder why," Amissa stated. "It seems like there have been some issues between your mother and father."

"I have no idea," Jarah murmured. Was there something wrong with her father? Had something happened with her parents while she had been gone? There was a long pause as they watched the boys sparring with each other.

Reia suddenly shuddered and whispered. "I hope we're never in a real fight."

Amissa nodded in agreement. "It's fun to watch now, but actually being in a battle or just *seeing* a battle would be terrifying."

"If we do have enemies ahead, I hope they stay far away," Reia stated.

"Me too," Jarah breathed. The thought of her brothers, her father, and her friends going into war… she couldn't watch the boys with the same enthusiasm now.

"Let's go back and get dinner ready. The sun is starting to set," Jarah suggested. The girls, sobered now, agreed, all ready to get their minds off what could happen in the future.

ت

It was nighttime now. Eitan had lit a fire for dinner and stocked it well with firewood. Their family and friends surrounded the fire pit, singing songs of praise to Yahweh. Jaden played his reed flute and Ezra switched back and forth between his three instruments, the flute, castanets, and the lute.

One by one the family members went off to bed until only Jaden, Ezra, Lemuel, Jarah and Amissa were left around the campfire.

Jarah's eyes wandered around the vast Israelite camp. Fires were glowing everywhere creating little dots of golden light for miles around. The cliffs and sloping hills that surrounded their camp had turned from red and orange to a dark midnight blue when the sun had set. A crescent moon made the landscape shimmer with pale, silvery light. The desert was hauntingly beautiful at night. The hurried movement of the traveling Israelites during the day was gone. In its place were only soft whispers and other distance songs of praise echoing throughout the camp. It was peaceful, tranquil, and beautiful. Jarah took a deep breath of the cool night air. She wished it could always be like this.

"Well, I'm going to bed," Jaden declared, stretching as he stood up.

"Me too, Father. Good night everyone," Amissa said.

"Good night," the others replied.

Amissa gave Jarah a big hug and whispered in her ear, "I hope you had a wonderful day."

Jarah grinned and hugged her friend back. "It was wonderful. Thank you again for your gifts."

As Amissa and Jaden left the little circle, Ezra called after him, "I'll be there in a moment, Father. I'm going to put out the fire."

"Very well. Just don't stay out too long," Jaden told him.

"Yes sir," Ezra nodded.

Jarah approached her brother. "I'll see you in the morning, Lemuel."

"Good night little sister, and happy birthday." Lemuel gave his sister a kind squeeze. "Oh Jarah," he added, as if remembering something, "that dress Mother made looks beautiful on you."

"Yes, it really does," Ezra added.

"Thank you… both," Jarah replied sheepishly. She turned quickly and hurried into the tent to avoid Ezra's deep stare. Was Ezra just being kind to her, or was there something else behind the compliment?

ת

Asher crept into the tent, the sounds of music and singing and laughter faint in the distance. Today had been a good day. He'd been able to get his wagon wheel fixed with the help of his new friend, Ennis, who had stopped by for a visit. Asher always felt good when he worked with his hands. He had also enjoyed the celebrations of the last two days with Eitan and then with Jarah. And Mariel had been in a good mood, which meant that the whole family had been cheerful, too. He sighed in contentment. Yes, the last two days had been wonderful.

As he silently made his way towards his sleeping mat in the corner, Mariel turned to face him. Asher was a little surprised, thinking that she was already asleep. He hoped that he hadn't done anything to upset her. She seemed to be so easily upset these days. He approached her and gave her a genuine smile.

"Where have you been?" she hissed.

"Shh, Mariel. The children are asleep," Asher shushed her, gently and quietly. He got down on his mat and started to feel around in the dim light for his blanket.

"Where were you?" she whispered.

"At the campfire with Jaden and the rest, singing songs."

"Are you aware of our food situation?"

79

Asher groaned a little. Not that again. She'd been badgering them about food since before Eitan and Ada's betrothal. Jaden's family had contributed, and he knew that they were fine.

"Last I checked, Mariel, I thought we had food for about five days, if we ration it carefully. Ow!" His hand hit something sharp, and he realized it was the spear which he had thrown into the tent after their weapon's practice. "I need to put that away," he mumbled. "Where's my blanket?"

"Well when did you last check?" Mariel demanded.

"Last night after we packed up from the betrothal ceremony. Oh. Here it is." He wrapped the blanket around himself, shivering a little in the dark.

"Well I just checked before bed," Mariel began, "and I guess between all the extra celebrating more food has been eaten than usual. Asher, there's only food left for one or two more days."

"What?" Asher exclaimed in a loud whisper. Mariel put a finger to her lips to quiet him. Lowering his voice, he whispered, "Who's been eating so much?"

Mariel stared at him. "Asher, we have many growing children. They eat a lot of food."

Asher sat, deep in thought. "Well, maybe we'll have to kill one of our sheep."

"I thought we both didn't want to do that because of how much our flock has suffered in the last year. We wanted to save our sheep for the Promised Land!" Mariel protested.

"Well it's either starve or kill an animal for food, Mariel!" Asher said, exasperated.

"Can't you hunt for something?"

Asher rolled his eyes. "With over a million people moving through the desert, don't you think all the animals have been scared off by now?"

Mariel crossed her arms, upset. "Well it wouldn't hurt to check," she stated, pointedly.

"And I will!" Asher almost yelled.

"Shush!" she quieted him. "The children!"

Asher turned his back to her, trying to control the anger welling up inside of him. He finally composed himself enough to say, "Yahweh must have a plan, Mariel. I'm sure we'll be fine."

"Puh. Yahweh," Mariel muttered under her breath. She suddenly grabbed his arm and said, "Asher, I'm not familiar with these parts, but as far as I can tell we're moving away from the Promised Land, not towards it. I thought Moses said it was in Canaan. Well Canaan is north of us, not south, and that's where we're heading. Do you think this Moses and this cloud might be leading us the wrong way?"

Asher paused for a moment. He hadn't thought of that. "But Father said that Yahweh wanted to bring us somewhere to give us His laws for living in the Promised Land."

"But why does he have to lead us away from the land to do it?" Mariel persisted.

"I don't know!" Asher snapped at her. "Yahweh does what He pleases."

"Well, I think it's time we got out of this accursed desert and on to our new homes," Mariel said, sounding angry, too.

"I can't do anything about that, Mariel," he said, flopping down on his mat to show that he was done with the conversation.

"You could speak to Moses," his wife told him.

"What?" He flipped over and stared at her.

"You could talk to Moses and tell him that if he expects the Israelite nation to make it to the Promised Land without starving to death that something needs to be done," Mariel suggested.

"I'm sure Moses already knows about the situation. I'm not going to go talk to him."

"Fine, then!" Mariel said, sarcastically. "Just let your wife and your children starve. Sounds like a good plan to me!" She angrily laid down on her mat.

"Mariel, I'm not going to let that happen!" Asher fumed.

"Good night, Asher. Hopefully you'll get some good sleep to clear your mind and tomorrow you'll come up with a plan on how to get us more food."

"Fine! I will!" Asher countered, moving so that his back faced her again and then squeezing his eyes shut. His chest heaved with anger and frustration. Why was this so hard? Why couldn't Mariel just accept his answers and believe that Yahweh would provide for them as He always had? Surely Yahweh would do something for them by tomorrow morning. He had provided water. Couldn't He provide food if He wanted to?

He will provide for us. I know it. Mariel will see. We're not going to starve.

Feeling a little more relieved, Asher slowly allowed himself to fall asleep.

"WHAT IS IT?"

The next day Mother was particularly irritable and it didn't take Jarah long to figure out why. There was only enough food left for one day. They had no other source of food besides the sheep, goats, and chickens, and they would need these animals once they got to the Promised Land. Jarah heard her mother grumbling at Father inside of the tent.

"Asher, you *must* go and talk to Moses. This is absurd, staying here in the middle of the wilderness with little water and no food. I doubt the people will even have enough strength left to go to another campsite. There must not be any food for miles and miles. Go talk to him. Our children will starve if you don't," Mother demanded.

"Mariel, Yahweh will provide for us. He always does," Father assured her. But even Father's usually optimistic tone was weary and annoyed.

"You keep saying that. One day He'll just leave us alone," Mother proclaimed. "That cloud will just disappear. You watch!"

"Fine! I'll go talk to Moses, but I'm sure there's nothing I can do," Father snapped.

Jarah had never heard her father respond that way. Her parents had argued before, but not nearly as often as they had lately. And Father almost never raised his voice in anger. What was wrong with him?

Father exited the tent and walked with swift, heated strides towards the center of the camp.

"Father, where are you going?" Lemuel asked. But Father didn't answer. His brow was dark and furrowed and he almost seemed to be purposefully ignoring Lemuel. "What's wrong with him?" Lemuel asked, turning to Jarah with a raised eyebrow. "Do you know where he's going?"

Jarah shrugged. "I think Mother was trying to get him to talk to Moses about the food situation."

"What can Father do?" Lemuel wondered. His eyes followed his father. Father had stopped at Grandfather's tent and was now talking with him. Grandfather nodded gravely and walked away with his son.

"Maybe we should go with them," Jarah suggested. "I've never seen Father this angry before and I'm afraid there might be trouble."

"I feel the same way," Lemuel muttered absently. "Let's follow him."

"Wait, we have to ask Mother first," Jarah pointed out. She dashed into the tent and gained permission from Mother to go with Father.

They trailed Father and Grandfather through the camp. As they came closer to its center—where Moses supposedly was— the crowd thickened and it became difficult to move. Insults, angry shouts, and grumbling rang out from the group of Israelites.

"Let's stick together. I don't like the looks of this," Lemuel yelled over his shoulder to Jarah. He clasped Jarah's wrist and pulled her along behind him. She struggled to keep up with her brother's strong strides. They elbowed and forced their way through the people, trying to keep her father and grandfather in sight.

Finally there was a slight opening ahead. Moses, Aaron, Joshua, Moses' sister Miriam and her husband, Hur, stood by the opening of a large tent. Crowd members kept trying to force their way to Moses and Aaron, but Joshua and several men who appeared to be soldiers under Joshua's command held them back. Jarah stood on tip-toe to peer between people's shoulders and get a glimpse of what was happening. Grandfather was talking with Moses, and Jarah could see that her grandfather was upset. Moses nodded grimly and held up his hand for silence. Grandfather stepped away from Moses and back next to Father. Eventually the shouts died down to a low murmur of constant noise.

"What is your business here today, sons of Israel?" Moses asked.

"We want food!" a nearby man shouted.

"Yes! Yes! We're hungry!" A chorus of voices enveloped Jarah from every side. The people were becoming riotous. Jarah looked uncomfortably at Lemuel, but his eyes were glued to their father.

"It would be better to have died by Yahweh's hand in the land of Egypt, when we sat by the pots of meat, when we ate bread to the full; for you have brought us out into this wilderness to kill this whole assembly with hunger," another man accused.

"Where's Yahweh now? Does He not hear us and know our plight?" someone else demanded.

"We want food! My family is hungry!" Father urged.

More shouts and exclamations filled the air. Jarah sucked in her breath. What had gotten into her father? Grandfather was talking in low tones with him, but there was an angry glint in Father's eyes. Jarah's eyes drifted to the pillar of cloud.

Yahweh's right here, leading and guiding us. Yet it's still so hard to trust that He will give us just what we need. I want to trust Him. I want everyone else to trust Him, too. But it's still so hard. Why can't we just believe and trust in Him no matter what?

People were pressing all around Jarah now. The crowd was starting to get out of control. Lemuel's grip on Jarah's arm tightened. Jarah peered up into his face.

"I don't think we should've come along," Lemuel yelled above the crowd. "This is getting dangerous." Jarah followed Lemuel's eyes. Lemuel was staring at their father, hopelessness and fear on his face.

"Should we go?" Jarah yelled above the throng.

Lemuel tried to answer, but Jarah didn't hear him. Aaron was calling out, loud and clear. "At evening you will know that the Lord has brought you out of the land of Egypt; and in the morning you will see the glory of the Lord, for He hears your grumblings against the Lord; and what are we that you grumble against us?"

Moses added, "This will happen when the Lord gives you meat to eat in the evening, and bread to the full in the morning; for the Lord hears your grumblings which you grumble against Him. And what are we? Your grumblings are not against us but against the Lord."

Jarah was close enough that she heard Moses say to Aaron, "Say to all the congregation of the sons of Israel, 'Come near before the Lord, for He has heard your grumblings.'" Aaron shouted the words to the assembled crowd.

As Aaron was speaking, the pillar of cloud began to shine. The light grew in intensity, until it was brighter than the sun.

"It's the glory of the Lord!" an elderly man by Jarah's side cried out in terror. Jarah was disoriented and confused. The cloud was growing brighter.

The shouts of the people turned from anger to fear. The light nearly blinded Jarah. She shielded her eyes with her hand. Moses stared intently at the pillar of cloud and seemed to be listening. Slowly, the light grew dim and died away. Jarah blinked several times then turned her attention back to Moses.

Once again, Moses raised his voice to the crowd.

"Thus says the Lord, 'I have heard the grumblings of the sons of Israel; speak to them, saying, "At twilight you shall eat meat, and in the morning you shall be filled with bread; and you shall know that I am the Lord your God."'"

The crowd was so still and silent that Jarah could hear her heart pounding in her chest. She couldn't get the vision of the bright, blinding light out of her mind. Her eyes still ached and her stomach felt unsettled from fear of the Lord.

Slowly, the people melted away. Lemuel and Jarah went up to Father and Grandfather and walked home with them. Grandfather was a little annoyed that they had not been given food immediately, and Father seemed discontent and irritable.

The day wore on monotonously. No one felt like doing much. Most rested in the seclusion of their tents. Lemuel sat wearily on a distant rock, watching the herd. Jarah sat under a scraggly bush, treasuring every inch of shade. Squatting beside her, Yanni dragged his short fingers through the sand in interesting designs. Eventually Yanni gazed up at Jarah and said in a hoarse voice, "Jah-Jah, I'se hungy."

Jarah sighed in irritation and explained, "Yanni, we don't have much food left. We're saving what we have for tonight and in the morning. Just keep playing. We'll eat something in a few hours."

"Jah-Jah, I'se hung-y!" Yanni persisted.

"Don't yell. You'll wake up Mother," Jarah ordered, all sweetness gone from her voice.

"Jah-Jah, I wanna eat!" Yanni demanded. He stood up and stomped his foot on the ground.

"Yanni, stop it. I don't have any food to give you."

"Me food now!" Yanni started jumping up and down and screaming.

"Yanni, stop right now or I'll get Father."

A deep voice bellowed, "Yanni!"

The little boy spun around and found Father's shadow hovering over him. Father's eyes shone with rage. Yanni hung his head under his father's glowering stare.

"Go to your mat immediately," Father commanded. "You are never to behave that way, and you know it!"

"Yes, Papa," Yanni replied. He jutted out a trembling lower lip in a pathetic pout and walked slowly towards the tent, scuffling his feet in the dust. Father watched his son with a terrible, unfamiliar look on his face.

"Is there something troubling you, Father?" Jarah ventured to ask, timidly.

"No," her father snapped, "nothing's wrong."

"I'm sorry, it's just that you—" Jarah stopped short as her eyes met her father's rebuking look. "Never mind," she finished, quietly.

Father sighed, resignedly. "I'm sorry, Jarah. I'm just trying to provide for my family." Without another word, Father walked away towards the tent. He disappeared inside and Jarah soon heard her Mother's heated voice arguing.

"I can't listen to this," Jarah muttered to herself. Tears were stinging her eyes. She rose stiffly from the ground and walked towards Lemuel. Climbing up the rock, she sat next to him. The vast valley spread out around them; a land of orange and red-colored cliffs and sand. The rough mountain peaks rose up on all sides of them far into the distance. Lemuel's strong, youthful face looked calm, but Jarah could tell that he was very troubled. His eyes roamed back and forth over the landscape and he didn't make eye contact with her.

"Are you all right?" Lemuel broke the silence.

"Yes. Just thinking," Jarah responded mechanically.

"Me too," Lemuel whispered.

There was a drawn-out pause. Jarah debated whether or not to pry into Lemuel's mind.

"Thinking about Father?" Jarah finally ventured to ask. Lemuel nodded. "What's gotten into him, Lemuel?"

"I don't know. That's the problem. Eitan doesn't know, either. This new anger has been creeping up on him for a while. I can tell he's trying to get rid of it, but he's struggling with... some inward passions, I suppose. There's only one thing that I can think of..." Lemuel's voice drifted away.

"And what's that?" Jarah prodded.

"Father once mentioned that if you live with a contentious wife she has the possibility of tearing down the whole household. Perhaps with the combination of traveling, facing starvation, the heat, and Mother's irritation, he's just been worn down."

"But he's never been like this," Jarah exclaimed, tears filling her eyes.

"I know. That's what makes it seem so strange." Lemuel shrugged his shoulders.

Jarah slid closer to her brother. "What can we do?"

"That's what I'm trying to figure out." Lemuel reached out and laid his hand over Jarah's. He still didn't look at her but Jarah felt a sense of love, peace, and protection in that touch.

Then a sweet sound floated to her ears. It was Ezra's flute. She craned her neck over Lemuel's shoulder to see the player. Ezra sat in the shadow of his family's tent sending tranquil, yet sorrowful notes into the air. The music matched Jarah's feeling exactly and soothed her soul. Even Lemuel seemed moved and a small smile softened his face.

"Do you remember that song that Ezra's playing? He taught it to us the night of your birthday."

Jarah nodded, but she couldn't trust herself to say anything. Lemuel started singing, slowly and softly, along with Ezra's flute:

> "God will make a way,
> A straight and narrow way.
> He will lead us onward,
> He will lead us homeward.

> "Against us none will stand,
> When we come to our own land.
> He will lead us onward,
> He will lead us homeward."

Jarah swallowed her sobs and quietly joined in.

> "His promises will stand,
> He'll guide us by His hand.
> He will lead us onward,
> He will lead us homeward.

> "He will make a way,
> A straight and narrow way!
> He will guide us safely... home."

The notes of Ezra's flute drifted away, and then he started a new song. Lemuel and Jarah simultaneously drew in a long, deep breath.

"Everything's going to be fine, isn't it?" Jarah spoke the question aloud, but she really meant it for herself.

"Of course. Everything will be fine." Lemuel spoke with confidence and gave his sister's hand a reassuring squeeze. Jarah sighed comfortably and felt almost peaceful inside.

A shadow fell across her face and Ezra's song stopped abruptly. *Is it nighttime already?* Jarah wondered. As she looked up, her jaw dropped. There were quail flying close over their heads. And not just a few lone birds—a whole flock of fat, juicy quail. In fact, there were scores and scores of flocks. Millions and millions of birds darkened the sky, descending into the Israelite camp. Lemuel leapt to his feet.

"Come on," he urged. "We need to catch as many as we can!" Lemuel caught Jarah's hand in his and the siblings scrambled down the large rock.

The quail on the ground were strutting around, unconcerned by the humans nearby. But there were so many quail in a constricted space, the birds began to pile on top of each other. Jarah's hands snatched one and struggled to hold it firmly. Lemuel scooped up a quail in each hand and started working his way towards camp, kicking birds to and fro as he struggled through the sea of feathers. Jarah followed in her brother's footsteps, laughing aloud with relief and joy. She heard Lemuel laughing, too.

They met Shayna and Eitan at the entrance of their tent. Eitan was decapitating birds as fast as Shayna caught them. Mother was stoking the fire and putting a pot of water on to boil.

"Mother, where did the water come from?" Jarah asked.

"Ask your father," Mother snapped, hobbling back into the tent.

"A hidden well was discovered nearby," Father announced, throwing a pair of birds into the boiling water. Father was smiling and his mellow chuckles filled the air. Lemuel and Jarah exchanged a happy glance. His anger had subsided, for the moment.

That night their little encampment of relatives and friends had quite a feast, even more plentiful than the day before. Jarah went to bed that night cheerful and comfortably filled with food. She smiled to herself as she stared up at the moon.

"Yahweh *is* faithful to provide," she whispered. "We must have peace and trust in Him, no matter what."

א

It was late as Ezra adjusted the stakes on their tent. He was happy and full. Yahweh had provided, as always. Though he had been worried for a little while, Ezra had a peace that everything would work out. And it had.

Voices close by startled him. It was his father and Asher.

"Asher, I asked you to come out here because I needed to talk to you about what happened today. I don't know what has happened to you, but for the past few weeks you've been rather irritable and haven't been around your family much at all. And then today something just seemed to snap. What happened?"

Asher sighed deeply. "I don't know, Jaden. Mariel has just been nagging me constantly about everything she needs and about our food situation. But I can't give her anything else! We're not in the middle of a marketplace—we're in a desert! I've done all I can to make her comfortable, but she just keeps complaining. I just—I had to get away from it all."

"Running away isn't the right choice, Asher. You know that," Jaden confronted him.

"I know... You're right. I shouldn't have been upset at her, or at Yahweh for that matter. I guess this trip has just been wearing on me."

"And perhaps you're not spending the time you need for your relationship with your family or with Yahweh, but are simply thinking of yourself," his friend said, pointedly.

"You're probably right," Asher mused.

Ezra slowly rose from the ground. He knew he shouldn't be listening. He crept into the tent and laid down on his mat. But he could still faintly hear his father and Asher's voices.

"So what's going to change, Asher?" his father was asking.

"I—I need to be home more. I need to seek Yahweh more," Asher replied, resolve in his voice.

"And maybe love your wife more," his father finished.

"Yes," Asher agreed. "Yes. I'll give more of myself. I promise you that, Jaden."

"Good. I'll be keeping you accountable to that, Asher," his father said, gravely.

"Thank you," Asher said. "I needed to be confronted on that. Thank you, Jaden."

"You're welcome."

The men parted ways. Ezra's father threw back the tent flap and came inside. His shadow moved quietly to the other side of the tent where Ezra's mother was resting. Ezra rolled over to his side, trying to get comfortable. He barely heard his father and mother's voices whispering together.

"Do you think he's going to change, Jaden?" his mother asked.

His father exhaled. "I'm not sure. I hope so. But... something didn't look right in his eyes. He needs to truly repent, not just talk about repenting."

"Jaden, I think Ezra might have heard some of that conversation. He came in just a few minutes ago," his mother said, quietly. Ezra's body stiffened. What was his father going to say to that?

"It's fine, Sanne. Ezra's a man now. He's responsible, and I know he won't go talking about Asher to anyone. In many ways, it's better if he knows. He can be watching Asher and keeping him accountable, too. He's around Asher's family even more than I am. Ezra's starting to be firmly rooted in his faith, and he'll know if there's trouble." There was a slight pause.

"I know Yahweh is going to do great things with our son," his father finished.

Ezra's heart swelled with pride. It was all he could do to keep from jumping up and exclaiming, "Oh thank you, Father!" But instead he just flipped onto his back and gazed out of the tent flap at the stars in the deep blue sky. Father trusted him. Father had faith in him. Father said that he could see Yahweh's work in his life. To Ezra, there was nothing else he could ever hope to ask for.

ב

runch!

"What?!" Jarah jumped back. She had been the first to wake up that morning, but as soon as her feet left the tent she had stepped on something hard. She looked down and felt very bewildered. Along with the morning dew that sparkled in the sunlight, something flaky lay on the ground and spread out as far as the eye could see.

Someone came up behind her.

"What's—" Eitan didn't finish.

"What is it?" Jarah asked.

Eitan shrugged his shoulders and shook his head, looking bewildered. "I have no idea."

"Do you think it's anything dangerous?"

"I don't know. I don't think so. It almost looks like some sort of flat bread, maybe?"

Father and Shayna joined them at the tent entrance.

"What should we do, Father?" Eitan asked.

"I suppose we should talk to my father or Moses," Father responded, almost hesitantly. "This looks very strange."

"I'll go with you," Eitan offered.

The two men started to walk across the white stuff. It cracked under their feet. Shayna and Jarah looked at each other, confused.

"Do you know what it is?" Jarah asked. Shayna shook her head. "I have no idea."

"Girls, be quiet! People are trying to sleep here. Or at least they *were*."

"Yes Mother," Jarah said, quickly. The girls closed the tent flap and quietly sat down on their mats.

In a few minutes, everyone inside was awake, and they all wanted to go outside.

"No," Shayna told them in a tone that warned them to not ask again.

"Why can't we?" Raphael persisted.

"Because there's something strange on the ground and we're waiting for Father and Eitan to come tell us what it is," Shayna repeated for the fourth time.

"I still don't see what that has to do with anything," Raphael muttered, sitting down again.

Shayna rolled her eyes. But suddenly she exclaimed, "Where's Yanni?"

Jarah glanced up from where she was folding a blanket. Yanni was gone.

Lemuel sprang to his feet. "Yanni, Yanni!" he called. He and Jarah made it to the tent flap at the same time. They both bolted outside and began searching.

"Yanni!" Jarah cried.

She rounded the tent and found Yanni sitting on the ground, shoving the white stuff into his mouth.

"Yanni no!" Jarah jerked the flakes from his hand and quickly picked him up. Yanni started wailing.

"Me want more!" he screamed.

"Jarah, did you find him?"

"Yes, Lemuel. Over here, quick! He's eaten some of it!"

Lemuel ran up to them. He looked very worried. Yanni, upon seeing his older brother, reached out for him pleadingly. Lemuel pulled Yanni into his arms and the little boy's sobs subsided.

"What are we going to do? He's swallowed it." Jarah was panicked.

"Muel, me want more," Yanni begged.

"Well, it doesn't seem to have done anything bad to him," Lemuel said slowly. He crouched down and picked up a broken piece of the flaky stuff. Almost gingerly, he nibbled at it. His face lit up.

"Jarah, this tastes good! Try it. It tastes sweet."

As Jarah knelt to try some, Yanni starting whining again, "Muel, pwease. Me want some!"

Jarah took a bite. "You're right. This is good." It was light but satisfying, and tasted like honey.

"I'm pretty sure it's harmless. It's almost like this stuff was just dropped here, for us," Lemuel said.

"Like bread from Yahweh? Bread from heaven?" Jarah wondered. Lemuel nodded in agreement.

"Come on," he said, handing some bread to Yanni, "let's bring some to the others. It's after breakfast time."

In no time at all the children were running around wildly, collecting more bread then they could eat. They brought it back to their parents, who in turn put it into baskets.

Father and Eitan returned soon, bringing Grandfather with them. Moses' instructions about the bread were that every person was to get an omer each. Once everyone had gathered what they wanted, no bread would be leftover on the ground or it would all melt away. The bread was called "manna." They were not to leave any bread through the night.

But the next morning, Jarah was awakened by a scream.

"Asher! Come here!" Mother was shrieking. She was staring into a basket. Everyone surrounded Mother, trying to get a glimpse of the basket. The girls all gasped in disgust. The manna Mother had saved from yesterday had worms in it. Fat, slimy worms.

"Eitan, get rid of this," Mother ordered in disgust. Eitan obediently took the basket outside and threw out the bad manna and the worms.

"Mariel, Moses said not to keep any manna through the night. Why did you disobey the Lord's instructions? See, there's manna outside for today." Father motioned towards the open tent flap. White, flaky manna once again covered the ground.

"I—I just thought, well, maybe there wouldn't be any. Moses hasn't always provided for us, you know," Mother stated, defensively.

"Mariel, these aren't Moses' instructions. They're *Yahweh's* instructions. And Yahweh has always provided for us, even when it may not seem like it. We've had a lack, but we've never had an overwhelming need. Yahweh's trying to teach us to trust and follow Him, and He's always to be obeyed, Mariel."

Mother backed away. Father looked very stern and determined. Though Mother didn't acknowledge her defeat verbally she looked very small, insecure, and confused.

The next day was the day before the Sabbath, and Grandfather came telling them that they were to gather twice the amount of manna that day. Moses said that since the next day was the Sabbath that Yahweh didn't want them to work and gather manna and that the manna would stay good overnight. Mother was obviously worried.

"Before it didn't keep through the night, but now we're supposed to gather enough for two days? I don't know about this," she grumbled under her breath.

Jarah and Shayna helped Mother gather what they thought would be enough for two days. Jarah couldn't help but wonder if the manna would stay good. She was trying very hard to trust in Yahweh, but His instructions didn't always make sense.

"What do you think of Yahweh's commands?" Amissa asked Jarah that night at dinner.

"I honestly don't know. I'm trying hard to listen to whatever He says, and not question Him. But I don't understand it at all. Why would the manna go bad one day but then suddenly not go bad another day?"

Amissa shrugged. "I've been thinking and praying about it all day. But since Yahweh has provided the manna in the first place He must be able to bless it and do whatever He wants with it, right?" Amissa's eyes stared into Jarah's questioningly.

Jarah pushed the hair back from her face. "I hope so," she murmured.

The next morning was the Sabbath. Jarah woke up just as Mother was coming into the tent, her brow clouded and her countenance dark.

"There wasn't any manna, was there?" Father spoke with confidence.

"Of course not," Mother threw at him. "I—I was just making sure," she added with self-assurance and a haughty air.

"Did the manna go bad last night, Mother?" Jarah queried, almost hesitant to ask.

"No, and I don't know why," Mother snapped, obviously very irritated. Father turned his head and his shoulders shook with silent laughter.

Jarah sighed a deep sigh, feeling her shoulders relax and joy flood into her heart.

Yahweh keeps His word, Jarah assured herself. *We're in His good hands.*

AN UNEXPECTED ENEMY

The Israelites had been traveling for almost a week since the manna first fell. They finally reached another campsite, but once again it was full of rocks and sand and sparse vegetation. With Mother being with child and grandmother traveling with them, Father took things a little slower for their sakes, and the family straggled into camp nearly at the end of the great procession.

As Jarah was boiling water and watching the last remnants of the traveling Israelites trickle into camp, she suddenly stopped, squinted, and peered into the distance.

"Father?"

"Yes, Jarah?"

"Weren't there more people than that behind us? There was that elderly man and his wife that we helped today, remember? She was very sick. And that young couple with the three little children. I haven't seen them pass by yet."

"You haven't?" her father asked, taking the yoke off the oxen and tying them to a tent stake.

"No." Jarah shook her head.

"You could've missed them, Jarah," her father suggested, shrugging.

"I don't think so," Jarah answered, more to herself than her father. He didn't seem to take any notice of her and went away to tend to the sheep.

Jarah knit her brow pensively, feeling a cold knot in her stomach. Something about this didn't seem right.

Why do I have a bad feeling about this?

א

The next day the crowds trudged along through the dust, sand, dirt, and heat. Heads drooped and shoulders sagged. Even the shade from the cliffs on each side weren't enough to dampen the sun's heat, absorbed and thrown back by the rock. Jarah felt like they had been winding in and out of passes for hours. Everyone was exhausted and miserable. She couldn't wait to set up camp again and rest.

Eitan suddenly halted the wagon.

"What are you doing, Eitan?" Mother demanded from where she lay sprawled out in the bed of the wagon.

Eitan didn't answer for a second. His head was cocked to one side as if he was listening. Lemuel, next to the wagon with the sheep, stopped and listened, too.

"Do you hear that?" Eitan asked. He sounded alarmed.

"Hear what?" Jarah rose to her knees, gripping the side of the wagon and straining to hear a sound besides the tramping of feet and the braying of the animals. Father, Grandfather, Rishon, and the other men around them were also pausing in their tracks and looking backwards.

In the distance, Jarah heard what sounded like a horn and then a distant roar.

"That sounds like an attack!" Grandfather exclaimed.

Jarah's heart stopped beating. *An ambush? Who's attacking us? Where?*

Eitan pulled a short sword from under the wagon seat and leapt to the ground. "It's coming from behind us. Someone's attacking the back of the line where the sick and the weak are most vulnerable!"

In seconds the men had weapons in their hands; slings, swords, spears, or staffs.

"You women keep going," Grandfather ordered, taking command. "We'll go back and assist our brethren. Spread the word. Someone go find Joshua or someone who can help."

Grandfather's little company of friends and family broke into a run back into the depths of the passes. Men all around Jarah were springing from their wagons and flying after them. Mother had clambered up into Eitan's vacated seat and was goading the oxen forward.

"Jarah," Grandmother called, "you and Shayna take the donkeys and try to get through the people. We need to follow your grandfather's orders and try to find Joshua and other men to help. If this is an ambush there's no telling how many people could be attacking us."

"Yes Grandmother," Jarah replied. She slipped off the wagon and ran over to Tirzah who was sitting on the donkey, eyes wide with terror.

"Get off. You need to stay with the little boys." Jarah tried to make her voice sound confident despite the fears that grasped her heart. *Suppose we're attacked? No one is here to guard us. And what if Father, Eitan, Lemuel, or Ezra are—* She couldn't. She shouldn't think that word.

Tirzah was off the donkey in a moment and Jarah was soon trailing Shayna through the throng of Israelites. The distant sounds of fighting had spurred the Hebrews into panic. The women frantically tried to keep control of their animals and children as their husbands and sons rushed to join in the fray. The fear of unknown enemies behind them was driving the people almost mad with terror. Jarah struggled to keep the donkey from running away with her. She searched the face of every man and boy who ran pass her, hoping to see Joshua or Pagiel, her tribe's leader. Shayna was way ahead of her now, weaving her way in and out of the petrified masses.

Maybe she'll find Moses or one of the other leaders first, Jarah hoped, allowing her donkey to run as she craned her neck, trying to keep Shayna in sight.

A trumpet blast directly to Jarah's right made her scream. The donkey shied and bucked, almost throwing Jarah from its back. Jarah looked up to see Joshua standing on a large rock, a sword in one hand and a horn in the other.

"Men of Israel, an enemy has fallen upon us! They are destroying the weak and sick and aged! Come join me! Come fight! Fight for your friends! Fight for your families! Fight for your nation, and fight for your God!" he bellowed over the noise and chaos.

A passionate shout erupted from every side as men rallied to him, answering the call.

Jarah wheeled her donkey out of the way as the infuriated Israelites charged towards the sounds of the fight. Her heart was beating in her ears and all she could think was, *Yahweh, please protect them. Please protect them. Don't let anyone die. Please, oh please.* Jarah found that she was crying. She saw Shayna emerging from the crowd and felt relief wash over her. She had never been so happy to see her sister in all of her life.

"Let's try to get back to Mother," Shayna was saying. Her face was pale and she seemed very scared.

The girls tried to make their way back, but it was no use. The terrified women and animals were moving at a rapid rate out of the pass and into a long, narrow valley. The girls managed to follow the other Israelites into the flat plain. They eagerly searched for their mother and eventually found her. Their herd of animals was struggling wildly in fear, and Jarah and Shayna fought to get them controlled and in line.

"I wish the boys were here," Shayna growled.

Jarah was about to say, "Me too," when a thought struck her so hard she almost cried out from the fear of it.

What if the boys never come back? Jarah bit her lip, trying hard to blink back tears.

"Jarah, help me," Shayna snapped, grabbing a staff from the wagon and chasing down a stray goat. Jarah slid down from the donkey and hurried to help her sister. She swallowed hard, hoping and praying that her friends and family were still alive.

ב

E zra clutched his sword, keeping up with his father and Eitan as they dodged terrified animals and people.

Who's attacking us? What are we going to see? What if we get hurt, or killed? Ezra's thoughts ran through his head as fast as his legs moved. He was trying not to be scared, but he was shaking a little from nervousness.

"Up there!" Sethur yelled, pointing with his sword. Dark silhouettes of men in helmets and leather armor stood on the cliffs, shooting arrows into a screaming mass of frantic men, women, children, and animals. Ezra watched with a sickening knot in his stomach as he saw women and children struck by arrows and falling to the ground, wounded or dead.

Instantly the nauseating fear inside of him turned into a rage he had never known before. What were these men thinking, killing weak and innocent people? The cowards!

"Eitan, pick them off!" Rishon was grabbing stones from the ground, putting them into his sling, and hurling them at the men on the cliffs. Eitan's sling started launching stones at the men on the other side of the cliff. A soldier cried out as one struck his head. The man grabbed his head, toppled, and fell off the cliff, crashing to the ground below with a thud.

Ezra raced towards the cliff, his father at his heels, and started to scale it. They had to try and hold off another barrage of arrows. More men followed him.

Below him He heard Sethur shout, "Forward!"

Out of the corner of his eye he saw Sethur leading almost one hundred men down into the canyon. He could see at a glance that foreign soldiers and horsemen were in the pass ahead of them, killing Israelites at every stroke of their swords.

Ezra focused his attention back onto the cliff above him. He was almost to the top. His hands gripped the side of the cliff and he heaved himself up, rolling over the edge. A large boulder was right in front of him. He ducked behind it, relieved to see that the soldiers, about fifty yards away, had their backs to him and hadn't noticed his presence. It would only be a matter of seconds before other Israelites were with him on the cliff. But Ezra quickly realized they didn't have any protection against the enemies' arrows. He looked up to heaven, saying a brief but silent prayer to Yahweh.

Then he noticed something—this wasn't the top of the cliff, only a large ledge jutting out from its side. Twenty feet above him was the true top, littered with large rocks. And currently, there were no enemy soldiers up there.

Ezra took a deep breath and bolted for the higher ground, scaling its sloped side in just a few seconds. He took a sweeping glance of the landscape. He was standing in a field of large boulders. If only he were strong enough, he could roll them down on top of their enemies.

He heard the noise of scrambling feet and drew his sword, preparing for an attack. Lemuel's head popped up over the edge of the cliff and he pulled himself up.

"What are you doing?" Lemuel panted.

"The boulders. If we could just move them, we could roll them down on those archers before they shoot any more people."

Lemuel rose to his feet, still panting. He looked at Ezra and they both nodded.

"Let's do it," Lemuel agreed.

The boys braced themselves against a boulder.

"On three. One, two, *three*," Ezra counted, heaving with all his might. Lemuel groaned besides him as the stone slowly moved. The rock tore and ground against the gravel as it tottered on the edge of the cliff and then fell, careening towards the enemies. Ezra and Lemuel collapsed to their knees and peered over the edge, trying to stay invisible. A soldier, seeing eminent death, started yelling to the others. But it was too late. The boulder plowed over three men and sent them head-first down the cliff.

"Again!" Ezra urged. He and Lemuel each thrust a smaller boulder down the rock face. More soldiers fell to their deaths.

"Hurry, Ezra! They're targeting our fathers," Lemuel urged.

They picked a great boulder, the biggest one they had yet attempted to move. Straining, the boys shoved it. It barely budged. Ezra grunted, digging his toes into the ground. He and Lemuel mustered all their strength for a final effort. The rock started to move. Ezra put his back against it and pushed with all his might. The rock groaned into movement and then suddenly plummeted over the edge. As he felt the boulder fall out from beneath him, Ezra tried to step forward but lost his balance.

In a horrible flash of a second, his body began to fall to the ledge below. For a moment, time seemed to stop as he found himself looking down to his death. Then he felt a hand grasp his own, pulling him to safety before his feet had left the ledge. Lemuel held him up while Ezra regained his balance. They were both trembling and sweating from exertion and excitement. Ezra backed away from the edge, realization finally setting in.

"Thanks," he whispered hoarsely.

"I owed you one. We'll call it even," Lemuel said, a half-grin on his face.

They saw their fathers and the other Israelites charging the remaining foes on the ledge below them. A brief struggle ensued, but the Israelites quickly gained the upper hand, killing the men outright or throwing them over the cliff. Ezra and Lemuel slid down the cliff's side and joined their fathers. Ezra pulled his sword from its sheath and stabbed a man who was about to attack his father from behind. A flash of horror gripped his heart as he saw his own sword take life and come back out of the body, dripping blood. However, there was no time to think about the fact that he had just killed a man. Enemies were everywhere, and Ezra found himself in close combat, trying to fend off the sea of soldiers before him. He saw Lemuel force a man off the cliff. In a blur, another enemy fell dead at Ezra's feet.

Ezra heard a blasting horn and a victorious shout. His assailants suddenly turned and ran, disappearing into the clefts and crags of the rocks. Ezra looked from the cliff and saw a large group of Israelite men sweeping through the pass, trampling the enemies before them. In just a few seconds their attackers had turned and fled, almost seeming to vanish from sight.

"These men are crafty. They set a good ambush, and they sure know how to disappear and use this terrain to their advantage," Ezra's father muttered under his breath.

Now that the immediate danger was over, Ezra realized that he was trembling from head to toe. His throat was completely dry and he was gasping for air. He wiped the sweat from his brow and found his hand stained with blood. He started a little and turned to Lemuel. In the heat of the battle he hadn't even realized that he was injured. Lemuel's eyes filled with concern as he untied his sash and held it up to Ezra's head, applying pressure to stop the bleeding.

"It's just a cut. I think I'll be fine," Ezra said, trying to shake it off. But he was beginning to feel a little light-headed.

The boys quickly surveyed their fathers and friends. Rishon and Eitan, still below them, had stayed back using their slings and were unharmed. Ezra's father had a swollen eye and bloody nose, and Lemuel's father had several scrapes. However, no one was seriously injured.

"We've all been very fortunate," Ezra said, releasing his breath slowly.

Lemuel was staring down into the pass. "We didn't save many of them. Look."

The boys looked down in sorrow as they saw the bodies of men, women, and children littering the ground below them.

"The cowards." Ezra felt his teeth and fists clench.

"We've got to get back and find our families. Who knows how many soldiers we're up against and if they've attacked the main body," Ezra's father said.

"I doubt it. These men seem to be only assaulting the weak and sick. But all the same, we should head back," Asher assented.

The descent from the cliffs was precarious, but they soon reached the bottom and found Sethur. He had a bandage around one arm as he clutched his spear with the other and was muttering under his breath.

"The cursed Amalekites."

"Who?" Lemuel questioned.

"The Amalekites. They're the ones who attacked us." Sethur was holding a leather breastplate that he had taken from a dead soldier. Designs and strange words were burned into it.

"But why are they here? We aren't anywhere near their territory," Asher asked.

Joshua approached them. "Thank you all for your help. I came as soon as I could, but your work here was invaluable. Sethur, thank you for helping lead the charge."

Sethur lowered his head in reverence and gratitude before saying, "Joshua, this can't happen again. We need a guard or some other form of protection."

Asher stepped forward. "Joshua, my daughter noticed that several families seemed to vanish a few days ago. Is it possible that these small ambushes have been happening for a long period of time?"

Joshua nodded his head, gravely. "A man just told me that some of his friends disappeared a few days ago. I don't know why I wasn't made aware of this until now. I'm going to get some of the men that I've been training and have them stationed down the lines with horns. The people of Amalek are cowards. This display of arms should warn them that we are not to be trifled with. Spread the word of the attack and have your weapons prepared and at the ready at all times. You're right, we don't want this to happen again."

Everyone agreed, hoping and praying that Joshua was right and that the Amalekites would stay very far away.

ג

"Jarah, pay attention! You're burning the quail stew," Mother scolded. "Oh. Sorry, Mother," Jarah murmured. She grabbed a heavy cloth and pulled the pot from the fire. How had she not noticed the smell of burnt quail before?

"Mother, when will they be back?" Raphael whined.

"How should I know?" Mother grumbled. Jarah sat down next to Raphael, anxiously picking at a woven mat.

"Jarah, pour the soup into bowls. We aren't going to wait," Mother ordered. Jarah hurried to obey.

When will they be back? Is everyone safe? Thoughts swirled through her mind as she dished stew into wooden bowls. Raphael and Yanni were clambering for their food. Jarah absentmindedly gave them their dinner and then sat down again. A squeal from Tirzah startled her.

"There they are!"

Jarah saw her father, brothers, friends, and relatives walking through the camp towards them. Everyone was there, and while there were a few bandaged limbs, they all looked safe. In absolute delight, Jarah, Tirzah, Shayna, and her aunt and grandmother raced towards them.

"You're back!" Jarah cried. Lemuel gave her a big hug.

"Yes, we're back. We're all right."

"What about the attack? What was it?"

Grandfather spoke, his voice hoarse with anger and emotion. "The Amalekites attacked the back of our line, killing men, women, and children. We were able to stop them, but not before they killed many Israelites."

Everyone was silent for a minute, sobered by the news. Father and Mother started talking in low tones. Grandfather and Grandmother walked away towards their tent. As Ezra turned to go, Jarah gasped a little and exclaimed, "Ezra, your head."

"It's just a scrape. I'll be fine," he said, wiping some dry blood from his cheek.

"Lemuel, Jarah, it's dinner time," Shayna shouted.

"Coming," Lemuel called. Turning to Ezra he said, "Take care of that cut."

Ezra grinned, but the grin was a little shaky. "I will."

Jarah and Lemuel went back towards their tent. Lemuel released a long sigh.

"What's wrong, Lem?"

"I don't like battle, Jarah. It's… It's hard to watch people die. To kill people, I mean. And to see them murder men, women, little children, and older people in cold blood. I hope I don't experience that again any time soon." Lemuel shuddered. Jarah slowly nodded her head. It had been hard enough waiting for them to return. She couldn't imagine seeing someone die.

"I'm just glad that everyone's safe," she said, softly.

Lemuel patted her shoulder. "Me too," he breathed. "Me too."

ל

It was late that evening when Asher finished securing the animals and came into the tent to sleep. Mariel was still up, sitting on her mat, staring off into space. Remembering Jaden's words, Asher sat down next to her and put an arm around her shoulder.

"I'm glad you're all right," Mariel murmured.

"Me too," Asher said, releasing a shaky breath. "I hope we never have to face them again." Mariel nodded. There was a pause. Asher looked at his wife and saw a tear slide down her cheek. "Are you well?" he asked, a little concerned.

"Yes, yes," Mariel responded, a little gruffly. "I'm just with child and emotional, that's all." She forced herself to laugh a little.

"Is there anything I can do to help you?" he asked.

Mariel looked up at him in surprise. "What's gotten into you?" she asked a little gruffly. Asher's heart stung at her words.

"Look, Mariel. I'm sorry. I haven't behaved right towards you for this whole trip. I've been avoiding you and not really caring about how to make you more comfortable. Will you forgive me for that?"

Mariel blinked and seemed shocked. "I will," she finally said, softly.

"I'm going to try to help you through this, but you've got to help me too, all right?" Asher prodded.

"All right," Mariel agreed, looking down at the mat.

"Now, what can I do for you?" Asher questioned.

Mariel sighed a little. "I'm still worried about our food situation." Asher suppressed a groan. She was always talking about that. But this time her voice didn't sound upset or accusing as she added, "We have the manna every day, but not much meat left, and we can't live on just manna. And we always seem to be low on water..."

"So... What do you suggest I do?" Asher asked, hesitantly, almost fearing her answer.

Mariel's hazel eyes met his. "Maybe you need to do some hunting. I know that might be difficult with all these people around, but maybe we should at least try. Or perhaps we need to consider killing an animal.

Or maybe trading for some flour. Just… something—anything—to have a change in our diet."

"Maybe Yahweh will provide us with more quail," Asher began, but Mariel interrupted him, sounding annoyed.

"He's provided us with quail *sometimes*, but there's no sense in waiting for Him to bring birds down from the sky for us if we can go out and hunt and trade and get our own food, Asher. Are you becoming lazy?" she demanded.

"No. Of course not," Asher replied, a little defensively.

"Well then? Don't you agree?"

Asher nodded. "Yes. You're right. I'll see what I can do then."

Mariel looked up at him and smiled, but Asher thought he caught a hint of smugness in that smile.

"Good," she stated, lying down on the mat. There was a pause as Asher contemplated whether there was anything else that he needed to say. Then he heard Mariel say, "Thank you, Asher," in soft, genuine tones.

Asher took her hand, brought it to his lips, and kissed it.

"You know I love you, right?" he whispered.

Mariel turned so that she could see him. "Of course. You wouldn't have married me otherwise," she answered, smiling a little. Asher chuckled and laid down on his own mat.

Maybe this will be easier than I thought… he told himself. *Besides, now that I've met that neighbor, Ennis, I have a way to do trade. If I can't find anything while out hunting, it'll be easy enough for me to get what we need. Yahweh has provided for us, but I guess Mariel's right. It's time that I go out and do this on my own and don't rely on food miraculously coming to us all the time. I guess I have been lazy…* he thought as he dozed off.

ה

Three days passed. Joshua had stationed men along the length of the line of the travelers. Their presence gave everyone protection and some comfort. So far, nothing had been seen or heard from the Amalekites. Everyone felt relieved and began to relax.

"I think we've scared them off," Lemuel told Jarah at the end of the third day as they set up camp.

"How can you be so sure?" Jarah asked. "It's only been three days."

"Yes," Amissa agreed. "I'm still really worried. I mean, the Amalekites could be hiding anywhere."

"I think we'll be fine," Lemuel soothed. "Now that we have guards, the Amalekites know they won't be able to kill people as easily. I doubt we'll hear from them again."

"I hope so," Jarah replied. She was still uneasy, but Lemuel's words gave her confidence and peace.

"I hope so, too," Amissa whispered as Lemuel walked off. Jarah faced her friend.

"I think Lemuel's right," she said. "It's been a while. If they were that close, they could have easily attacked us again."

"I guess you're right..." Amissa agreed reluctantly. But there was a strange look in Amissa's downcast eyes.

"What's wrong, Amissa?" Jarah prodded.

Amissa raised her head and attempted a smile. "It's nothing, I guess. I just have a weird feeling about all of this." She shrugged and tried to make light of the situation with a nervous little laugh. Jarah tried to laugh, too, but a thought haunted her.

The last time Amissa said she had a weird feeling we were attacked by the Egyptians on the beach... But maybe she's just nervous and it's really nothing. We'll pray that it's nothing. We just need to trust Yahweh for protection.

With that thought, Jarah hastened to finish setting up camp before nightfall, and her worries began to melt away.

$$\rceil$$

Another blazing afternoon. Sweat dripped down Jarah's back as she tried to ease her aching shoulders against the side of their jostling wagon. Yanni was curled up in her lap, sound asleep. All around her the wagons were creaking and the animals' feet were making heavy thudding noises on the packed sand. Jarah was beginning to become bored of this monotonous 'freedom' and days and weeks of traveling.

When will we get to the Promised Land? When will we ever get out of this dry, thirsty desert?

"How much further to the campsite?" Tirzah whined from where she sat on the donkey with Shayna. "Why are we always last to get anywhere?"

"We're not *always* last," Jarah retorted. "There's a lot more people with us besides our four families." Jarah looked at her mother who was dozing in the back of the wagon. Her father was riding on the other donkey and attempting to help Lemuel keep the sheep and goats in some kind of order. A few armed soldiers on horses were riding back and forth along the line, patrolling the area.

At last they came to the top of a small incline and found themselves looking into a long pass, closed in by cliffs on both sides. Beyond this, tiny colored spots told Jarah that the Israelites were setting up camp.

"We're almost there," Eitan shouted over his shoulder.

Raphael, Manni, Manuel, and Joleen slipped down from their wagons and started climbing around on the cracks and ledges of the cliffs, laughing and collecting stones.

"Stay ahead of the wagons, children," Father called. "We don't want you to be trampled."

"Yes Father," Raphael shouted back, scampering on ahead.

"Jarah," Lemuel called, "can you come help me get this lamb back in the herd?" The animal had slipped past the reach of Lemuel's staff and was climbing up the cliffs.

"Sure," Jarah replied. Gently moving Yanni, she jumped off the back of the wagon and clambered up the cliff after the lamb. She heard a sudden noise above her almost as if someone—or something—had stepped on a pebble and sent it clattering down the side of the cliff. Jarah looked up. Her mouth dropped open in horror. For several seconds she couldn't force her limbs to move. Then, wheeling around, she slid back down to the others screaming,

"It's the Amalekites! We're being attacked!"

As Jarah shouted the alarm, men appeared at the crest of the cliffs, some armed with bows and arrows and others with swords. Bronze breastplates, gleaming in the sun, covered the nobles on horseback while the footmen wore protective leather. Jarah's cry alerted some of the Israelite soldiers, but many were caught off guard as a volley of arrows descended into their midst. An Israelite guard blew a long blast on his horn, summoning others to their aid.

Jarah raced to her family and friends. Eitan had goaded the oxen into a canter and Shayna and Tirzah were already galloping away on the donkey. Their flock of sheep and goats were running around chaotically and several were struck by arrows.

Jarah heard footfalls behind her and peered over her shoulder. Three Amalekite soldiers with drawn swords were on her heels. In terror, Jarah pushed herself to go even faster and ran towards the exit of the pass. She stepped on a rock and pain surged up and down her ankle. With a suppressed cry, Jarah fell. She struggled to rise but the three men were now almost on top of her. Jarah couldn't move. She was gasping for air and felt paralyzed and senseless from fear.

Suddenly, a large stone struck the foremost of the soldiers on his leather head covering. The man staggered and fell forward, senseless. Eitan was on the ground, a sling in his hand and Rishon by his side. He was hurling stone after stone at the enemies. Rishon was doing the same.

Jarah heard her name called and found herself looking into Ezra's face. He was holding his family's horse and extending a hand in her direction. Jarah clasped his arm and Ezra pulled her to her feet. A small sword was in his hand and he quickly cut down the second soldier who had been chasing her. The third soldier lay dead on the rocks, dispatched by Lemuel's staff.

"Get her out of here," Lemuel yelled to Ezra above the clamor of battle. Ezra nodded and swung onto the horse's bare back before assisting Jarah to clamber up after him. He dug his heels into the horse's ribs, urging it into a gallop.

Jarah craned her neck to peer over Ezra's shoulder and saw that their worst problems were not yet over. Ahead of them, more than a score of horsemen were charging forward. Several had bows and were loosing arrows; the rest had long swords. Father, on the donkey, had already cut one horseman down and trying to force his way through the crowd. Mother was driving the wagon through the wreckage in an attempt to escape.

Twisting around, Jarah saw more horsemen were charging upon the rear of the Israelite band. The Israelite soldiers were trying valiantly to fight them off, but they were severely outnumbered.

Suddenly Ezra exclaimed, "Hold on!" Jarah spun her head around and found that a horseman was almost on top of them. His sharp sword was just descending on Ezra's blade. Before Jarah could blink they clashed. *Clang! Clang!* The blows were followed up quickly as the horses circled around and around, whinnying. Ezra swung his sword about wildly but his face remained calm and determined. Jarah clung to Ezra, hiding her face against his back.

"Yahweh, please protect us," she frantically whispered.

The next instant Ezra deflected the Amalekite's sword and plunged his own blade into his opponent's side. He quickly pulled his blood-stained weapon back and the soldier toppled from his horse.

He did it! I can't believe it, Jarah thought in complete amazement.

Ezra breathed a slight sigh of relief as he snatched the reins of the other horse. "Thank you Yahweh," he breathed. He yanked the enemy's horse around to face them and then commanded Jarah, "Quickly, get on!"

Another volley of arrows descended upon them. One whizzed past Jarah's ear. She clambered onto the other horse, noticing at the same time that Ezra's arm was deeply cut. She gasped, but Ezra didn't seem to notice.

He suddenly uttered a low exclamation. Jarah followed his gaze and felt her face drain of its color. Raphael, Manni, Manuel, and Joleen were all on the nearby cliffs, leaping rapidly from boulder to boulder and screaming in terror. Joleen was just reaching the ground when an arrow stuck fast in her shoulder. Joleen clasped the wound and leaned unsteadily against a large rock. Uncle Daton vaulted from the front seat in their wagon and ran to Joleen's assistance. Rishon instantly took his father's place, urging their donkeys forward.

Jarah heard Raphael's familiar cry. She saw her little brother tumbling down the cliff. He landed softly on the sand only a few feet below, but over him stood the dark frame of an Amalekite, his back toward them. In complete panic, Raphael cried for help at the top of his lungs and flung up his hands to shield himself. As the soldier drew back his sword to strike, Lemuel leaped forward, drawing a dagger from his tunic. The blade sank deeply into the man's back, and the soldier dropped his sword and fell forward, dead. Lemuel picked up Raphael, saw Jarah, and started to run towards her.

As this was happening, Ezra kicked his horse into a run—back towards the ambush.

"Ezra, what are you doing? Don't go back! You'll be killed!" Jarah shrieked.

"I've got to get my brothers!" Ezra yelled back. Manni was almost to the ground and ran, arms outstretched, towards his protective older brother. Manuel was still climbing down the rock-face. Ezra lifted Manni up onto his horse and reached for Manuel. The little boy was standing on a drop-off just above his brother's head. But then Manuel's body jolted, then quivered and collapsed. Ezra caught him, and Jarah saw what had happened—Manuel had been shot in the back by an arrow.

Cradling his little brother, Ezra steered the horse towards the Israelite camp. Lemuel now reached Jarah and shoved Raphael up onto the horse's rump.

"Go, now!" he told her.

"What about you?" Jarah asked in alarm.

"I'm helping the others. Get out of here!" Lemuel smacked the horse's rump. The horse sprang forward. Jarah peered over her shoulder and saw Uncle Daton swiftly carrying Joleen towards her grandfather's wagon. An assailant was right beside him and struck at him with his sword. Uncle Daton tried to duck to avoid the blow but the weapon still sliced deeply into his upper-arm.

"Lemuel, Uncle needs help!" Jarah yelled.

"I'm going!" Lemuel called back.

However, Grandfather had already brought his thick shepherd's staff crashing down on the soldier's head. The man was killed instantly and Uncle Daton was in the wagon.

Grandmother sped their cattle towards the exit. Jarah followed, and they all burst out of the dangerous pass into the blinding glare of the sun. The beginning of the Israelite's camp was thousands of feet away on the plateaus of the cliffs. Their four wagons, along with two other families that Jarah did not know, were the only ones who had made it through. The echoes of agony and cries of war mixed with the sound of metal against metal and the baying of animals. A party of more than two hundred armed Israelites raced past them and towards the cliffs.

"I hope they can save the others," Jarah murmured, panting from fear and exhaustion. She looked around, finally grasping that she wasn't dreaming and that this was a terrifying reality. Uncle Daton's right arm was bleeding profusely and Jarah thought she could see the bone. She quickly turned her eyes away from him. Her grandmother was cuddling Joleen who appeared to still be conscious. Aunt Zuriel was leaning over her little daughter with careful tenderness. Eitan, Lemuel, and Rishon had some scratches but otherwise seemed unharmed. Raphael's arms were wrapped around Jarah's waist and he was sobbing uncontrollably. Jarah turned to comfort him and noticed drops of blood sliding down his left leg.

"Raphael, you're bleeding," Jarah exclaimed.

"The—the soldier dropped his sword on my leg," Raphael choked.

"It's going to be all right," Jarah soothed him. She squeezed his hand.

Ezra was surrendering the body of his little brother over to his mother and Ada. Sanne's eyes filled with tears but she said nothing as she took the limp form. Ada cradled the boy's bruised head. Jaden hesitantly leaned over and felt for Manuel's heartbeat. Ezra shook his head.

"It's no use. He's dead, Father," he whispered in an almost inaudible voice. He paused and then said, "I'm sorry. I didn't get to him in time." Jaden nodded, smiled weakly, and then slapped the reins on the backs of their donkeys.

Jarah's heart stopped. Manuel was dead? Manni was staring longingly into his twin's pale face, silent tears streaming down his white cheeks. Ezra's face was as immovable as a stone. It didn't seem like it was possible.

They straggled into the camp. Now that the immediate danger was over for them, everyone's thoughts turned to bandaging the wounded, caring for the animals, and finding water for them all. There had been hardly any water yesterday and practically none today.

Lemuel and Eitan appeared dazed from what had just happened and went mechanically through the chores of settling the animals and preparing the tent. Ezra helped Raphael down from the enemy's horse and Jarah slid down to the ground. As soon as she put weight on her left ankle she felt a stab of pain. A low cry escaped her lips.

"Are you hurt?" Ezra's face held genuine concern.

"No, not really. It's just my ankle. I think I twisted it or something." Jarah uncomfortably shifted her weight to her right leg and tried to erase the look of pain from her face.

"Here, let's get you to your tent." Ezra offered her his arm for support and brought her over to where Lemuel was putting pegs in the tent.

"Jarah, what happened?" Lemuel asked in alarm.

"I twisted my ankle when I was running. I think it'll be fine. I'll probably just need to rest it."

Lemuel examined her foot. "It looks a little swollen. Here, use my staff." He handed Jarah the rod and then said to Ezra, "Thank you."

Ezra nodded slightly, looking down at the ground. Lemuel looked at his friend with compassion and said, "Ezra, don't blame yourself for what happened to your brother. I know it's hard. I couldn't imagine." He put his arm reassuringly around Ezra's shoulders. Ezra winced.

"Are you hurt?" Lemuel asked.

"It's just my arm," Ezra replied quickly.

"That's a pretty deep gash. It needs to be bandaged," Lemuel observed.

"Yes, I know. I'll get Ada to do it."

Jarah could tell that Ezra was trying to hide his true emotions and wisely decided to leave the two friends alone for a few minutes. She sought out Amissa, who was sitting in her family's wagon, sorting through crates of belongings. She was crying softly.

"Amissa?"

Amissa jumped, startled.

"Are you all right?"

Amissa stared at her friend blankly, shaking her head. Jarah clambered up next to her and hugged her. Amissa clung to her, sobbing.

"I'm so sorry," Jarah whispered, holding her friend tightly.

Amissa finally let go and sat back. "Did you see his body, Jarah?" she asked, wiping the tears from her face.

Jarah nodded, biting her lip and blinking back her own tears.

"He was so limp and pale and…" Amissa choked on a sob. "He's gone, Jarah. He's dead. It hurts. It hurts so bad. And I know it'll hurt more when we get over the shock of it all and realize that he's truly gone…" Amissa's voice trailed away and she brushed away her tears.

Jarah felt sobs rising in her own throat. She took her friend's hand. "Yahweh will help you through it," she ventured to say, tentatively.

Amissa nodded. "I know He will. But I don't know how."

"Yes, I know." Jarah sighed. She didn't see how any good could come out of this. Her best friend's little brother was dead. She had seen him die. What could Jarah say to comfort her? Nothing. All she could think to say was to trust Yahweh, just like Amissa had told her so many times. But she couldn't bring herself to say it. Besides, Jarah knew that her friend knew the truth. Or at least,what Jarah believed to be true. But right now, it didn't feel true to her, either.

Why did Yahweh allow this? she thought, sorrow settling over her. *And so many other people died, too. I thought He was guiding us and protecting us. Where was He when we got attacked?*

Amissa suddenly stated, "I can't let this get the better of me and make me doubt Yahweh or His power. I know He's with us. He's right there." She pointed towards the pillar of cloud in the distance. "It had to be for a reason. And maybe one day—" She stopped short, took a deep, shaky breath and continued, "Maybe one day I'll know why."

Jarah was taken aback by Amissa's strength in such a terrible time, but she drew encouragement from Amissa's words. She was right. Yahweh was right there. He hadn't left them alone. He was still watching over them.

Jarah again put her arm around her friend's shoulders. "I know you'll find out why one day," Jarah assured her, tears welling up in her eyes. "And I also know that Yahweh's going to bless you for your faith in Him. You're always so strong, and you never doubt Him, even in hard times." Tears were falling down Jarah's cheeks now. "I want to be more like you, and have the kind of faith you have," she finished, whispering.

Amissa looked up, surprised. "But Jarah, you can! You just have to ask for it. He'll give it to you! I know He will."

Jarah gave Amissa another hug. Both girls were crying together now.

"I love you, Amissa," Jarah murmured.

"I love you, too," Amissa replied. "You're the best friend that I could ever have."

ﾔ

Finally the tents were erected, and the families slunk wearily into them. Shayna, who was a wonderful nurse, set out at once to sew up Joleen's and Uncle Daton's wounds. Joleen was very brave, and though she screamed and cried from the pain while the arrow was removed, she calmed down quickly. Uncle Daton was pale and weak. Raphael's leg was bandaged tightly. Everyone was quiet, serious, and mournful.

"Asher, we must find some water," Mother ordered.

"Mariel, where am I expected to find water in a place like this?" Father asked, somewhat defensive.

"There has to be a well or something. We must have water for the animals and to keep the wounds clean."

"I'll go look in a little while," Father muttered, obviously annoyed and exhausted.

At that moment Eitan entered the tent. He glanced at his parents and then at Jarah. She gave him a knowing look and then lowered her eyes. Eitan nodded, realizing there was tension in the air.

"Eitan, did you find any water?" Mother asked.

"No, Mother. I didn't realize I was supposed to be looking for some," Eitan said, trying to be calm.

"Well, when there's no water left you could have *supposed* that you should find some," Mother snapped. Eitan wisely remained silent. "Don't just stand there! Asher, take your sons and go find a well."

"Very well. I'm going," Father mumbled under his breath. He stomped out of the tent with Eitan and Lemuel at his heels. Mother sighed and sat down in a chair with her eyes half-closed, resting.

"Jarah, you'll need to start dinner soon," she said lazily.

"Yes Mother. I will," Jarah responded. Jarah limped over to where Shayna was sitting next to Raphael. He had fallen asleep with his leg propped up on some fabric. Shayna aimlessly fingered the frayed edge of the mat and stared off into space, a vacant expression on her face.

"Will he be all right?" Jarah asked.

"Oh, he'll be fine," Shayna said, dismissively. "He was just scared more than anything."

There was a long pause as Jarah looked at Raphael's sad and pale face. Shayna broke the silence by sighing despondently.

"Shayna, is something wrong?" Jarah asked almost timidly, worried that her sister would snap at her for prying, but hoping that everyone's injuries weren't worse than she feared.

"Oh no, nothing's *wrong*," Shayna replied, "except that Rishon has had more than a month to get to know me again and he hasn't asked about a formal betrothal, which should be taking place very soon. But no, nothing's *wrong*." Shayna lapsed back into a sullen silence.

"Oh… I haven't been thinking about that," Jarah replied.

"Of course you wouldn't. It's not *your* marriage or *your* life. You've got other things to worry about, like Ezra." The sneering, sarcastic tone was still in Shayna's voice and eyes and the way she said 'Ezra' made Jarah's cheeks flush.

"Why would I be worried about Ezra?" Jarah asked, a little defensively.

"Oh…" Shayna exhaled and leaned back on her heels, frustrated. "Well," she began at length, "Father's going to talk to Rishon sometime soon. I just want to know what he thinks of me."

Jarah could understand that. "Well, you know, Shayna, Rishon's very quiet. He doesn't talk much, even around Eitan, who seems to be his best friend. And when he does speak he's very blunt and frank. He doesn't show much emotion, either. So maybe he really does like you but just hasn't shown it," Jarah said logically.

"But he hasn't spent time with me at all, Jarah. He acts so indifferent," Shayna said, sounding almost ready to cry.

Jarah shrugged. "I don't know." It was true. Rishon hadn't really spent much time with Shayna, except for in their family groups. He had treated Shayna with cold politeness, not seeming to care much for her. Did he find her beautiful older sister attractive at all?

Perhaps it's just an awkward situation for Rishon to be in, Jarah thought. *At least we'll find out soon.*

"Mariel, can I come in?" Grandfather called from outside the tent.

"Yes. What is it?" Mother responded.

Grandfather entered, looking grim. "I went to report the attack to Joshua, but he had already heard about it. Moses has asked Joshua to prepare the men for battle. Tomorrow, as many men as are able who are twenty-years-of-age and older are to assemble in a main body under Joshua. We are going to go through the passes until we find the Amalekites and, with Yahweh's help, we'll defeat them. We also hope that one of your sons will be able to join us to carry supplies like water, food, weapons, and bandages. We don't know how far we'll have to travel until we find the main camp of our enemies."

Jarah's face turned white. A battle? The Israelites were actually going to take part in a battle? But these Amalekites were crafty and clever. They had set ambushes and killed so many people. Could they defeat them? What if something happened to her father or brothers? What would they do without them?

Mother's face went pale and her body was rigid. She was silent for a moment. She moistened her lips with her tongue before replying, quietly, "I'll let Asher know as soon as he comes back. He's out trying to find water."

"Very well. If I find him before you I'll make sure he gets the message. I need to talk to Jaden and Ezra now. Please let us know if you find any water, too. We're all in desperate need of it." Grandfather left the tent, his face grave.

A few minutes later Father, Eitan, and Lemuel reentered the tent. Father sank to the ground.

"Did you see your father?" Mother asked. "Did he tell you about the battle?" She looked genuinely concerned and worried. She kept looking from Father to Eitan to Lemuel with nervous eyes. Father met her gaze and nodded in assent.

"Yes, I saw him. We talked. The boys and I will begin sharpening our weapons and preparing provisions immediately."

"Did you find some water?" Mother asked hopefully.

"No," Father sighed. "There are no wells or springs anywhere in this area. I've asked everyone I can think of." Father shook his head. "First an unknown, silent enemy, and now no water. Our strength will be gone. This whole fight will be worthless. And everything is so dead here, there's no hope of finding water at all." Father's shoulders sagged.

"No, Father. It's not hopeless. Not yet." Eitan looked deeply into his father's brown eyes. Father looked away uncomfortably and hung his head.

There was a long silence. "That does it!" Mother stamped her foot on the ground and rose hastily.

"Does what?" Lemuel questioned.

"I'm not sitting here idly any more. First heat and exhaustion, then an attack by enemy soldiers, then no food, and now no water! And Joshua is thinking of sending you and all of these other men into battle? Has he gone insane? It's time that we go back to Egypt, and Moses needs to know just what we think of him and his pathetic God. Come." With that, Mother snatched Father's wrist and began to drag him out the door.

Jarah jumped up. "Back to Egypt? But Mother—"

"No buts, Jarah. Don't forget to start dinner," Mother snapped. She walked out of the tent and Father reluctantly followed. To Jarah's eyes, her father looked like a slave following his master.

"Eitan, you can't just let them go! What's Mother thinking?" Jarah almost cried.

"I don't know… I don't know," Eitan moaned. He looked down at the dirt, thinking hard, but despair rested on his face. Jarah couldn't believe what she was watching. First Father and now Eitan were giving in to despondency. *No, Eitan. Please, not you, too.*

Finally Eitan roused himself. "Let's go after them," he said to Jarah, "and see if we can't change Father's mind, at least. You try and talk to Mother. She'll listen to you more than she'll listen to me.

She's still mad because I stood up to her when Father was teaching us about Yahweh back in Egypt." He took Jarah's hand in his and they hurried out into the late afternoon sunlight. Mother and Father were already out of sight.

"Let's use the horse and catch up to them." Eitan climbed onto the enemy horse's bare back and pulled Jarah up after him. He turned the horse towards the center of the camp where Mother and Father had probably gone.

As they rode, Eitan said, "Jarah, I think Mother is really worried about all of us and that's coming out in anger towards Father. You just need to try to pacify her, to help her see that everything will be fine. I'm going to try to get Father to remember Yahweh's power and His provision for us. He's given us water before, and He can again." Eitan sounded resolute now, like his old self. Jarah's heart lifted a little and she felt a resolve seeping into her bones.

"Yes, Eitan. I'll do it," she agreed.

Jarah and Eitan were soon at the edge of an angry mob. Eitan jumped to the ground and threw the horse's reins over the branch of a straggly tree before pushing his way into the midst of the people. As he threaded his way through the Israelites, peering through shoulders and over heads in search of his parents, Jarah struggled behind him, attempting to follow her brother's path. Her ankle was throbbing, but she tried to ignore the pain.

"There they are," Eitan announced. Mother still had a strong hand on her husband's arm and Father grimly followed her, looking like he would rather die.

Eitan forced his way towards their parents but Mother was already at the edge of the circle, glowering at Moses. Father was studying the ground, looking quite irritated and bitter. Jarah wanted to cover her ears. Everyone was shouting at once. Only around Moses did there seem to be any order. Joshua stood by Moses' side, his hand on the hilt of a long sword as if he was ready to take the rebellious Hebrews in hand personally.

"Give us water that we may drink!" shouted someone from the crowd. This was followed up by yells of agreement from those surrounding the man.

"Why do you quarrel with me?" Moses asked the people. "Why do you test the Lord?"

"We're thirsty!"

"We need water now!"

"My family is going to die if we don't get water soon!"

"We can't go into battle without water!"

The people were becoming dangerous.

"Eitan, maybe we should go," Jarah suggested, having to yell in order to be heard. Eitan was vainly trying to get Father to leave, but Mother stood in his way, not letting him pass.

"Why have you brought us up from Egypt, to kill us, our children, and our livestock with thirst?" Mother questioned angrily.

Moses looked at the yelling and angry throng of people around him and threw up his hands in aggravation. He said something to Aaron and then hastily entered the big tent.

"What's he doing? Where's Moses going?" the Israelites wanted to know.

Aaron held up his arm for silence. "Moses has gone to talk with Yahweh."

A murmur of complaints swept through the multitude.

"I wonder how long it will take for Yahweh to respond this time," Mother grumbled to Grandfather, who had come up beside them. "Yahweh will probably give Moses an answer *after* we have all died of thirst, or are killed by Amalekites. We should have never left Egypt or the Egyptian gods."

"No, we should have left Egypt," Grandfather stated slowly and calmly, "but probably not with Moses as our leader. Perhaps we should consider someone else. He cannot be following Yahweh's leading. Moses has gotten us into too much trouble between all of these enemy attacks and now the lack of water." Several people around Grandfather nodded their heads in silent agreement.

"Father, please, let's leave this matter in Yahweh's hands and pray. This horde of people is becoming too restless. Someone could get hurt."

Jarah's attention now focused on Eitan and her father. Father's expression was dark and he was obviously flustered.

"Let me be, Eitan. Praying won't do any good now." Father shrugged Eitan's hand off his shoulder and turned his back on his son.

"Mother, please, let's go back and leave this in Yahweh's hands," Jarah insisted, tugging on her mother's sleeve. "There's nothing we can do now. We've all stayed safe and well, and I know that Yahweh will provide for us, just like He has before, and protect us from the Amalekites, too. We don't have to be afraid of them."

"No, Jarah," Mother exclaimed, pulling away from her daughter. "I won't go back, not until Moses has fixed this problem. And what are you doing here? I told you to make dinner!"

Jarah couldn't believe the scene around her. Looking about, all of the hundreds of Israelites she could see were angry and upset.

People aren't just doubting Moses—they're doubting Yahweh! she thought. *Surely He'll give us water. I don't know why He's letting this happen to us again, but we need to start trusting Him and stop doubting Him, just like Amissa said. Yahweh's still here. He's still with us. I just wish He didn't make it so hard to trust Him... But we must trust Him! We must!*

"I'll tell you one thing," a man was saying to Grandfather, "if I see Moses again and he hasn't done anything to help us, we need to replace him with someone who *can* lead." The man picked up a large, red stone and clenched it in his fist.

Jarah gasped. Were the people thinking of stoning Moses? Someone had to warn him.

"Eitan!" Jarah pointed towards her grandfather who was trying to convince the other man to take things cautiously. Eitan's face was pale and he stared at her helplessly. Jarah frantically looked around and saw that many other people were holding stones in their hands.

"They can't do this! They can't do this! Father, please!" she cried, her heart pounding in her chest.

"Jarah," her father began in annoyance, "your grandfather is right. Someone else needs take control now."

"But Father, the cloud! We've been following the pillar of cloud! We're not following Moses. We're following Yahweh!" she pleaded, gripping his arm tightly. Her father just shook his head and turned away.

"Moses can't be hearing correctly, Jarah. Yahweh promised to lead us to a new land, and Moses is only leading us farther and farther away."

"It's not Moses! It's the cloud! It's Yahweh!" Jarah argued.

Eitan put a hand on Jarah's shoulder and looked his father directly in the eyes.

"Listen to her, Father," was all that he said.

Just then Moses stepped out of the tent. He was holding his staff—the same staff that had turned the Nile into blood. He motioned for Aaron, Joshua, Grandfather, and three or four other elders of Israel to follow him. He started heading up a small, yet steep hill on which perched a very tall rock. It was almost sixty feet high and was tall and narrow, almost like a finger pointing towards the heavens. The throng of Israelites followed their leaders to the rock in a noisy, grumbling mass. Moses drew back his arm and struck the rock with his staff. For a moment, nothing happened. Then there was a loud *crack!* Starting from the top of the rock, a crack ran through the stone, dividing it in half. With a crumbling sound, the rock split into two equal parts, only connected at the base, and a torrent of water began to flow down the steep incline and form a deep pool at the bottom. The people gasped and screamed in delight and began to kneel at the new little river and drink to their heart's content. Grandfather, standing on top of the hill, beheld the scene in shock and disbelief.

Jarah sunk down by the pool of water forming at her feet and drank gratefully. The water was cool and clear. More of it continued to crash down the sides of the hill. There would be no lack.

As she and Eitan went back to their tent to start dinner and have Lemuel get water for the rest of her family, a happy thought struck Jarah. She realized that she had not doubted Yahweh. She had really believed that Yahweh would provide water for them. After all, He had provided food and water for them before. Couldn't He do it again if He chose to?

Maybe my faith is getting stronger, little by little, Jarah thought with a smile and a heart warmed by the love she was beginning to feel for Yahweh.

SORROW

A little ways from camp, in a deserted red plain, a solemn group of thirty people met. The sun was getting low in the sky, and the heat was starting to abate. A hole had been dug in the rocky soil, and in it lay a body covered in faded white linen.

Ezra, Jaden, Rishon, Grandfather, Lemuel, and Father scooped up the freshly turned earth using buckets and their hands, and soon filled in the hole. Sanne stood close by with Manni in her arms. Manni didn't even look upon his brother's grave; instead, he hid his face against his mother's shoulder and his body shook with silent grief. Amissa's arm was wrapped around Jarah's waist and tears flowed down her cheeks. Eitan stood with Ada, tenderly holding her hand. He smiled at her sorrowfully and she looked back at him with a wet face. Jaden's countenance was remorseful. Ezra's face was very white and his jaw was set as he rapidly and determinedly threw the dirt down into the hole.

At last the little funeral was over. Slowly, everyone drifted away until only Amissa, Jarah, and Ezra were left. Ezra sat on the ground, staring into the distance with unseeing eyes. Amissa wiped away the tears and then murmured, "I should go help Mother." She smiled at Jarah and squeezed her friend's arm. "Thank you."

"You're welcome," Jarah said. She smiled cheerlessly as her friend turned to head back towards camp. She started to follow but something in her heart stopped her. Jarah looked back at Ezra who sat as still as a statue, hardly even blinking.

"Ezra."

He didn't reply. He didn't even move.

"Ezra," Jarah repeated a little louder. There was still no response. Almost hesitantly, she knelt by his side. "Ezra, it's out of your hands now."

"Well, it wasn't *then*," he muttered, his voice trembling with emotion. He still didn't look at her. Jarah very slowly stretched out her hand and laid it on his arm, right above the deep gash.

"Ezra." This time he met her gaze. The defiance and anger were gone. In their place was a sad, lonely, and empty stare. "It's not your fault," Jarah said. "You were there for him. It was Yahweh's will."

"I know that."

There was a long pause. "Then what's troubling you?" she finally asked.

"It's just—I was his protector, his leader, Jarah. He was younger than me. I should've died before him. I'm sure it happened for a reason, and I can learn to live with it. It's just… hard. It's an all-consuming grief." Ezra shrugged as if he was trying to shake off his sorrow.

He looked down at the ground, and Jarah felt that she should leave him alone now that she knew he wasn't angry with Yahweh like so many other people had been today.

She withdrew her hand. "I'll be praying for you."

"I appreciate it." There was a cold edge in his voice, but Jarah could tell Ezra really meant it.

As she walked back to her tent she came across her father, sitting with Lemuel and Eitan in the shade of a large boulder.

"Oh, I'm sorry. I didn't mean to interrupt." She started to back away but her father stopped her.

"It's quite all right, Jarah. Actually, you should join us. This is something I want you to hear, as well."

Something was not quite right in her father's voice. "What is it?" Jarah asked hesitantly. She sat down across from her father.

Father paused and then began, "Jarah, I want to ask your forgiveness for the way I've been acting towards you and the rest of the members of our family. I haven't been leading like I should, and I know it's left you all in difficult situations. Do you forgive me?"

"Of course, Father," Jarah replied emphatically.

"Thank you," Father breathed in relief, "and I will try to do better, I promise. There's just… a lot of tension between your mother and I right now. We're trying to figure out how to take care of our family, away from everything we've ever known and loved. But it should go away soon." Father smiled at his children. "And I also want to thank you for pointing me in the right direction, even if I don't seem to accept it." Father looked at Eitan and clasped his son's shoulder, and then smiled kindly at Jarah.

"It's fine, Father. We know you want to do what's best," Eitan assured him.

"Yes, Father. We forgive you," Lemuel added.

Father looked upon his sons with gratitude. "Now," he said, "let's go and give the animals their dinner and then get any weapons ready that we can find. We also need to fill the skins with water and pack provisions. Who knows how long we'll be gone."

Jarah rose to follow her father, and though she was glad that he had recognized the error in his ways, something was still not quite right. There was a distant look in his eyes that Jarah could not describe or understand. It scared her. Was Father really repentant? Or was something holding him back from getting rid of all of his bitterness?

As she was thinking about this, Rishon came towards them. Father looked at his children and said, "You go on ahead. I'll be there shortly."

A smile stole across Jarah's face as they headed back into camp.

"What's so funny?" Lemuel wanted to know.

"I know why Father's talking with Rishon." She gave Lemuel a knowing smile. He looked at her inquisitively and then starting grinning.

"Then I know, too."

Jarah giggled and Lemuel suppressed a laugh.

"I hope Father will tell us what comes out of that conversation," Lemuel said. Jarah nodded, still smiling. But then she noticed that Lemuel wasn't smiling any more.

"What's wrong?"

Lemuel looked at her. For the first time in a very long time Jarah saw that he was scared.

"Jarah, there's a battle tomorrow. We're going to try to find the Amalekites, or they'll find us. Almost all of our male family members and relatives will be in it. It's just suddenly occurred to me that—" Lemuel stopped short.

"Something might happen to them?" Jarah finished for him.

"Yes." Lemuel exhaled. "I know Yahweh defeated the Egyptians. But this time, it just seems so much bigger, so much more horrible." Jarah felt a cold shiver run up her spine. Lemuel's eyes looked into hers. "We need to be praying for them. And we need to pray that we fight the Amalekites on our ground instead of trying to find them in all these mountains. On a plain it would be bad enough, but in the canyons and passes of the mountains, a landscape we don't know, we'll be as good as done."

Jarah gulped, but her mouth suddenly felt dry and her stomach was hollow. "I'll be praying. I'm praying now," she managed to say.

Lemuel nodded. His face was still pale. He pulled Jarah into a close hug.

"Yahweh is on our side, Jarah. Whatever happens is for His glory, right?"

"Right," she breathed, fighting back tears. But inside she was crying, *Oh Yahweh, please protect us…*

א

Ezra sat by himself for a long time, staring at the heap of stones that marked Manuel's grave. He was too numb to cry. He could barely even think straight. He couldn't think about the upcoming battle. He couldn't think about his family. He couldn't think about the pain inside. All he could think was, *I let this happen. I let this happen. I failed. Father shouldn't have put so much confidence in me.* His brother's terrified face would be forever etched into Ezra's mind. He wanted to go back to his family and comfort them. But wouldn't his presence just be a reminder that Manuel's death was because of him? For a few moments his thoughts cleared enough for him to contemplate running away.

But I can't live without them, especially not now, Ezra thought as he stared hard at the pile of freshly turned sand and dirt. Ezra peered up into the darkening sky, searching for answers.

"Yahweh," he whispered, "I know you have a plan like Jarah said... But I can't accept it now. I can't! I'm so sorry. I want to, but I can't. Please help me. Show me why." Ezra's voice broke into sobs and he laid his head on his knees and allowed the tears to fall.

"Ezra? Son?" It was his father's voice.

"Yes sir?" Ezra responded, wiping the back of his hand across his wet eyes.

"It's getting late. Don't you want to eat?"

"No. No thank you, sir," Ezra muttered, trying to keep his voice from shaking. His father sat down next to him.

"At the very least, you need to help get ready for the battle," his father urged.

"But—But I'm not twenty years old yet," Ezra said, surprised. "I thought I was staying here to guard the women and children."

"Many of the younger men are, and some of the older men, too. But lots of the young men are being armor-bearers and carrying supplies. I thought you could help me," his father suggested.

Ezra met his father's gaze, feeling bewildered. "You—you want me to come help you in battle?"

"Yes. Why is that a surprise to you?" Father asked, attempting to smile. Ezra could see the deep sadness in his father's eyes.

"Well, because… because I—I failed in this last skirmish. I didn't get Manuel out. I—I thought you would want me far away so that I wouldn't mess anything up again," Ezra faltered.

"Oh, Ezra." Father put a strong arm around his son's shoulders. Ezra embraced his father and found that tears were streaming down both of their cheeks.

"It wasn't your fault, son," his father finally managed to say, crying softly. "There was too much chaos, too many things happening. They were too far out of reach. No. Nothing could have been done to save him. You did your best."

Ezra knew that no matter how old he got, he would always feel comforted by his father's embrace. But even his father's strong, kind arms couldn't take all the hurt away, especially because he knew that his father was hurting even more than he was. He'd heard what people said about how hard it was to lose a child and a sibling. Now he was finding out. And he knew it was only the beginning. He felt his father's chest getting tense and saw tears dropping onto his father's tunic.

"Ezra," his father choked out, "you really were courageous in that fight. You ran back into the fray to get your little brothers. You're brave and strong. You have a good, calm head on your shoulders. I couldn't ask for anything more."

Ezra nodded, taking a deep breath. His father's words did little to encourage him. He was still a failure, even if he'd done so many other things right. He wished that he could say something to encourage his father, but he didn't know what to say or what to do besides return his father's hug and be there for him as much as he could. His father's chest was heaving with silent sobs, and it was several minutes before he had controlled himself enough to speak again.

"I need you out there to support me tomorrow, son. We both have to get our minds off this and onto what lies ahead. We've got to protect the rest of our family. We don't want to lose any more of them."

"Yes, Father," Ezra whispered, swallowing a sob.

Father stared into his eyes, as if reading Ezra's thoughts. "Oh son," he whispered. "You didn't fail. You did all that you could possibly do. That's not a failure at all." Father paused, wiped a few tears from his cheeks, and then spoke again with determination, as if he was speaking to both of them.

"It's times like this that we'll need to rise up and take the challenge that Yahweh has set before us. We need to work together as a family and keep our eyes focused on Him. That's the only way we're going to get through this battle, and through these next weeks and months."

Ezra nodded, silently agreeing with his father.

"I'll do my best Father, and... I'm sorry. I'm so sorry," Ezra apologized, holding his father tightly. He couldn't stop the tears now. The father and son sat on the sand, crying together and praying for strength for whatever lay ahead.

ב

"Shayna, there's someone here who wants to see you. Is now a good time?"

Shayna looked up towards the tent flap into the late evening shadows. A whiff of the bread that Jarah was preparing for dinner floated in. Her father's frame blocked the opening.

"Yes, Father," Shayna replied, wondering who it could be. To her amazement, Rishon stepped into the tent. Her father left, though Shayna did not doubt he was standing right outside.

"Rishon! How nice to see you!" Shayna was sure her voice conveyed great shock though she tried to smile and seem at ease. "Won't you sit down?" she added, putting on a flirty air as she batted her eyes and motioned dramatically to a chair by her side.

"No, thank you," Rishon said. There it was, that cold, almost rebuking tone. Was that his natural response to everyone? No, it couldn't be. She had heard a lovely warmth in his voice whenever he spoke to his little sisters. Why was Rishon so different around her?

"Shayna, you should know by now that I'm a blunt and honest person. So, I would like to get right to the reason that I'm here," Rishon declared, crossing his arms over his chest. Shayna felt a sense of foreboding.

"Yes...?" she asked, softly.

"Shayna, I'm sorry to tell you this. I don't want to cause you this pain, but... I do not believe we can become betrothed. You see," he continued after a disbelieving gasp from Shayna, "you don't appear to be a lover of Yahweh. You've taken after your mother in your beliefs and the way you act around others. In my short life I've seen that there can only be one leader in a household and that families can become separated and confused when the mother and father are leading two different ways. Your beliefs and my beliefs would clash and cause anger and strife. I can't marry you with a clear conscience. And—if I may be so bold—until you come to know Yahweh and act like a child of His instead of being stubborn and self-focused, I don't believe you'll find a husband who will be a good leader for you."

"But—but—" For once Shayna was at a loss for words. "You can't just leave me!" she finally blurted. "Our marriage was arranged by our parents. You have to consult my father before you go after some other girl. My father would never let you be so dishonorable."

"I've already talked to your father," Rishon replied calmly, yet directly. "He's agreed with me that it's not in your best interest or mine to have a formal betrothal."

There was an awkward pause.

"Shayna," he continued, "when you were younger, you were much sweeter, kinder, and seemed to love everyone and everything. Your beautiful heart only added to your outward beauty. That's what first attracted me to you and made me think that you would be the kind of woman I would want for a caring wife. But these last six years have changed you drastically from the sweet, innocent girl I used to adore, to a selfish, cold-hearted young woman. Shayna, I do care for you, and I believe that deep down inside you have a good, kind heart. But until you decide to obey your father, and your God, I can't marry you."

Rishon looked penetratingly into Shayna's hazel eyes. She looked down at the floor in shame, completely emptied of any self-conceit and haughtiness. "I understand," she whispered.

Rishon nodded and left the tent, leaving Shayna alone with her thoughts.

ג

"That's what he told me, Jarah!" Shayna sobbed, trying to sniff back her tears.

Jarah was not quite sure which shocked her more: that Rishon had been so direct with Shayna, or that Shayna had actually come to her for comfort. She always went to Ada for counsel and friendship. Rishon had touched something in Shayna's heart that no one else had been able to reach before. With his forward personality and simple, yet honest words, he had brought Shayna to a breaking place, and she now had to decide which way to turn.

"I'm really sorry, Shayna," Jarah soothed, though she truly felt inadequate for this conversation.

"It's—it's all right." Shayna was beginning to collect herself again. "I'll just find someone else, that's all. He's not the only handsome young man out there," Shayna said confidently, though a bitterness slipped into her voice as her eyes wandered towards the bright stars in the sky. She breathed deeply.

"He would've made a wonderful husband," Jarah murmured, more to herself than to Shayna.

"Don't you think I know that?" Shayna exclaimed. "I loved him, but he's gone and ruined everything." Tears began to roll down her cheeks again.

"Perhaps everything isn't lost. Perhaps if you change—"

"I can't change! I like the way I am! And even if I wanted to change, I don't know how. Besides, he doesn't love me and never will. He just said he cares for me. Even if I did decide to act a little differently, his mind is already made. You know how he acts, Jarah. He's so straightforward and stubborn." Shayna sighed again. Jarah could tell she was wrestling with deep, inward passions.

"Shayna, do you really like the way you are?" Jarah asked softly. "Are you filled with joy?"

"Yes. Yes, I am," Shayna declared resolutely.

"Really, Shayna?" It wasn't a question. It was more of a challenge.

Shayna stared into Jarah's face. As she looked into Jarah's eyes, it seemed as if her whole self was shedding its old skin and that Jarah was looking at a new young woman; a young woman who was empty, sad, lost, yet full of new potential, if she would only look to the right One for help—Yahweh.

Shayna slowly moved her eyes away and whispered, "No. No. I guess you're right. It only feels good for a little while." Then she looked at Jarah, earnestness in her eyes. "Is this why I don't make friends easily? Why the only person I feel close to is Ada? Am I really that selfish?"

Jarah bit her lip, not knowing what to say. Only her eyes spoke as they met Shayna's.

"I can't believe it," Shayna muttered. "I feel so blind, so dumb." Shayna looked away and whispered, "I don't know what to do."

"Do what Rishon suggested," Jarah told her.

"And what's that?" Shayna asked, dejectedly.

"Decide—deep in your heart—to obey Yahweh, to follow our father's instructions about believing in Yahweh, and to look out for others' good ahead of your own." Jarah felt that there was nothing more for her to say. She laid a tender hand on Shayna's arm and gave her an encouraging smile. Shayna looked back with a solemn face and tried to smile through her tears. Jarah decided to leave her sister alone with her thoughts and headed back towards the tent. Shayna remained on the rock, her face shining in the light of the moon, looking wistfully out toward the mountains.

ⴕ

Ezra and his father were up late that night packing supplies for the battle. It was possible that they would be gone from the camp several days as they tried to find the Amalekites and then defeat them. Hardly anyone else in the camp seemed to be stirring. Most were resting in preparation for tomorrow. Ezra could see the dark silhouettes of men standing guard on the tops of the craggy rocks in the distance.

A sudden *crash* startled both of them. It sounded like someone had run into their wagon. They heard a muffled cry and a few low, angry words. They hurried towards the noise. In the dim moonlight, they saw Asher coming out of the shadows. He was holding a big bag that seemed to be full of something soft. In his other hand was a small money pouch.

"Asher, what are you doing out so late?"

Asher looked up in shock. A slightly guilty expression was on his face. "Oh, umm… Did I wake you?" he stammered.

"No. Ezra and I are packing up for the battle. But what are you doing?" Ezra's father demanded.

"Oh. I'm—Well, Mariel wanted more grain before I left. My friend Ennis has a surplus, and he was willing to sell me some. I'm heading to bed right now," Asher explained. He seemed a little nervous.

"Sleep well, then. Will we see you in the morning?" Father asked.

"Of course. I'll be ready," Asher responded, waving his hand as he headed back towards his own tent.

"He didn't seem right," Ezra stated in a low voice, watching him walk away.

"You're right, son," his father replied. He took a deep breath before finishing, "I'm worried about him. Something is definitely wrong."

ה

Asher silently made his way through the tent and around his sleeping children. Mariel was sitting up, waiting for him. "Did you get the grain?" she asked in a low voice.

"Yes. I did. It's in our wagon." He clutched the money pouch at his side so that the coins didn't jingle together. He didn't want Mariel to see how little was left. He quickly and quietly stuffed the pouch under some of his belongings. They both laid down.

"Are you going to the battle tomorrow?" Mariel questioned. He was touched that her tone sounded worried.

"Yes, I am."

He heard Mariel take in a long, deep breath. "Be careful."

He swallowed hard before reaching out and taking her hand. He stroked it tenderly with the back of his thumb. Her hand was calloused and worn with labor. "I will." He leaned over and kissed her cheek, feeling some of the old love that he had for his wife. "I believe I'll come back."

"I believe you will, too." Her voice sounded thick with emotion. The tent flap blew back for a moment and Asher saw a tear on her cheek. She quickly brushed it away.

"I never expected to be with child in the desert," she said with a forced laugh, as if trying to make light of the situation. Asher chuckled a little bit and kissed her hand.

"Mariel, you do know that I really do love you, right? That I'm really trying to do what I can to help you and everyone else?"

Mariel nodded. "I know." She slowly turned onto her side. "Just come back safe tomorrow."

He laid on his back, staring out at the pillar of fire. "I'll do my best."

THE ISRAELITES' FIRST BATTLE

"To arms! To arms, Israel! The time for battle is at hand!"

A crier ran through the camp, startling Jarah from her fitful slumber. It was very early and inside the tent it was still dark. Outside she could hear the crackling of a newly lighted fire. Eitan and Father's beds were vacant and Lemuel was gathering up his sling and stones. His shepherd's staff was close at hand.

The day of the Israelites' first battle had arrived. Jarah would have given anything in the world to skip this day and pretend that the ambushes had never happened. But then she remembered Manuel's grave and felt her throat constrict and a cold knot form in her stomach.

Jarah dressed rapidly, her heart pounding with fear. Wrapping a shawl around her shoulders, she stepped outside into the cool darkness. A dark, wet mist hung in the air. Around the campfire Mother, Father, and Eitan were eating a hurried meal. Looking across the camp, Jarah saw Reia talking softly with Rishon by their fire. Next to their tent Grandfather was strapping on a protective breastplate of leather. Amissa and Ezra were getting their meal ready. Everyone was hurrying about in a state of silent urgency.

Jarah tried to eat the baked manna, but it was dry in her mouth and hard for her to swallow. Butterflies danced in her stomach as she watched the men preparing for war.

Soon every man and young man from their group had assembled. Father, Grandfather, and Jaden would be the only ones actually in the combat. Uncle Daton was still very weak from his injury and offered to stay behind with Lemuel to guard the women in case the Amalekites should attack the camp while the majority of the men were gone. Eitan, Rishon, and Ezra would serve as armor-bearers, carry the supplies, help the wounded off the field, bring water to those in need, and deliver messages to the camp.

Jarah focused her attention on the men preparing to leave. The older men looked grave and determined. Rishon's face was—as usual—immobile, and his eyes were cold, hiding any emotions that he felt. Defiance filled Ezra's eyes, but his face was pale as he and Lemuel shook hands.

"Stay safe," Lemuel said simply.

Ezra grinned weakly. "I plan to."

After hugging her father and saying good-bye to the others, Jarah slipped inside the tent to check on the sleeping Yanni and let her tears flow freely in private. She had never felt so scared for her loved ones in all of her life.

"Eitan, must you go? You really don't have to be so close to the battle. Only men twenty and older are fighting. Please, I don't want you to get hurt." Jarah heard Ada's voice from behind the tent pleading tearfully with Eitan.

"Ada, they need the young men to carry provisions, take care of the wounded, and deliver messages. Don't worry. I'll be fine," Eitan tenderly assured her.

"But I have a feeling that you won't be." Ada burst into tears. Eitan put his hands on her shoulders and Ada looked up into his face.

"I'll be fine," he repeated, slowly and directly.

"Please, don't put yourself into any unnecessary danger," Ada begged.

"I won't. I promise. I'll come back. I know I will."

Jarah peeked out of the tent flap and saw Eitan kiss Ada's hand before turning and hurrying away. Ada darted off towards her own tent, crying. Jarah heard the group of men depart and she prayed aloud, "Yahweh, please protect my family and friends and give them strength to win the battle today. Please Yahweh, please be with them. Please let us win."

א

The boys stood at the back of the main company. Groups of other young men carrying weapons and bundles of provisions surrounded them. Through the swirling morning mist, Ezra saw the men and boys who were staying back to guard the women and children ascend the nearby hills and cliffs. Eitan came back with several skins filled with water.

"Any word from the front lines yet?" he asked.

Rishon shook his head. "No."

Ezra shivered a little. "How much longer do we have to wait? I can't stand just sitting here doing nothing."

"Have patience, my friend. They'll be moving soon," a strange voice by Ezra's side assured him.

Startled, Ezra spun around.

"Adriel?" The two friends embraced with brotherly affection.

"Who's your friend, Ezra?" Eitan asked.

"Everyone, this is Adriel. Jarah and I stayed with them when we were lost," Ezra explained.

"Do you mind if I help you all?" Adriel asked, a little hesitantly. "I don't know many others my own age and I would love to accompany you."

"Of course. You're welcome to join us," Eitan said, extending a hand to Adriel. "You seem a little anxious."

"Who can help it?" Adriel said, exhaling shakily.

Eitan chuckled softly. "We all can't help but worry about the outcome today."

Adriel nodded, studying the ground and scuffling his foot in the dirt. "I've never seen a man die or even been near a battle," he murmured softly.

"We were exposed to battle twice already," Rishon said quietly, thinking of his father's wounded arm.

"Really? How?" Adriel's eyes widened.

Eitan quickly interjected, trying to make light of the situation, "That's a long story for another time. I'd be glad to share it with you when we've both grown old."

Ezra appreciated the fact that Eitan was trying to divert the subject. He felt a tear threatening to fall from his eye at the thought of Manuel and the death that they had already seen. He quickly brushed the tear away.

"Then you know what battle feels like," Adriel whispered. "I just don't know if we can do it. If *I* can do it," he finished under his breath.

"Come on. What's wrong with your faith?" Ezra gave him a joking prod, trying to hide his own feelings and push the thoughts of his dead brother from his mind.

Adriel's face broke out into a grin. "A lot, but nothing that can't be fixed with time, I suppose."

The four boys laughed, glad for a break in the tension of waiting.

"Keep trusting in Yahweh, my friend, and He'll see you through," Ezra assured Adriel, slapping a hand on his shoulder and trying to smile.

"I know. It's just hard sometimes. Father's been helping me."

"He's a great man," Ezra said genuinely.

"Yes, he is."

There was a long pause. Some movement in the main body of soldiers aroused them from their thoughts. Asher emerged from the group and came towards them.

"We've decided on a plan. From this camp there are three passes that we could take to find the Amalekites. We hope and pray that they aren't too far away since they attacked us just yesterday afternoon. Our tribe will be taking the pass farthest on the left, along with the tribes of Reuben, Ephraim, and Manasseh. Joshua will be our leader. Caleb, the son of Jephunneh, and Palti, the son of Raphu, are the other two leaders. We will have men scale the cliffs and watch for signs of ambush. If we're able to find the Amalekites, then we'll blow the horn to alert the other bodies of men. Then we can surround their camp and attack them on all sides. At least, that is the plan.

"You boys aren't supposed to be in the combat. You should stay back, far from the back of the line. Be prepared to help the wounded, provide food and water to the soldiers, and take messages to the camp or to the other boys who are helping the other two bodies of soldiers. Is that understood?"

"Yes sir, we understand," the boys answered, almost in unison.

"Eitan, as the oldest one here—and my son—I'm putting you in charge of your friends. I trust you to make wise decisions and keep them from harm. And I trust the rest of you to listen to him and obey whatever he says," Asher continued.

"Yes sir," Rishon and Adriel said together.

"Of course," Ezra replied.

"Who is this?" Asher asked, pointing to Adriel, who he seemed to have just noticed.

"Adriel. We stayed with his family when Jarah and I were lost," Ezra answered.

"I'm more than willing to obey you and your son's instructions, sir," Adriel said respectfully.

"Thank you. I'll be praying for your safety." Asher smiled grimly at them, embraced Eitan, and then disappeared into the main body of soldiers. Ezra noticed that Eitan's face was very pale. He was blinking back tears and it almost looked like Eitan had matured by ten years in just those few moments. The responsibility on his shoulders concerning their little group was visible on his face. It was several seconds before Eitan could face them again with a composed countenance.

"The line is starting to move. Let's put these bundles on our backs and be ready to march with the men."

The others instantly obeyed Eitan's command, shouldering the weapons, skins of water, and bundles of bandages and food. Slowly, cautiously, the procession started to move forward. The boys had to wait for what seemed like ages until they, too, were walking into the pass. The high cliffs rose up on either side of them, ominous and threatening. Ezra watched as hundreds of men climbed the cliffs and then walked on the top of them, ears and eyes alert. No one spoke. They were a silent, moving throng. The stillness and the weight of the anticipation was gnawing away at Ezra's heart. He took a deep breath and wet his lips.

They came to the top of a low hill. From here they could see even more passes and cliffs and mountains spread out all around them. In the far distance, Ezra saw three figures standing on the highest hill of all.

"Who's that?" he asked in wonder. "Are they enemies? Scouts?"

"No, that's Moses," Rishon stated.

"I heard someone say that Moses was going to be watching the battle today. He brought his staff with him. I hope that Yahweh will give him divine power to help us win," Eitan said, quietly.

"But who's with him?" Ezra persisted.

"I believe it's Aaron and his brother-in-law, Hur."

Ezra squinted, trying to make out the men in the early morning light and the fog. If only what Eitan said was true and Yahweh would somehow give them the victory through Moses.

Yahweh, you know what's going to happen today. Please help us, guide us, and protect us. And Yahweh, if it be your will, please help us win.

ב

They hadn't heard anything yet. Jarah fidgeted uncomfortably as she stirred quail stew for their lunch. If only she could know what was going on and how she could help. No one had brought them any news. No horns had been blown. No sounds of war reached their ears.

"You worried?" Lemuel asked.

"Not really," Jarah said quietly, but her strained voice revealed her emotions. She didn't move to face her brother.

There was a low chuckle. "You don't have to hide it from me, Jarah. I know what you're feeling, even without looking at your face. You're very worried."

"Well, I'm trying not to be," Jarah retorted.

There was silence between them for a few minutes, then Lemuel sighed. "I'd better go get some more water for the flock." He had a hard tone in his voice.

"What's wrong with *you*? Are *you* worried?" Jarah challenged.

"What do you mean?" Lemuel was slightly taken aback.

"The way you just said that. You don't seem as happy as you're trying to be." There was an awkward pause. "You don't have to hide it from me, Lemuel," she said, repeating her own brother's words.

He grinned a little, and then exhaled slowly. "I didn't want to be left behind, Jarah. The only reason I'm worried is because I can't be there to help. Instead, I'm back here, in the camp…"

"Like a coward?" Jarah finished for him.

"Yes," Lemuel said, bitterly.

"You're not a coward, Lem," Jarah soothed. "Men have to stay and protect the camp. What if the enemy attacks us? We'd be completely defenseless if all the men were gone. Besides, it takes courage to watch your friends and family just… walk away." Jarah swallowed a sob.

"I suppose," Lemuel assented. He grinned cheerlessly at her. "I need to check on the animals."

Jarah nodded, straightened her back, and gazed out towards the mountains. This waiting was killing her.

What's happening?

Then her heart stopped beating. She heard a long, loud, frantic trumpet blast.

א

Ezra plodded behind Eitan, who walked about one hundred yards behind the last soldiers. His shoulders were already aching from carrying all of this baggage, and they'd only been walking an hour.

His heart suddenly skipped a beat. A horn sounded from high above them, so loud that it made Ezra's ears rings. His heart was instantly racing in his chest.

"Stop right here," Eitan ordered, throwing down his bundle and grabbing his shield and sword. The others followed his example. They heard a wild battle cry. The ground shook underneath their feet and a sound like thunder filled the air.

"What's that?" Adriel exclaimed, his face white.

"Horsemen." Eitan turned to face them. He looked scared. Ezra gulped. He heard the neighing of horses. The ground felt like it was rocking back and forth. From where the boys were standing, on a bit of a hill, they could see the Israelites frantically trying to muster their few horsemen and stand at the ready. But it was too late. The Amalekites crested the hill in front of them and charged down upon the unprepared Israelites. At every blow of the enemies' swords Israelites were falling. It looked like it was going to be pure slaughter.

"Yahweh, please help us now," Ezra panted out. His chest felt like it was constricting. The suspense and terror were making it hard to breathe. He heard Joshua blowing short and repeated blasts on his trumpet.

"The others aren't going to make it in time," Adriel exclaimed, tightening his grip on his sword.

Rishon took a confident step forward and stood next to Eitan. "Just pray," he said, low yet firm.

Ezra looked up to heaven, silently begging Yahweh for help. He then noticed Moses, standing on the hill in the distance. He was raising his staff and holding his hands up to heaven as if he, too, was crying out to Yahweh. A battle cry rose up on either side of Ezra. The soldiers and slingers who had been standing guard on the top of the cliffs had arranged themselves in close, compact companies and were running along the cliffs towards the conflict. The slingers were launching stones at the horsemen. Left and right, Amalekites were dropping from their horses.

"It's working! It's working!" Ezra shouted, jubilant.

The boys raised up a cheer. The Israelites at the bottom of the cliffs were rallying and moving forward, pushing the battered and broken Amalekite horsemen before them. But before they had a chance to celebrate, a long, deep, resounding note was blown from a foreign horn. It was followed by a deafening shout that seemed to shake the mountains.

"What was that?" Adriel asked, trembling.

"The rest of the Amalekite army." Eitan's voice was hoarse and his face portrayed no emotion. The boys watched, silently, as the Amalekites' horsemen fled back to safety behind the hill. Ezra stared at Moses who now stood, hands down, leaning on his staff anxiously.

ד

Asher stood on the front lines panting for air, his sword dripping blood. He had narrowly escaped death several times and his heart was pounding in his ears. He vaguely realized that blood was flowing down his face.

"Everyone hold your lines! Prepare for the attack!" Joshua was commanding.

The earth was shaking under Asher's feet and he could hear the armor and shields of the enemy clanking together. Their helmets appeared over the hill, then their chests, then their sandals. The first row of men was descending upon them... then the second row, and the third. They were racing towards them, swords drawn. Asher braced for the attack. The first Amalekite was charging down upon him, yelling. Gritting his teeth, Asher ran towards the man and their swords clashed. Around and around they spun.

"Asher!"

Asher rotated around to see another Amalekite coming up behind him. In a swift movement he swept the man's legs from under him and turned to see that the first attacker had been stabbed in the back by his father.

"There's more coming," his father said.

More and more men were pouring down upon them in a blur. Asher didn't know how many he killed or injured. He barely realized a pile of dead soldiers was forming all around him. Terror and passion gave him the energy to keep fighting. His father was beside him, dealing magnificent strokes with his sword.

"Asher, Joshua's in trouble!" he heard his father yell. He broke from the circle in which they were fighting and Asher struggled to follow him. They could just see Joshua and several of his hand-picked soldiers fighting in a close-packed knot, almost back to back. They

145

were fending off the Amalekites successfully, but the Israelites were outnumbered and more Amalekites were joining by the moment. The odds were overwhelming. Asher saw Israelites falling on every side, but he didn't have time to think about it.

He and his father fell upon the assailants surrounding Joshua and assaulted them from the rear. The Amalekites were taken by surprise and for a moment they fell back, allowing Joshua and his commanders to fight free of their position. Joshua raised his horn to his lips and blew two short blasts.

"Forward!" he cried.

Asher and his father followed Joshua as he started the charge up the hill into the midst of the enemy. For a moment it seemed like it would work—the Amalekites were giving way and the Israelites were penetrating the enemy's line. Other Israelites joined in. Asher looked up to see Moses standing on the mountain above him, hands outstretched to heaven.

Please keep holding your hands up, Moses. We need your prayers and leadership.

A sharp pain in his arm forced him back to attention. An arrow was embedded in his flesh. Asher grimaced and broke off the shaft. An enemy was approaching him, sword above his head, ready to end Asher's life. Asher ducked, grabbed a spear from the ground and thrust it into the man's chest. The soldier fell, dead. But the fight was far from over.

Yahweh, give us your strength; give us your victory.

ה

Ezra was bandaging up a man's arm when Eitan exclaimed, "We're forcing our way forward!"

Ezra gave the man water, helped him to his feet, and then peered up at Moses. Moses was still standing on the side of the mountain watching, but it was obvious that he was exhausted. His hands dropped to his sides. Ezra's eyes widened.

"Eitan, Moses dropped his hands!"

Before anyone could say anything else Rishon practically screamed, "Eitan!"

A shout was heard overhead. The next few seconds were a blur. Out of the corner of his eye Ezra saw Rishon throw Eitan to the ground. Arrows were raining down on them from all sides.

"Make a barricade," Ezra yelled to Adriel, diving behind his pack of skins, water, and bandages. Adriel was beside him in an instant. They were piling up the baggage to make a protective wall when Ezra heard a frantic cry.

"Ezra! Ezra!!"

Ezra peered around the edge of his bundle. Already arrows were driving deep into their provisions. His heart stopped beating. Eitan was dragging Rishon behind a rock. Rishon had an arrow deeply embedded in his side.

"Stay here. I've got to help Eitan," Ezra shouted to Adriel above the noise of whistling arrows and the screams of wounded men. Adriel nodded at him, face completely drained of color. Ezra grabbed a shield, gripped it tightly, and bolted towards the boulder. An arrow whizzed past his ear and another one struck his shield and glanced off. Ezra dodged another arrow and landed right next to Eitan.

"Cover me," Eitan panted. He had pulled off his tunic and was tearing it into bandages. Rishon's chest was billowing and he was gasping for air. Ezra felt his heart grow cold in his chest as he placed his shield in front of Eitan's back, shielding all three of them as best he could.

"Eitan, just get out of here," Rishon panted out.

"I won't do that," Eitan stated, forcing back tears of fear. He laid a hand on the arrow to pull it out.

"Eitan don't!" Ezra shouted, urgently. "It's in too deep. We've gotta get Shayna or someone to help him. We're just going to make it worse."

"You're right." Eitan was stricken. "Ezra, he took the arrow for me. He shoved me out of the way." There was a slight pause as Eitan applied gentle pressure to the wound, trying to stop the bleeding. His hands cupped the arrow, trying to keep it from sliding farther into Rishon's flesh. Rishon's face was contorted in pain. "I can't let him die," Eitan said, determination and desperation written on his face.

"We've got to get him out of here," Ezra stated.

"Yes, but how?" Eitan's forlorn gaze met his, begging for help.

A horn blasted close-by. Ezra peeked over the rock and saw the Israelites climbing up the cliffs in an effort to stop the enemy archers. The Israelites who remained on the ground were hurling stones up at the enemy in an attempt to distract them and do as much damage as they could. The Amalekites' attention was now drawn away from the wounded men and boys in the rear and they turned their arrows on the main body of Israelites. Ezra realized that now was his only chance to help get Rishon to safety.

Moses, please lift up your arms. Please give us Yahweh's power.

Ezra could barely see Moses from where he was hiding. He saw that Moses was trying so hard to keep his hands up, but he was so exhausted that he could no longer lift them. His arms flopped to his sides and he collapsed to his knees.

No! Please don't! Yahweh, we need you!

Aaron and Hur were by Moses' side in an instant. They seemed to be talking to him, then they both ran away and disappeared from view. Moses again tried to raise his arms, but to no avail. The noises of galloping horses, the screams and moans of wounded and dying men, the whoosh of arrows, and the clashes of metal against metal were ringing in Ezra's ears and seemed to be closing in around him. He flattened himself against a rock as a stray horse bolted towards him.

An idea flashed upon him like lightning. The horse was about to gallop pass him, whinnying and bucking in fright. Ezra dashed towards the animal and managed to grab hold of its reins as it passed him. The horse reared and kicked, but Ezra held on, trying to calm it down. The horse's sides were heaving and sweat glistened on its brown body.

"Shh, it's all right. Calm down," Ezra soothed, rubbing the horse on the nose as he pulled it towards Eitan. They were behind the rock now, but the horse was so big that it wasn't completely concealed.

"This will help you get out of here," Ezra said. Eitan glanced up at him, a small flicker of hope in his eyes. He and Ezra raised Rishon's body and helped him to sit on the horse. Eitan quickly leapt upon the horse's back, grabbing Rishon to stabilize him. Rishon was reeling, almost unconscious. The horse was prancing, scared and confused. Ezra grabbed the reins as Eitan situated Rishon as comfortably as possible and then laid low against the horse's neck. Ezra untied his sash and wound it through the straps of his shield.

"Tie this around your waist," he told Eitan, putting the shield on Eitan's back for protection. It was done in a moment, and Ezra turned the horse's head towards the camp.

"I'm praying you'll make it through," he said.

"Thank you, Ezra. Stay safe," Eitan instructed. Ezra nodded, let go of the reins, and smacked the horse on his rump. The horse took off like an arrow from a bow, galloping for all it was worth away from the noise and terror of the battle. Ezra watched with a beating heart as an arrow struck Eitan's shield and bounced off. In a few moments, they were out of range of the archers. Ezra looked around and saw that the archers were, at least temporarily, aiming elsewhere. He darted back to Adriel, who was still huddling behind the baggage. His eyes were wide with fear.

"I don't think I can do this," he barely whispered. "I can't handle it anymore."

Ezra hunkered down besides him. The relief that Eitan and Rishon had gotten safely away only slightly lessened the fear for his own life and for his friends' lives. But he had to stay strong for Adriel's sake.

"Yes, you can. Yahweh's with us. Pray," he urged. "He'll help you and give you the peace you need. Just ask for it. Pray."

"I can't." Adriel was literally trembling.

"You can." Ezra grabbed Adriel by the shoulders and looked straight into his eyes. "I'm going to pray for you right now." Ezra bowed his head, silently begging Yahweh for His strength and courage and victory.

He was startled by a low cry from Adriel. He was peering around the edge of the barricade, eyes filled with horror. Turning around, Ezra saw Emmitt, Adriel's father, climbing the cliff. He was almost to the top, but a soldier on the crest had seen him and, drawing back his bow, shot him in the chest. Emmitt's body shuddered. He tried to keep his grip on the cliff face, but he couldn't. He dropped, crashing to the ground at the foot of the cliff.

"Father!" Adriel sprang into action, running from the safety of the boulder and to his father's aide.

"Adriel! No!" Ezra yelled, but Adriel didn't hear him. Quickly glancing around, Ezra made a dash to keep up with his friend. They were both in great peril, but they had to get Emmitt out of harm's way. Adriel was just reaching his father's side. Ezra grabbed an abandoned shield and held it over Emmitt's body, trying to shield him as best he could from the arrows. Thankfully, where Emmitt had fallen, they weren't visible to the soldiers above them.

"Father!" Adriel wrapped his arms around his father's shoulders. Emmitt's eyes were closed and he wasn't moving.

"We've got to get him out of here," Ezra urged. "I'll get his feet. You get his shoulders. Stay close up against the cliff. The soldiers can barely see us here. We need to get back to the barricade for water and bandages."

"Right," Adriel acknowledged. He took a deep, unsteady breath and lifted his father's shoulders. Ezra grabbed his legs and together they lifted him and carried him back to the barricade and to safety.

"Adriel, he's not moving," Ezra said, as they hunkered down behind their barrier.

Adriel's eyes grew wide with a different fear.

"Father, come on. Wake up!"

Adriel checked for Emmitt's pulse. Emmitt's face was gray and his chest was still.

The two boys realized the horrible truth—Emmitt was dead. Adriel's hungry, hurt, and pleading eyes looked into Ezra's, seeming to ask him if it was really true. Ezra swallowed hard and nodded. Adriel appeared to be stunned. Tears welled in his eyes and his head dropped to his chest. Ezra reached over Emmitt's dead body and put a hand on his friend's shoulder. He gazed up to heaven, trying to hide his own emotion.

Suddenly he noticed something and his eyes grew wide.

"Adriel, look!"

In the distance, Aaron and Hur were back, rolling a large stone. They set it on the edge of the cliff, helped Moses from the ground to sit on the boulder, and then one stood on each side, holding Moses' hands up towards heaven.

Suddenly on either side of them, horns were blown. A deafening shout erupted from the cliffs above them.

"Are there more Amalekites?" Adriel asked, panic-stricken.

"No, look!"

Sweeping through the Amalekite archers was the other company of Israelites headed by Caleb. The overwhelming surge of people took the Amalekites by surprise. Almost all of the archers were killed within minutes.

"Look back there!" Ezra exclaimed. The Israelites led by Palti were attacking the rear of the enemy line. The Amalekites were being pressed in by all sides. Everything was chaos and confusion among their ranks.

"We're winning!" Ezra jumped to his feet, celebrating.

The boys watched as the Amalekites were pressed closer and closer together. Finally, the Amalekites broke ranks and fled. They were retreating into the mountains. With a great cry the Israelites pursued them, annihilating Amalekite soldiers.

"The battle is as good as won! Yahweh has given us the victory!" Ezra shouted, grabbed Adriel's hand and hauled him to his feet. The boys looked up at Moses who sat, absolutely exhausted, on the rock that Aaron and Hur had brought for him. They still held up his arms towards heaven. Ezra knew that it was only through Yahweh that they had been given the victory. However, a low sob from Adriel made Ezra's heart sink. He glanced at his friend who was staring off into the distance. His eyes were moist with tears. Yes, Yahweh had granted them an amazing victory. But it had not been without great cost.

ו

"Jarah! Jarah!"

A desperate cry reached Jarah's ears. She jumped to her feet from where she sat in front of the tent. Aghast, she stared at Rishon's bloody body as Eitan pulled the horse abruptly to a stop in front of her.

"Rishon," she exhaled in horror.

"Get Shayna, quickly!" Eitan yelled, sliding from the horse's back.

Wordlessly Jarah dashed into the tent. "Shayna, Shayna!" she gasped.

"Jarah, what is it?" Aunt Zuriel asked in alarm. Shayna turned to face her sister, a curious eyebrow raised.

"Rishon—Rishon is—"

"Rishon? What's happened?" Aunt Zuriel leapt up, overturning the stool on which she sat.

"He's hurt. Shayna, you need to help him."

Shayna stared at her sister like she was a ghost. Reia's already pale face turned ashen and she fled from the tent.

"Reia, wait!" Lemuel tried to grab her arm, but she raced past him. He, Jarah, Aunt Zuriel and Shayna ran outside. Reia was staring at her older brother, scarcely breathing. She stumbled forward and would have fainted if Lemuel had not caught her.

"I'm—I'm all right." Reia slowly regained her balance but couldn't keep her eyes from the arrow in Rishon's side.

"Rishon!" Aunt Zuriel cradled her son's face.

"Shayna, he needs help, quickly," Eitan urged. Shayna nodded.

"Let's get him inside," she said, trying to force confidence into her voice.

ƚ

S hayna crouched next to Rishon, examining his wound. His eyes were closed and he was taking quick, shallow breaths. Eitan anxiously sat by his friend's side, praying silently for his healing. Ada stood by Eitan, a gentle hand laid on his shoulder.

Finally Shayna sighed slowly. "It's bad. I've only seen one wound worse than this, and that was when the man who lived next to us in Goshen was stabbed with a spear for disobedience. I was with his wife when we saved his life. But the arrowhead is in here deeply and it might have punctured his lung. If I can get it out, I'm still not sure he will recover." She turned to Aunt Zuriel and Reia, huddled together in the corner and crying softly.

"Isn't there anything you can do?" Aunt Zuriel begged.

"I'll do everything in my power, but it will be painful. Very painful." Shayna looked down at Rishon, planning her next steps. She hadn't had much training with puncture wounds of any type, especially with something this serious.

Rishon forced his eyes open and stared up into Shayna's face. It took a great effort for Rishon to focus on her face, but the meaning in his expression was undeniable. Shayna saw it, and it made her heart leap with both sadness and hope. His eyes were filled with trust. He trusted her.

Laying a hand on Rishon's arm Shayna asked quietly, "It will hurt. Do you want me to try to help you?"

Rishon looked from Shayna to Eitan's worried, pleading gaze. "Yes," he whispered almost inaudibly.

He trusts me. I have to do everything I can to save his life. I only hope I can.

"I think you should all leave," Shayna said, turning around and addressing everyone in the room. Silently, they all exited the tent. Everyone that is, except for Eitan.

At a questioning look from Shayna, Eitan stated, "He's going through this pain for me, and while there's something that I can do to help him, I'm not leaving."

Shayna nodded. "I'll be glad to have your help," she said, "but I'm afraid this is going to be gruesome." She went to the bucket of water in the corner, washed her hands, and then came back to Rishon's side. Her slender fingers worked themselves into the wound, trying to find the arrowhead. Rishon's face was distorted by pain and a loud moan escaped his lips.

"Stay with us, Rishon," Eitan told him, squeezing his cousin's hand comfortingly. "You can do this. Hold on."

ת

Jarah sat outside the tent, waiting. She kept hearing low groans from behind her in the tent. It hurt her heart deeply to hear it. She could only keep praying that Rishon would make it. She hugged her knees, blinking back tears and staring out towards the mountains.

153

The distant roar of the battle could be heard, but it seemed to be moving farther away. Was that a good thing?

She started. A figure was running towards them. She leapt to her feet.

"Ezra!"

Lemuel ran around from the other side of the tent and practically tackled Ezra with a mighty hug.

"Are you all right? What's going on?"

Ezra was beaming. "We've won! The Amalekites are in full retreat. The men are chasing them and killing them. How's Rishon? Did Eitan make it back?"

"Yes, they made it back. But... We don't know how Rishon is. Shayna still doesn't know if he'll make it," Lemuel finished, quietly.

Ezra bit his lip and his face darkened with sorrow. He sighed deeply and then said, "I've got to get back to help the wounded. Where's the horse that Eitan rode? I need to spread the word that the battle is over and bring more water and bandages."

"Back behind the tent. Come on." Ezra and Lemuel hurried to go get the horse.

"He's safe," Jarah murmured with a happy sigh. "He's safe."

ט

"The arrowhead has been removed, but Shayna believes it will be a long, difficult recovery, and he may not make it. He's lost a lot of blood and there's a great risk of infection, not to mention that his lung might've been punctured," Eitan reported grimly to Ada outside of the tent.

"Eitan, how did it happen?" Ada asked tearfully.

Eitan explained the particulars and then added, "He did it for me, Ada, for us."

"I know," Ada replied, nodding her head slowly. They stood side-by-side for several quiet minutes. Jarah watched them from the entrance of the tent, praying silently. She could only hope that no one else had been injured or killed in the battle.

❜

Darkness was beginning to fall, and Jarah was beginning to despair of seeing her family and friends before the end of the night when cheers and shouts suddenly echoed through the camp.

"Mother, the army's back!" Lemuel announced.

Jarah ran to the edge of the camp and climbed up on a rock, searching for any sign of her family or friends. A thrill of relief ran down her spine as she saw the familiar faces of her father, grandfather, Jaden, and Ezra. They had come back alive.

The men came back to camp bloody and bruised but exultant in the victory. The women saw to their wounds, and that night there was a splendid celebration in camp with feasting, singing, and dancing before the Lord.

Jarah came back into the tent a little before the others. She wanted to check on Shayna, who was still at Rishon's side. Peering over her sister's shoulder, Jarah saw that there was no change in Rishon. If anything he looked even worse than before. His face was chalk-white; his breathing irregular. His skin was clammy with a cold sweat and the wound in his side was still slowly oozing blood, saturating the bandage that was tied around his chest.

"How is he?" Jarah asked hesitantly, though she already knew the answer.

"Worse. He has a fever now." Shayna laid her hand on his forehead. Her shoulders were sagging and dark circles rimmed her eyes. "I don't think he'll make it through the night."

Jarah drew in her breath sharply. "Does—do Aunt Zuriel, Uncle Daton, and Reia know?"

"Yes, though I know that Reia is choosing to not believe it. Now that the immediate grief is over, Aunt Zuriel seems to be doing much better. She's trusting Yahweh and has given her son into His hands." There was a long, thoughtful pause. "I just hope I can help him, and by doing so help all of them." There was a new note in Shayna's voice, one of hope, compassion, and comfort. Jarah knew that her sister's heart was beginning to soften.

"Well, I think that Rishon couldn't have a more gifted healer," she said with affection, grabbing Shayna's hands and pressing them, encouragingly.

Shayna looked into Jarah's eyes and smiled, though it was a tired smile. "Let's see if I live up to that," she whispered, squeezing the reassuring hand.

TROUBLE

"Jarah, did you finish filling the skins with water?" Shayna called from the opening of the tent.

"Yes, Shayna," Jarah shouted back.

Eitan came walking towards her, carrying the blanket for Oved, the enemy horse that they had captured.

"Is it just me or have the days been getting hotter?" Jarah asked no one in particular. She mopped her face with her arm.

"It might just be you," Eitan said teasingly as he laid the blanket on Oved's back. "Or it could be the fact that summer is coming on quickly."

"What month is it now?" Jarah asked. The days had blended together and it was almost impossible to keep track of time.

"The middle of the fourth month." Eitan's voice was muffled as he was underneath Oved's belly tying on the blanket. Jarah couldn't help but laugh.

"Jarah, can you go see if Mother's ready?" Lemuel shouted from where he was trying to contain their herd.

"Sure Lem." Jarah started for the tent and then felt her jaw drop in surprise. "Rishon!" she squealed.

Rishon was supported between Uncle Daton and Shayna and was taking slow, gentle steps towards their family's wagon. Eitan ran towards him and quickly took Shayna's place by Rishon's side.

"It's good to see you up and about again, my friend," Eitan said with evident delight.

"It's good to be out again," Rishon said weakly, but still with a joyful smile on his face.

Jarah looked into Shayna's face. Shayna was beaming with delight. Yahweh had answered their prayers. Rishon was recovering. He was still very pale and weak, but the fact that he had been able to walk to the wagon after only seven days of recovery was a wonderful sign.

He will get well, Jarah thought. *He has to.*

א

Jarah was one of the first ones up the next morning. She looked at the cloud, seeing if it was lifting or moving at all. She sighed a little in relief—no movement yet. Maybe this morning wouldn't be as hectic and chaotic as the previous ones.

Jarah grabbed a basket from their wagon and began picking up manna from the ground. The manna sparkled in the dew and made everything white and fresh and clean. Other girls and children were running about and gathering manna, too. Some of the younger ones were shoving manna in their mouths as they ran along. Jarah grinned. She was happy watching them work.

The sound of a stifled sob came to Jarah's ear. She peered around. Who was crying? And why? She couldn't see anyone who looked sad or discouraged. But there was the sound again. Jarah approached a nearby boulder and peeked around it.

Amissa sat there, curled up in a little ball, crying.

"Amissa, what's wrong?" Jarah knelt at her friend's side. Amissa started, then met Jarah's gaze with very sad and round eyes.

"I—I miss Manuel," she sobbed out.

Jarah wrapped her arms around her friend and gave her a big hug. Amissa dropped her head on Jarah's shoulder and let herself cry. Jarah held her friend, gently rubbing her back, for a very long time. The cold, damp sand made Jarah shiver a little as it was pressed into her flesh, but Jarah continued to comfort her friend, not wanting to let go. It felt good to be needed.

As Amissa's crying slowly quieted, Jarah finally ventured to speak.

"I'm so sorry, Amissa," Jarah said, as kindly as she could. "I can't imagine what it would be like."

Amissa shook her head and wiped away her tears. "Father and Mother are so quiet. Manni looks so lost and confused without his twin. And Ezra..." Amissa choked back a sob. "Ezra still blames himself, I think. He seems to be keeping it all inside, and I don't know how to help him. I want to help all of them, but it hurts so badly." She started to weep again.

"I know it hurts. I wish I could help you, too," Jarah comforted, still holding her friend.

"I just don't know why, Jarah." Amissa turned pleading eyes to her friend's face. "I don't know why God had to take Manuel. Father keeps talking about Yahweh's plan and Yahweh's purpose, but I don't understand it. I want to understand it. But how can something good come out of something bad?"

"I don't understand it, either," Jarah admitted, hanging her head. The girls sat silently together, holding hands, each thinking. Amissa finally broke the stillness.

"But there's something I keep coming back to," she began, thoughtfully. "Things were bad in Egypt. I mean, we were slaves. We were beaten and worked almost to death. I didn't think anything good would *ever* happen. I just had to accept the bad things in my life and hope and pray for the good things, like one day being free. And now... we're free."

Jarah tightened her grip on Amissa's hands. "Then cling to that, Amissa. Cling to the fact that though nothing seems right, it really is right. Yahweh is working. Don't give up hope, and don't get angry at Yahweh."

"Oh I'm not angry with Him," Amissa hurried to say. "I just wish I understood." She looked down at the sand, tears again gathering in her eyes.

"Me, too," Jarah breathed.

"But I thought about this, too," Amissa added. "If our family hadn't been in that ambush, then we wouldn't have known that the Amalekites were still around. Maybe they would've come with the whole army and killed us while we weren't prepared. We might have all died, not just Manuel."

"I hadn't thought of that, but you're right," Jarah mused. "It was really Yahweh's way of saving our nation!"

Amissa nodded and smiled sadly, blinking back tears. "He's still in control," she whispered. "I just have to make the choice to believe that."

"I know you can make that choice," Jarah told her friend, confidently. "And I'll be praying for Yahweh to give you peace and comfort. You and everyone else in your family."

"Thank you, Jarah. You're the best of friends," Amissa said, smiling through her tears. She rose to go. "I'd better return to the wagon. Mother will be looking for me."

Jarah collected her basket and stood up, giving her friend another hug with her spare arm. "Yahweh loves you, and I love you, too. Don't forget that."

Amissa giggled a little and wiped away a few tears. "I won't." She hurried back towards her tent, a slight spring in her step as she ran. Jarah bent over and continued to collect manna. As she moved on to another patch of ground, she saw two figures sitting on a boulder close to their animals.

"That looks like Lemuel and Ezra," she thought out loud. She prayed that Lemuel was able to encourage Ezra just as she had been able to bless Amissa.

ב

L emuel was surprised to see Ezra already out this morning. The sun had just barely risen, and everything was still dim and wet. Ezra sat hunched up in a little ball on top of a low rock, looking tired, his staff resting listlessly in his hands.

"What're you doing out here?" Lemuel teasingly asked. Ezra jumped. Apparently Lemuel had startled him out of deep thought.

"Huh?" Ezra gazed at him blankly.

"I said I was going to take care of the animals this morning. You took a turn yesterday. You should be asleep!" Lemuel stated.

"Oh." Ezra shook his head a little, seeming to come back to the world. "I couldn't sleep, so I thought I might as well come out here and give you a break."

Lemuel felt very concerned as he sat next to his friend. For the past week Ezra had seemed very doleful and down, and there was such a sad expression in his eyes. He knew it was Manuel's death. Ezra was trying to deal with his grief silently and wasn't letting anyone else into his pain and hurt and sorrow. It worried Lemuel, but he tried to make light of the situation.

"But I said I didn't need a break, Ezra. In fact, I think it's the other way around. You look like *you* could use a break," he tried to joke.

Ezra didn't make eye-contact with his friend. He smiled grimly and said, "I'd rather stay busy right now, if you don't mind. You can head on back." Ezra's eyes scanned the landscape.

But Lemuel didn't head on back. Instead, he put a hand on Ezra's shoulder and forced Ezra to look at him. He felt Ezra shudder under his touch. "It's your brother, isn't it?" he probed. Ezra eyes immediately filled with tears and Lemuel saw that he was struggling to keep his emotion.

"I miss him," he whispered, almost inaudibly. "I keep thinking through that day over and over and over again, thinking what I could've done differently, how I could've saved him..."

Sorrow gripped Lemuel's heart, a deep, aching sorrow for his friend. He couldn't imagine losing either Raphael or Yanni. But Ezra couldn't wallow in his misery and pain. It wasn't Ezra's fault, and Ezra needed to realize that before his anger and bitterness turned into hatred for himself or for Yahweh.

"Ezra, you know it's not your fault—" Lemuel began, but Ezra angrily cut him short.

"Everyone says that. Father says that. Mother says that. Amissa says that. But I was supposed to be watching him. I should've gotten him and Manni first! I wasn't even thinking!" Ezra pounded the rock with his fists, rapidly blinking back tears. "Why did this happen?" he yelled. "Why? Why couldn't it have been me instead of him? Couldn't Yahweh have stopped it? Why didn't he? Why did it happen? Why?" Ezra looked up and shouted at the sun, "Why?!" He starting weeping and hid his face, his anguish pouring out of him all at once.

Lemuel sat silently, watching his friend, praying for him, and thinking. He finally heard Ezra whisper, "I won't believe that it wasn't my fault. It was. Everyone just wants to make me feel better, but it doesn't help." Ezra drew in a long, shaky breath. He finished, "I almost wish we hadn't left Egypt. Then maybe Manuel would still be alive."

Ezra slowly raised his head. His face was steeled and grim. He still didn't look at Lemuel, and he didn't say anything more. The boys just sat together, neither of them speaking. Lemuel continued to pray silently and waited to see if Ezra had anything else to say. When it was apparent that Ezra was waiting for him to speak, Lemuel thought for a moment before beginning.

"But Ezra, you helped save many lives. You helped cut a way through to get all of us out. You got Jarah and Raphael and Manni out of there. We were surrounded, and there were so many people that needed help. It's not your fault, and you can't continue to think that it was. It's only going to make the pain worse and turn you against yourself, and against Yahweh."

"I'm not against Yahweh," Ezra stated quickly, as if trying to convince both of them that it was true. There was a pause as Lemuel carefully calculated what to say.

"But you're mad at Him, aren't you? And mad at yourself?"

Ezra buried his face in his arms. "Yes," he choked out. His back shook with silent weeping. Lemuel laid a hand on Ezra's shoulder, silently praying for wisdom for himself and comfort for his friend.

"I just don't understand," Ezra yelled vehemently. "I can't understand! Why? Why did Yahweh do it?"

Lemuel tightened his grip on his friend's shoulder, letting him know that he was still there, still supporting him.

As Ezra's sobs began to subside, Lemuel asked, very quietly, "Ezra, do you believe that Yahweh is a good God?"

Ezra's head jerked up and he stared into Lemuel's face with squinting, questioning eyes. "What do you mean?"

"Do you believe that Yahweh is a good God?" Lemuel repeated.

"I suppose so...?" Ezra began, holding up his hands as if he didn't understand the question.

"You can't suppose so, Ezra. You need to believe it. Do you believe, really and truly believe, that Yahweh is a good God?"

Ezra shook his head. "I don't know if I can believe that right now."

Lemuel positioned his body so that he could look directly into Ezra's eyes. The sun struck him full in the face. "Ezra, think about this for me. Think of the good things that have happened in your life. What are they?"

Ezra sat for a while, pondering, and wiping a few stray tears from his cheeks. Then he quietly began to list things. "My family. Yahweh has blessed me with them. When we moved into the house next to yours when we were really little and back in Egypt, that was a good thing. You. Your family. The fact that we never starved. Our animals have thrived. We got Ada back from the palace. Yahweh freed us from slavery."

Lemuel nodded, encouraging him. "How about more recently, since we left Egypt?"

Ezra began talking, very slowly, "Yahweh delivered us from the Egyptians. He helped us find you again. He's provided us with food and water. He helped us defeat the Amalekites."

"Now," Lemuel began, still softly, "can you think of the things in your life that have seemed to be bad?"

Ezra's brow was furrowed. "Being slaves in Egypt. Ada being taken from us to serve in the palace. Being beaten or having times of sickness… Losing Manuel and others in all of the battles."

Lemuel nodded in agreement. "Now think for a moment. How many of those things have ended in good things?" Ezra gave him a puzzled expression, so Lemuel explained. "We're free now! We're not slaves in Egypt anymore. Ada was returned to you, and allowed to be betrothed to Eitan instead of being forced to marry Paki. And while this in and of itself wasn't a good thing, the ambush on our families alerted Joshua to the need to go to war before the Amalekites destroyed our nation. So even in that, Yahweh was working for good. So Ezra, can you believe that Yahweh is a good God?"

Ezra didn't make eye contact with his friend, but he was slowly nodding his head. "Yes. I can choose to believe it."

A smile broke over Lemuel's face. "Can you believe that Yahweh is right here with us, watching us and guiding us and leading us?"

Ezra's head came up again, and his eyes were pleading as he said, "But He wasn't watching out for Manuel!"

"Can you believe it, Ezra?" Lemuel countered, quietly, avoiding Ezra's statement. Ezra hung his head. Lemuel sighed a little and said kindly, gently, "Ezra. Look up." Ezra did and his eyes followed Lemuel's finger as he pointed towards the pillar of cloud.

Lemuel asked again, tenderly yet directly, "Can you believe that Yahweh is here with us?"

Tears spilled out of Ezra's eyes as he looked hard into the cloud. His lip was trembling. "Yes," he whispered. "He's here."

Lemuel smiled sadly at him. "I know you can't believe this now, but somehow, in some way that we don't understand, this is Yahweh's plan. I don't believe that He killed Manuel. Evil did that, and yes, I'm sure Yahweh could've stopped it, but He had a bigger plan in mind: Deliverance for our people. A new land, filled with promise and hope and new beginnings."

Ezra straightened his back and raised his head. In his eyes, a glimmer of the old spark seemed to kindle. His jaw was set and determined as he looked Lemuel straight in the eye and said, "You're right. I must *choose* to trust. I *choose* to believe, and to hope. I'll try my hardest to rest in His comfort and strength and stop blaming myself... or Yahweh. But..." Here the flicker in his eyes almost seemed to go out. "That will be very hard."

"It'll be easier if you let Yahweh and us help you and don't keep it all inside," Lemuel told him.

Ezra nodded, slowly realizing what Lemuel was saying. "You're right." He sighed, as if a weight was being lifted from his shoulders. "You're right."

Lemuel put an arm around his friend's shoulders. "I'm here for you, Ezra."

Ezra's eyes were again dim with moisture. But a small, peaceful smile rested on his face as he answered, "I know you are. And Yahweh's here, too."

The boys both watched the pillar of cloud, silently thanking Yahweh for being in their midst.

א

The sun was setting and the shadows were stretching out behind Jarah. Camp had been erected and she was cleaning out the wagon. She was shaking out some dusty blankets when she heard mischievous giggles from behind a large boulder. Jarah circled the rock, still holding a large blanket, and found Tirzah, Chanah, and Joleen. Yanni and Raphael were playing together a short distance away. It was obvious that the young girls were supposed to be watching the little children but they weren't being very attentive. Sitting together in a tight circle, they were talking in subdued voices, quite caught up in their conversation.

"Girls?"

A short scream simultaneously issued from the three young ladies. Seeing that it was only Jarah, they burst into relieved laughter.

"Jarah, don't do that to us," Tirzah exclaimed once they had gained control of themselves.

"Do what? Scare you, or rebuke you for not watching your siblings?" Jarah glanced at Yanni and Raphael, who were trying to climb a large

165

rock. She looked Tirzah in the eyes and her little sister's cheeks colored with embarrassment as she darted away to fetch the young children.

"We *were* watching them," Joleen stated in defense for Tirzah. "We were—just about to get them," she stammered.

"I see." Jarah drew out her words and raised an eyebrow knowingly.

"We were just surprised to see you, that's all," Tirzah puffed as she sat back down in the shade of the boulder, a squirming Yanni in her lap.

"And what were you talking about that made you so engaged in your conversation?" Jarah asked, draping the blanket over her arm.

The girls all exchanged a suspicious look. "Nothing you'd want to know about," Joleen said tersely, straightening her dress. Chanah and Tirzah gazed up at Jarah expectantly as if they already knew that Jarah was going to pry for more information and wished to drag out her suspense as long as possible.

"Why wouldn't I?" Jarah sat down with the other girls, folding the blanket in half as she did so.

There was a long pause. "We were… matchmaking," Tirzah said finally, suppressing a giggle behind her hand.

"Of course. If you're involved in *any* conversation romance *has* to come up," Jarah said with some annoyance. That was one thing she must talk to Father about—romance. Tirzah was too young to understand the harm in playing with emotions and she needed to be warned. "Aren't you girls a little young to be planning out who you're going to marry?" Jarah prodded.

"Oh, we weren't thinking about ourselves," Chanah asserted.

"No. We were talking about—" Here Tirzah smirked at her older sister. "Other people," she finished.

"Oh. And would I happen to be one of them?" Jarah asked.

"Well…" Chanah glanced at her other accomplices.

"Yes," Tirzah and Joleen said together.

"I see. You're trying to match up your older sisters, is that it?"

"Yes," all three replied in unison.

"Well now that I've dragged the whole thing out of you I might as well tell you that romantic topics are not appropriate for girls your age."

"But we were being very realistic," Joleen said gravely.

"Yes. We were only matching up the people that make sense," Tirzah added.

"See," Joleen began, "now that Rishon has refused Shayna we think he is going to marry Amissa."

Jarah couldn't see that match. "I don't see how—"

"And that Lemuel is going to marry Reia," Tirzah interrupted, plowing ahead.

"Yes. And you're going to marry Ezra," Joleen added for Tirzah. All three girls looked penetratingly at Jarah, trying to determine her thoughts. They were gratified to see that her face was turning crimson.

"You girls are ridiculous." Jarah could hear the strain in her voice as she stood up abruptly.

"But it's so obvious. Just the way he looks at you, Jarah. And you like him. We can tell," Tirzah said teasingly.

"I don't see anything obvious," Jarah stated. Now she sounded angry. "You've been matching Ezra with me for years, Tirzah, and he's never shown any interest in me."

Tirzah looked at her sister for a long time before she said anything. "You're blind, Jarah," she said, simply. "Remember that time with the snake?"

"Oh. That," Jarah muttered wryly, rolling her eyes.

"And all that he did for you when you got lost? You were raving about him for days."

"Tirzah, I have work to do. And I suggest you girls go and get the boys before they get hurt on those rocks." Jarah turned on her heel and stormed away feeling angry, frustrated, and confused.

"I don't like him. I don't," Jarah told herself. "Stop focusing on romance. You're just as bad as Tirzah."

But nothing that Jarah said to herself could erase the fact that her heart pounded in Ezra's presence and she felt her cheeks flush at all the random comments he gave her. And it couldn't hide that vague, far-away look in Ezra's eyes that she had caught a few times when he stared at her.

"He doesn't like me. He doesn't. He can't," Jarah whispered. But her words lacked emphasis.

She was back at the wagon now, folding the blankets and putting them away almost in a daze. Her cheeks were still red. She was startled to hear the sound of running footsteps from behind her.

"Excuse me."

Jarah wheeled around, trying to gather her scattered thoughts. A young man was standing in front of her.

"I'm looking for Sethur of the tribe of Asher. I was sent in this direction by Pagiel, leader of your tribe. Do you know him?"

"Yes, sir. I'll take you to him," Jarah said, leading the young man across the clearing to her grandparents' tent.

Grandfather wasn't in his tent. Jarah had to lead the young man all the way out to where the animals were grazing to find him.

"Grandfather, this man wants to see you," Jarah said.

Grandfather grasped the young man's hand firmly. "I'm Sethur. How can I help you?" He nodded to Jarah, signaling that her job was done and that she should go back home. Jarah sighed a little, wishing she knew what her grandfather and this man were up to.

Jarah headed into the tent, still thinking about her grandfather and what the little girls had said. She entered in the middle of another argument between her parents.

"Where have you been all day, Asher?" Mother was demanding.

"Taking care of things, Mariel," Father replied, irritated.

"If you're out talking to the children about Yahweh behind my back again, I'll—"

"No, Mariel," Asher cut her off, annoyed. "I've been doing as you asked and not speaking to the boys as much about that."

"I'm sure," Mother said, sarcastically.

"Mariel!"

Mother suddenly noticed Jarah standing silently in the corner. "Well? What are you doing here?"

"I finished cleaning and folding the blankets, Mother. You said to come back when I was done," Jarah answered, meekly. She was fighting back tears. It scared her and hurt her to see her parents fighting.

"Oh." Mother appeared surprised. "Get started on dinner, then. Check the wagon for some meat and make some stew."

"Yes, Mother." Jarah quickly ran outside, eager to escape the argument. She clambered into the wagon and began searching through their baskets and pots, but she didn't find any meat. She bit her lip, thinking about where else they might have stored their food. Her parents' heated voices were still audible from the tent. Sighing, Jarah slid from the wagon and went back inside.

"Mother?" she said, hesitantly.

"Yes? What is it?" Mother snapped.

"I can't find any dried meat."

"There's none in the wagon?"

"No, Mother."

"How about some vegetables or wheat?"

Jarah shook her head. "The only thing we have is manna. We ran out of vegetables and wheat last week."

Mother stood still, hands folded across her chest, tapping her fingers.

"Well, Asher, sounds like we have a problem."

"*We?*" Father exclaimed.

"Yes, *we*. Who's the provider for this family, Asher?"

"I am," Father muttered, darkly.

"Well then, aren't you going to do something about it?" Mother demanded.

"Look, Mariel, I've been trying to find people to trade with for a while now. Everyone is hoarding their own provisions. And hunting is also impossible. A group of people this big scares off all animals." Father was obviously exasperated.

Mother's hands were on her hips now. "Well, maybe you aren't trying hard enough!" she practically shouted.

"What else am I supposed to do?" Father yelled back, throwing his hands up in anger. Jarah cringed and backed into a corner.

"Get out there and do something about it!" Mother retorted, pointing at the door.

"All right!" Father spun around and stomped towards the door. A voice from outside made him pause and regain his composure.

"Asher? Son?"

"I'm in here, Father."

Grandfather opened the tent flap and stepped inside. He was smiling broadly.

"Moses' father-in-law, Jethro, has come, bringing Moses' family with him. I've been invited to a feast that Moses is holding in Jethro's honor. Should anyone come looking for me for any reason, see what you can do to help them in my absence. And if you can't be of assistance, you can tell them that I'm not sure when I'll be able to return but that I will help them as soon as I am able."

"Yes, sir. I'll be happy to," Father said.

Grandfather left them, still smiling. Father followed him out of the tent. Jarah eagerly ran outside, too. While she was excited that her grandfather was getting such attention from Moses and Joshua, that was of almost no significance to her in light of what was going on with her parents. They argued almost daily now. And what about their food? Could they live on just manna?

Ada's voice shocked Jarah out of her thoughts.

"Jarah! Can you come here for a minute?" Ada called, looking concerned. She and Ezra were standing in front of their wagon.

"Yes? Is something wrong?" Jarah wondered.

"We were just about to ask you the same question," Ezra stated. He looked very serious and worried.

"What do you mean?" Jarah was confused.

Ada glanced at Ezra before responding. "We heard a bunch of— yelling—coming from your tent."

Jarah felt herself grow tense. She hung her head. "Mother and Father have been arguing a lot. None of us know what to do to help them. Eitan and Lemuel were out with the animals this time and weren't here to stop it."

Jarah heard Ezra sigh deeply.

"I'm so sorry, Jarah," Ada murmured, sympathetically. "I've been praying for them. I know this trip has been hard on your Mother particularly, and I'm sure your Father is worried about her and that's taking a toll on your whole family."

Jarah just nodded. Her throat was tight, and she blinked back tears.

"Do you need help with anything?" Ezra asked.

Jarah shook her head. "No. We're just trying to find food. We don't have any wheat or meat left. We have manna, but my mother is sick of manna, and we don't want to kill any of our animals just yet…"

"You're that low already?" Ezra exclaimed.

Jarah nodded again, daring to meet Ezra's gaze. "Yes. We didn't realize how much was gone."

Ezra was biting his lip and looking past her absently, as if thinking hard. Ada laid a hand on Jarah's shoulder.

"I wish there was something we could do to help you," she said, kindly.

"Have you talked to Eitan?" Jarah ventured to ask. "Maybe he would know how you can help us."

"Not really. Eitan hasn't been around much lately. I guess between your family matters and helping with the animals he's been a little preoccupied…" Ada's voice trailed off. Jarah saw Ezra glance anxiously at his sister.

"I'm sorry he's so busy. I'm sure he wants to talk to you very much," Jarah assured Ada.

"I'm sure you're right," Ada agreed, smiling slightly.

There was an awkward pause as Jarah thought about what else to say. "I guess I need to go get my little siblings and get ready for dinner," she finally said.

"Yes, right. We'll see you tomorrow," Ada replied, waving in farewell. Jarah waved back and hurried off to find Tirzah, Raphael, and Yanni.

As she searched from tent to tent and through groups of people trying to find her little siblings, she wondered when her father was going to be back and if they would have anything besides manna for dinner. Every time there had been an argument between her parents recently, it seemed like her father would disappear for a while.

"He just has to sort things out, I'm sure," Jarah told herself. But it worried her and made her anxious. It also made her uneasy that Eitan seemed to be ignoring Ada. He loved her so much. Jarah knew that he did. But if he wasn't paying attention to her, of course it would make Ada upset. She could tell that it made Ezra a bit frustrated, too. Should she mention it to Eitan? Or should she let him figure it out on his own?

It was hard for Jarah to fall asleep that night. So many thoughts were in her mind. Mother had been very, very irritable, complaining about how all they had was manna to eat. How were they going to find more food? There was plenty of manna, but Jarah was beginning to get sick of eating just manna and quail all the time. Maybe Mother was right about needing a change in their diet.

Father had not come back after the argument. Jarah wondered where he was, and where he always went. She kept tossing and turning, trying to get comfortable and go to sleep. She heard Eitan stirring, too. Mother also seemed to be dozing in and out of a restless sleep.

Suddenly the tent flap moved aside. Eitan's dark silhouette jerked to a sitting position.

"Father?" he whispered.

"Yes, son. Go to sleep," Father answered, gruffly.

Eitan lay back down and Jarah remained perfectly still. She watched Father's tall shape maneuver quietly to the other side of the tent. He appeared to be carrying a heavy burden.

"What's that?" she heard her mother's voice ask in a low whisper.

"I've got some grain. It should last a while," Father replied. He sounded tired and strained.

"Finally," Mother said, sarcastically.

There was a pause as Father flopped down onto his mat. His voice was shaking with emotion when he said in return, "I'm glad you approve of something I do, Mariel."

Mother's tone was softer as she said, "Asher, I'm sorry. I'm just worried about our family's situation."

Father didn't say anything for a moment. Then in a husky voice he muttered, "Good-night, Mariel."

No more was said. Tears rolled down Jarah's cheeks as she closed her eyes and slowly drifted off to sleep.

ٮ

Jarah was awakened from a deep sleep by angry yelling. She started up to a sitting position, her heart pounding.

"It's you! You did this! Give it back to me, *now!*" a man's voice bellowed.

Her father's heated voice answered, "It wasn't me! I swear!"

"Don't lie to me! My neighbor saw you! You can't deny it!"

"And I look just like any other Israelite man! How do you know it was me?" Father accused.

Eitan leapt from his bed and dashed outside. Tirzah and Raphael clambered from their bed and raced to where Shayna was sitting, concerned and nervous, and sat in her lap. Mother rose to one elbow and demanded, "What's happening? What's going on?"

Lemuel rose and crouched by the tent flap, peering outside. "I'm not sure, Mother, but Eitan's there. He'll help sort things out," Lemuel assured her, but his brow was furrowed and he was worried. The heated voices were still arguing outside.

"If I went into your tent right now," the other man yelled, "I know I'd find my missing grain!"

"You have no right to enter my tent and take things that don't belong to you!" Father exclaimed.

"Oh? And what about what *does* belong to me?" the other man shouted.

"Father, what's this man talking about?" Eitan asked, trying to get a word in edge-wise.

"It's none of your concern, Eitan," Father snapped at him.

"Well I'm just going to go in and see for myself!" the other man stated.

"I won't allow you to do that," Father roared.

The brief sound of a scuffle ensued. Lemuel's eyes grew wide, and he made a movement as if to jump away from the door. But suddenly a strange man stormed into the tent, knocking Lemuel to the ground in his haste. His dark eyes darted around the hut, surveying everyone and everything with distaste and suspicion. He spied something and his eyes grew round. He stomped towards Mother. Lemuel raced towards their mother and jumped in front of her, shielding her.

"What are you doing?" Lemuel exclaimed.

"Finding this!" the man announced. Eitan and Father came running in as the man reached past Mother and pulled out the large bag of grain that Father had brought home last night.

"That's ours," Father growled.

"I don't think so," the man snorted. "You'll notice that this bag is made out of wool, whereas most bags imported to Egypt are made out of burlap. My wife weaves cloth and made these bags so that we could tell ours apart from a family that is sharing our wagon."

"My wife weaves cloth, too, so what makes you think that this couldn't be one of ours," Father accused.

The man looked at Father, a gleam of triumph in his eye.

"This."

The man flipped the bag over and showed a design made out of coarse red thread. The design was two diagonal lines crossed in the middle.

"As I said, my wife marks our bags of grain to tell the difference between our food and the people who are using our wagon. This is our mark."

Father stood still, speechless. Jarah looked from Eitan's stricken face to Lemuel's open-mouthed astonishment. Eitan took a step forward. "Father? Did you... You couldn't have..."

Father brushed Eitan aside and looked the man directly in the face.

"This is our grain," he said in a low, dangerous tone.

The man glared at Father and tightened his grip on the bag. "I demand that you come with me to Moses' council and see what he has to say about this. If you're the thief that I think you are, you deserve judgement."

Jarah drew in her breath sharply. Her father a thief? No! Of course not! Father appeared slightly taken aback and his face turned a little pale. But he straightened his shoulders and replied, "Yes, I'll go with you. Let Moses decide between you and me."

The man nodded and both he and Father left the tent. Eitan's eyes followed his father. Jarah rose to her feet and walked over to him.

"Eitan, Father didn't really steal anything, did he?"

Eitan slowly shook his head. "I can't imagine it. But it didn't completely line up in his favor."

Shayna stood up, still holding Raphael. "Maybe we should go get Grandfather. He's familiar to Moses and—"

"We can't," Lemuel interjected. "Grandfather's with Moses and Aaron right now at the feast for Jethro, Moses' father-in-law. At least, I think he is. He wasn't back late last night."

"I'll go see," Eitan offered.

"You do that," Mother ordered, stretching as she sat up. "Girls, get started on finding manna for breakfast. And don't any of you fret about anything. Your father is just trying to provide for his family, and Moses will see that."

"I hope so," Jarah heard Lemuel whisper under his breath. He walked outside and Jarah followed him.

"Lemuel, do you really think that Father stole that grain?"

"I don't believe that, Jarah, no."

Jarah paused, thinking of the right words to say. "You don't believe it, but is it possible?"

Lemuel sighed. "I'd like to think not, but for some reason, I can't completely say no to that right now."

"But—"

"Jarah," Lemuel interrupted. "I don't know. Let's just let Moses sort it out, all right? We can trust in Moses' decision and pray and hope that Father is completely innocent."

Jarah nodded and swallowed hard. Lemuel gave her a half-hearted smile, grabbed his staff, and moved away to take care of the animals. Jarah suddenly felt a soft touch on her arm.

"Jarah?"

"Ada! You startled me. Is something wrong?"

"No, not really. I just wanted to see Eitan, that's all," Ada replied. She was smiling, but the smile seemed forced.

"He just left to see if Grandfather is back home. There was… an issue with Father this morning," Jarah said, carefully choosing her words.

"Oh. All right." Ada looked down at the ground and turned away.

"I'll tell him that you're looking for him as soon as he gets back," Jarah offered.

Ada gave Jarah a sad smile. "Thank you."

Jarah grinned back and watched Ada walk away.

"Eitan really needs to pay more attention to her," she whispered to herself.

"Jarah! Hurry with breakfast!" Mother's voice barked from inside the tent.

"Yes, Mother."

Jarah grabbed a basket from the wagon and started collecting manna from the ground. The sun was already bright, and in some places the manna was melting, but there was still an abundant supply. Jarah was startled to hear running footsteps behind her. She spun around to see Eitan returning to the tent. Before he ducked inside, Jarah called to him.

"Eitan, is Grandfather back?"

"No," Eitan yelled back, shaking his head. He pulled back the tent flap.

"Eitan," Jarah called again, darting up to him. "Ada wants to see you. I think she's really missed you. You need to talk to her."

"I'll get to her later, Jarah. We have to sort this out first."

"But Eitan, she seems so sad. She really wants to talk to you."

"I know, and I'll talk to her. I just—I need to do this first." He moved away again, but Jarah grabbed his arm.

"Don't neglect her, Eitan."

Eitan returned her gaze. "I won't. I promise. Just let me talk to Mother." And he went inside. Jarah drew in a deep breath.

So much is going on all at once. Did Father really steal? I can't believe that he could do that. But he's been acting so different, and we're all so irritable... Could he just be desperate to help us? But surely he would never steal. Yahweh, please help it to not be true. Please don't let Father be stealing.

ה

It was late afternoon and neither Father nor Grandfather had returned. Jarah was baking manna on the hot rocks surrounding the fire pit for dinner. She heard Raphael's voice announce, "Grandfather's back! And Father!" Eitan and Lemuel came running from taking care of the animals. Jarah leapt up to greet her father and Shayna and Mother stepped out from the tent. But as soon as they saw Father's face, everyone instantly froze.

Something was very wrong.

Grandfather looked upset, even angry. Father walked with stooped shoulders and a head hanging with shame. His cheeks were very pale, but in his eyes a defiant, irritated spark was burning.

"Father, what's wrong?" Eitan asked worriedly. Grandfather raised his hand as if bidding everyone to be silent.

"Asher has something to say to you all. I want you all to not interrupt but to simply listen to what he has to say." Grandfather looked straight at Mother as he said this. Jarah found that she was holding her breath. Her heart was beating in her ears.

Father glanced up at their faces, and then fixed his gaze on the ground again.

"I—I went to see Moses and Aaron with that man, Cham, to see about the grain that he found in our tent. We had to wait for hours to even see Moses. He is very overworked, and your grandfather says that Jethro is doing things to help Moses manage these people. But when Moses heard the case, he ruled in favor—" Father stopped and gulped. "He ruled in favor of Cham and said that I stole the grain."

"But Father, you didn't steal it, did you?" Jarah interjected, pleading.

Her Father's eyes met hers, but he didn't say anything. Grandfather glared at his son as if commanding him to speak. Father sighed deeply and whispered, "I did steal it."

Jarah's jaw dropped. Shayna and Tirzah drew in their breath. Eitan and Lemuel's faces drained of color. Mother stood as if frozen.

"You... stole?" she managed to ask.

"I didn't want to!" Father insisted. "But you kept badgering me about how I wasn't providing and how much everyone needed more food, or at least different food, and no one was selling any that I could find, and—"

"Oh, so now this is *my* fault?" Mother exclaimed. "Asher, I didn't tell you to steal!"

"Well what else was I supposed to do when you wouldn't listen to me and kept telling me to get more food for us! Mariel, I'm trying here, and—"

"And now you're in trouble with Moses and the law! Asher, what were you thinking?" Mother shrieked.

"Silence, both of you!" Grandfather roared.

Immediately, silence reigned. Jarah uncomfortably noticed that many of the neighbors were staring at them with condemning eyes. Tears were gathering in Father's eyes. Jarah's body was in shock. She could barely breathe, barely think. The only thoughts circling through her head were, *Father broke the law. Father disobeyed Yahweh. Father stole.*

"Asher is not in trouble with Moses. The grain was given back to Cham, and Asher is to repay him back with three more bags of grain, or three bags of money. If there's another incident, then the punishment will be much more severe. Moses understood that what Asher did was out of desperation, and though that doesn't excuse his crime, he didn't give a harsh sentence."

Mother crossed her arms. "And just where are we supposed to get all of this grain or money, Asher? Where?" she demanded.

"Mariel, I—"

Grandfather held up his hand. "Stop it, both of you! Come into the tent and we'll discuss this. Eitan, if you could join me momentarily I would appreciate it."

"Yes, Grandfather," Eitan murmured.

Grandfather and their parents entered the tent, and the children could hear angry shouts coming from within. The neighbors shook their heads and returned to their normal business. Eitan turned and looked at them, his face absolutely downcast. Shayna and Tirzah were crying. Jarah felt tears in her own eyes. Lemuel's arm slid around her shoulder and he held her close. Jarah could feel his chest heaving.

"Eitan, how could Father do it?" Shayna asked, sobbing.

Eitan shrugged. He started to say something, but then shut his mouth again. He raised his head and slowly met their eyes. "I don't know. But we've got to figure this out. Just pray. Pray really hard." He shook his head and took a deep breath. "Let's get back to our chores," he finally said.

Shayna and Tirzah nodded, heading towards the wagon to get water for dinner. Lemuel squeezed Jarah one more time, took up his staff, and headed around the back of the tent. Jarah knelt in front of the fire pit and blew on the coals to rekindle the fire. Her tears dropped onto the hot coals and made them hiss and steam. She tried in vain to swallow back her sobs, but her throat tightened up and it was hard to breathe. Out of the corner of her eye, she saw Eitan pause in front of the tent. He appeared to be fighting back his own emotions. Mother and Father were still yelling at each other.

A voice startled Jarah. "Eitan!"

Ada came running towards them, looking happy but also a little concerned. A small smile spread across Eitan's face.

"Ada." He reached out to take her hand.

"Do you have a minute to talk, please?" she queried.

Eitan smiled at her sadly. "Ada, I'm so sorry, but there's trouble with my parents and I have to talk to them and my grandfather. I'll come find you afterwards, and—"

Tears glistened in Ada's eyes. "Please, Eitan," she begged.

"Ada, I really have to deal with this," Eitan asserted, starting to move away.

Ada took a step forward. "Eitan." Eitan turned on his heel and faced her. "You've told me that you'd see me before, and we haven't talked in over a week." Her voice was calm, but direct.

"I know, I'm sorry. I didn't mean to lie to you. Really. But something is really wrong right now Ada, and—"

"So wrong that you can't even tell *me* what it is?" Ada accused.

Jarah could feel the tension between her brother and Ada. She quietly threw some twigs on the fire as she watched her brother's inner struggle.

"No. I can't. Not now. But I will. I just have to figure this out with Grandfather, and then—"

"Eitan, you're not the man of the family. You can't do it all. You can't sacrifice our relationship trying to fix your parents' relationship!" Ada almost yelled. Jarah was startled to see the anger on Ada's face.

"Ada, please," Eitan entreated.

"No. You have to hear me out," Ada said, forcibly. "You can't let your father's struggles become your own. I know you're not spending time praying and talking with Yahweh like you used to. You've practically ignored me for two weeks. You're getting caught up in trying to fix everyone's problems. But it's not your job, Eitan! You can't do that! You just have to stand strong and realize you need to be preparing for your own family—our family! Please Eitan! Please realize your mistake." Ada burst into tears and ran off.

Eitan started to go after her, but then stopped in his tracks. He hung his head. Jarah came to him and put her arms around his waist, partly to hide her own tears, partly to comfort him. She felt Eitan's body trembling.

"She's right," Eitan whispered, talking to himself. "She's right. But I don't know what to do... I have a responsibility here. I'm the heir of this family. If Father doesn't follow his role, then who will? Who will help the rest of you?" He stared down into Jarah's face. "What do I do?" he asked.

Jarah caught her breath as she realized that Eitan was genuinely asking her opinion. *Yahweh, give me the right words*, she prayed silently. She breathed deeply and looked into his face, fighting back tears.

"Eitan, I believe you have to do what Father always told us to do. If our relationship isn't right with Yahweh first, we can't do anything right. And besides, we can't fix anybody's problems. Only Yahweh can help people. We're just supposed to pray and love them no matter what. Even—even Mother and Father," she finished softly, focusing hard on the ground in an attempt to see through her tears.

"You're right. My relationship with Yahweh has suffered... Which means my relationship with everyone else has suffered... But Jarah, I've prayed so hard for Mother and Father. Why doesn't Yahweh step in and help them?"

Jarah paused, not knowing at first what to say. "I think," she began slowly, "that Yahweh doesn't always fix things right away. What I think we all learned in Egypt through the plagues was that Yahweh always answers our prayers. It probably won't be right away, or when we want it, or in the way that we want it. But He'll answer somehow, because He always knows what's best."

"But how is this best, Jarah? How is Father stealing the best thing for us?" Eitan asked. He was crying now, too.

"I don't know," Jarah replied, voice quivering. Eitan reached out and brushed away her tears. A thought struck Jarah and she fixed her gaze on his face and said earnestly, "Eitan... It's drawing both of us closer to Yahweh. So maybe it *is* Yahweh's best for us right now. Maybe He wanted us to be closer to Him and that's why. And maybe Father and Mother will get over their fighting as soon as all of us children learn to be content and close to Yahweh and accept His plan for us."

Eitan stood as if frozen, gazing down into her eyes.

"Jarah, I think you're right. If the best thing is to be close to Yahweh, then He'll do whatever it takes to help us draw closer to Him." He grabbed her hand and squeezed it. They both smiled at each other through their tears.

Then Eitan's eyes moved to stare past Jarah. Following his gaze, she saw Ada in the distance standing with Ezra, crying. Ezra had an arm around his sister's shoulder, but he was looking at them. And he didn't look happy.

"After you talk with Grandfather, go talk to Ada and you both pray together," Jarah suggested. "I think she needs that right now, and you do, too."

Eitan nodded his head. "Yes. I will. I promise you I will." He turned quickly and went into the tent. Jarah heard the yelling inside stop. She took a deep breath and quickly wiped away her tears. She threw more twigs onto the fire. She sat down in front of it, occasionally blowing on the fire to make it blaze bright. She turned the manna to keep it from burning. Over the constant murmur of noise that always rested over the Israelite camp, Jarah heard footsteps coming towards her. She looked up, startled, and saw Ezra. He put a finger to his lips as if to tell her to be quiet and sat down beside her.

"Did you hear what just happened?" he asked, softly. Jarah nodded.

"Did he listen to anything my sister had to say?"

"Yes, he did. He's going to talk to her soon," Jarah whispered back.

"Good," Ezra nodded, letting out a little sigh. "I was worried. She was, too."

"I know," Jarah assented, turned away from his gaze.

Ezra abruptly asked, "What's wrong?"

Jarah was slightly taken aback by the question. She fumbled for words. "What do you mean?"

"I saw that something big happened over here with you all. What's wrong?"

Jarah wanted to tell him, wanted to tell him everything. But tears threatened to spill over again and she knew the last thing she should do was cry in front of Ezra. She forced the tears back and responded, "I really can't tell you right now, but I'm sure someone will tell your family soon."

Ezra nodded and bit his lip as if thinking hard. Jarah saw Shayna and Tirzah coming towards them with pitchers of water. Ezra rose quickly and murmured, "If there's anything you or your family need, just let me know. Father and I are watching out for you all and doing all that we can to help." Then he left.

What did that mean? Jarah wondered.

"What did Ezra want?" Tirzah demanded.

"He just wanted to know if something was wrong with Father," Jarah replied, dismissively.

"Did you tell him?" Shayna pried, looking alarmed.

"No. Of course not," Jarah retorted. Then she caught herself and whispered, apologetically, "I'm sorry, Shayna."

Shayna nodded and said, "It's all right. We're all a bit uptight today."

Eitan stepped from the tent, looking almost pleased. "Father's going to repay Cham the money in just a moment, and I'm going to see Ada. It looks like the worst is over." He smiled, a real smile. Jarah grinned back.

"I'm so glad," she stated. Eitan hurried off towards Ada's tent. Jarah's eyes followed him and she couldn't help but think, *But how long will it stay like this...*

א

In the rosy light of dusk, Eitan stood in front of his tent, taking deep breaths and smoothing back his hair. He watched Ada busily working by her family's fire pit, throwing things into a heavy pot to make quail stew. He could smell the savory smell from here. He breathed in deeply and looked hard at Ada's face. Her face was sad and her eyes seemed to hold an aching pain. He sighed.

"I caused this," he murmured to himself. "Well, Eitan, it's time to go make things right."

He strode quietly across the camp, coming up behind Ada as she was rummaging in their wagon. She was talking to herself.

"Where did I put that pitcher of water?" she was saying, frustration in her voice. Eitan peered around and saw a pitcher leaning up against the tent, nearly hidden in the shadows. He ran and grabbed it and appeared in front of Ada, triumphantly holding out the pitcher.

"Looking for this?" he asked, grinning teasingly at her. Ada jumped a little, and then laughed nervously. She was trying to smile, but it was a very tense smile.

"Yes, I was. Thank you," she replied, reaching to take the pitcher from him. Eitan moved the jar out of her reach and shook his head with mock severity.

"No, no, no. I'm carrying it. You tell me what you want me to do with it."

Ada's smile grew more genuine and less tense. She giggled and then motioned towards the fire pit. "I was going to pour some more water into the pot. The stew's too thick."

Eitan and Ada walked towards the fire and Eitan started to pour the water into the thick liquid. Ada watched him, carefully monitoring his work.

"That's good!" she quickly announced. She picked up a wooden spoon and stirred the stew until it whirled around and around and bubbled. Eitan found himself watching her closely. He was constantly amazed by the grace and dexterity with which she did even the most menial of chores. As she scurried around the fire, setting out dishes and cups and watching the soup to make it sure it didn't burn, she almost seemed to be floating. A few curls escaped from under her head-covering, and she pushed them back with a smooth gesture. She suddenly looked up and caught him staring at her. She blushed and looked even more beautiful, in his opinion, with the pink color on her cheeks. She spun away from him. Eitan walked over to her and gently touched her shoulder.

"Ada," he whispered. She slowly moved to look him in the eyes. "You're beautiful."

Tears sprang to Ada's eyes. Her lips were quivering as she opened her mouth to reply to him, but then shut it again as she tried to swallow her emotion.

"Ada," Eitan began, apologetically, "I'm sorry. I'm here to make things right."

Ada began sobbing. "Oh Eitan, I'm so sorry. I didn't mean to yell at you. I know you're having a hard time, and—and…" Ada couldn't continue as she hid her face in her hands.

Eitan reached out and put his hands on Ada's shoulders. "Ada, it's all right. It's my fault. You were right."

"But I should've been more—more gentle," Ada sniffed, daring to meet his gaze.

Eitan smiled at her, giving her shoulders a little squeeze. "Sometimes men need to be told the truth that bluntly or we don't understand it."

Ada grinned a little through her tears. "Really?"

Eitan nodded, his smile broadening. "Really."

He watched Ada wipe the tears from her cheeks and hesitantly reached out to brush a tear away, himself. Ada slowly began to collect herself, and Eitan waited for her sobs to subside before saying anything else. He finally said, "Ada, we do need to talk about things. You need to know what's been happening at home."

Ada nodded and replied, a little quiver still in her voice, "I would like that, Eitan, but…" A smile broke like sunshine on her face. "Can I finish making dinner first?"

Eitan chuckled. "Of course. I'm sorry. I forgot."

Amissa suddenly appeared from the tent and began, "Ada, Mother wants to know how long until—Oh! I'm sorry! I didn't realize you were talking." She looked apologetic and backed away as if to leave.

Ada beckoned to her. "It's all right. We were just finishing."

"Do you want me to finish dinner?" Amissa offered.

Ada peered up at Eitan, questioningly. Eitan nodded and replied, "That would be wonderful. Thank you, Amissa."

Amissa grinned and gave her sister a playful nudge. "Anything to let you two spend time together." She sent them both a teasing look before hurrying away to tend the fire.

Eitan eagerly snatched Ada's hand and playfully dragged her with him around the tent and to a nearby rock. Ada laughed as they ran, and then collapsed panting on the rock, smiling up at him. Eitan plopped down next to her. For a moment they just sat silently, staring up into the deep blue curtain of sky and watching the stars as they slowly began to shine through. Eitan felt peace passing over him like a slow wave. It felt good to just sit and be at rest and be with Ada. He loved that he felt perfectly comfortable around her and didn't even have to say anything to break the silence.

"Your sister is kind to let me steal you away," Eitan finally said.

Ada nodded, smiling in the dark. "She's so sweet and so good to me. So is Ezra."

Eitan suddenly felt a cold shiver run up his spine. He had barely noticed how much the temperature had dropped with the setting of the sun. Peering over his shoulder, he saw the orange lights of many fires in the camp just behind them. They looked warm and inviting, but what he needed to say should only be for Ada's ears alone. Turning to face her, he realized that she was hugging herself and appeared to be shaking a little.

"Are you cold?" he queried.

Ada nodded again. "A little. I can manage."

Eitan quickly pulled off his outer tunic and threw it around Ada's shoulders. The sudden rush of cool air against his skin made it prickle. Ada pulled the cloak around her and gazed up into his face.

"Thank you," she whispered, meaning it. "Now, what's wrong?"

Eitan sighed a little. He wasn't sure where to begin.

"Well, you know, something's been wrong with father."

Ada nodded in assent. "I know Father's tried to talk to him."

"Yes." Eitan exhaled. "No one seems to be getting through to him. Not even Grandfather! I just—I don't understand. He was so happy when the trip started. We all were. I mean, the traveling has been hard, and a lot longer than we all anticipated, I know. Mother is really irritable, but I don't feel like it's been much worse than in Egypt. Maybe now it's because he's around her all day when he didn't use to be... I don't know. It seems as though he's... doubting himself as a leader, and beginning to doubt Yahweh. But he was so strong in Egypt! He encouraged us in our faith and strengthened us and encouraged us to believe in Yahweh. I don't understand why."

Eitan felt tears threatening to fill his eyes. He quickly blinked and drew in a few deep breaths. He felt Ada's cold, gentle fingers close around his in the dark. She squeezed his hand, encouragingly.

"I also think that his new friends are having a bad influence on him," Eitan added.

"Father thinks so, too," Ada agreed.

Eitan ran his hand through his hair before continuing. "I just... Today showed that he's so confused and so far from Yahweh... So much farther than any of us realized or thought was possible."

"What happened today?" Ada prodded.

Eitan slowly moved to meet her questioning look. Her big eyes searched his face. He took a deep breath and said, "Father stole a bag of grain."

Ada drew in a breath, shocked and surprised. "What? Why?"

"Mother's been badgering him about not having variety in our food. We might have enough manna, and some quail meat, but our flocks haven't done well all year and we can't possibly kill any of them right now. I think she was pressuring him to find more food, or at least different food. But she herself said that she would never have asked him to steal!"

"How was he found out?"

Eitan shared the whole story, with Ada asking occasional questions.

"Well," Ada said after the story was over, "now I feel really bad for getting upset at you."

"Ada, I already told you that I deserved it. You and Yahweh need to be first in my life right now. But I'm going to need to ask you to be even more patient with me as I try to handle things at home and still become my own man. Not that you're not patient, of course," he added quickly as Ada gave him a funny look. Ada squeezed his hand again and smiled.

"I understand. As long as you're aware of it and I'm aware of it and we make time for Yahweh and for each other, everything will be fine."

"Thank you, Ada. You're amazing. I don't know what I did to deserve you."

She laughed, embarrassed, and turned pink again.

"You're beautiful when you blush," he said simply, which sent Ada into peals of laughter. Eitan joined in. Ada finally composed herself and drew Eitan's tunic closer around her shoulders.

"I'm cold, and it's getting late. Why don't we pray together and then head back before dinner gets cold?" She grabbed both of his hands in hers.

"Good idea," he agreed. "Your turn to pray first."

The reunited couple grinned at each other and bowed their heads in prayer to Yahweh. Eitan knew that no matter what happened, he and Ada's bond would always be strong, safe, and sure. She was his foundation in a world of chaos and uncertainty, and he would do everything in his power to provide stability for her.

༃

Three days later Jarah raced out of the tent and into the scorching desert heat. She barely noticed the difference in the temperature. Blinding, angry tears made it hard for her to see. Panting, she threw herself down in the shade of a boulder and started sobbing.

"What's wrong, Jarah?"

She looked up through tear-dimmed eyes to see Lemuel standing over her, his dark eyes filled with worry. She was crying too hard to respond.

"Is it Mother and Father?" he pressed. Jarah gulped back a sob and nodded. Lemuel sighed, sat down next to her, and put his arm around her shoulders.

Another voice startled her. "Jarah, is everything— Oh. I'm sorry." It was Ezra. "Is she all right? I saw her leave the tent upset." He directed the question towards Lemuel. Jarah hid her face against Lemuel's shoulder and forced back the tears.

"There's a lot of tension between our parents right now, with everything that happened a few days ago," Lemuel explained. "It's weighing on everyone."

Jarah brushed the tears away and managed a weak smile at Ezra. His brow knit with concern, Ezra sat down opposite them.

"Yes, I know," he said sympathetically. "I heard what happened with your Father."

"It's just—really hard," Jarah sniffed. "Father's trying his best. I know he is. But his faith in Yahweh is shaken. I don't believe what my mother says about the Egyptian gods. But sometimes she sounds so convincing and it almost makes me doubt. I know it's not true, but to see Father waver... I wish we could all believe the same thing. They argue so much now about food and provision and about Yahweh and the Egyptian gods and it hurts to hear it." Tears welled up in Jarah's eyes again. Lemuel's arm was still around her waist and he gave her an affectionate squeeze. Jarah slowly raised her eyes to meet Ezra's. His deep brown eyes seemed to be gazing deeply into her own. She uncomfortably looked away again.

"I've been praying for your family. Ada and your grandfather have told me a lot of what's been going on. I know I can't relate, but just know that we're here for you whenever you need it." Ezra looked right at Jarah when he said that. Her heart skipped a beat.

"Jarah!" her mother's shrill voice shouted. "Get over here!"

Jarah quickly rose to her feet, feeling dread creep into her heart. She paused for a moment, looking at Lemuel pleadingly, almost afraid to go back.

"Go on. You can do it," Lemuel encouraged. Jarah nodded, blinked back tears, took a deep breath, and hurried back towards camp.

Yahweh, I need your strength more than ever. Please take away this fear and doubt. Please give me peace and help my parents stop arguing. And Yahweh, I don't know if this is possible... But can you have my mother believe in you, please?

As Jarah came back into camp she saw Pagiel talking with her grandfather. Her grandfather looked very pleased.

I wonder what's going on. I hope it's good news. I don't think I could handle any more bad news right now.

"Jarah, get started on dinner!" she heard her mother yell from inside the tent.

"Yes, Mother," Jarah replied meekly.

As Jarah lugged a pitcher of water from the wagon, Pagiel walked past her, also looking very happy.

"Sethur is your grandfather, isn't he?" Pagiel asked her. Jarah was a little taken aback to be suddenly addressed by such an important person.

"Yes, sir," she sputtered.

"He's a great man," said Pagiel. "I'm happy to have him as one of the elders of the tribe."

"Is there something he did, sir?" Jarah questioned, feeling very surprised.

"Moses and Jethro have been appointing different men of the nation as leaders of thousands, hundreds, and fifties. The workload on Moses in leading and judging the people has been too much. Your grandfather has just been appointed a judge of a thousand people of our tribe."

Jarah's heart swelled with pride. "Thank you, sir," she gasped out.

Pagiel smiled. "It's wasn't me, my dear girl. It was Moses and Yahweh. But your grandfather has certainly distinguished himself and deserves the recognition and respect." Pagiel turned and disappeared into the center of the camp.

"What an honor," Jarah whispered, rushing to begin dinner. "Yahweh must be smiling down on our family." She felt a flicker of hope in her chest. "Maybe things will get better now..."

ת

It was very dark inside the tent. Acenith lay perfectly still, waiting for Yachne's and Adriel's breathing to become regular. She wanted to make sure they were asleep.

She turned her head, listening. There was no sound except for heavy, deep breathing. Confident that everyone was unconscious to the world, Acenith silently rose and slipped outside. She ran across the cool sand to a large rock about one hundred yards from their tent. She sank to the ground and let herself cry long and hard. She couldn't show her emotions around Adriel, Yael, or Hava. The only people she had ever opened up to in her whole life were Jarah, Yachne, and Emmitt. And now... Emmitt was dead. Just like Bes. Just like her mother. And Yachne was struggling so much that Acenith kept her pain and hurt to herself. Emmitt had been the father that Acenith had never had. He had loved her, taught her, prayed for her, made her feel important and like a somebody instead of like a piece of trash. And now... he was gone. His body was buried miles and miles away. She would never see him again.

"And he told me that Yahweh was loving and kind. He's not. He *can't* be. A loving, kind god would never do this to me!" she wailed up at the moon. Her heart was like ice in her chest. She could never love anyone, never trust anyone again. Everyone she had loved and trusted had been stripped from her arms.

She longed to see Jarah. She had looked for her several times over the past few weeks, but to no avail. Jarah was gone, just like everyone else. Acenith hugged her legs, not bothering to brush away her tears.

"No. It's better to be alone, to not trust anyone, to not love anyone. And it's better to have no god," she murmured, bitterly. She buried her face in her knees.

"Acenith?"

The voice startled her. Acenith jumped and cowered, staring up at a shadow that loomed over it.

"It's only me," the voice said, soft and comforting. It was Adriel. He sat down next to her.

Acenith tried hard to choke back her tears. "I thought you were asleep. I want to be alone," she said, coldly.

She could tell that Adriel was smiling a little. "Well, I wasn't asleep." Then his voice became very serious. "And Acenith, I know the last thing you want is to be left alone."

Acenith's head jerked up and her eyes met his. She wanted to say something cold and mean and make him go away. But at the same time, she longed for him to stay with her and tell her that he would take care of her and not turn her out or leave her alone.

"Acenith, I know you're hurting just as much as the rest of us. He was your father, too. I know he was. I know you feel very, very alone. You feel abandoned by everyone who loves you. I can see it in your face. Mother knows it, too. She knows that you don't give your love and trust easily. But you loved and trusted Father, didn't you?"

Acenith could only nod. Tears were streaming down her cheeks.

"Me too," Adriel said. His voice was trembling.

Acenith started to sob. "Adriel, he said that Yahweh was loving and kind. How could a loving and kind god do this to me—to us! Surely you don't believe in such a god."

"Oh, Acenith, don't blame Yahweh for this," Adriel said, compassionately.

"What do you mean? I thought Emmitt said that Yahweh was in charge of everything, even life and death." Acenith choked back her sobs.

"He is. But He's not a cruel god and He doesn't send us sorrow for no reason. I'm sure there's a purpose, and I'm sure we'll know what it is someday. But some people had to give their lives so that the rest of us could live. Maybe we were too close to Father, and he had to be taken away so that we could become closer to Yahweh..." Adriel's voice trailed off.

"I can't believe that," Acenith stated, her voice hard and bitter.

Adriel sighed. "I know you can't right now. Frankly, I can't right now, either. But we need to try. Try really hard." He paused. Acenith sniffled and wiped away her tears.

"Can you try with me?" he asked.

"I—I'll have to think about it," Acenith whispered, avoiding his dark eyes.

For a moment, they said nothing. Then Adriel took a deep breath and turned to face her.

"Acenith, I know you don't really trust me, or Yahweh, or anyone right now. But we're still a family. We love you. We want you to stay with us. I consider you to be my sister, and I promise to love you, protect you, and help you as much as Father would've done. But I need your help. I can't do this by myself. I don't know anything about leading a family. You're strong and kind, respectful and obedient. You were in charge of your little family back in Egypt. I need you if we're going to make this family work. I can't do it without your help. You help Mother and take care of Yael. I can't do that. I need you to help me. I *want* you to help me."

Adriel was crying now, too. His eyes looked into hers, intense and pleading. "Please, Acenith? I promise you, as long as I'm alive, I'll be the best replacement father and brother I can possibly be to you. But please… please help me."

Tears streamed down Acenith's face. She couldn't stop them. She had never felt more sad, or more loved, in her entire life. But her heart wouldn't let her believe what she was hearing.

"You—you still want me?" she sobbed out. "You still… love me? I—I can stay?"

"Of course," Adriel whispered. He reached out and brushed a tear from her cheek.

Acenith burst into tears. Adriel reached out and put his arms around her, pulling her into a warm, comforting, brotherly embrace. Acenith buried her face against his chest and wept. She vaguely realized that his chest was heaving and that hot tears were dropping onto her hair.

"We're in this together," Adriel choked out. "We can make it through this."

ט

The sky was turning a light gray in the distance. Jarah's shoulders sagged. Her eyelids were drooping shut. She shook her head, trying to make herself stay awake. She was riding on Oved and she didn't want to fall off.

The Israelites had been traveling by night for several days now. While it was wonderful to not travel in the heat of the day, everyone was having a hard time coping with the change and they were exhausted. Jarah found herself sighing.

"Are you all right, Jarah?" Lemuel asked. He was herding their sheep and goats next to her.

"I'm exhausted," Jarah grumbled. "We've been wandering in and out of passes for days. I just want to rest."

Lemuel smiled at her. He looked tired, too. There were dark circles under his eyes. "Yahweh will give us rest soon. I'm sure of it."

"I hope you're right," Jarah replied with a sigh.

Abruptly, they came out of the pass and saw before them a vast, sprawling plain. A little sliver of sunlight shone brilliantly over the cliffs and mountains. Towering above the plain was a particularly dark, gigantic mountain. The pillar of fire stopped its travel and rested on the very top of the mountain. A murmur of amazement and wonder rippled through the Israelites. Many pointed up at the mountain, dumbfounded by its majesty and size.

"Mount Sinai," Jarah heard her grandfather say.

"What is it, Grandfather?" Tirzah queried.

"I believe that is the mountain Jethro told Moses about. He called it Mount Sinai."

"Mount Sinai," Jarah breathed.

THE MOUNTAIN OF GOD

The ominous shadow of Mount Sinai seemed to engulf the plain in which the Israelite people were camped. The pillar of cloud rested at the top of the mountain, hiding the summit from view. Dark gray storm clouds slowly revolved around the pillar of cloud. The distant sounds of strong wind and rumbling thunder made the whole camp feel eerie, yet somehow holy. Occasional flashes of lightning made Jarah jump as she collected sticks and twigs for their morning fire. She was nervous and didn't want to stray far from their family's tent. There was a fear deep within her heart that Yahweh would strike them with lightning or fire. She couldn't help but wonder why Yahweh had brought them here. She heard rumors that they were going to be given the laws that Yahweh wanted them to use in the Promised

Land, but was that true? As much as she wanted to trust Yahweh she was still scared by His awesome power and strength.

Jarah straightened her back and stretched. Branches and twigs were scarce. She had only found one armful. Another peal of thunder made Jarah start. She cast her eyes up to the mountain and squinted. It almost looked like someone was moving up the mountain. Was it Moses? She couldn't tell from here.

I wonder what's going on.

א

"Mother! Mother!" Raphael dashed into the tent, almost pulling the tent flap off in his excitement.

"Careful!" Jarah exclaimed, hurriedly putting the flap back in place to keep out the blinding rays of the sun. Yanni was asleep.

"Raphael, hush!" Mother scolded. "Your brother is taking a nap!"

"Mother," Raphael said again, lowering his voice to an excited whisper, "Father said I'm done helping and that the tent's all the way up and there's nothing left in the wagon and Lemuel doesn't need my help. Can I go play and explore, please? Please?" he begged.

"Jarah, can you watch him? I'm too tired to keep up with his antics today," Mother said with a long sigh. She was reclining on her mat, resting, her swollen stomach looking bigger every single day.

"Yes, Mother," Jarah replied, smiling. She was aching to explore the campsite around Mount Sinai and to have some fun with her friends, too.

"Then hurry along," Mother shooed them away. "I need some sleep!"

"Yes, Mother!" Raphael said, louder than was necessary.

"Shh!" Jarah hushed as they hurried out into the late afternoon sunlight. The threatening clouds that rested above the mountain did little to abate its light and heat.

"Jarah! Over here!" Raphael called to her. He was running toward Amissa's tent to join Manni, Tirzah, Joleen, and Chanah. Jarah felt a smile creeping across her face. Their faces and eyes were so eager, so excited. After days and nights of traveling, everyone was thrilled to be doing something fun together.

THE MOUNTAIN OF GOD

"So, what are we going to play?" Jarah asked, looking into every happy little face.

The children shouted out so many different ideas at once that Jarah was startled and stepped back, trying to comprehend it all. "Hold on! Hold on! One at a time!" she said, laughing.

"Me first! Me first!" Chanah jumped up and down, waving her hand in the air.

"Yes, Chanah, what do you want to play?" Jarah motioning with her arm for the other children to quiet down as she turned her attention toward the little girl.

Chanah's eyes sparkled. "Can we please play the game where everybody hides and one person tries to find them?"

"Yes! Yes! Let's play that!" the other children chorused, delighted.

"Who wants to be the person to find everybody?" Jarah asked.

"I'll do it!" Joleen volunteered.

"Everyone go hide!" Raphael ordered. "Joleen, close your eyes and don't look until you can't hear us running around anymore."

"Fine." Joleen covered her eyes with her hands and the children scattered, muffling their laughter and squeals.

Jarah watched where each child ran to hide. She was the oldest person there, and as the supervisor, she didn't want to lose anyone in the crowd or have a child hide and never be found again! Raphael and Manni dove into her grandparents' tent. Tirzah hid in Mother's old chest that hadn't been brought inside yet, and Jarah saw Chanah attempting to climb a short, scraggly tree. A thought struck her.

Wait! I have to hide, too! Jarah spun around, frantically looking for a place to hide that would be big enough for her. She rushed towards Amissa's wagon, hoping that Joleen hadn't opened her eyes yet.

I could climb in there, but that's too obvious, isn't it? Jarah leapt into the wagon, not seeing any other alternative, and she landed on something soft. Straw and hay filled the bottom of the wagon. Jarah grinned, an idea flashing into her mind.

I'll bury myself in straw!

Jarah quickly dug up a bunch of the straw and was about to lay down and cover herself again when someone said her name.

"Jarah!" Amissa was standing on her tip-toes, peering into the wagon. "What are you doing?"

"Quiet!" Jarah urged. "I'm hiding from Joleen! Come on, Amissa! Jump in, quick, before she sees you!"

"Jarah, I have to help with dinner soon."

"Come on! She'll know where I am if you don't hide now, too! She might be looking for me already!"

"All right." Amissa gave in and climbed up, ducking out of sight behind the walls that made up the wagon box. The girls quickly covered each other in straw and then hunkered down in their little burrows, facing each other. Jarah could just barely make out Amissa's face through the hay and dust. Both girls were trying vainly not to giggle.

"Isn't this fun?" Jarah pressed in a soft whisper.

"Yes, but it'd be more fun if the straw wasn't itching me all over!" Amissa laughed. Jarah's hand flew to her mouth to try to silence her giggles.

"Stop making me laugh!" she hissed. "You're going to give us away."

"I can't help it!" Amissa snorted.

A voice abruptly yelled, "I found you! Raphael, Manni, get out of the tent!"

"Aww!" the boys groaned. Jarah heard them talking with Joleen about where everyone else might be hiding.

"She found them really quick," Amissa murmured.

"Shh! They're not that far away! Don't talk!" Jarah shushed her.

Each minute that crawled past seemed to last an eternity. The girls listened intently as Joleen saw Chanah in the tree and helped her down. They heard the boys join Joleen in their search as they flipped over baskets and looked in chests and finally found Tirzah.

"Now where's Jarah?" Joleen wanted to know.

"I don't know," Raphael responded. "I didn't see where she went."

The children all started to look for her. They looked in the different tents, went out to the flocks and herds to see if she was out with the animals, and seemed to be searching behind every rock and under every wagon. They were only a few feet away from Jarah and Amissa at times, and each time the girls had to cover their mouths for fear of giving themselves away.

Eventually the children seemed exhausted and disgruntled. They were sprawling a few yards away on the sand, complaining about how they couldn't find Jarah and didn't know where else to look. Straw was jabbing into Jarah's back, and the dust made her want to sneeze. She was getting really hot. Sweat was dripping down her back. Everything was stuffy, too.

"Should we climb out?" Amissa whispered.

Jarah was about to respond when she heard Ezra talking to the children.

"What's wrong with you all? You look so sad on such a nice day!"

"We're playing a game and we can't find Jarah," Tirzah grumbled.

"You can't find Jarah?" Ezra talked in an overdramatic way, as if he might know where she was.

"Does he know?" Amissa asked, sounding a little concerned. "I didn't see him when I jumped into the wagon."

"How should I know?" Jarah answered, exasperated.

"Lemuel, do you know where Jarah is?" Ezra was questioning, an obvious and teasing tone in his voice.

"I have no idea," Lemuel replied, but Jarah knew that he was being sarcastic.

"They know!" Amissa squealed. Jarah clapped a hand over Amissa's mouth.

"Shush!"

Ezra spoke again, and this time he sounded like he was coming towards them. "Hmm... I wonder where she could be..."

"I don't know," Lemuel said, seemingly eager to play into Ezra's little game. "Did you all check the tents?"

"Yes," came the children's frustrated reply.

"Did you go look out by the animals?"

"Yes," they stated again, still sounding upset.

"Did you look in all the chests and baskets?"

"Lem, Jarah couldn't fit in any of those!" Tirzah retorted, obviously not happy.

There was a sound as if Lemuel had smacked his head with his hand. "Of course! I forgot about that." Chanah was giggling.

Ezra's voice again. He was right next to them!

"Did you look in all of the wagons?"

Joleen sounded distressed. "Yes! There's nothing left in the wagons and they couldn't hide in there. There's just old straw."

Ezra was chuckling. "Or is there...?"

Without warning, the whole cart began to shake violently back and forth. Jarah and Amissa began to slide back and forth and before they could brace themselves they banged into the sides of the wagon. Both girls screamed and sat up, flinging straw everywhere. Brushing the hay and dust from her face, Jarah found Lemuel and Ezra each gripping a side of the wagon and giving them their silliest grins. The children were laughing and jumping up and down and shouting, "We found you! We found you!"

"We?" Ezra protested. "Excuse me? I believe it was Lemuel and I who saw them climb into this wagon ages ago and found them for you."

Amissa stood up, cheeks pink, as she shook the straw from her dress and tried vainly to brush it out of her hair. Jarah joined in the merriment, but she felt her face turning red, too, as she was sure they must be a sight. She felt Ezra and Lemuel's eyes resting on her and knew that, while they didn't say anything and were trying very hard to suppress their own laughter, they were thoroughly enjoying themselves.

"Jarah," Tirzah crowed, "you have straw all in your hair!" The little girls were again shrieking with laughter as Jarah quickly combed her fingers through her hair and saw the hay rain down all around her. Reia came running up to the little circle, eyes wide with surprise.

"What happened?" Reia's voice was a mixture of shock and bewilderment.

"The girls decided to hide from Joleen under the straw in the wagon," Ezra explained. His teasing eyes rested on Jarah and then turned towards Amissa. Amissa was shaking out her head-covering, which had slipped off her hair, and was tying it hastily around her chin.

Reia was grinning as she offered, "Here, let me help."

Amissa was about to climb down from the wagon when Lemuel offered her his hand and said, with overdramatic gentility, "Please, allow me." A smile returned to Amissa's face as she let Lemuel help her get out of the wagon. She nodded her head in thanks.

"Jarah?" Lemuel reached out for her and Jarah jumped. He caught her and placed her safely on the ground.

"Thanks," Jarah said, grinning in spite of herself.

"I must say," Ezra began in a jesting tone, coming around from the other side of the wagon, "you two picked a pretty creative hiding place." His eyes were glinting with mischief.

"That was Jarah's idea," Amissa explained, poking her friend in the ribs. Jarah looked into Amissa's face, worried that her more cautious friend would be upset at her. She was relieved to find that Amissa was grinning from ear-to-ear.

"I'll help fix your hair if you want," Reia offered, quietly.

"You girls might want to take her up on that," Ezra said, trying to be sober, but Jarah saw him flash a wink at Amissa.

"You look so funny, Jarah," Chanah teased, hiding a giggle behind her hand.

"I know I do," Jarah replied, tapping Chanah's nose with her index finger. She felt Reia take her hand.

"Come on," Reia said with a smile. "Let's go to my tent and I'll fix your hair while we talk." She took Amissa's hand, too, and the three girls ran off together, laughing and spreading straw throughout the camp.

As Reia seated the two girls on stools in the tent and gave them rough wooden combs, Jarah settled herself where she could watch through the entrance. Ezra and Lemuel were playing with the children, building tiny houses out of sticks and twigs and rocks, and Ezra seemed to be telling them a very entertaining story.

Jarah realized that she was staring at him. She blushed and looked away. In the midst of the camp, she caught sight of her father; he almost seemed to be sneaking away somewhere. She wondered if Lemuel had noticed, but he seemed too caught up in Ezra's story and their game to have seen their father wandering off. Jarah sighed a little.

"Jarah, is something wrong?" Reia inquired.

"No, it's fine. I just thought I saw something," Jarah responded in a light tone. She shifted her weight on the stool so that she wasn't looking at the boys anymore and instead focused her attention on her friends. Reia had already combed through all of Amissa's hair and had it almost completely woven into a beautiful thick braid.

"Reia, that's beautiful! You're really good at this," Jarah said. Reia blushed a little from the praise and shrugged modestly.

"Thank you. When you have two little sisters you get lots of practice. I'll do the same thing on your hair if you want, Jarah."

The girls talked and laughed and played with each other's hair, enjoying the time to just sit and relax and spend time together.

"Well, I need to go start dinner," Amissa finally said with a slight sigh, rising from her stool and adjusting the shawl on her head to cover her hair.

"I should probably help my mother, too," Reia agreed, putting the combs and ribbons back into a small box.

Jarah started to follow them outside, but then a thought suddenly struck her.

"Amissa, Reia!"

"What?" the girls asked simultaneously, spinning around to look at her.

"This is what it's like to be free." Jarah watched as both of the girls' eyes grew wide and smiles spread across their faces.

"You're right," Amissa said, beaming. "We can have fun and laugh and sing and talk without being watched or beaten. We can live in peace and happiness, and we have Yahweh with us every moment."

"Being with Yahweh provides the real freedom," Reia pointed out. "Without Him we wouldn't have any of this."

"Freedom," Jarah breathed, sighing happily. "This is what it's like." She grinned at her friends. "I love it."

The girls all laughed together.

"If this is what it's like in the desert, I can't wait until we get to the Promised Land," Amissa announced.

"Me neither," Reia agreed.

"Me neither!" Jarah cried. "It's going to be so wonderful!"

"Hopefully we leave this camp in just a few days and we'll be there before we know it!" Amissa exclaimed.

"I hope so," Jarah replied, dreamily. "I really hope so."

ב

That evening, all of the elders were called together by Moses. Grandfather was asked to attend the meeting. The news he brought late that night made Jarah tremble with both excitement and fear. During the next two days all of the Israelites were to cleanse themselves and be in readiness. On the third morning, Yahweh Himself would appear at the top of Mount Sinai in the form of a cloud.

I can't believe it! We'll actually see and hear Yahweh!

"We must be very serious about the cleansing process," Grandfather was saying. "We don't want the wrath of Yahweh to fall on us or our children."

"Shayna, tomorrow I want you and Jarah to boil water and wash all of our clothes, then yourselves and the young children as well. Eitan, Lemuel, and I will use whatever water is leftover," Father instructed.

"But Father, using our precious supply of water? There's not much water around here. Shouldn't we save it for us and the animals?" Shayna protested.

Father stared at Shayna, his face dark. "Shayna, didn't you just hear what your grandfather said? This is a serious matter. We must sacrifice whatever we can to obey Yahweh's instructions and to do His will."

"Father's right," Eitan asserted. "Yahweh's done so much for us— freeing us from slavery, drowning the Egyptians in the Red Sea, giving us victory over the Amalekites, and leading and guiding us every day. He has provided us with manna, quail, and water, not to mention His own presence to lead and guide us. It's the very least we can do."

Shayna still didn't seem convinced. Mother snorted and muttered, "The least we could do is to preserve ourselves and our children in this accursed desert."

Father's eyes flashed with sudden anger. "Mariel, you must stop this grumbling and complaining against every single thing I tell you to do. Do you want Yahweh's anger on us?"

"Yahweh, Yahweh, Yahweh, that's all I hear about!" Mother yelled. "What about me? What about us and our children? This monster of a

God has bewitched you, Asher! You're risking the lives of your family to obey the ridiculous commands of this Yahweh."

"Mariel, that's enough!" Father roared. "I—"

Eitan jumped in between his parents and grabbed his father firmly by the shoulders.

"Father, stop this, please," he begged. Jarah's heart sank to hear the deep sadness in Eitan's voice.

"Shayna, help me inside. I need to get off my feet. I shouldn't be out in this desert when I'm this far along with child." Mother clutched Shayna's arm and threw a smirk over her shoulder at Father. "I won't be silenced, Asher. You know I'm right. Consider what I've said."

"Mariel!"

But Mother and Shayna were already inside the tent. Father pushed Eitan's hands from his shoulders and stormed towards the desert.

"Father!" Eitan dashed after him but his father swung around and glared at him

"Leave me alone. I don't need your help, son. I know what I'm doing."

Father spun on his heel and stormed away. Jarah heard one of their neighbors say, "There they go, arguing again." Jarah's cheeks flushed with anger and embarrassment.

Of all the times that my parents had to be against each other, we have to be surrounded by hundreds of Israelites who see and hear everything we do, she thought, swallowing an angry sob. *Yahweh, why are you letting this happen?*

Eitan was still frozen to the spot. His shoulders were sagging. Jarah quietly approached her older brother. Tears were threatening to spill out of her eyes. She held Eitan's hand and laid her cheek against his arm.

"I'm sorry, Eitan." Jarah swallowed hard, trying to keep the tears back.

Eitan sighed deeply. The sound seemed to come from the very depths of his soul. "Me, too," he whispered, so low that Jarah could scarcely hear him.

Jarah didn't know what else to say. She just stood with her brother, gently rubbing his arm. She slowly gained control of her emotions and said, softly, "But we'll still obey Yahweh, right, Eitan? Even if Mother says no?"

Eitan's arm suddenly went around Jarah's shoulder and he kissed the top of her head. He laughed a little, but Jarah could tell now that he was quietly crying.

"Yes, Jarah, of course." He hugged her and then murmured in her ear, "Thank you for your love and support. It makes me feel like—like a man now."

Jarah looked up at Eitan, eyes glistening. "I'm so glad," she mumbled, trying hard not to cry, too.

א

The next morning Jarah was lugging pitchers of water from their wagon and dumping the contents in their largest pot.

"Jarah, no more! We have enough," Shayna said, throwing another branch on the fire.

Jarah set the pitcher down. She could tell that Shayna was worried. Shayna seemed to be oscillating back and forth between wanting to follow Yahweh and being stuck with her mother's beliefs. Ever since Rishon had refused to marry Shayna she had been different: less bossy, more quiet, and more outwardly focused. But Jarah still didn't know if Shayna had really decided to change like they'd talked about a few weeks ago.

"Shayna?" Jarah stopped. She didn't want to ask. What if Shayna got mad at her?

Shayna's eyes glared into hers. "What?" she demanded.

Jarah sighed and cringed a little as she replied. "Do you—do you want to obey Yahweh? Or do you think that Mother's right?"

Shayna threw a few more twigs on the fire and turned her back to Jarah, crossing her arms anxiously. Jarah waited silently, scuffling her foot in the sand. There was a sudden sob, and Jarah stopped abruptly.

"Shayna?"

Shayna slowly moved to face Jarah. Her cheeks were wet. "I—I don't know." She grabbed a pile of the soiled clothes and threw them into the hot water. Jarah wordlessly handed her the soap. Shayna broke off a piece and dropped it into the water.

"I wish I knew," Shayna continued tearfully. "I want to believe in Yahweh so badly. But sometimes it's hard for me to ignore what Mother says. This whole cleansing process seems so unnatural and demanding. But His power is undeniable," she continued, musing. "What He's done for us... I know He's there."

Jarah bit her lip, carefully choosing her next words.

"So... What's holding you back from believing in Him?"

Shayna shrugged her shoulders and brushed away her tears. She vigorously stirred the water, making it swirl and bubble. The clothes spun in circles. "I don't know."

"But since you've seen it and you know it, why can't you believe it?"

Shayna started crying again. "I don't know. Something's holding me back. I don't know if it's Mother or if it's me." Shayna's eyes met Jarah's. "I just need a little more time to think it all through. If I change then maybe I can believe. But I don't think I can do this by myself. Change is—it's so hard."

"But you don't have to do it by yourself, Shayna. You have Yahweh to help you, and you have us."

"But not Mother," Shayna said, lowering her eyes. Jarah nodded. "I just need some more time," Shayna finished, sniffing.

"Of course. Let me know if you have any questions. I'll try to help you any way I can," Jarah offered.

Shayna gave her a half-smile. "I have all the answers. I just need the faith to go along with the answers."

"Girls? What's going on out there? If we're supposed to be serious about this cleansing thing you both are moving way too slow. Isn't that laundry done yet?"

"We're working on it, Mother," Jarah called, trying hard not to be irritated.

"Well hurry up. I need some water for my bath."

Shayna used the stick to lift clothes from the water. "This is sure a lot of work," she mumbled.

"We have to be our best for Yahweh," Jarah said, throwing some more garments into the water.

"Yes," Shayna breathed out. "I just hope it's enough…"

Jarah gulped. She hoped so, too.

א

It was the third morning. Though the sun had risen a few hours ago the sky was still overcast and dark. Their little group was eating a quick breakfast, each feeling anxious and cold under a sharp, biting wind that came from the clouds.

Suddenly a bolt of lightning split the darkness. Flashes of light surrounded them. Thunder peeled. Horns sounded, deafening. The ground shook. Jarah grabbed Eitan's arm as he leapt to his feet. All eyes turned to Grandfather. The elder smiled grimly.

"It is time."

ד

The Israelites moved slowly and with trepidation towards the mountain. Jarah was jostled a bit as all of their friends and relatives reached the gathering place where millions of Israelites were already assembled. Rishon sat on their horse, Oved, and Raphael sat with him, getting a good vantage point to see over the crowds.

"Don't go any closer," Grandfather warned sharply, gently guiding Jarah backwards. "If you get close to the mountain and touch it you will be put to death." Jarah drew in a deep breath, horrified. She stepped closer to Amissa and Reia. The eyes of both girls were round with wonder and fear.

Unexpectedly a pillar of fire shot from the black clouds and lighted on the mountain top. Jarah felt the heat strike her face even from such a great distance. The ground began to tremble, slightly at first, but the shaking quickly increased until Jarah could scarcely stand. Amissa shrieked, stepped backwards, and threw her arms around her father for balance. Reia clutched Lemuel's arm and he put an arm around her protectively. Oved was neighing in fright and it was all that Rishon could do to control him.

207

Jarah started to move towards Lemuel when a sudden impulse knocked her to her knees. Rocks started to tumble down the mountain. A large boulder struck the ground with tremendous force only a few yards from Jarah, and she could feel the ground under her fingers reverberating from the strike. Gasping, Jarah tried to crawl backwards and away from the mountain.

A voice beside her commanded loudly, "Get down. There's no use in trying to move." A firm hand was on her back, forcing Jarah to lie flat on her face. She heard rocks falling all around them, their heavy *thump, thump* startling her. What if she were hit? The hand still rested on her back and Jarah chanced a glance sideways to see who her protector was. Despite the dangerous situation, Jarah felt her cheeks flush. It was Ezra.

Before the thudding of the rocks ceased a loud burst of trumpets rent the air. Jarah's hands flew to her ears. Where were the sounds coming from? Were they heavenly trumpets? They were so loud, clear, and magnificent, yet terrifying. Jarah scarcely wanted to look at the cloud representing Yahweh's presence.

The earthquake slowed in its intensity. As Jarah rose to her knees she saw that Moses was slowly ascending the mountain. He was soon swallowed up by the dense cloud. There was a murmur of sounds as the blasts of the trumpets died away. The fire, smoke, thunder and lightning remained, but everything seemed relatively calm compared to what they had just been through.

Ezra and Jarah got to their feet and stepped even further away from the mountain.

"What do we do now?" Amissa asked Ezra in an awestruck whisper.

"I suppose we wait for Moses to come back," Ezra whispered back. Jarah inched towards Lemuel.

"Are you all right?" he questioned in concern.

"Yes, fine. Just..." Jarah searched for the right words.

"Amazed and frightened?" Lemuel suggested.

"Exactly."

Lemuel nodded solemnly. "Me too."

For almost an hour there was no sign of Moses. Then someone shouted, "There he is!" Moses was just leaving the cloud and coming back down the mountain.

When he reached the bottom, Moses conversed with Aaron and then lifted up his voice and addressed the people.

"Yahweh says to warn you that none of you, neither man nor priest, are to break through the line and come up the mountain to the Lord, or He will break forth upon them. I am taking Aaron up with me once again after the Lord speaks."

Then a voice like the crashing of thunder, deep, bellowing, warm, and incredibly strong filled the air. The voice of Yahweh. And He spoke directly to the Israelites.

I am the Lord your God, who brought you out of the land of Egypt, out of the house of slavery. You shall have no other gods before Me.

"You shall not make for yourself an idol, or any likeness of what is in heaven above or on the earth beneath or in the water under the earth. You shall not worship them or serve them; for I, the Lord your God, am a jealous God, visiting the iniquity of the fathers on the children, on the third and the fourth generations of those who hate Me, but showing lovingkindness to thousands, to those who love Me and keep My commandments.

"You shall not take the name of the Lord your God in vain, for the Lord will not leave him unpunished who takes His name in vain.

"Remember the sabbath day, to keep it holy. Six days you shall labor and do all your work, but the seventh day is a sabbath of the Lord your God; in it you shall not do any work, you or your son or your daughter, your male or your female servant or your cattle or your sojourner who stays with you. For in six days the Lord made the heavens and the earth, the sea and all that is in them, and rested on the seventh day; therefore the Lord blessed the sabbath day and made it holy.

"Honor your father and your mother, that your days may be prolonged in the land which the Lord your God gives you.

"You shall not murder.

"You shall not commit adultery.

"You shall not steal.

"You shall not bear false witness against your neighbor.

"You shall not covet your neighbor's house; you shall not covet your neighbor's wife or his male servant or his female servant or his ox or his donkey or anything that belongs to your neighbor."

The people were reacting in sheer terror. The voice of Yahweh was too wonderful, yet too terrible to listen to. Many started to cry out to Moses and Aaron, "Speak to us yourself and we will listen; but don't let Yahweh speak to us, or we will die!"

As the thunder and smoke diminished slightly Moses announced to the Israelites, "Do not be afraid; for Yahweh has come in order to test you, and in order that the fear of Him may remain with you, so that you may not sin."

While the Israelites stood at a far distance, Moses and Aaron approached the thick cloud where Yahweh was and were again hidden from sight.

For over two hours the people waited. The time seemed long, and yet short at the same time. Jarah did not get tired. Her gaze was transfixed to the cloud, wondering what was happening to Moses and what Yahweh was telling them. The words of the commandments that Yahweh had spoken to them reverberated in her ears and replayed themselves in her mind.

Then she saw Moses and Aaron coming towards them. A hushed silence reigned as they waited for Moses to speak the words of the Lord.

Moses proclaimed, "The Lord said, 'Thus you shall say to the sons of Israel, "You yourselves have seen that I have spoken to you from heaven. You shall not make other gods besides Me; gods of silver or gods of gold, you shall not make for yourselves. You shall make an altar of earth for Me, and you shall sacrifice on it your burnt offerings and your peace offerings, your sheep and your oxen; in every place where I cause My name to be remembered, I will come to you and bless you."'"

Moses added, "Tomorrow we shall build an altar and sacrifice to the Lord. For now, go to your tents and ponder what Yahweh has spoken to you and what you must obey."

Jarah was glad to go home away from the noise, the smoke, the terror. She had not known that Yahweh could be so frightening, and so big and glorious at the same time. She sank down on her mat, feeling fatigued from the intensity. Of all that Jarah had learned that day one thing stood out to her the most: Yahweh was to be feared above everything else. He was more powerful than anything, and none of the Egyptian's statues could ever compare to Him.

ה

The next morning the whole camp again assembled at the same place as the day before. Moses was there next to an altar that he had built. Twelve pillars of stone surrounded it; one to represent each tribe of Israel. From where she stood, Jarah could see Moses placing large clay bowls on the altar. She wondered what they were for. To her surprise, Jarah saw Moses approach her grandfather and begin speaking with him. Whatever they were talking about seemed to please her grandfather.

She was still more astonished when Moses pulled Lemuel, Eitan, Rishon, and Ezra from the group.

"You will be some of the young men offering peace sacrifices to the Lord," he told them. "Go and find several pure young bulls and bring them back here." Jarah saw the boys' faces glowing with pride as they hastened to do Moses' bidding.

An awed silence rested over the entire assembly. Jarah kept staring at the altar, pondering, thinking, and praying about what this might mean. Many others around her appeared to be praying and thinking, too. It was strange to Jarah that Yahweh would want sacrifices like the Egyptian gods. But this peace and sorrow she saw around her wasn't how the Egyptians had acted when they offered sacrifices. They were often weeping and wailing for mercy and deliverance. Yahweh had already delivered them, hadn't He?

Jarah's attention was suddenly drawn to Eitan and Lemuel who were emerging from the crowd. Lemuel was leading a young bull. The boys brought the cow up the sloping side to the top of the altar where Aaron stood, holding a long glistening knife. Aaron raised the knife high above his head and then brought it down with a quick motion. Jarah's heart skipped a beat as she saw the blood flowing from the bull. She felt nauseous and for a moment she had to look away, taking deep breaths to regain her composure. It was hard for her to reconcile the fact that innocent animals had to die for the sins of humans.

We're really the ones that deserve to die. The thought made Jarah's stomach turn inside out. She gasped a little, tears welling in her eyes. *Yahweh has been merciful and not killed* us. *He's putting our sins on these animals instead, and no matter how sad it is, we are free. He gives us the sacrifice so that we can live without His anger. We don't deserve that at all. But that's what Yahweh gives us…*

Eventually, the nausea subsided and the tears of amazement and sadness stopped. Jarah was able to look back to Aaron. Eitan and Lemuel were placing logs and dry sticks around the bull's dead body. Rishon was collecting the blood from the animal's neck. Ezra came forward with a lighted brand and started the fire. Jarah was mesmerized by the flame as it slowly licked up the wood and spread rapidly. In a few moments the sacrifice was completely engulfed in fire.

Meanwhile, Rishon had climbed off the altar and brought a bowl of the blood to Moses. Eitan and Lemuel brought another young bull forward and stood gazing into the fire, waiting for the first sacrifice to be consumed. Jarah bowed her head and prayed, asking the Lord to forgive her sins and her bitterness about the heat and the desert and the lack of privacy and the issues in her family. She heard other murmured voices around her praying to Yahweh, too.

I hope Yahweh is pleased with our love, sacrifice, and respect. I understand now more than ever how much we should worship Him and put Him first before everything in our lives.

Jarah looked up and saw Moses moving towards the altar. He took the blood from the bowl and sprinkled half of it on the altar. Then Moses repeated all of the words that the Lord had told him yesterday for the whole congregation of Israel. Jarah listened hard, taking in every word, trying to remember every single commandment so that she would please Yahweh and obey Him as best she could.

When Moses finished retelling the words of the Lord the Israelites unanimously shouted out, "All that the Lord has spoken we will do, and we will be obedient!" The roar of their voices was deafening.

Then Moses took the blood of that sacrifice and of the second sacrifice that had just been offered and put it into different basins. He divided the blood into two equal sections. With one half of the basins he walked in and among the people, sprinkling the blood on them.

Jarah watched with some disgust as Moses came closer and closer to her, sprinkling it onto the people.

"Grandfather, what's the purpose of putting blood on us? I thought we were supposed to be cleansed and clean, not covered in blood." Jarah shivered a little.

Her grandfather's grave eyes looked down upon her. "It's the blood of the covenant—the blood that was shed for us. It shows that Yahweh is identifying us as His own people and that we have agreed to abide in His will. It's Yahweh's way of distinguishing us and showing us that a sacrifice was made to enter into this covenant."

Jarah's eyes were glued to Moses as he approached her. *Do I really love Yahweh enough to have blood sprinkled on me and to be under His covenant and to be His child?*

Moses was right in front of her now. His eyes met hers for a moment and he smiled tenderly. Feeling a glow of warmth in her heart, Jarah thought, *Yes, I do love Yahweh that much.*

She bowed her head as Moses sprinkled the blood onto her and the others around her. While he did this he said, "Behold the blood of the covenant, which the Lord has made with you in accordance with all these words."

Jarah fixed her gaze on Moses as he moved down the line. She didn't know why, but a new joy and love seemed to be growing in her heart. She felt a smile spreading over her face.

Soon, Moses took the elders of the tribes with him along with Aaron, Aaron's sons, and Joshua, to the foot of the mountain. The rest of the people were sent home. Jarah could not wait to hear what Yahweh and Moses were going to say to her grandfather.

Lemuel was grinning from ear to ear when they reached their tent.

"Won't you wipe that silly grin off your face?" Jarah teased.

"Jarah, you don't know what it feels like, being chosen by Moses to offer sacrifices to Yahweh. There were many boys to pick from, but he picked me! I felt so important, so close to Yahweh's will. Like—like I was living out what I believe."

"I can understand that," Jarah said, nodding her head.

"I wish you could feel the same way I do. I wish I could feel this way for the rest of my life," Lemuel said, passionately. Jarah laughed. This morning had been so peaceful, as if Yahweh was a completely different God, a God of love and peace and stillness; not just Someone to be feared, but Someone to be reverenced, loved, and honored.

'He's just and merciful, Jarah,' she remembered her father telling her time and time again.

Now I've seen it, both sides of Him, she thought with a smile. *I feel like I'm beginning to know Him, if only a little. I'm sure I'll never know all about Him. But today I've experienced His love and forgiveness and mercy towards us by placing our sins on innocent animals. It's more freeing and awe-inspiring than all of the miraculous signs He's done in our behalf. He is truly an awesome God.*

ﾞ

Grandfather did not come back that night. No one dared to go near the mountain; the cloud had been shining brightly with the glory of Yahweh ever since the sacrifices had been offered.

The next day they heard the magnificent blast of trumpets again. In a moment, the cloud turned into a blazing and consuming fire. From where Jarah sat, she saw a dark speck that looked like a man entering the fire. She gasped. There was no doubt in her mind that it was Moses.

The fire died down and soon it was just the dark, billowing cloud again with thunder and lightning surrounding it.

What did Yahweh do to Moses? Jarah thought in fear. *Is he just up there getting more instruction, or did Yahweh actually do something to him?* She wished that her grandfather was back so that she could ask him. *But maybe he'll come back soon,* she assured herself.

Grandfather did come back later in the evening and around the late dinner campfire he told everyone about what he had been doing.

"We came up to the foot of the mountain and sat down. And then, suddenly, we saw Yahweh Himself! He was huge and brilliant. It hurt our eyes to look at Him. But we could see that He stood on a sort of pavement that looked like sapphires. And He did not harm us, or stretch out His hand. Instead, He provided food and drink for us. We ate there in Yahweh's presence and saw Him. Then He called Moses to come up. Joshua went up with him to a certain distance. Moses said that Aaron is here and is to judge the people in his absence."

"What do you think has happened to Moses?" Father asked.

"I can't say for sure. He said to wait for him, but…" Grandfather's voice trailed off. Everybody was thinking the same thing. They might never see Moses again.

COURAGE AND COWARDICE

It was late as Asher crawled onto his mat next to his wife. He realized with surprise that Mariel was still awake, staring up at the roof of their tent.

"I didn't realize you were awake," he whispered, looking about to see if any of his children were up. They all seemed to be lost in their dreams.

"I was just… thinking," Mariel murmured absently.

Asher settled onto his mat and pulled a blanket over his chest. Loose grains of sand seemed to pierce through his clothes and made his back itch. He rose partially, brushing off the sand as he said, "You've been really quiet for the past two days, ever since we went to the sacrifices." Mariel just nodded. This silence was something new to Asher. "What are you thinking about?" he asked, very gently, situating himself in a more comfortable position.

The answer struck him like a thunderbolt. "Yahweh."

He sat bolt upright, speechless. "What?"

She slowly sat up and moved across from him, looking him in the face. Her eyes shone in the dim light.

"I've been thinking about Yahweh, His commands and the sacrifices that He demanded."

Asher stumbled over his words, not sure what to say. "Then… What did you think?"

She sighed and lowered her eyes. "Asher, I've seen enough now to keep myself from believing that He's not real, that He doesn't exist. I didn't want to see in Egypt, and I didn't want to see it out here in the desert. But I can't deny it anymore."

Asher reached out eagerly and embraced her. "Mariel, that's wonderful!" he almost shouted.

"Shush! You'll wake the children!" Mariel hissed as she pulled away from him, seeming to shun his embrace. "And Asher, that doesn't mean that I trust Him. I don't. I just believe that He's real."

Asher blinked, not fully comprehending. "I don't understand."

Mariel sighed, seeming slightly exasperated. "Yahweh is real. I know that now. I believe that now. But I can't trust Him."

"But why not?" Asher persisted. He realized that it almost sounded like he was whining.

Mariel now looked up to meet his gaze. "He's not predictable. I can't understand Him."

"But Mariel, no one can understand Him! He's all-powerful! He's our God!"

"Then why does He let so many bad things happen, Asher? Why did he let my parents die when I was just a little girl, when I didn't have anyone to help me and protect me?" Mariel's voice was choked with emotion. She quickly wiped her hand across her face as if trying to erase memories. "Why did he allow me to be whipped to the point of death and my leg injured for life? What about the plagues on the Egyptians? Why did he have to kill so many people just to let us go? And why did He allow the Amalekites to attack us from behind? Why did He allow them to kill Manuel? Why did He make us fight the Amalekites and lose so many Israelites in war? Why did He lead us all the way out here to suffer in the desert instead of just bringing us to the Promised Land? And why does He order so many animals to be sacrificed just to appease Him? I thought you said He was merciful and gracious, but now He's acting just like the Egyptian gods, if not worse than them."

"Oh, Mariel, Yahweh didn't make all of those things happen, He—"

"Then who did make all those things happen, Asher?"

Asher opened his mouth to speak, and then shut it again.

"See? You don't know," Mariel stated.

"But that doesn't mean that Yahweh's not in control, Mariel. Maybe He does it for our own good, to show us His deliverance and His power."

Mariel stared at him. "I can't believe that."

"I know you can't. It'll take some time," Asher assured her.

"Then why do you believe in Him?" Mariel asked. Asher was surprised to hear that she didn't sound accusing. She just sounded curious.

"Well…" Asher paused, thinking about it as he pulled the coarse blanket around his shoulders. "I've seen His wonders. I've felt His love in my life. I know that He is true. He's with us right now, guiding us and leading us."

Mariel sighed. "Again, we can't seem to agree."

"If you've come to believe that Yahweh exists, you'll eventually come to trust Him too, Mariel," Asher said, kindly.

Mariel reached out and grabbed his hand. "Asher, I can't. I've thought about it for a long time now, and I can't. I won't."

Asher hung his head. At least this was progress. This was exciting. A feeling of love for his wife crept into his heart.

"Asher." Mariel broke the silence. "We can't go on like this."

His head jerked up, suddenly. "What do you mean?"

"Our family is falling apart. They have no clear guidance. You and I are fighting all the time. We've come to an understanding of each other. Now we need to come to an agreement. We can't stay this way, both of us believing that we're right. Someone has to give in to make this family work and grow. We have another little one on the way and we need to take this even more seriously now with Eitan's marriage and a new baby coming."

"I agree."

"So…" Mariel stopped. "Who's going to give in?"

Asher felt some heat coming to his face. "It's not going to be me."

"Well, it's not going to be me," Mariel retorted, some of her old attitude coming back into her words.

Asher paused, thinking. "Let's both get some sleep and talk tomorrow."

"Asher, my thoughts won't change by tomorrow."

Now it was Asher's turn to sigh. "I don't know then, Mariel."

"There's nothing in you that doubts Yahweh?" Mariel persisted.

"No, there's not," Asher said, getting defensive.

Mariel laid down, looking out the tent flap and gazing at the moon. "Then we're choosing conflict, Asher."

"We can make this work," Asher pleaded, that almost whining tone in his voice again.

"No, we can't, Asher, and you know it," Mariel stated, matter-of-factly.

Asher laid down and angrily pulled the blanket up over himself, turning his back on his wife. She was right, and he knew it. But he wasn't going to give in and desert Yahweh now. Mariel would change. She had to. Otherwise, she was right. Their family was falling apart.

His thoughts went back to Mariel's words, Mariel's reasons for not trusting Yahweh. Was there any chance that she was right? That Yahweh really didn't have as much control as he had originally thought? Many bad things had happened in this world…

No. He couldn't go there. Couldn't think that. He wouldn't let his faith in Yahweh fail. He still believed. But with a cold feeling in his stomach, he realized that now, a very tiny part of him had begun to doubt.

א

The next morning, while there was a slightly anxious feeling in the air because of Moses' absence, everything else felt peaceful and relaxed. The dark clouds that had covered the sky yesterday seemed to be clearing and the sun was peeking out in a few places. Jarah was keeping her siblings occupied outside of the tent. Mother and Father were having a semi-heated discussion inside.

She was thankful that it was only *semi*-heated. It seemed like they might actually be coming to an agreement about something.

Wouldn't that be a relief, she thought, sighing a little.

Tirzah, Raphael, and Yanni had collected tiny twigs and were dipping them into the cool, black coals that were left from the fire yesterday. They used the twigs to draw coal pictures on the rocks surrounding the fire pit.

"Look, Jarah, it's you!" Tirzah pronounced, holding up a small rock with a figure sketched on it. Jarah could barely make out the girl's dress and curly hair.

"Very nice," she said, nodding her approval. Tirzah eagerly put the stone back in its place and picked up another one.

"I made a sheep." Raphael showed Jarah his rock.

"Look! Sheep!" Yanni cried. He held up his rock to display it. It was a picture of indiscernible lines, but Jarah still praised him and his work. She even grabbed a stick and joined them in their fun.

In a few minutes some of their little friends seemed to magically appear and start drawing with the coal, too. Jarah sat back and watched them, giving them ideas and encouraging them in their fun.

Lemuel and Ezra soon came around the corner of the tent, staffs in hand. Jarah gasped in delight. Lemuel was carrying a new baby lamb. He was beaming.

"Jarah, look! Old Anna finally had her baby! I'm going to show Father and Eitan and finish drying her off before I bring her back to her mother. We need to bring some hay for Anna, too."

Jarah ran over to him and gently patted the little lamb's head. It was still damp.

"She's precious, Lemuel," Jarah said, in awe of this little life.

"Is Father inside the tent?" Lemuel asked.

"Yes, but Mother and Father are talking, and we probably shouldn't interrupt them right now," Jarah explained, soberly.

Lemuel bit his lip, looking concerned. "Are they arguing, or...?" Ezra took a step forward so that he could see Jarah's face, and he was also worried.

"No. I don't think so. It almost seemed like they might be coming to an agreement or an understanding or something. But I still think you should wait."

A flicker of hope flashed across Lemuel's face as he heard that their parents seemed to be having a normal discussion. A satisfied smile rested on Ezra's face, too, as if he was happy for them.

"Well, then, where's Eitan?" Lemuel asked.

Jarah arched her eyebrows and made a face. "Where do you think?"

The boys both exchanged a knowing glance. "With Ada, right?" Lemuel grinned. Jarah nodded her head. "Well, I'll walk over there and show him the lamb. Then Ezra, maybe you can help me bring some straw and water back for Anna?"

"Of course," Ezra responded. He moved over to where the children were still drawing their designs and ruffled Manni's hair, paying particular attention to his little brother's picture. Jarah's heart ached a little as she saw a momentary look of sadness cross Ezra's face. She couldn't imagine losing a little sibling.

As Jarah scanned the happy little faces around her, she realized that Tirzah wasn't there anymore.

"Joleen, where's Tirzah?"

Joleen didn't look up from her play and just shrugged her shoulders. "I don't know."

"Tirzah!" Jarah called.

"I'm right here!" Tirzah answered. She came running up to Jarah. "Jarah, Mother wants you to get some wood from the wagon and get started on baking some manna for our lunch."

Jarah glanced up. The sun was getting higher in the sky.

"All right, but Shayna was supposed to help me. Where is she?"

"She's fetching water," Tirzah told her. She settled back down on the ground, but kept stealing glances behind her as if looking at something. Jarah had an uneasy feeling that Tirzah might be up to some mischief.

"Tirzah, is something wrong?" Jarah demanded.

Tirzah's innocent round eyes looked up into hers. "No. Why?"

"No reason. I was just wondering." Jarah threw a few twigs into the fire pit and then started to head towards the wagon to get the bigger logs. Ezra stepped up to cut her off.

"Do you need any help?" he asked, graciously.

Jarah felt a funny little fluttering in her chest. "No, it's just a few logs. I'll be fine. But thank you for asking."

Ezra nodded and grinned at her as she walked past him and towards the wagon. She was lifting the latch to open the back of the wagon when Tirzah screamed, "Jarah! Look out!"

Jarah stepped back, startled, and anxiously searching the area for something that could've alarmed Tirzah. Something on the ground caught her eye and she screamed herself. A snake was curled up against the wheel of their wagon, just a few feet from her. Terror gripped Jarah's heart as she frantically thought about what to do. Should she run? Should she freeze? Should she jump into the wagon? What about the children?

Before she could do or say anything, she heard Ezra's commanding voice. "Jarah, don't move!" In an instant he was by her side. He lifted his staff into the air and brought it down with tremendous speed on the head of the snake. The snake's head was crushed into the sand and it's body twisted a little and then lay motionless.

Jarah leaned up against the wagon, head spinning. She vaguely realized that Ezra had taken her arm to support her. He was breathing hard as if he, too, had been scared.

"Are you all right?"

Jarah nodded and gulped. "Yes. Fine," she managed. She heard running footsteps and put a hand to her head, trying to stop the dizzy feeling. The children came crowding around them, looking at the dead snake, and Jarah heard Eitan's voice in the distance.

"Is everything all right?" Eitan and Lemuel were running towards them and Ada was walking behind, carrying the new little lamb.

"We're fine," Ezra assured them as soon as Eitan was close. "There was a snake by your wagon. Jarah discovered it. I think I've killed it."

"A snake?" Lemuel exclaimed. He knelt by the body of the dead snake and used his staff to poke and examine the body. Jarah noticed that Tirzah seemed to be fighting back a smile.

"Odd," Lemuel muttered. "This is exactly the same kind of snake I killed yesterday afternoon. Tirzah found one like it close to the animals and told me about it. It's the same size, too. I hope there's not a nest around."

"Maybe we should go look," Ezra suggested. "We don't want anyone to get bit."

Jarah heard a choking sound. It was coming from Tirzah.

"Tirzah, are you choking?" Eitan asked, concerned. Tirzah shook her head. She was grinning and it was now obvious that she was laughing.

"Tirzah, it's not funny," Eitan said, sternly. "Jarah almost got bit by a snake!"

But Tirzah couldn't stop laughing now, and she was staring at Ezra and Jarah with such a mischievous, teasing look.

Lemuel suddenly snapped his fingers as if he had just remembered something. He rose to his feet, his face dark. "Tirzah." Lemuel grabbed her shoulder. "Is this the same snake that you found the other day?"

Tirzah gave him a taunting look. "Maybe…"

"Tirzah!" Lemuel was shocked. Eitan looked angry. Ezra's jaw dropped and Jarah felt her cheeks turning bright red. Another wave of dizziness passed over her as she realized what had just happened.

Tirzah had set up the whole thing with the body of an already dead snake.

"Oh, no," she moaned, turned her back towards Tirzah and Ezra. She could feel Ezra's eyes resting on her.

How embarrassing! she groaned inwardly. *Of course Tirzah would try to set up something that seemed romantic to her if she had the chance!*

"Tirzah, why did you do this?" Eitan interrogated.

"I just thought that it'd be funny!" Tirzah explained, still grinning mischievously. "Lemuel told me to do something with the snake, so before I buried it, I thought I could play a trick on Jarah and Ezra because of the whole snake incident back in Egypt."

Jarah felt Tirzah's eyes staring her down as if to say, "I told you that you liked him and that I was going to prove that he liked you, too!"

Jarah was furious. She was so mad she almost wanted to hit her little sister.

"Tirzah." Eitan knelt down and grabbed her shoulders, making her look straight into his eyes. "You've been a very foolish, careless girl."

The mirth left Tirzah's eyes and she dropped her head, scuffling her foot in the sand.

"You set up an unkind, unfeeling prank. You know that Jarah hates snakes. It was cruel of you to do such a thing, and to alarm all of us, as well. You're supposed to be looking out for your family and friends and be kind and respectful of them. And you showed no wisdom by your actions and have upset many."

"I'm sorry, Eitan," Tirzah murmured, sadly.

A thought struck Jarah. Spinning around, she demanded, "Tirzah, did Mother really tell you to have me start a fire for lunch."

Tirzah's head hung even lower. "No."

"Tirzah!" Eitan rebuked. "You lied?" The little girl slowly nodded her curly head.

"Tirzah," Eitan began, upset and exasperated, "did you not listen to anything Yahweh has said to us through Moses and through His cloud over the last few days? Nothing? What was one of Yahweh's commands?"

Tirzah shifted her weight, uncomfortably. "He said something about not being a false witness."

"Yes, and what does a false witness do?" Eitan pressed, still keeping his hands firmly on Tirzah's shoulders.

"Tell lies," Tirzah whispered, almost inaudibly.

"Tirzah, you must ask for forgiveness from Jarah and Ezra."

Tirzah slowly approached her big sister and pleaded with tearful eyes, "Will you please forgive me?"

Jarah was mad. She was furious. She had been embarrassed in front of Ezra and so many others for no other reason other than to please Tirzah's romantic fantasies. She wanted to snap back at her sister and yell and be upset. She took a few deep breaths to control herself before answering, as calmly as she could, "I forgive you."

Eitan nodded his head in approval. "Now Tirzah, ask Ezra for forgiveness."

Tirzah moved to Ezra and with the same sorrowful face asked for his forgiveness. Ezra smiled kindly at her and patted her shoulder. "Of course I forgive you."

He's a much better person than I am, Jarah thought, still fuming inside.

Eitan beckoned Tirzah to come to him. He was very grave.

"Tirzah, you've just asked for forgiveness, and they have forgiven you. But asking for forgiveness means that you have to really and truly repent. You must seek wisdom and stop playing silly, childish pranks. Most importantly, you need to think before you speak and before you act. If you continue to tease people or play pranks on them, your punishment will become more severe. For now, we're going to take you to Father and see if there's anything else that he needs to do with you."

"Yes, Eitan." Tirzah hesitantly slipped her hand into his as the brother and little sister headed towards the tent.

Ada handed the lamb back to Lemuel and told the other children to head back home. "It's almost lunchtime and your parents will be looking for you." She took Manni's hand and steered him back towards their tent. She looked over her shoulder and gave Jarah a kind smile that told her that she was truly sorry for what had just happened. Jarah tried to smile back, but she couldn't.

Lemuel nudged the body of the dead snake with his sandaled foot. "I'd better bury this so no more harm can happen because of it," he muttered. Jarah could feel that Ezra was looking at her again, and she felt like she had to say something.

"Thank you, Ezra. I'm so sorry about this. I had no idea, and—I mean—well..." Jarah stammered over her words. Ezra grinned down at her, a funny look in his eyes. "I'm sorry you had to kill it again," Jarah finally blurted.

Ezra looked a little surprised, and then burst into laughter. Lemuel was laughing, too, and when Jarah realized what a ridiculous thing she had said, she giggled and knew that she was turning pink again.

"Well," Lemuel gasped out, recovering his composure, "at least we know that Ezra's really good at killing snakes. Next time I see one I'll just call him and it will be doubly dead when he hits it once!"

Ezra chuckled again, shaking his head. "I guess I'm just fated to keep girls from being bitten by snakes, whether the snakes are alive or dead." He gave Jarah a teasing grin.

"Well, I hope you don't make any more of a habit out of it," Jarah replied. She tried to sound teasing, but she really, truly meant it. Tirzah was going to get an earful about this later.

"Seriously though, Jarah, are you all right?" Ezra queried, the jesting look leaving his face and being replaced by a look of concern.

"I'm fine. Really." Jarah tried to prove it by giving him as big a smile as she could. Ezra nodded, satisfied. Lemuel stepped up to her and put an arm around her, comfortingly.

"You're one strong young lady," he said, encouragingly.

"Thanks," Jarah murmured, lowering her head to hide her blush.

Lemuel squeezed her gently and the little lamb nuzzled her with its nose before Lemuel said, "Ezra, let's go take care of Anna and then we'll see about burying that snake."

"Sounds good."

The boys walked off together with the baby lamb and some straw and water, talking animatedly about the whole prank, while Jarah sulked off towards the tent, tears of frustration filling her eyes.

"I'm trying not to like him, but it's really hard when he's so nice to me and Tirzah keeps putting me in these awkward situations," she grumbled. She took in a few deep breaths and prayed, quietly, "Yahweh, take these feelings away, please, if that's what You want."

Feeling a little more relieved and a little less angry, she went into the tent to check with Mother and see if she really should get a fire going and start baking manna for lunch.

ב

Ten days. Fifteen days. Twenty days. Still Moses did not appear. Everyone was anxious and uneasy. What had happened to Moses? Perhaps Yahweh had swallowed him up and killed him! What would they do then?

It was on the twenty-ninth day that Jarah was outside tending the fire. She noticed a man striding through the camp. He looked

227

vaguely familiar, but Jarah couldn't quite figure out where she had seen him before. He looked like someone very important. He was tall and strong, about Aaron's age, and he looked very dignified. Then Jarah put it all together. It was Hur, brother-in-law to Moses and Aaron. What was he doing here?

Hur stopped and looked around like he was trying to find someone. Then he approached Jarah. She didn't know what to do. She felt so insignificant in this man's presence. Hur had a warm smile on his lips and Jarah could see in his eyes how much he loved Yahweh. She wondered if she should run and try to find her father or Eitan to talk to this man. What did he want?

Humming contentedly, Hur drew nearer to Jarah. He asked in a soft, yet powerful voice, "Excuse me young lady, I'm looking for Sethur, one of the elders of this tribe. Do you know where I can find him?"

"Yes, sir," Jarah answered, rising to her feet. "He's my grandfather."

"How blessed I am that the Lord pointed me to you," Hur said giving Jarah a smile that made her feel completely comfortable.

"Please, follow me." She motioned with her hand.

Jarah led Hur to her grandfather's tent. She was glad to see that he was sitting outside, relaxing in front of his tent. She was surprised to see that Rishon, almost completely well thanks to Shayna's nursing, was sitting by her grandfather's side, in earnest conversation with him. Eitan often spent time with Grandfather, gleaning his wisdom, but though Rishon and Eitan were close friends, Rishon was quieter and rarely initiated a conversation with her grandfather.

At this moment, Grandfather noticed Hur and Jarah coming towards them.

"Hur, what a pleasant surprise! What brings you here?" he stood up and greeted his guest warmly.

"Thankfully for both of us I have not come with a legal matter." Hur's continual smile widened.

"I think I should be going now, Sethur," Rishon excused himself, rising to leave. "I'm sure you have something important to discuss and I don't want to be in the way."

"Me, too," Jarah added.

"No, please stay," Hur insisted. "I always enjoy having young people around."

Rishon and Jarah glanced at Grandfather, who nodded his approval. They both sat down across from Hur.

"Well, if it isn't a legal matter, what can I do for you?" Grandfather asked, picking up the conversation where it had left off.

"I've heard that there are some among your relatives and intimate friends that are very skilled in metal work." Here Hur threw a questioning glance at Rishon before continuing. Rishon's attention was immediately glued to this important man. "When we get to the Promised Land there will be an abundance of work in this area. In fact, my sons and I are making weapons even now. As you know, Sethur, my son and grandson used to be in the pharaoh's close service." There wasn't a hint of pride in Hur's voice as he said that. "Uri and Bezalel—my son and grandson—are looking to take on an apprentice or two, someone who can help us with the work, lessen the burden, and learn from what they can teach."

Rishon's eyes lit up but the rest of his face showed no emotion. Grandfather smiled warmly.

"You're in luck. I know a fine young man who I am sure would be more than willing to help. This is Rishon, the son of Daton and a cousin of my daughter-in-law."

Rishon extended his hand. "It's nice to meet you, sir."

"And you as well. You are quite skilled in your work?" Hur asked.

"I wouldn't say skilled," Rishon began, modestly, "but I work hard at what I do."

"Your family worked in a forge back in Egypt?" Hur pressed further.

"Yes, sir."

"Do you have any work that you could show me?"

Rishon's brow furrowed. "Most of the things I made were left in Egypt. I don't know if—"

"Wait, Rishon!" Jarah pulled the necklace that he had made for her from her neck and handed it to him. Rishon smiled and passed it to Hur. Hur examined it carefully.

"This is a most excellent piece of work. The skill, precision, and attention to detail are very obvious." Hur looked penetratingly at

Rishon. "You seem like a diligent, honest young man. Could you bring me to your parents?"

"Yes, sir," Rishon replied with confidence. He gave Jarah back her necklace and she watched Rishon walk away with Hur. Her heart was bursting with pride and joy for Rishon. She knew that he loved metal work, and now, to be able to work alongside Hur and his relatives, of all people! For Rishon, it had to be a dream come true.

ג

Very early the next morning, Jarah was outside collecting manna. She heard quiet voices and saw Rishon talking with Uncle Daton in front of their tent. They clasped hands and then Rishon strode off into the early morning mist. Uncle Daton disappeared into the tent and in a moment, Reia came out to start their fire. Jarah ran over to her.

"Where's Rishon going?"

Reia was smiling, but also looked a little sad, too. "Rishon is starting his apprenticeship with Uri and Bezalel today. We're so excited for him. It's such an honor for us. Rishon will be a great apprentice, I'm sure. But we'll all miss him." Reia quickly brushed away a tear and tried to smile.

"Will he be gone a lot?" Jarah asked.

"Yes. For almost twelve hours a day. There's a lot of work to do making weapons for the people," Reia explained.

"I didn't realize he'd be gone so much," Jarah murmured.

"We know it's the right thing, though," Reia said, emphatically. "Rishon will be using his talent for Yahweh. It's what he's always wanted."

"Yes, of course," Jarah said, trying to sound encouraging. Out of the corner of her eye, she saw her father walking away from their tents. It almost looked like he was sneaking off again.

"Father, where are you going?"

Father looked up, looking a little sheepish.

"I'm going to meet up with my friend, Ennis. He's helping me do some trading and some carpentry work," he explained.

"All right. When will you be back?"

"I'm not sure," her father called over his shoulder as he headed into camp.

Jarah sighed a little and watched as Reia threw another stick on the fire. Her eyes gazed towards the mountain. A distant rumble of thunder came to the girls' ears.

"Moses still hasn't returned," Reia whispered.

"No. He hasn't. Tomorrow will be thirty-one days he's been gone," Jarah said, more to herself than to Reia.

Reia's big eyes looked into Jarah's face. "Do you think something has happened to him? Why hasn't he come back?"

Jarah shrugged. "I don't know. I was wondering the same thing."

The girls stared up at the mountain, silently prayed to Yahweh to let Moses come back to them.

ז

Thirty-four days. Mother was incredibly cross and irritable. She and Father regarded each other with sullen anger and silence. They almost never talked any more, and the pressure that it put on the rest of the family was unbearable. Jarah and the others were so disheartened. A few weeks ago they appeared to have reached an understanding and had been working together. But it now seemed as though both of them had decided to not give in to each other for any reason, all their words were now fueled by anger and bitterness.

"What has happened to Moses?" Mother grumbled.

"No one knows, Mariel." Father sighed in exasperation.

"Well, someone ought to know. What if he's dead?" Mother asked.

Father shrugged.

"He's not dead, Mother. He's receiving Yahweh's law," Eitan said boldly.

"For thirty-four days? Really, Eitan. Doesn't that seem a bit long?"

"Yahweh does what He pleases," Eitan replied.

"I don't think He cares. You've seen what Yahweh has done. He caused earthquakes and terror, demanded hundreds of animals to be slaughtered to appease His wrath, and now He's probably killed Moses. Is this the 'gracious' God who supposedly led us from Egypt?"

"Mariel, stop. That's enough," Father commanded in anger.

"No, I won't!" Mother almost screamed. She rose to her feet, stamping her foot on the ground in rage. "What if Moses *doesn't* come down? What are we supposed to do then? Who will lead us to this Promised Land? Who even knows if it exists? I've told you, Yahweh can't be trusted!"

Suddenly Mother cried out in pain and fell to the ground. She clutched her swollen stomach and looked up at Father, terrified.

Father's eyes grew wide and he said quietly, "Jarah, go get your aunt."

ה

"**A**unt Zuriel! Aunt Zuriel!" Jarah tugged on the door to the tent and her aunt quickly appeared.

"Jarah, what is it?" she asked with some alarm.

"Mother's in labor!" Jarah exclaimed.

"What? She's not due for quite some time! This could be very serious. Are you sure?"

"Yes, yes, I'm sure!" Jarah persisted.

"I'll be right there. Go get Marnee and Sanne. I may need their help. And is Shayna there?"

"Yes."

"Good. Now go, quickly!"

ו

The labor lasted for hours and continued on into the night. Eitan, Lemuel, and Raphael slept in Aunt Zuriel's tent while Jarah, Tirzah, and Yanni slept with Amissa's family in their tent. Jarah tried to sleep, but the constant moans and cries from her mother kept waking her up right as she was drifting off to sleep.

Finally, she slipped outside to sit by the dwindling coals of Amissa's family's fire. Father sat by the entrance to his tent, his head in his hands. Jarah did not venture to go towards him. He seemed like he wanted to be alone.

232

The night was chilly but Jarah barely noticed. Her brain was whirling with thoughts. What was happening to Moses? What would happen to the Israelites if he didn't come back? And what was happening to her mother?

A loud wail from Jarah's tent startled her. It was followed by a very weak, constant cry. A baby's cry. It was here.

A few minutes later an exhausted Aunt Zuriel slipped from the tent, a very tiny bundle in her arms. She handed it to Father. "It's a girl," she said softly. "Mariel has named her Ximena."

"She's so little," Father whispered.

"She's very premature," Aunt Zuriel said. She fell silent. She opened her mouth to speak, but no words came. Hesitantly she began, "Asher, I don't believe she'll live long. She's very weak."

"I know," Father choked. After a pause he asked, "How's Mariel?"

"That's also what I wanted to talk to you about. The labor was hard. She's lost a lot of blood. We're not sure if she will ever fully recover."

Father sat as if stunned. Jarah felt her heart stop beating. How could it be? Her new little sister would soon be dead, and her mother would be an invalid for life? Why? Why would Yahweh let that happen? Turning, she fled into the tent, threw herself upon her mat, and sobbed herself into a fitful sleep.

๒

Ezra lay awake, watching Jarah's body shake with sobs. He couldn't help but sigh. He had heard what Zuriel had said.

Yahweh, this poor family... They've gone through so much with the tension between Mariel and Asher over the past few months, his stealing and lack of leadership in the family, and now this! And Ada's going to be a part of this family... I don't know if she can do it. I wish I could help. I mean, I help Father talk to Asher and encourage Lemuel, Eitan, and Jarah as much as I can. But I wish there was more I could do.

Tears gathered into Ezra's eyes as he thought about what to pray next. It still brought pain back into his heart whenever he thought about it.

Yahweh, I know what it's like to lose a sibling. Please... Don't let that happen to them. Please don't let them experience that pain and sorrow. I don't know if they can bear it... I know I almost didn't. I don't know if I can help them if their little baby dies.

He saw Jarah's body relaxing and could tell that she was falling asleep from sheer exhaustion.

Be with her, Lord. She needs you. We all do, but right now Jarah and this family need you more than ever. Be there for them, Yahweh. Please help me know how to be there for them, too.

ת

Two days had passed. Jarah slumped down by the fire pit, letting her shoulders sag. The hot desert sun beat down upon her, but Jarah didn't care. She stared at the ground and let the tears flow down her cheeks.

"Jarah, how are they?" Amissa appeared by Jarah's side. Reia sat down on Jarah's other side and took her hand, lovingly. Jarah choked back her sobs before replying.

"Worse. Mother's fever is slowly climbing. If it gets much higher Aunt Zuriel said it could be very dangerous." Jarah's chest heaved with sobs.

"And Ximena?" Amissa prodded.

Jarah shrugged. "She's so weak and little. We fear it's just a matter of time for her. We're just hoping that Mother doesn't get worse. If she doesn't get better in the next few days..." Jarah couldn't stop the tears any more. She was too tired and sorrowful to care what her friends thought of her now. Reia's arms wrapped around Jarah's neck. Amissa squeezed Jarah's hand.

"Jarah," Amissa began, "everything will work out for good. It might not seem like it now, but we know that it will. Yahweh's in control and He loves your mother and baby sister more than even you do."

Jarah nodded her head. "I know that. But—but it's hard to believe it," she finished, sniffing. "Especially because Mother... Mother doesn't believe in Yahweh. What will happen if she does get worse?

What happens if she dies?" Jarah looked searchingly, pleadingly into Amissa's face. Tears glistened in Amissa's eyes.

"I—I don't know," Amissa whispered. "But Yahweh has a plan. He always has a plan, even now when nothing makes sense. When Moses is gone and your mother and sister are sick, I know He must seem very far away. But Jarah, look up."

Through her blurred vision Jarah did look up. The dark, ominous clouds were still there. The flashes of lightning, the rolling of thunder far, far away. Yahweh's presence was there, right with them. Surely He must know what was happening. There was still hope left. As Shayna had said, "As long as there's life, there's hope."

"I just need to keep praying—and—hoping..." Jarah was sobbing violently now, but at the same time, she began to feel more at peace.

Amissa wrapped her arms around Jarah as Reia squeezed her tight and whispered, "That's all you can do, Jarah. It's not hopeless yet."

The girls heard pounding feet behind them. Rishon bolted around the tent, his face very white. He saw Reia and panted, "Reia, where's Father?"

"With the animals. What's wrong?" Reia asked in concern, rising to her feet.

"I've got to talk to him," was Rishon's only response. He darted away towards the open desert.

"What's wrong?" Jarah wondered aloud. "Rishon never acts like that."

Reia shook her head.

"I'm not sure. I hope it's nothing serious."

In just a few minutes, Uncle Daton and Rishon came back into camp. Uncle Daton's countenance was dark and worried. Rishon's face was still white, but now shock and sorrow were mixed in his eyes.

"Reia, go get Sethur, please," Uncle Daton instructed.

"Yes, sir." Reia obeyed immediately and soon returned, bringing Grandfather with her.

"Daton, Reia said you wished to see—Rishon, what's happened? Your face is as white as the moon," Grandfather exclaimed.

"Sir, something terrible has happened." Rishon gulped and looked from Grandfather to his father. Uncle Daton nodded, encouraging Rishon to tell his story.

"I was working with Bezalel and Uri today. We've been sensing all day that something wasn't right. Then we heard the noise of a mob. Looking out, we saw men and women who looked very angry. They were passing our tent and going towards Aaron's. We were worried that something was wrong or that they might try to hurt Aaron, so we grabbed weapons and followed them. We didn't know what was happening, but we knew there was trouble..." Rishon paused in his story. He was staring out towards the mountain, sadness on his face, and a look of remembering in his eyes...

ט

Rishon stood at the edge of an infuriated throng. The noise of the angry mob was deafening.

"Father, what's going on?" Bezalel shouted.

"I don't know, but we must get to Aaron. He might need our help," Uri yelled back.

Rishon clutched the short sword by his side, swallowed hard, and plunged into the crowd of Israelites, trying to keep Uri in sight. He and Bezalel endeavored to push their way through, but it was only a few moments before they lost sight of Uri and couldn't regain their sense of direction. They stopped for a minute, bewildered and confused. Rishon tried to distinguish the voices around him and figure out what had started this whole commotion.

"What's this all about?" a newcomer asked a man.

"We've had enough of this!" he shouted back.

"Enough of what?"

"Camping in the desert and following every whim of a cloud! Moses is the one who led us here, and now he's gone. We want a new leader and a new representation of Yahweh, something that we can see and feel and something that will really go before us to the Promised Land!"

"But Moses is coming back, isn't he?" the first man asked.

"He's been gone for a month," the other man scoffed. "Everyone knows he's dead. Besides, we want nothing more to do with Moses. And we want nothing to do with this mystical 'pillar of cloud.' We want a god we can see and feel. And we want a leader who thinks as we do!"

"Do you think Aaron will listen to our demands?" the first man questioned, seeming to warm up to the idea.

"He'd better. Hur resisted us, and you'll never hear from *him* again. If Aaron doesn't listen to us there will be trouble." The second man picked a large stone from the ground and gripped it tightly in his fist.

Rishon's eyes grew round with fright and he turned to Bezalel, whose face was filled with alarm.

Hur's been murdered? Is it true? Or is it only a rumor… We've got to get to Aaron!

Gripping Bezalel's arm, Rishon shouldered his way forward, hoping to find a way out of the crazed mob of people.

In a moment he broke out of the crowd and saw Aaron standing in front of him, surrounded by soldiers. Uri was already there.

"People of Israel," Aaron was crying out, "what do you want from me?"

"We want you to make us an image of Yahweh!" the Hebrews declared.

Aaron was stupefied. "But Yahweh told us to—"

"Aaron!" A man who seemed to be one of the ringleaders stepped from the crowd.

"Ennis?" Aaron seemed confused and fearful. Ennis moved closer, his eyes kindling with passion.

Rishon drew his sword and put it against the man's chest. The man stared Rishon down.

"What are you thinking boy, trifling with me?" Ennis growled.

"I'm only protecting the man of Yahweh, sir," Rishon said as respectfully as he could. His heart was pounding.

"It's all right. Let him come," Rishon heard Uri command. He slowly backed away and let Ennis advance. Ennis glared at Rishon as he marched over to Aaron. Uri signaled for Rishon and Bezalel to back down and to let the elders deal with the situation. Obediently, Rishon and Bezalel melted into the front ranks of the crowd.

"Come, make us a god who will go before us; as for this Moses, the man who brought us up from the land of Egypt, we do not know what has become of him." Ennis took another step forward until he was right in Aaron's face. "We want a god who will go with us into battle and lead us to the Promised Land, and not leave us to wander around this wasteland following a cloud."

"But—But the commands of Yahweh said not to! I can't do this," Aaron stammered, throwing up his hands.

"You will do it! Or you'll end up dead just like your brother Moses," Ennis threatened. Aaron backed away, terrified. Uri grabbed Ennis's arm and pulled him away from Aaron. Several other soldiers stepped forward to join him.

"Fine! Do whatever you want to me!" Ennis roared. "But Aaron, I'm not the only one! See these thousands of people? Even if you kill me, that won't stop this crowd from having their way. Your few bodyguards won't be able to protect you from their wrath!"

Rishon looked around, suddenly feeling hopeless. Ennis was right. There were thousands of people in the mob, and at most only fifty who were standing up for what Yahweh said was right. They were dreadfully outnumbered.

Yahweh, I'm willing to die for you if I must. But please, don't let this happen. Please let us soften their hearts and point them towards You.

Aaron's wild eyes searched the crowd.

"All right!" he almost screamed. "I'll do it!"

Rishon's jaw dropped.

What? Aaron has just given in to them?

An evil gleam rested in Ennis's eyes.

"You made the right choice," he hissed.

Aaron looked out at the crowd and shouted, "People of Israel, tear off the gold rings which are in the ears of your wives, your sons, and your daughters, and bring them to me."

A few cloth sacks were produced from somewhere, and the people began dumping any gold jewelry they possessed into the bags. Over the hubbub of clinking jewels and rejoicing people Rishon heard a voice which shocked him out of his daze. It was Uri. He turned to see Uri staring Aaron down, face red with rage.

"How could you do this, Aaron? How could you?" he said, his voice low and dangerous. "I would rather die knowing that I had some small part in preventing this sin than live to see it destroy my people!" Uri continued, his voice rising to a bellow. "I will have nothing to do with this Aaron. Nothing! I refuse to help you make this image or commit this great sin. All responsibility falls upon you!" Uri turned on his heel and disappeared into the crowd. Aaron stared after him, looking frightened.

"You boys." Ennis was suddenly there, holding out an empty sack to Rishon and Bezalel. "Help us gather more gold for our image." He thrust the sacks in their hands. Bezalel backed away, horrified.

Rishon took a step forward and straightened to his full height. Looking directly into Ennis's eyes he declared, "No. I can not and will not disobey my Lord's commandments or support you in this act."

Ennis's eyes were snapping with indignation.

"You'll regret this," he spat into Rishon's face.

Rishon didn't move. He stood strong and determined, feeling the strength of Yahweh fill him. He knew that what he was doing was right and he wasn't going to back down. Ennis seemed to falter under Rishon's cold stare and finally turned back to his evil work. Rishon felt Bezalel's hand on his arm.

"We've got to get out of here. If something happened to my grand-father—" Bezalel stopped short, took a deep breath, and blinked back tears. "If something happened to my grandfather," he began again, "we need to move our tents. People know where we are and if they know we made a stand against this idol they could kill us and our families. We have to protect them."

"Yes, you're right." Rishon swept his eyes across the faces of the Israelites in the crowd. They were so happy, so jubilant.

Don't they realize what a horrible, terrible, wicked thing they're doing? Rishon thought. Anger and sorrow gripped his chest and made it hard to breathe. His gaze finally rested on Aaron who was nervously wringing his hands.

"Let's go," Bezalel urged. Rishon slowly nodded his head in assent and the boys fought their way through the Israelites and into the middle of the camp where everything seemed still, quiet, and deserted.

"We did the right thing, didn't we?" Bezalel asked softly, almost as if he was talking to himself.

Rishon took a deep breath. "Yes. We did the right thing. Now we can only pray that Yahweh's favor and protection rests on us and our families."

׳

After that Uri and Bezalel moved their tent somewhere else to keep their families safe," Rishon said, concluding his narrative. "That was a wise idea," Uncle Daton muttered softly.

"But Sethur, what are we going to do? How can we stop this madness?"

Grandfather's brow was furrowed and he gazed at the ground, deep in thought.

"I will try talking to Aaron, but at this point I doubt there's anything I can do."

Rishon breathed a sigh of relief as Grandfather left them. He and Uncle Daton continued talking in low tones. Jarah, Amissa, and Reia said nothing for several minutes. They were stunned. The cowardice and madness that had struck the people seemed almost inhuman. What had happened to them? Had they really murdered Hur? How could they have possibly killed one of their righteous leaders?

"What's going to happen?" Amissa finally broke the silence. Her blue eyes were very wide.

"I don't know," Jarah whispered. "I don't know."

כ

Two more days passed. Ximena clung on to life, still very weak and sickly. They tried everything to nurse her to health, but nothing seemed to be working. Mother seemed to be getting weaker, too.

240

She rarely walked around anymore but stayed on her mat, resting. Shayna was almost constantly by their sides. Dark circles rested under her eyes. Every night Jarah cried herself to sleep, begging Yahweh to make her mother and little sister well.

Nothing had been heard about the image that Aaron was making. They all hoped that what Grandfather had said to Aaron had discouraged him from this dreadful act.

Nothing prepared them for what happened next.

ל

"Shayna! Shayna!"

Hurried steps were heard outside the tent. The tent flap was rudely thrown open and a handsome young man entered. Jarah groaned softly. It was one of Shayna's good-for-nothing friends. Before Rishon's injury, Shayna had spent most of her time in the company of three lazy youths. But ever since Rishon had told Shayna he couldn't marry her she had distanced herself from them and now avoided them all together. The leader of the little group, Mayer, was the one who now stood before Shayna.

"Mayer, be quiet. Mother's sleeping," Shayna hushed him in annoyance.

"Oh. I didn't realize," Mayer said, though Jarah doubted that he cared.

"What do you want?" Shayna sighed in exasperation.

"Come with me," was Mayer's reply. He playfully took Shayna's hand and attempted to lead her from the tent. She pulled away in disgust.

"Mayer, I told you I'm not going to join you or Yaphet or Zephon anymore. Don't seek me out. I want to be left alone."

Maybe I should go get Eitan, Jarah pondered. *But then that would leave Shayna alone with Mayer. What should I do?*

"And why not?" Mayer asked, faking a wounded look. "Have you found another young man more handsome than me? Perhaps that one you've been spending so much time with recently. Does he really compare to *me*?"

"Mayer, the only reason I was with him was because I was tending his wounds. He doesn't care for me, but at least *he* was courageous and actually helped on the field of battle," she snapped at him.

Mayer stepped backwards, his face turning red with embarrassment and frustration.

"Look, Shayna," he began, annoyed, "I didn't come here to have an argument. I came to ask if you want to have a little fun with me." Mayer advanced towards her, forcing Shayna to back up, a little nervously.

"I'd rather not," she announced boldly.

"But you don't even know what I wanted to tell you about yet," Mayer said, putting on a pleading air.

Seeing that he would give her no rest, Shayna sighed again and questioned, "What is it?"

"There's a big feast going on in the middle of the camp. There's dancing, wine, good food, lots of handsome men, singing and music. Come with me, just for a few hours," Mayer pleaded persuasively.

"Why is there a feast? What's happened?"

"I suppose you haven't heard. Aaron has made us an image of the god who led us out of Egypt—a golden calf. Everyone's gathering to worship it. Now we have a god to lead us to the Promised Land, one that we can actually see and feel and who will cater to our wishes. There have already been sacrifices to it. Please come."

Jarah's eyes grew wide. A statue? Aaron had really made a graven image?

"But Mayer—"

"What's going on?" Mother sat up, rubbing the weariness from her eyes. "A golden calf, did you say?"

"Yes," Mayer said. He seemed quite pleased that Mother was now taking part in the conversation.

"A golden calf," Mother mused. "Yes, sacred cattle like the Egyptians worship. At last. Aaron has made a good decision."

"So, are you going to come with me?" Mayer demanded. He had taken Shayna's hand again.

"But Moses said—"

"Shayna, it doesn't matter what Moses said. He's dead. Besides, we're still worshiping Yahweh. You can just see Him now. Come on. I told Zephon and Yaphet I wouldn't be long."

Shayna seemed to be wavering. *No*, Jarah thought. *Please Yahweh*, she begged, *help Shayna. Give her strength.*

"Go with him, Shayna. I think I'm going to try to get up and go myself," Mother said, rising from her mat and limping over to a nearby chest which held her clothes and jewelry.

"But I—"

Before Shayna could finish, Mayer grabbed her hand in both of his and dragged her from the tent. Jarah followed them, worried that Shayna would give in.

I've got to find Eitan or Lemuel. Where are they? Jarah eyes darted around, but it was mid-afternoon and hot and there was no one in sight to help them. Everyone was resting in their tents.

"Come on, Shayna," Mayer urged, still pulling Shayna after him. But Shayna yanked her hand away and stood still, staring at Mayer. She glanced at Jarah and saw her sister's worried, pleading eyes.

"Now is your moment to change, Shayna," Jarah murmured softly.

Shayna stared at her sister, then slowly turned back to Mayer. She drew in a slow breath and said, quietly but firmly, "No. I'm not going with you."

Jarah had never been more proud of Shayna than in that moment. But her joy quickly faded to fear as Mayer lunged forward and grabbed Shayna by the shoulders.

"You *will* come," he commanded between gritted teeth. "I'm not leaving you. I need you, Shayna. Let's go back to the way things were."

"No, Mayer!" Shayna cried, struggling against his painful grip.

"Come with me!"

"No!" Shayna aimed a kick at his shin, but Mayer simply laughed at her attempts. He grabbed her and held her close, leading her towards the celebration. Shayna struggled desperately, but he was too strong for her to get away.

"Eitan! Lemuel! Help!" Jarah screamed.

Someone dashed past her, nearly knocking Jarah down. It was Eitan. Grabbing Mayer, Eitan spun him around and punched him—

243

hard—in the face. Mayer staggered and fell to the ground, his eyes spinning and his nose gushing blood. Tears of pain streamed down his cheeks. Shayna ran to Eitan, clinging to him. Jarah had never seen Eitan more angry, passionate, and strong as he looked in that moment. Mayer groveled at Eitan's feet, consumed by fear.

"Get out of here—*now*," Eitan said slowly and directly, his voice trembling with rage, "and don't you *ever* come back. If I see you near Shayna again I'll really give you something to cry about. Do you understand me?"

Mayer nodded and bolted away, wiping the blood from his face. In a moment he disappeared into the camp.

Eitan turned and quickly looked at Shayna, making sure she was unharmed. He looked searchingly into her face and under his tender gaze Shayna burst into tears. Eitan took her into his arms, comforting her until the sobs subsided.

"Eitan, what happened?" Father said, coming around the tent. "I thought I heard a scream."

"Asher! Come in here!" Mother commanded from inside the tent. Surprised by the strength in his wife's voice, Father entered the tent. The others followed him.

Mother was dressed in an Egyptian garment. Gold bangles adorned her wrists and she wore an anklet and long earrings. With the sleeveless dress and Egyptian finery Mother looked exactly like the pagan Egyptian women. Jarah wrinkled her nose in disgust as Mother pulled her hair back with a ribbon.

"Well, are you coming or not?" she asked Father.

"Coming where? What are you doing? Mariel, you're too weak to be going anywhere right now."

"Nonsense! I've been resting all day and I feel much better. Besides, this is an important occasion."

"What's going on?" Eitan asked, looking first at Mother then at Father.

"Didn't you hear what Mayer said? Aaron has made us a golden calf to worship as the god who led us out of Egypt. There's a great feast with food, wine, and dancing in the middle of the camp." Mother's flashing eyes turned upon her husband. "Now is the time to take things into our own hands and get out of this accursed desert and on to this Promised Land."

"Mariel, I can't let you do this," Father interrupted.

"I'm going whether you come with me or not," Mother announced, starting for the door. "And you, Asher," she said directly, "if you know what's good for you, you'd better come with me."

Jarah's jaw dropped to the floor. No one moved. Father stood rooted to the ground. He said nothing, but his eyes glistened with dark emotion.

At that moment, Lemuel, Tirzah, and the two young boys entered. Lemuel opened his mouth to say something but quickly shut it again. He instantly realized that there was serious trouble. Ximena started to whimper.

"Tirzah, please take Ximena and the boys outside," Eitan commanded in a quiet but firm tone.

Tirzah nodded and quickly obeyed Eitan's request. Lemuel was going to follow her but a look from Eitan stopped him. He quietly stepped to Eitan's side.

"I might need your help," Eitan whispered.

Mother suddenly took a few more steps towards the door. Father did not follow. Jarah breathed a sigh of relief, but it was premature.

"Well?" Mother barked. "Are you coming or not?"

Very slowly, Father moved towards his wife. In alarm Eitan leapt in front of his father.

"No, Father!" he cried. "Don't do it! It's against Yahweh's law given to Moses! Don't you remember? Yahweh clearly said that the Israelites shouldn't make or worship any graven image."

Father scowled at his son. "Eitan, Moses is dead. Everyone knows that. Besides, we're worshipping Yahweh through this image. He's obviously given your mother new strength, and your mother wants to worship Him. This is a cause for celebration."

Jarah saw a smug smile creep over her mother's face and a gleam of triumph come into her dim eyes. Jarah's heart was sinking. *How can this be happening?*

"But Father, Yahweh said—"

"Eitan!" Father rebuked. "You have no right to argue with me. I can do whatever I want. Yahweh said that you, as my son, must honor and listen to me. And I want to go with your mother to see this golden calf."

Before Eitan could respond Father stormed out of the tent, a gleeful Mother at his heels. Eitan gazed after them in shock. Lemuel laid a compassionate hand on Eitan's shoulder. Eitan looked sorrowfully at his three younger siblings.

"Eitan, what are we going to do?" Shayna asked tearfully.

Eitan obviously saw the confusion and pain in his sister's eyes. He sighed softly and looked at the ground for several long minutes, thinking. Then he squared his shoulders.

"I don't know what's happened to Moses," he began slowly, "and I don't know what's gotten into Aaron, or why Father is listening to our mother." He looked up, a new light kindling in his eyes and courage in his voice. "But our God is not a god made with human hands, and I will continue to obey and serve my God and listen to His voice alone as long as I live."

Tears sprang to Jarah's eyes as she nodded in agreement. They had to serve Yahweh. Who else was there to serve and trust? She had to rely on Him, especially now that her family was in shambles. She needed Yahweh and His strength more now than ever before.

A NEW GOD

"I tried to stop him, but Mother has been influencing him too long. He refused to listen to me."

"I'm so sorry, Eitan."

"I knew that this was going to happen sooner or later." There was a slight pause. "Did your parents go, too?"

"Well," Ada sighed, "one of Mother's friends dragged her off to the 'festivities' earlier this afternoon. Father went to go get her and hasn't come back yet. I think that he was convinced to stay..."

"Hmm. Grandfather has also disappeared. Uncle Daton went with Reia. Rishon and Aunt Zuriel managed to stay behind with Grandmother. But so many others have gone—men, women, and children. They just don't see the harm in it." Now it was Eitan's turn to sigh. "There's nothing we can do to stop it," he murmured.

"Yes, there is, Eitan," Ada whispered, softly. "We can pray."

"Yes. That's right. We can."

Jarah heard the couples' muffled prayer from where she sat in front of the fire. In the far distance she heard the faint swells of music, laughter, and feasting. She still couldn't believe that her father and mother were gone and were wallowing in sin with everyone else. She thought they would come back at nightfall, but it was now past midnight and there was still no sign of them. She wished there was something she could do, something to bring them back.

Suddenly, she thought of something.

Eitan never went looking for them. Perhaps if I go I can find them and beg them to come back to us, maybe, just maybe I can get them to listen to me.

Jarah slipped off into the night without bothering to tell Eitan where she was going. He thought that she was asleep with everyone else, and she didn't want him worrying about her in case her plan didn't succeed.

She tip-toed through camp, coming closer and closer to the screams, the laughter, the clang of tambourines and trill of flutes. Then before she knew it, she had stepped from the line of tents into a vast, open area. Thousands upon thousands of people filled it. Food and wine were everywhere. People were drunk and dancing hysterically. Many women were dressed in the immodest fashion of the Egyptians. Jarah cringed at the wickedness and sin that was surrounding her on every side. Gulping audibly, she melted into the shadows of the tents, trying to keep away from the light of the huge bonfire. She looked for any sign of her parents but saw only dark silhouettes of people in the orange glow of the flames.

This is hopeless! Jarah thought, agonized. Then she saw it—the golden calf.

High on a platform, a golden cow glistened in the eerie glow of firelight. She saw the bodies of animals sacrificed to it at the foot of the platform. People were kneeling in front of the statue and dancing wildly around it. Jarah's stomach dropped and she felt like she was going to be sick.

Two thoughts surfaced in her mind. The first was, *How can they do this?* and the second was, *I've got to go back.* Jarah forced her feet to slide backwards. Slowly, ever so slowly, she pushed herself away from the terrible scene. She turned to flee but felt weak from the horror of what she had just witnessed. Conflicting voices raged in her head.

Go. You can worship it. What harm will it do? After all, it's just an image of your God. You'll be paying Him respect, the first voice said.

No! You can't! Yahweh said not to! the second voice replied.

But Yahweh's not around any more. And if He is He's not the god you thought He was. Look what He's done to Moses. Look what He's done to your mother and baby sister. Go. Just enjoy the dancing and food. That's not wrong.

Yes, it is! See the pillar? It's still there. Yahweh is still here. Just leave, Jarah. Run. Go!

No—Stay—

Jarah turned and glanced at the statue one more time. She was suddenly conscious of someone's presence quite close to her. She whirled around and found herself face to face with a very attractive young man.

"Would you like to dance?" the young man asked, holding out a hand in her direction.

Jarah was disoriented and stunned. Hebrew people never danced with members of the opposite sex. She had seen the Egyptians do that though, and it had looked innocent enough. "Well, that—that's very kind of you. But—but really, I think, I—"

"Oh come on! It's just a little fun. You don't want to miss out, do you?"

The young man slipped his hand into Jarah's and she felt a thrill of excitement run through her. Jarah felt her flesh giving in but the second little voice was screaming at her, *No! Don't do it!*

"Well—I—" she stammered.

"Jarah?" Someone said her name. The next instant, she felt a hand grab her arm. Jarah started and found herself looking up into Ezra's face. Ezra scowled at the young man, who instantly let go of Jarah's hand and backed up, looking very nervous. Staring into Jarah's face, Ezra said darkly and forcefully, "We need to get out of here."

Jarah had no choice but to follow Ezra. He was still holding her arm and was pulling her along rapidly into the midst of the tents and away from the people. Jarah's head was spinning.

Ezra stopped once the sounds were far away. He looked Jarah squarely in the face, a strange expression in his eyes.

"Ezra—" she began, about to defend herself.

"Why were you there?"

The bluntness of his question startled Jarah. "Please, Ezra," she began, trying desperately not to make a fool of herself, "I didn't mean to. I mean—I meant to go, but I didn't mean to get caught up in anything. Really I didn't."

"What were you doing?" Ezra's face was fierce.

Jarah had no choice but to answer. "I was trying to find Mother and Father."

"I see. And you went without Eitan's consent, didn't you?" Jarah hung her head. "Didn't you?" Ezra repeated, a little louder this time.

"Yes," she whispered. "I didn't want him to find out in case I didn't find them."

"That was foolish, Jarah," Ezra reprimanded. "A young woman like you out in the middle of the night by yourself? What were you thinking? Eitan is your protector. And there's no way you would've found them amidst all of those people. You know that."

Jarah could only nod pitifully. Then a thought struck her. She stared into Ezra's eyes and challenged, "Why were you there?"

"Eitan discovered you were missing and he and Lemuel and I were looking for you," was Ezra's simple reply.

Jarah hung her head again, tears welling in her eyes.

"I'm sorry," she whispered, sobbing. "I'm so sorry."

"It's fine. I understand." Ezra sighed. He sounded so sad. "Let's head back. We need to get Eitan and Lemuel," Ezra said, after a long pause.

Jarah followed him back to their tents. Her head was swarming with so many thoughts. *Does Ezra really care that much for me to make sure I stay safe? He's such a strong spiritual leader.* Then she thought about the golden calf. The terrible images of what was happening back there seemed to be consuming her.

How could they do this? How could they after seeing all that Yahweh has done? I don't understand.

"Ezra?" she asked softly.

"Yes?"

"How could they do it? How could they make a golden calf and worship it? Why, after they've seen all that Yahweh's done for us?"

Ezra exhaled again and his shoulders drooped. "Yahweh made us in His image. Now they're trying to change Him into *our* image to do what we want. They want to control Yahweh."

"But they can't, can they?"

"No," Ezra said emphatically. He glanced over his shoulder. "And those people are going to learn that lesson the hard way."

א

"Please, Adriel," Acenith begged, kneeling in front of him. "It's not that late yet! I can go for just a little bit and come back."

"Acenith, for the last time, no! It's against Yahweh's law!" Adriel commanded, turning his back towards her.

"No, it's not," Acenith said, tearfully. "Just because they're having a party with some Egyptian customs doesn't mean that they're against Yahweh."

"There's an idol there, Acenith," Adriel said, exasperated. "Yahweh said not to make any images. We can't disobey Him. Didn't you see what He did to the Egyptians who didn't obey?"

"That was just the pharaoh's fault," Acenith sobbed. "And I don't want to worship it. I just want to remember Egypt. I miss it. I miss—I miss Bes... and our customs. No one understands me here. No one! I just—I just want to do something for fun to help me forget it all." She curled up into a little ball and cried. Adriel knelt by her side and his arm slipped around her shoulders.

"I'm sorry, Acenith," he whispered. "I know it's hard for you. I don't think about how you left your old world behind. You're right. We can't fully understand you and your struggles. I know these past months haven't made anything easier for any of us, either..." Adriel's voice trailed away and he cleared his throat. Acenith laid her head on his shoulder, wiping away her tears.

"You can go if you want," Adriel finally said in a low, husky voice. Acenith started and looked him full in the face.

"Really?" she gasped.

"Yes. I know you don't believe in Yahweh but please, don't worship the idol. Just promise me that." Adriel's piercing eyes bored into hers.

"I won't. I promise," Acenith stated. She rose to her feet. "Will you come with me? Just for a little bit? Just to get some food and make sure everything is all right?" Adriel fixed his gaze on the ground. "Please, Adriel?" Acenith pleaded. She knelt and took his hand in both of hers.

He finally looked into her face. "All right," he assented. "But just for a few minutes. Just to have some fun and forget it all, like you said."

"Yes," Acenith murmured, a happy light twinkling in her eyes. "Just to have fun and forget it all..."

ב

The next day dawned dark and overcast. The air was oppressive and hot. The feasting was still taking place and none of their relatives had returned. Eitan and Lemuel were downcast and Shayna was unusually reserved. Jarah was just preparing lunch when she happened to glance back up at Mount Sinai. She gasped. Something—or someone—was coming down the mountain.

"Eitan! It's Moses and Joshua! They're back! Moses has returned!"

In a few moments all of their friends and relatives who were not at the feast were running towards the mountain. They ran through the center of the camp, through the merry-making, and stood close to the mountain waiting for Moses and Joshua.

And indeed it was them. By now they were very close. Jarah could see that Moses held in his hands two tablets that appeared to be made of stone. And she could see his face, as white as marble, his eyes kindling with a terrible rage.

With a mighty shout, Moses threw the tablets from his hands. They crashed onto the rocky ground at the base of the mountain and shattered. At the sound of Moses' cry and the resounding crash of the rocks everything in the camp came to an abrupt halt. Everyone stared at Moses: some with expressions of guilt; some with anger; some with reverence.

Moses surveyed the scene, his face turning from white to crimson. Slowly, very slowly, all of the people dropped what they were doing and stepped towards the mountain, most of them hanging their heads in shame.

Suddenly Moses cried out in rage and ran through the camp. Joshua followed him. Moses pushed the golden calf from its high place. It fell with a heavy *thud* into the large fire that had formerly been used to offer incense to the idol. Moses grabbed a stone hammer that he found at the base of the altar and began to beat the calf. Joshua and several other Levites soon joined him, breaking the graven image into pieces and grinding it into flakes of gold and dust.

Jarah watched with a pounding heart. Her eyes filled with tears. What the people had done was a terrible, wicked thing. What would Yahweh say? What would Moses say?

The destruction complete, Moses scooped up handfuls of gold and dust and threw them into buckets nearby. Grabbing the buckets, he rushed towards the small brook that ran through the middle of the valley. He sprinkled the gold into the water and commanded, "Drink! All of you, *drink!*"

From the awful terror and anger on Moses' face, Jarah knew she should not disobey. She knelt down and drank, feeling tremors of fear run through her body. Jarah gulped up the water, tasting the cold, metal taste of gold in her mouth. It was bitter and sour. Jarah couldn't make herself swallow. She gagged, willing the water to go down her throat. She wiped her mouth with the back of her hand, feeling guilty and dirty, as though she was drinking sin. Groans of disgust and anguish filled the air as other Israelites tried to drink the water, too. Glancing up, Jarah saw Moses talking heatedly to Aaron, who looked extremely embarrassed and anxious.

After the multitude of Israelites had drank of the water, everyone stood by the brook facing Moses. He stood at the entrance of the camp many yards away. Moses glared down upon the people. Jarah glanced about and saw many different expressions on the Hebrews' faces. She saw anger. She saw fear. She saw repentance. She saw people who were not repentant. Did they not understand what a horrible, sinful thing they had done?

"Whoever is for the Lord, come to me!" Moses bellowed. There was a long, silent pause. No one walked across the open ground to meet Moses. Jarah wanted to. Every muscle in her body yearned to show Moses that she wanted to obey, that she was for Yahweh. But she felt rooted to the ground.

There was a slight commotion. From the crowd of Israelites over three thousand Levites came forward, crossed the sandy soil, and stood behind Moses. Many had swords at their sides. Their faces were as immovable as stones. Moses turned back to the people.

"Who is for the Lord? Who?"

A few others walked forward and joined the Levites.

"People of Israel! Who is for the Lord?!" Moses was practically screaming. Tears were streaming down his cheeks. Jarah saw someone starting to walk forwards. She gasped with delight. It was her father.

"Asher!" A chilling voice cut through the silence. Mother stood at the head of the line, glaring at her husband. Father froze. He looked at his wife, and then back towards Moses. He stood perfectly still, torn between Moses and his wife.

"Father, please." Eitan stepped forwards, Ada by his side.

Moses' tearful, pleading countenance darkened into a scowl. He turned to the Levites and instructed in a deep, forceful voice, "Thus says the Lord, the God of Israel, 'Every man of you put his sword upon his thigh, and go back and forth from gate to gate in the camp, and kill every man his brother, and every man his friend, and every man his neighbor.'"

Jarah's jaw dropped. Surely they wouldn't...

As a man, the Levites broke into a run towards the camp. The next few minutes were a blur. The Levites rushed past Father and ran past Jarah. Lemuel grabbed his sister and pulled her back towards himself and Ezra.

Later she remembered clinging to Lemuel and seeing Ezra moving his arm protectively in front of her and Amissa. Ear-splitting screams and cries of war and agony filled the air. Through all of these Jarah heard her mother cry out again, "Asher!" But this time she didn't sound angry. She sounded like she was in pain and needing help.

Jarah frantically searched for her mother. She saw her kneeling on the ground, and though she didn't look like she had been wounded, she was shrieking in pain and grasping her stomach. Father was beside her now, but then chaos hid them from view.

Eitan ran towards his parents, leaving Ada in the care of Rishon. He too was quickly swallowed up by the Israelites running frantically in all directions.

Within minutes the Levites had finished their work. Three thousand unrepentant people had been slain. The Levites came back to Moses, faces grim and sorrowful. Moses spoke to them, and his voice was trembling as if he was crying.

"Dedicate yourselves to the Lord—for every man has been against his son and against his brother—in order that He may bestow a blessing upon you today."

The Levites all nodded their heads in assent and slowly filed away. Everything in the camp seemed to settle down. Quiet crying and the soft sounds of feet walking across the sand were the only noises in the entire camp.

Jarah felt stunned and scared. She was still clinging to Lemuel. Her aunt and uncle came up behind them with Reia. Grandfather and Grandmother emerged from the throng of Hebrews. Grandfather's eyes were confused and he looked tired and grim.

"We should go back," he whispered. Slowly, everyone departed to their tents.

When Jarah entered their tent, she saw that her father, mother, and Eitan were already there. Father was bending over her mother, who was moaning softly.

"Father, what is—"

Eitan grabbed her by the shoulders and pulled her back. "Come with me," he whispered in her ear. He herded the rest of the little children out of the tent and towards the dying embers of their afternoon campfire. Shayna came out of the tent as well, tenderly cradling a whimpering Ximena.

"What's wrong with Mother?" Lemuel asked with some alarm.

Eitan sighed slowly. "She's in a lot of pain. She shouldn't have been out so long, being so sick. She might be…" His voice faded away.

"Dying?" Tirzah gasped in horror.

Eitan just nodded. No one said anything for a long time. All Jarah could think was, *Mother is dying.*

"Did Father or Mother say anything about going over to Moses?" Lemuel spoke slowly.

"No. Father seems very confused and distraught. I can't understand the struggle that's going on inside of him." Eitan's face was pale and he looked so worried. Jarah squeezed her brother's arm affectionately.

"We must pray for them, Eitan," she reminded, simply.

"Yes. Yes, of course." The children knelt on the ground and Eitan started to pray. His voice was trembling and his cheeks were wet with tears. Tears streamed down Jarah's face.

What's going to happen to us? What's going to happen to our people? And what's going to happen to Mother?

MERCY MIXED WITH JUSTICE

Mother died that night.

The whole family was surrounding her and praying for her when she took her last breath.

As Jarah saw the life leave her mother's eyes she felt her heart grow cold with shock. They were really and truly motherless. She watched in disbelief and horror as Eitan and Lemuel draped a cloth over their mother's still, cold form. Father sat in the back of the tent, his hands over his face. He was frozen like a statue. Tears streamed down Shayna's face as she herded the little ones to bed. Tirzah's grip tightened on little Ximena, who was whimpering pitifully. Eitan tenderly took Ximena from her and led Tirzah off to her own bed.

Tirzah laid down, but she didn't go to sleep. She stared at the sheet that hid her mother's body from view, shivering from grief and fear.

Jarah remained rooted to the spot, so stunned she couldn't make her body move. Lemuel's arms went around her shoulders. Jarah slowly turned and buried her face in Lemuel's chest, crying silently. A hot tear landed on top of her head and Jarah knew that Lemuel was crying, too.

א

The sun was high in the sky when Jarah finally awoke. Eitan and Shayna sat in the corner of the tent, talking in low tones. Shayna was spooning goat's milk into Ximena's mouth. Jarah looked around and saw that no one else was awake. Tirzah was still curled up next to her, a tear trembling on her eyelashes. Jarah quietly got up and went over to Eitan and Shayna. She shivered a little as she came close to her mother's dead body. She noticed that her father's place was vacant.

"Where's Father?" she whispered.

Eitan shook his head, sorrowfully. "He left early this morning. I believe he either went out to the plain to grieve in private or to see Ennis."

Jarah slowly nodded. Ximena started to cry. Shayna held her close and rocked her back and forth, trying to comfort her. There were dark circles under Shayna's eyes and her eyelids were red and swollen.

Jarah swallowed a lump in her throat and said, "I'll make breakfast."

"Thank you, Jarah." Shayna looked up at her with a half-smile.

"Jarah," Eitan began as she turned to leave the tent, "we'll be burying Mother this afternoon. I'm about to leave to go hear Moses' rebuke about the golden calf. I saw Grandfather this morning and he said that many people have died during the night. He believes Yahweh has sent a plague among us to kill those who weren't repentant," Eitan explained.

Like Mother... Jarah thought.

"Can you please go tell Ada's family and Uncle Daton that we'll have the funeral service this afternoon?" Eitan asked.

Jarah gulped and nodded. Already moisture was welling up in her eyes.

I've just woken up and I'm already crying, she thought, almost feeling mad at herself. She didn't want to talk to her grandparents. She didn't want to go around the camp telling everyone, "Mother's dead." She wanted to curl up into a little ball and hide from the world. She wished she could have slept for days.

Maybe this is just a dream and I'll wake up soon, she hoped in vain. *Then it will all be a nightmare and I'll soon forget about it.*

But as Jarah walked outside and felt the desert sun strike her face, she knew that it wasn't a nightmare. It was real—terribly real.

And somehow, she also knew it was only the beginning of hardships and troubles for their family.

ב

Ezra's heart was pounding and tears blinded his vision as he helped Lemuel, Rishon, his father, and Daton shovel dirt over Mariel's dead body. He quickly blinked back the tears. He wanted to stay strong for his friends' sakes.

He scooped the dirt up faster, hoping to get his mind off what was happening. The expressions on their faces were terrible to him. Eitan's face was pale, almost gray, and it was cold and stunned. Tears were flowing freely down Shayna's cheeks and onto baby Ximena. Shayna rocked herself back and forth as if to comfort both of them. Lemuel was sobbing quietly, but trying to hide it. The responsibility on his and Eitan's shoulders was evident by the way their bodies drooped. Tirzah clung to Amissa, her eyes hollow with fright and terror. Raphael and Yanni were scared. They didn't understand and they wouldn't understand for quite some time. Their grief would come out slowly as they missed their mother being around and it finally became evident to them that she wasn't coming back.

But Jarah's grief was the worst to see. She just stared straight in front of her, not appearing to see anything. Her lips were trembling, but she wasn't crying. It almost looked like her whole body had turned into ice and she was hiding everything deep down inside.

That was what worried him. She couldn't do that. He had tried to hide his grief inside when Manuel had died, but it had made it worse and one day had all come pouring out of him. He remembered that terrible day when his whole body has just seemed to crash to the ground, and he had spent hours alone begging, pleading, and praying for Yahweh to take away the guilt and the pain and forgive him. He remembered his talk with Lemuel and when he had realized that, in hiding his grief, it had taken root in his body and that it had affected his relationships with his family and with his God. Jarah couldn't do that. He would make sure that didn't happen.

Finally, the hole was filled. Everyone came forward mechanically and put stones on top of the grave as a marker. The last in line was Asher. He walked slowly to the grave and put a large stone at the top of the pile with shaking hands. He wiped away tears with the back of his hand. Everyone else slowly moved away but Eitan, Lemuel, and himself. Asher still stood, staring at the pile of rocks.

"Father." Eitan put a hand on his shoulder. "Please come back with us. We all need you now." Eitan's voice was trembling.

Asher didn't answer. He didn't seem to hear Eitan's voice or feel the touch of his hand.

"Father?" Lemuel asked, laying a hand on his father's other shoulder.

Asher's head jerked up. He gazed at Lemuel, and then slowly turned to look at Eitan.

"I'm sorry, boys," he said in a choking voice, "but not now."

Before Eitan or Lemuel could say anything, Asher turned on his heel and strode off quickly towards camp. Eitan's eyes followed him. As his father disappeared from sight, Eitan sank to the ground and buried his face against his knees. He was crying. Ezra went over to him and placed a hand on his shoulder, silently praying for him. Lemuel stood next to them. His cheeks were wet, too.

It was several minutes before Eitan raised his head and met Ezra's gaze.

"I'm trying to give him the chance, Ezra. I'm trying to give him the chance to once again become the man Yahweh meant for him to be. I believe that he thinks that he failed our mother. Maybe he did. But he shouldn't take that as defeat. He still has all of us, and we still need him. How can I convince him to come back home?"

Ezra had to turn away from Eitan's hungry, pleading eyes. For once, he didn't know what to say. There was a long pause and Ezra tried to think of something—anything—to say to his hurting friends.

"Keep praying. Keep giving him the opportunity. I'll try to talk to Father about it, too. Perhaps my father and Sethur can speak to him in ways that we can't."

Eitan nodded. "All right."

Ezra took a deep breath in and slowly released it.

Yahweh, do a mighty work in this family now.

א

After dinner, Eitan asked Ada and Jaden to take a walk with him. They went out to check on the flocks and make sure they were all settled for the night.

"Jaden, I know this might seem a little abrupt, but, well—I was wondering what you thought about our marriage taking place in a few weeks' time." Jaden's raised eyebrows showed that he was greatly surprised. "I know we were going to wait until we got to the Promised Land," Eitan continued, "but with my Mother's passing and my Father being in the state of depression that he's in, I've been forced into a role of leadership. Shayna also expressed to me that she's not quite sure how well she'll be able to run the household with Ximena being so sickly. I know that it would give me, at the very least, some comfort having Ada's helping hands around as everyone gets used to their new duties."

"Eitan's right, Father," Ada interjected. "I've been thinking all day about the possibility of my helping to bring some sort of order to their family."

Jaden stood for a moment with furrowed brow, thinking. "You're both right," he finally said, sighing slightly. "This is a huge adjustment for your family, Eitan, and though it will be an adjustment for you both to be married, you'll be able to draw strength from each other. I have no objection to moving the marriage to two weeks from now. But Ada," Jaden swallowed a sob, "we're going to miss you, more than you'll ever know."

"But Father, I won't be far away. You'll see me every day." Ada wrapped her arms around her father's neck.

"But it won't be the same. You know that."

"Yes, of course I do. But it's Yahweh's plan for my life," Ada said with confidence.

Jaden squeezed his daughter affectionately and said, "I'll give you both a moment alone. But don't be out for more than a few minutes."

"We won't," Eitan promised.

As Jaden walked away, Eitan reached for Ada's hand and held it close to his cheek. Ada's head drifted to his shoulder and she felt Eitan trembling slightly. She realized that he was crying.

"Thank you, Ada," Eitan whispered, his voice shaking. "You have no idea what a comfort you are to me." He looked down into her eyes and lowered his voice even more. "I love you." It was the first time he had said that. A thrill of joy ran through Ada's body.

"I love you, too, Eitan," Ada whispered, her eyes full of love, adoration, and hope.

א

Cries and moans and wailing surrounded Acenith as she poured water on their little fire, extinguishing it with a blast of smoke and steam and crackling coals. She watched the fire sizzle out as tears gathered in her eyes. The desperate, terrible ache in her heart since Emmitt had died had never gone away. In fact, it had gotten worse. She thought that going to the feast with the golden calf was the answer. Some time away to have fun, to be reunited with her Egyptian customs and beliefs, and to forget her worries. That should've brought her joy. But now, as she listened to the groans of dying men and women, the sounds seem to attack her from every side.

It was a plague, the elders said, a plague to smite down those who had been disobedient to Yahweh and worshipped the golden calf. So many were dead or dying. So many lives were torn apart and broken. So many families would never be the same.

Am I next? Acenith wondered. Surprisingly, she realized that thought didn't scare her. She almost longed for death. Life was too confusing, too terrifying, too full of hurt and pain. Just when she had begun to think that Yahweh might be a loving god who was guiding them towards a future and a hope, He had done this. He was killing people, again. Just like He had killed Bes. Just like He had killed Emmitt.

How can this be a god who loves us, who guides us to a Promised Land? I don't want to go to any land where He's in control. Bitterness welled up inside of her and made her cheeks flush with anger.

"Take me," she whispered fiercely to the pillar of fire on top of the mountain. "If you're a god who delights in killing people, then take me. I don't have anything to live for anymore. You've taken everything away. I'd rather die than live in the constant fear of knowing that You're going to keep killing everyone I love. Take me. Come on! Do it!" She had no purpose, no hope, nobody to live for. Why didn't he strike her with this plague? She deserved it, didn't she? She had disobeyed Him and His laws.

A soft sound from behind her made Acenith start a little. It was Yachne, singing a lullaby to her children as she put them to sleep. Yachne's voice was so tender and gentle, but her voice was trembling as if she was crying. She was singing of Yahweh, of His many miracles in Egypt. But she sounded discouraged as if she, too, doubted Him now.

But then another noise, besides the cries of the dying and the soft music of Yachne's voice, fell upon her ears. Someone was crying. She turned around, looking for the source of the noise. She found it. Adriel was silhouetted by the moonlight, sitting on a rock next to their animals. His face was buried in his arms, and he was sobbing.

Fear suddenly gripped Acenith's heart. Was he sick?

Oh no! Please, she begged, *take me, not him! His family needs him.*

Acenith found herself running towards him and climbing up on the rock to join him.

"Adriel, are you sick?" she gasped out, fear clutching her heart.

Adriel turned a tearful face to hers. "No… No. I'm just so upset with myself." He looked away. His body shook with silent sobs as he again hid his face from her. Acenith wrapped her arms around his shoulders, endeavoring to comfort him. Her cheek was pressed against his curly hair. She didn't know why he was upset at himself, and she didn't know what to say to comfort him or make him tell her. As Adriel's sobs began to quiet, he spoke.

"I shouldn't have allowed you to go, or gone with you. I've made Yahweh very angry. I deserve to die."

Acenith wrapped her arms even further around him, holding him tightly. "No, Adriel. It's my fault. I pressured you into going with me. I shouldn't have asked you to go, or asked to go, myself."

"But I'm the leader!" Adriel insisted, his voice fierce. "Ever since Father died, I'm in charge! I'm supposed to be leading everyone towards Yahweh! And—I haven't been able to do it. I've—I've failed." His voice trailed off into a whisper.

"No, Adriel, you haven't!" Acenith exclaimed, trying to encourage him.

"But Acenith, you don't believe in Yahweh," Adriel said, looking her squarely in the eyes. "Yael and Hava still don't seem to completely understand, and I know that Yael doubts because of how sickly he is."

"But my rejecting Yahweh isn't because of what you have or haven't told me," Acenith explained, trying not to let bitterness slide into her voice. "I don't believe in Him because of what He's done to me. To us," she added.

Adriel nodded and drew in a deep, shaky breath. "I know. I doubt sometimes, too…"

Acenith hugged him again and then moved back, looking at his face, hoping he wasn't upset at her.

"Are you angry with me?" she finally asked, hesitantly.

"Of course not!" Adriel exclaimed. "I'm actually beginning to understand more and more where you're coming from, Acenith. There's so much about Yahweh that I don't understand."

Acenith paused, thinking about what to say next. Her heart thrilled with a hope that Adriel understood her. She wondered what he was going to do from here. Was he really considering giving up his belief in Yahweh? She didn't know if she could ask him to do that.

But before she could say anything Adriel stated, emphatically, "I don't understand, but I'm going to keep doing what I can to learn more about Him. I was just thinking: if I knew everything about Yahweh, then He wouldn't be God. It means I would be God if I could understand Him. And I definitely don't want to be God. So I just have to continue to try to understand Him and trust Him."

Acenith sat back, nodding her head in resignation. If she was really, truly honest with herself, it was her desire to understand Yahweh better, too. But she couldn't bring herself to do it. Every time she did she learned more about Him that seemed to be hard and cruel.

Adriel voice broke through her reverie.

"Are you feeling all right? You're not getting sick, are you?" He sounded so concerned for her.

"No, I'm fine," Acenith assured him, quietly. She gave him a faint smile and said, "I don't think you're going to die. I don't know much about Yahweh, but He seems to honor hearts like yours—hearts that want to do right and want to know more."

Adriel grinned at her and reached out and squeezed her hand. His fingers were cold, but his touch was warm and kind. "Sometimes I don't know what I'd do without you, Acenith. You're such an encouragement to me, and mother. We're so glad you're here with us."

Tears sprang into Acenith's eyes. She choked back a sob before asking, "Really?"

Adriel smiled at her. "Yes, really."

Acenith suddenly realized that she *did* have a purpose. It was to help Adriel. He needed her. He wanted her to stay there and help him. She would do it, and gladly. She sat back on her heels on the rough rock, looking back up at the pillar of fire.

If it's all right, maybe… Don't take me yet? she silently spoke to the fire. *I'd like to stay here a little bit longer.*

ה

Three days passed. They hardly saw Father. No one knew where he went. He came back late at night and disappeared early in the morning. He had somehow avoided Grandfather and Jaden's attempts to talk to him. Jarah knew that something was very wrong. Eitan and Lemuel always seemed to be talking quietly together. Shay anxiously watched the tent flap as she tried to get Ximena to drink goat's milk.

But that wasn't the only thing wrong. Jarah knew that Yahweh was angry with the Israelites. Jarah sighed. Yahweh had every reason to be angry with them. He had every right to be angry at *her*. She had sinned. She shouldn't have gone anywhere near the golden calf and then given in to the temptation. If Ezra hadn't stopped her…

Ezra.

No, don't you even start to think about Ezra, she rebuked herself. She felt her cheeks coloring. Last night after dinner, he had come up to her, genuinely concerned about how she was doing. He had looked so worried and caring.

You need to stop thinking about him.

Suddenly Father stepped into the tent. Jarah gasped a little in surprise and delight.

"Father!" Shayna exclaimed. "Where have you been? We've been looking everywhere for you."

Father's eyes were glazed over. He started a little like he had just heard Shayna's voice and gazed at her, almost unseeing.

"I'm—I'm sorry, Shayna. I guess I was… preoccupied," he mumbled.

Eitan came through the tent flap, surprise and joy on his face.

"Father! I'm glad to see you," Eitan began, but Father interrupted him.

"I just came back for some food. I'm supposed to meet with Ennis soon. Shayna, do we have anything to eat?"

Tears pooled in Shayna's eyes as she took some manna from a basket and handed it to him. Eitan stood as if stunned, looking hurt and sad.

"Thank you," Father muttered. He turned on his heel to go, but Eitan grabbed his shoulder and held him back.

"Father, please." In vain, Eitan tried to blink back tears and stop his ice from trembling. "Father, we need you. We need your leadership, comfort. I'm not you. I can't lead this family. I can't be there for one and comfort them. I know you're hurting. I can't imagine in, and I won't pretend to. But we're still your family. You still Right now, we need you more than ever. Please—please come e our father once again, instead of a shadow of a man who to care," Eitan pleaded.

Father's eyes were fixed on the ground. Jarah found that she was holding her breath. She could tell that Eitan's plea had touched their father deeply. She stepped forward, timidly, and laid a hand on his arm.

"Father, please," she whispered, holding back a sob.

Father slowly raised his head and stared at her for what felt like a long time. He suddenly shook his arm away from Jarah's hand and moved to face Eitan.

"Eitan, you can't know my grief. But that's not it." Father took a deep breath and straightened, a hardened look coming into his eyes.

"I'm not the father I used to be, Eitan. You know that. Ever since we left Egypt I haven't been able to lead. Your mother grated on me. She made me irritable, frustrated. She was never content or happy with whatever I did for her. I tried to put distance between us, but then Jaden told me I wasn't being a good husband or father. So I came back. But your mother kept putting demands on me. I realized I wasn't providing well for her, or anyone else. That's when… the whole issue happened with Moses. And I tried to change! I did! But nothing I did was good enough for her. And in the end, I've failed her. I didn't protect her. I didn't give her the food and care she needed to get well." He was crying now, but it wasn't because he was sad. It was because he was angry.

"Father, you can't blame yourself for that. Many others died the night after the golden calf was destroyed. Moses said it was a plague from Yahweh to destroy those who were unrepentant. You had nothing to do with that," Eitan urged.

"But Eitan, it's not just that. Everything I've touched or tried to fix on this trip has crumbled in my fingers: my relationship with your mother, my relationship with you all, my relationship with Yahweh. We never seem to have enough water, or food. I've failed at providing for you all. I can't be in leadership anymore. I've messed up too many things."

"No, Father!" Eitan exclaimed. "That's not true!"

"You tell me one thing I haven't destroyed or made worse, Eit One thing!" Father roared. Eitan took a step back, startled and prised. He opened his mouth to speak, but then mechanicall it again.

"Nothing," Father said despairingly. "There's nothing I've done right since we've left, Eitan. Nothing."

"But Father, that can change," Eitan persisted. "You haven't failed completely. We still want you here. We still need you. Please, Father, focus on deepening your relationship with Yahweh and with us. You can become a godly leader again. You can become a good father again."

"But I'll never be a good husband again," Father said as if he was talking to himself.

Eitan paused, carefully choosing his words. "It's not too late, Father. Grandfather and Jaden will help you. I'll help you. Please, just let us."

Father shook his head. "I need time, Eitan. I need time away." He strode towards the door.

"Where are you going?" Eitan called after him.

"To see Ennis!"

"Ennis won't help you now, Father," Eitan yelled. But Father was already gone.

Eitan lowered his head and wiped away his tears. His body was shaking with sobs that he was trying to stifle. Jarah ran to him and threw her arms around his waist. He held her close. Jarah could hear that Shayna was crying, too.

Yahweh, please. You have to help us now, Jarah pleaded.

א

Ezra saw Asher storm from the tent and disappear into the camp. He knew at a glance that something was wrong. He considered pursuing him, but quickly changed his mind. He needed to tell father that he had actually seen Asher. He hadn't been around three days. He wished there was something he could do besides tittle-tale. He sighed deeply. If only he could help their family.

ꞇ

It was late evening. Ezra and his father were covering the coals of their fire with sand in an attempt to keep them alive until morning. Ezra was startled to see a shadow creeping around their tent.

"Father." He motioned towards the shadow. It was Asher.

"Asher!" Father called.

Asher froze, almost in mid-step.

"I'm sorry. I didn't realize anyone was still awake," Asher mumbled.

Father stepped up to Asher and put a firm, yet reassuring hand on his shoulder. "What's going on, my friend? You haven't been around much at all. Your family needs you. We're all worried about you."

"I'm fine," Asher said, fiercely. Father was a little taken aback.

"Asher, that very response shows me that you're *not* fine."

"Look, Jaden," Asher growled, "I don't need your help. I can do this myself. I just need some time away to think through things. I have to be able to come back and be the provider and protector that I used to be. Right now, everything I touch breaks or falls apart. Really, they're better off without me."

Asher moved as if to go, but Father held him fast. "Asher, every family needs their father. They're not better off without you. You're straying from Yahweh and His plan for what a man close to His heart should be."

"I don't need you to lecture me, Jaden," Asher said, annoyed. "I know what I have to do. I know all that you're going to say. I just need time alone to think through everything and grieve."

Father stared into Asher's eyes. Asher uncomfortably looked away.

"What are you really doing, Asher?" Father said, slowly and directly.

Asher shrugged Father's hand from his shoulder. "Nothing that concerns you. I've been spending time with friends. They're helping me forget… Helping me get over it."

"Asher, you need to stop right now. Sin can't bring peace and joy back to your heart. Only Yahweh can do that. You need to change your perspective and come back home—come back to Him."

Asher glared. "Change. I already told you, I *can't* change. Not now, anyways. I need time away to think."

Father shook his head. "The longer you put it off, the harder it will be to change your habits and actions. Don't wait, Asher. Change right now. Don't wait."

"I can't! I've tried!" Asher exclaimed in exasperation.

"That's the problem, Asher. You're trying too hard. Cry out to Yahweh and ask Him to be your strength, comfort, and help."

"But I don't want to, and I don't really know how," Asher persisted.

"Then let us help you. Your father and I are here, ready and waiting to point you back to Yahweh," Father pleaded.

There was a long pause. Ezra's heart was pounding. *Please say yes, Asher. Please say yes,* he begged.

Asher finally met his father's eyes.

"I can't," he stated simply. Then he turned and walked away into the blackness.

Ezra bit his lip. He walked over to his father and laid a hand on his shoulder. His father exhaled deeply. He looked Ezra in the eyes.

"We need to pray even harder," he said. "Only Yahweh can soften his heart now."

ת

Jarah and Tirzah were making stew the next afternoon. Jarah saw Grandfather walking towards them. He looked very distraught. Lemuel hurried towards him. The bucket of water that he was carrying sloshed around.

"What's the matter, Grandfather?"

"Yahweh's very angry with us, Lemuel," Grandfather sighed. "I just came from a meeting with Moses. He said that Yahweh is almost ready to desert us! Unless we turn our hearts completely towards Yahweh, He won't lead us to the Promised Land and His blessing won't be upon us."

"That's terrible," Lemuel exclaimed, his eyes wide. "What are we going to do?"

270

"The only thing we can do. Examine ourselves and pray that Yahweh will break our stubborn, willful spirits. Tomorrow morning we will worship the Lord."

Jarah nodded. She had been convicted in her heart over the last few days that she was very bitter inside about the death of her mother. She was angry and bitter towards Yahweh for the suffering He had brought to her. But didn't she deserve it? Hadn't she, too, disobeyed Yahweh's commands and gone to see the golden calf? She had almost given into temptation then. Jarah realized that she had to repent of her sins, too, and believe that Yahweh's will was best.

But it seems so hard, Jarah moaned. She turned back to her stew but tears ran down her cheeks and obscured her vision. Could she really surrender *everything* to Yahweh? Her life, her dreams, her hopes? Even her family and her little baby sister?

I will try, she vowed. *I will try to surrender, no matter what.*

ט

J arah was startled from a deep sleep. A trumpet was blowing loudly. Several others joined the first trumpet and their calls echoed around the camp. Jarah rubbed her eyes. It was still very dim outside. What time was it?

"Everyone must go outside, quickly," she heard Eitan urge.

Jarah nodded, realizing what was happening. They were supposed to go and worship Yahweh. She rose to her feet, yawning, and grabbed the half-asleep Yanni from his bed. Shayna lifted Ximena up and held her close. Lemuel was herding Raphael and Tirzah towards the tent flap. Jarah suddenly saw that their father was there, sleeping on his mat in the corner. Eitan was shaking him and telling him to get up. He was grumbling and complaining, but he was getting up and going with them.

Everyone hurried outside the tent. In the early morning light, they fixed their eyes on Moses, who was ascending a large hill nearby on which the tent of meeting, a place of worship to Yahweh, had been erected.

As Moses entered the tent, the pillar of cloud descended down upon it with a sound like a whirlwind. Yahweh was talking to Moses. Everybody instantly knelt on the sand, praying silently for Yahweh's blessing and forgiveness. Jarah poured out her heart, confessing all of her sins, her hurt feelings, and her bitterness towards Yahweh. Her hot tears fell fast onto the ground.

Yahweh, please forgive me. Please take over my life. Free me from my anger and bitterness. I don't want to be mad at You. I don't! I want to love You no matter what. I want to follow You no matter what. Please help me do that. And please... please forgive me.

Jarah heard sobs next to her. Shayna was rocking back and forth, holding Ximena who was whimpering. Her lips were moving in fervent, yet silent prayer. A little thrill ran down Jarah's spine. Her sister was praying to Yahweh. She was changing. Jarah knew it.

Lemuel and Eitan had their foreheads touching the sand in absolute prostration and dependence. Then Jarah saw her father.

He was on his knees, but his head wasn't bowed in worship or prayer. He stared, unseeing, into the distance. His face was hard, cold, and immovable. Jarah's heart sank.

Yahweh, my father needs to repent. He needs to ask forgiveness for the way he treated my mother, for going to worship the idol, and for those things he stole a long time ago. I think he's become calloused towards You and Your commands. He's trying to hide his guilt, his fear, and his grief, and in doing that he's hiding from you. Please reveal Yourself to him. Soften his heart.

Yahweh... I want my father back.

Jarah looked away. She tried to stifle her sobs, but she couldn't. More tears filled her eyes. She bowed her head, wanting so desperately to stop crying. But she couldn't stop thinking, *I want my father back. I just want my father back.*

After what felt like an eternity, the cloud lifted from the tent of meeting and Moses appeared at the entrance.

"Today, I go back up Mount Sinai to once again receive the law from the Lord. I will be gone for quite some time. Each one of you, listen to Yahweh's commands and obey His voice until I return." Moses then reentered the tent and disappeared from sight.

"Moses is going away again?" Tirzah whispered, a little fearfully.

272

"Yes," Eitan murmured.

"But what if something happens again, like last time?" Tirzah pressed.

Eitan shrugged and shook his head. "I don't know." There was a long pause. Eitan took a deep breath and looked at their father. He still appeared to be in a daze.

"Father, would you lead us in prayer?" he asked, hopefully.

Father jumped a little. "Uh… No, son. Why don't you lead us?"

Eitan bit his lip. It looked like he wanted to say something. But instead he sighed and assented. "Yes, Father." He bowed his head. "Yahweh, we pray that You would be strengthening our faith. Please show us the path to take. Please be our comfort, our guide, our heavenly Father. We ask that You would keep us from stumbling, that we would obey all of Your commands, and be drawn closer to You through Your commands. We also pray for our nation, that they would repent and truly seek to do Your will and worship only You. Please protect us, every single one of us. Amen."

The little family remained kneeling on the ground for several long minutes before Shayna finally broke the silence. "It's getting late. We should have breakfast."

"Yes, of course." Eitan rose to his feet.

"Eitan," Father said, "I'll be out for most of the day. I'm going to see my father for a while."

"Very well," Eitan said, smiling a little. "Thank you for telling me."

He's going to see Grandfather, Jarah thought in delight. *Maybe his heart is softening. Maybe Grandfather can help bring him back!* She smiled as she went with Shayna to collect manna. Looking back over her shoulder, she saw the children gathered around the fire pit, and Father was with them. She sighed a little. *Everything will be all right now.*

❧

A sher ate his manna slowly, watching as the rest of the family slowly dispersed and went about their jobs for the day. Lemuel went to tend to the animals. Eitan was rummaging through supplies in their wagon, seeing how much quail meat they had left. Shayna was

273

in the tent trying to get Ximena to eat. Asher was glad they were out of his sight. He loathed the thought of his little daughter. He felt that her birth had caused Mariel to be taken from him. Angry tears came to his eyes, but he forced them back. No, he was just going to keep distancing himself until he got over this and stopped making everything worse for his family.

Jarah was milking their goat over by a small bush. Tirzah, Raphael, and Yanni came out of the tent carrying baskets. They were going to find leftover manna.

"Good-bye, Father! Have a good talk with Grandfather," Tirzah said, skipping over to him and hugging him. Asher put his arm around her. A feeling of tenderness crept into his heart. He swallowed the lump in his throat and pushed the feeling from him.

"Good-bye, Tirzah," he said, as coldly as he could muster.

The little girl looked at him, her amber eyes round and sad. The look wrenched his heart. She quickly brushed away a tear and ran off towards the camp. The boys followed her, looking bewildered. Asher shook his head. He stood up to go, steeling himself. He wasn't going to feel tenderness, or love. Tenderness and love had ended up hurting him more than he could've ever imagined. No. There was no place for love in his heart.

Asher started to walk towards his father's tent. When he was a few steps away, he looked behind him. No one was watching him. Asher quickly bolted behind a tent and ran off in another direction. He chuckled to himself. Asher wasn't going to see his father. His father would say things that he didn't want to hear. No, he was going to see Ennis and see if he could do better today than yesterday.

ב

Jarah was walking a little lighter this morning. She was smiling and humming. Her father had seemed better this morning. He was going to talk with Grandfather. Things would get better. They had to! She collected up their bowls from breakfast in a large basket and started to head towards a nearby spring to wash them.

"Jarah! Wait up!" Jarah turned to see Amissa and Reia running after her, both holding baskets full of their own dishes. Jarah greeted them warmly and smiled.

"May we join you?" Amissa asked, smiling in return.

Jarah made a straight face and promptly replied, "No."

Reia and Amissa stopped in mid-step, staring at her. Jarah grinned and started to giggle. "I'm just teasing! Of course you can come with me!"

Amissa and Reia laughed in relief. "For a moment we thought you were serious!" Amissa gasped out between her giggles.

"You must be in a good mood this morning," Reia commented, composing herself.

"I am," Jarah said as the girls headed towards the spring. "Father seemed better this morning. He's going to talk to Grandfather today. I know that Grandfather will help him."

"That's wonderful!" Amissa encouraged. "I've been praying so hard for him, and for you."

"Thank you." Jarah grinned. "It's working! Yahweh is listening!"

"When do you think that Moses will come back?" Reia asked, turning to the other most pressing question at hand.

"How long was he gone last time?" Jarah wondered. Her life had been one big blur recently and it was hard to keep anything straight.

"I think forty days," Amissa told them. "So maybe it'll be forty days this time, too."

Jarah nodded.

"How's Ada?" Amissa queried. "I haven't seen her for a few days."

Jarah noticed a hint of sadness in Amissa's eyes. "Do you miss Ada?"

Amissa colored a little bit and looked down. "Yes. She's still around, but it's not the same."

The girls reached the spring and put down their baskets before Jarah put a kind hand on her friend's shoulder and said, "I'm sorry."

"No. It's fine. It's better this way, for your family at least, and Father has time to give us children more attention now, too." Amissa smiled.

"Well, I think Ada's fine. Raphael, Yanni, and Ximena really make her tired, though. She's not used to adoring little boys begging her for food and love and attention. Yanni doesn't give her a moment's rest!"

Amissa snickered. "I can see that."

The girls continued to wash their dishes, chatting together. Jarah suddenly felt cold water splash all over her. She gasped, shocked by the cold rush. Amissa and Reia burst into peals of laughter.

"Amissa!" Jarah squealed, brushing the water from her face.

Amissa was holding her stomach, laughing hard. "Just trying to see if I could dampen your spirits!" she joked.

"Not funny!" Jarah exclaimed, scooping up water in her hands and throwing it into her friend's face.

As Amissa sputtered, Reia called, "Jarah!" Jarah turned to look at her shy cousin and saw that Reia was standing in the spring and was now kicking water onto her dress.

"Reia! Stop!" Jarah leapt to her feet, now thoroughly soaked. By now Amissa was splashing her, too, and Jarah laughed and joined in the fun. The other people at the spring looked on, smiling. Some of the girls started splashing their own friends. Mothers and grandmothers shook their heads to hide their smiles. But Jarah, Reia, and Amissa didn't care as they laughed and played and felt the worries of the world slide from their shoulders as they were covered in cold, clear water.

ל

Ezra, sitting and guarding his herd of animals, saw the girls in the distance and couldn't help but smile. He loved seeing his sister and Jarah having some fun. Seeing a smile on Jarah's face warmed his heart. He knew that she was having such a hard time, and was glad to see the cloud of sorrow lifted from her face, if just for a little while.

He was startled by a little voice calling, "Lemuel! Lemuel!" Looking down from his perch, he saw Tirzah running around, calling for her brother.

"Good morning, Tirzah!" he shouted to her. Tirzah squinted up at him and waved.

"Shalom, Ezra! Where's Lemuel? Eitan told me to find him."

"I don't know. I haven't seen him this morning."

Tirzah crossed her arms and stood there, thinking hard. "But Eitan said that he was with the animals."

"Sorry. I haven't seen him."

Tirzah sighed and walked over to him, as if determined to wait with Ezra until her brother appeared. A sudden splash and scream made both of them jump. Ezra saw that Jarah had slipped and fallen into the spring. Amissa and Reia were pulling her up, the girls all chortling and screaming with glee and the cold temperature of the water. Ezra smiled. He heard Tirzah giggling.

"What are you looking at, Ezra?" she asked in a teasing, sing-song way.

"The girls playing in the water," he replied, looking down at her.

"Well, then, which *one* were you looking at?" she pried.

"What do you mean?" he asked, smiling a little.

Tirzah was giggling. "You were staring at Jarah."

Ezra felt the hair on the back of his neck began to prickle. "No, I wasn't," he said defensively.

"Yes, you were."

"No, I wasn't."

"Yes, you were!"

"Just because she fell down in the water and I wanted to make sure she was all right."

Tirzah crossed her arms across her chest and gave him a knowing look. "Uh-huh."

"Tirzah, it's not like that," Ezra started, but Tirzah interrupted him.

"I know you like her. All of us girls do!"

"What?" Ezra exclaimed.

"Yes! And—" Tirzah suddenly stopped short and hung her head, embarrassed. Looking about quickly, Ezra saw with relief that Lemuel was standing in the shade of the rock, glaring at Tirzah.

"Tirzah, that's enough," he said in a kind, yet forceful way. "Eitan and I have talked to you about this. You promised to repent and do better. Are you listening to us and obeying Yahweh's commands?"

Tirzah slowly nodded her head and murmured, "No."

Lemuel sighed in exasperation. "Go find Eitan. I'll be right there to talk to both of you."

Tirzah raised a disappointed face to meet her brother's gaze. "But Eitan told me to come get you!"

"Then tell Eitan I'll be right there." Tirzah's shoulders drooped and she walked slowly back towards the tents. Lemuel shook his head and climbed up next to Ezra.

"I came in right at the end of that conversation, so I don't know who she was teasing you about, but I'm sorry about that. Eitan and I have been talking to her a lot about her fascination with romance and with teasing people and prying into secret matters, and it just hasn't sunk in yet, as you very well know." He sighed a little as he watched Tirzah's sad form.

Ezra cleared his throat, awkwardly. "It's fine. I'll just tell her to be quiet next time."

Lemuel grinned. "I hope she listens. It's hard to get that one to stop talking." He clapped a hand on Ezra's shoulder. "I'll be back soon and give you a break."

"I'm all right. No hurry," Ezra said, graciously.

"Thanks." Lemuel leapt off the rock and raced to catch up to his little sister. Ezra smiled slightly as he watched the two of them walking back to camp.

"That girl," he muttered, shaking his head slowly from side to side. "She's trouble. Good thing she was teasing me and not someone else who would actually get upset." However, a concerning thought slowly formed in his mind.

"But she did say that 'All of us girls know that you like Jarah,'" he thought out loud. "Am I really acting like...? No. I'm sure everything's fine. Tirzah's always prone to exaggeration and gossip. I'm sure she didn't really mean it."

Feeling a little relieved, he faced the herd again and swiftly counted to make sure that none of them had slipped away in the confusion. Content that all the animals were still accounted for, he relaxed and turned his gaze towards the three older girls, who were packing up their dishes and sloshing back towards camp, their wet hair and the hems of their dresses dripping water. He grinned, getting great enjoyment out of watching them and knowing that they were having fun together.

מ

It was two days later as their little family sat around the fire pit eating manna. Jarah could hardly taste it today. Father was here this morning, but he was upset and irritable.

"Father? How did your talk with Grandfather go the other day?" Lemuel asked.

Father looked up questioningly. "With my father?"

"Didn't you go see him two days ago?"

"Oh! Umm… Yes. I did. But your grandfather was occupied and we weren't able to talk," Father said.

"You should try again," Lemuel suggested.

"I'll see…"

"Or talk to Jaden. Jaden was asking for you yesterday," Lemuel pressed.

Father glared at his son.

"I'll see, Lemuel, but I'm perfectly capable of managing myself," he said, sternly.

"Oh. Yes, sir. I'm… sorry." Lemuel glanced helplessly at his older brother.

"Father, did something happen to you?" Eitan questioned, cautiously.

Father shook his head, a dark scowl on his face. "Just some trouble with a friend, Eitan. I can handle it."

"Is there something we can do for you?" Eitan asked, trying to be respectful.

At this moment, Ximena started crying. Shayna held her close, quietly humming. There was a short pause before Father suddenly exploded.

"Yes! Yes, there is something you can do," he exclaimed, jumping to his feet. "You can get her to stop crying!"

Tirzah gave a little scream and inched closer to Lemuel. Lemuel put one arm around her and the other around Jarah. Yanni climbed into Jarah's lap, sucking his thumb. Raphael, Eitan, Ada, and Shayna sat still as if frozen. Their father's face was red with anger and he was staring darkly at little Ximena.

"Father," Eitan soothed, "we're trying the best we can. She's weak and sickly, and—"

"That's not enough, Eitan!" Father roared. "Every time I see that baby I can't help but remember she caused my wife's death. I don't want to hear her. I don't want to see her! I wish she had never existed!"

Jarah gasped. Lemuel held her closer. Eitan rose to his feet.

"Father, I know you don't mean that," he began.

"I most certainly do," Father stated emphatically. "If you want me around, Eitan, you need to make her be quiet and keep her out of my sight, or pray that she'll go ahead and die."

"No!" Tirzah cried. She hid her face against Lemuel, wailing.

"Father," Eitan said, low and dangerous, "We're not going to pray for Ximena to die, or just let her die, either. I don't know what's gotten into you."

"It's her, Eitan! Not me!" Father accused, pointing a shaking finger at the little baby. Shayna scooted herself backwards and away from her father.

"Father," Eitan began, his voice getting a little louder, "it's not Ximena's fault that Mother is dead. Mother didn't repent after she worshipped that idol. She was struck down by Yahweh because of her sin. Ximena had nothing to do with it."

"But she was sick and dying even before she went to see the golden calf, Eitan," Father argued. "You know that. I'm telling you, it's her fault!"

"No, it's not!" Eitan told him, taking a step forwards.

"Then whose fault is it? Yahweh's? Fine then. If it's His fault, then I want nothing to do with Him! Nothing! Do you hear me, Eitan?" Father was yelling. He suddenly raised his hand and slapped Eitan across the face. Jarah screamed. Eitan staggered backwards, barely catching himself against their wagon. Lemuel leapt to his feet and rushed to his brother's aide.

"Asher! Asher!" Ezra raced towards them, his face pale. He planted himself directly in between Eitan and their father.

"What are you thinking? What are you doing?" Ezra blurted.

"It's none of your business, Ezra," Father growled, darkly.

"Yes, sir, I'm afraid it is. I'm not just going to stand by and let you hurt your own children. Don't you see what's happened to you? Don't you see who and what you've become?" Ezra demanded.

For a moment, Father didn't move. He simply looked at Ezra. Jarah saw a flicker of doubt and sorrow cross his face. Tears trembled in his eyes. He suddenly swung around and ran towards the desert. Ezra moved as if to follow him, but Eitan stopped him.

"No, Ezra," Eitan commanded as Lemuel helped him stand up. "There's nothing we can do for him right now but pray," he finished. Eitan's nose was bleeding, and the blood was smeared across his face.

"Tirzah, run and get some cloth," Lemuel told her. Tirzah tremblingly obeyed.

"Are you all right?" Ezra asked in concern.

Eitan nodded and swallowed hard. "I think I'll be fine. I just—I never thought my own father would hit me like that." He looked at Ezra with hollow, pleading eyes. Ezra put a hand on his shoulder.

"I'm so sorry," he sympathized. "I can't imagine."

Tirzah was back with the cloth. Eitan pressed it to his nose.

"Eitan," Jarah ventured to ask, "did he really mean that? All that he said?" She blinked back tears. Her heart was pounding in her chest.

All eyes were glued to Eitan as he slowly lifted his head to look at them.

"I don't know," he finally whispered. "I don't know."

ל

It was late afternoon. Jarah was trying to mend the little boys' tunics. They were both outgrowing their old clothes. Shayna was weaving some cloth. The *clack, clack, clack* of the loom reminded Jarah of old times and soothed her troubled soul. Ximena was sleeping peacefully in a cradle at Jarah's feet. Jarah was happy to see that there was a little color in her thin cheeks today. Her fingers weren't looking so scrawny. She was slowly gaining weight.

How could Father have ever wanted her to die? she thought remorsefully. *I'm sure he mustn't have meant it. He couldn't have meant it.*

The tent flap opened. Jarah glanced up, expecting to see Eitan. Instead, she saw her father. At first she felt joy. But then she felt fear. Was he still angry? What did he want?

"Shayna, where's Eitan?" Father asked.

"I believe he's out with the animals. One of the goats was about to give birth," Shayna explained. "Do you want me to go get him?"

"No. No, it's quite all right." Father hesitated, trying to decide whether or not to leave. "Shayna," he finally said, "I need to apologize to you, and Jarah, and everyone, really. I haven't been myself, but that doesn't mean that I shouldn't be around to help you. I know I've been a burden to you all, and I'm going to change. I promise I am."

Shayna didn't know what to say. There were tears on her cheeks as she replied, "Thank you, Father. We—we forgive you."

"Can I do anything to help?" Father asked.

"Well, Eitan said that the spokes are loose on some of the wagon wheels. He was going to try to fix it a few days ago, but he hasn't had time since he's getting ready for the wedding. Maybe you could help with that."

"I will," Father assented. He looked at Jarah and smiled. It was a small smile, and there was still a dark look in her father's eyes, but at least he was smiling. Jarah tried to smile back. Her father moved to the tent flap.

"Father," Jarah called after him. He turned to face her. "I—I forgive you, too," she said, quietly. Father's smile got a little bigger. He left the tent.

He's coming back. Father's back. Jarah sighed in contentment. He was taking steps in the right direction. Ximena opened her eyes and looked up at Jarah, cooing. Jarah gently rocked the little cradle, singing softly:

"Night, night, the wind grows strong,
Night, night, the trees rustle,
Night, night, a star is singing,
Go to sleep, blow out the candle."

All of a sudden, a *crash* sounded from outside. Shayna and Jarah leapt to their feet and rushed out of the tent. One of the wagon wheels had come off and lay, shattered, on the ground. The wagon seat had cracked in two and the whole wagon had toppled over. And their father was pinned underneath!

"Eitan! Lemuel!" Jarah shrieked. She and Shayna strived in vain to pick up the wagon. Ezra suddenly appeared by Jarah's side.

"Here, let me help!"

Together they lifted the wagon and their father rolled out from underneath it. Eitan and Lemuel dashed up, both very alarmed.

"Father, are you all right? What happened?"

"No, I'm not all right," Father snapped.

Eitan and Lemuel helped him to his feet as Shayna asked, "Are you hurt?"

"No. This is exactly why I shouldn't be here," Father yelled.

"What do you mean?" Eitan pressed.

"I mean that everything I touch gets ruined, Eitan! Everything! I can't try to fix something without making it worse. I can't be around you all without getting angry or upset. I can't lead because... You're better off without me."

"No, Father! We still need you! We want you!" Lemuel pleaded.

"You want things to be worse? No, Lemuel. I can't do that. I can't." Father spun around on his heel and disappeared into the people and tents, leaving his four children standing bewildered, shocked, and sad by the broken wagon.

Asher sat next to the glowing embers of their dying fire. It was very late. No one was stirring. The distant roar from the pillar of fire was the only sound in the still night.

"Asher?"

Asher started. "Yes?" The figure of his father emerged from the dark.

"Eitan told me what happened today. Are you all right?"

"Of course," he snapped.

His father sat down besides him. "Asher, you made steps in the right direction. You apologized. You tried to make things right. Why do you keep backtracking on any progress you've made?"

"Because I keep failing," Asher said, bitterly. "I wasn't a good husband to my wife. I didn't provide enough food for my family. I've failed you as a son, and Jaden and Daton as a friend. My children are afraid of me and don't want me around."

"But they do," his father said, gently. "No one should be without the presence of a Godly father."

Asher opened his mouth and then closed it again. He took a deep breath before admitting, "But I'm not a Godly father." He sighed. "I've failed in that area, too."

"No, you haven't, Asher," his father stated. "You haven't. Look at your children. Right now they are all following Yahweh. They are stronger in their faith and their love for Him than they have ever been before. Mariel didn't give them that desire or that passion. You did."

"But right now, I don't want to follow Yahweh or believe in Him," Asher protested.

"Why do you say that, my son?" his father asked, bewildered and surprised. "For years you've stood firm in your beliefs. You helped your children learn about Yahweh and know who He really is. And somehow, you were still able to love Mariel and not adopt her beliefs. I admire you for that. I know you're hurting. I know how much you did love her, even though you didn't always get along. I told you from the beginning that it was not advisable for you to marry, but you loved her so much and you've stayed strong in your faith. That is, until now." He paused. Asher hung his head.

"Examine your heart, my son." His father sounded so sad. "Yahweh's right there, waiting for you to come back to Him." He motioned towards the pillar of fire.

"If He wants me, then why did He take my wife away?" Asher suddenly cried, leaping to his feet. "Answer me that, Father!"

His father just looked at him, seemingly helpless. "I don't know the exact reason, son, but—"

"Of course you don't. That's because there *is* no reason. I used to think Yahweh was merciful, but I realize that His cruelty wasn't just towards the Egyptians. It's now been turned towards me. Wait until you experience loss and you'll know what it feels like," Asher spat.

He ran off into the night. His father hung his head and spoke, in a low tone, as if to his departing son.

"Asher, what you don't realize is that without trials we'll never really know Yahweh's mercy, love, tenderness, or His plan. If everything were perfect, we would never need Him. We would never learn to live in His strength or to experience His love and joy. These things were brought to test your faith, Asher. And you're failing the test miserably."

"I WANT FATHER BACK"

Jarah couldn't go to sleep. Four days had passed since the incident with the wagon. Lemuel and Eitan had almost finished repairing it. But something was obviously not right. Father was gone almost every day and didn't come back until very late at night. Eitan and Shayna always looked anxious. The tent flap stirred. Jarah quickly sat up. Her father crept into the tent.

"Father?" she whispered. Her father froze in mid-step. "Is everything all right?"

"Yes. Everything's fine. Go to sleep," he ordered.

"Yes, sir," Jarah replied, softly. She lay down, tears on her cheeks.

He's not loving and kind like he used to be, she gulped and tried to still her sobs. *Yahweh, I want my father back. I know You're my heavenly Father, but I can't feel You here right now. Please, give us our father back.*

א

Ezra was returning from the spring with another load of water for his family and Jarah's family. It was the afternoon of Ada's wedding. Everyone was washing clothes and trying to get themselves cleaned up for such a special occasion. He was nearing their tents when he saw Asher striding through the camp. Ezra set down the jugs and ran after him, weaving in and out of people and tents.

"Asher!" he called. Asher stopped and turned to face him.

"My father's been looking for you. Can you come back with me? We haven't seen you in days, and we've had several questions about the wedding this afternoon."

"It's this afternoon?" Asher exclaimed.

"Yes, sir. Did you not know?" Ezra asked.

"I—I'll have to come back later. I have a commitment, and—"

"A commitment more important than you oldest son's wedding?" Ezra scoffed, incredulous. Then he stopped himself. "I'm sorry, sir. That wasn't respectful. Please forgive me."

"Of course," Asher muttered, looking distressed.

"Please come with me. My father really needs to talk to you," Ezra said, pleading with him.

Asher exhaled slowly and reluctantly assented. "Very well. Take me to your father."

"Yes sir," Ezra said. He couldn't hide his joy.

Father will help him, he thought. *Father will help all of them.*

ב

Asher followed Ezra, scowling. How could he have forgotten that today was Eitan's wedding? He was in serious trouble. Ennis was waiting for him—and that payment. But if he didn't make an effort to be at his son's wedding he'd be letting his whole family down—again.

And now, thanks to Ezra, I have to listen to another lecture from Jaden. He angrily kicked at a stone.

"Asher! Thank goodness! We've been looking everywhere for you." Jaden came forward, slapping Asher heartily on the back. "Isn't it a glorious day?" he continued.

"Oh. Yes. Of course," Asher replied, trying to be jovial.

"Asher, I've wanted to talk to you about Ada's dowry. I have almost everything settled with Eitan, but I also wanted to include two ewes and a ram from our flock to help Eitan start his own herd. I wanted you to examine the animals with me and take your pick of which animals would be suitable to add to your flock."

"That's a very gracious gift, Jaden," Asher stated, eyes wide.

"We've been very blessed this year," Jaden said, smiling. "Our sheep and goats have multiplied quickly, and Yahweh has provided so much food that we haven't had to kill any of our own animals to eat. I know your flock has suffered over the last few months. It's the least I can do."

"Suffered because of me, you mean," Asher mumbled under his breath.

"What's that?"

"Nothing." Asher turned towards the outskirts of the camp. "Shall we go?"

"Yes. Of course. We only have two hours before the ceremony."

"Two hours…" Asher mused.

"Is something wrong, my friend?" Jaden asked in concern.

"Oh. Umm, no. Nothing's wrong. I just—I got my days mixed up and I have a friend I'm supposed to see. I was trying to figure out if I could see him before the ceremony. But he'll just have to wait, I suppose." Asher forced a grin at Jaden. But Jaden wasn't smiling anymore. He looked upset.

"Asher, who have you been spending time with?" he abruptly asked.

"I've told you, and Father, too. I've been spending time with Ennis," Asher said in exasperation.

"And haven't we both told you that it's unwise to be spending time with him?" Jaden demanded.

Asher felt anger welling up in his chest. "So you've said many times. But I told you—and Father just three days ago—he's helping me. He's helping me forget and move on."

"Is *he* what's really helping, or is there some *thing* that's really helping?" Jaden pressed.

"What are you talking about?"

Jaden sighed. "Asher, you're not happy. You've had a dark, angry spirit resting on you for the past few weeks. You've never been an angry man until the last few months. You're trying to hide something, I know it. You've tried to hide sin before, and it doesn't work. Now, what are you doing?" Jaden was close to Asher now, staring him straight in the face. Asher looked away, uncomfortably.

"I've told you the truth. I've been spending time with Ennis and some of his friends. Ennis is a carpenter. He fixes wagons and other things."

"But is that what you do when you're with them?" Jaden questioned, his voice growing louder.

Asher could no longer hold back his frustration.

"Listen to me, Jaden," he yelled, "you keep your nose where it belongs, and that's out of my business! I'm not a child. I didn't ask for your help, or Father's. I'm more than capable of getting through this by myself. From now on, I want both of you to leave me alone!"

Asher spun around and stomped away leaving Jaden alone, shaking his head.

"Be sure your sin will find you out, Asher!" he called after his friend.

But Asher didn't respond. He just turned his back and continued to walk away.

א

It was now twilight. Torches were lit and staked to the ground. The stars and the moon were coming out and casting their light onto the white canopy under which Eitan and Ada would be wed. The canopy under the stars was to ask Yahweh's blessing upon them and remember His promise to their father, Abraham, that the Israelites would number as many as the stars in the sky.

Jarah stood, surrounded by her siblings, watching Eitan's face as Ada was brought towards him by her father and mother. Once again, Ada was dressed beautifully. Her face was serene and happy. Eitan looked straight into her eyes. From the huge smile on Eitan's face, Jarah knew that he was bursting with joy.

Grandfather stood by Eitan as Sanne walked Ada seven times around Eitan, symbolizing the fact that Ada, as the new wife, would be a protective and loving light in their new household. Ada then stood next to Eitan, smiling up into his face.

Grandfather said, "Now, as you begin this life together, let the heads of the households come forward and pray for this young couple." Jaden and Uncle Daton stepped forward, followed by her father. Jarah could tell that something wasn't right with her father. He seemed troubled, not joyful and excited like everyone else. It was like a cloud was resting on him. Jarah bowed her head as her grandfather prayed.

"Yahweh, we're thankful for this pure love between Eitan and Ada. We thank You for the young man and the young woman they have grown up to be. We thank You that they are rooted in You and Your laws and words. We ask, Yahweh, that You bless this new union with joy, that they would never grow tired in their love for one another, that they would always serve each other selflessly, and that they always find delight in one anothers' company."

"Yahweh," Uncle Daton began, "rain down Your blessings on this faithful young man and young woman. May You be always first in their hearts and minds. Grant them wisdom that they may always discern Your voice."

Father cleared his throat. "Please give them strength, Yahweh, for whatever lies ahead for both of them." His voice sounded husky, as if he was holding back his emotion.

"And Yahweh," Jaden began, "let them have faith and trust in Your perfect plan. Let them be devoted to one another. Give Eitan the courage to lead, and the courage to love. Give Ada the same respect and submission for her husband as she has given to me. I—" Jaden suddenly stopped.

Jarah peered at him out of the corner of her eye. He was crying.

"I'm going to miss her presence in my home very much, Yahweh," Jaden finally admitted. His voice was shaking. He wiped away a tear before continuing. "But Yahweh, You've prepared her for this. She and Eitan need each other in order to be complete, in order to serve You to the utmost. We pray Your blessings over them. Amen."

"Amen," everyone assembled echoed.

Grandfather presented Eitan with a glass cup filled with wine. He prayed a blessing over it and then said, "Drink, Eitan, and then present the cup to your wife."

Eitan raised the cup to his lips and drank and then passed the cup to Ada, who drank the rest of the wine. Grandfather handed Eitan the plain gold ring that had belonged to their mother. Jarah noticed that Father looked away as Eitan put the ring on Ada's finger, saying, "Behold, you are sanctified to me with this ring."

Finally, Grandfather took the wine glass and laid it on the ground next to Eitan's feet, draping a rag over it. Eitan stepped on the glass, breaking it. Everyone cheered and applauded. Jarah found that she was both laughing and crying at the same time.

Eitan and Ada were now married.

א

The next week went by in a blur. Shayna and Ada finished constructing a small separate room to add onto the back of their tent so that Eitan and Ada had a place to put their belongings. Father, Eitan, and Lemuel made many trips back and forth from Ada's tent to theirs, bringing new clothes, rugs, pots, buckets, small trinkets, and whatever else Ada owned.

"Ada, I can't believe you kept all of this," Eitan told her at the end of the week, after they had finally moved over the last of her chests of clothing. Jarah followed, bringing in a bundle of candles that were a gift from Aunt Zuriel.

Ada looked around at the tiny, crowded room. "Maybe you should've moved to my family's tent and saved us all this bother," she joked.

Eitan's hand slipped about her waist and he leaned over and kissed her forehead. "You are never a bother, Ada," he said, meaning it. Ada blushed and laughed. Jarah smiled to herself and left her brother and new sister-in-law alone. She crept over to Ximena's cradle and leaned over the sleeping little girl.

"You're getting better, aren't you little girl?" she whispered. She sat down, gently rocking the cradle. A wave of exhaustion swept over her. She felt her eyelids drooping.

No. Don't go to sleep yet. You need to help Shayna fix dinner and milk the goats.

It seemed as if the chores had doubled for everyone with Mother's passing and Father's lack of help. He had been around for most of the week helping get everything moved. But something still wasn't right. Jarah didn't know what it was. She wished she knew. She had seen both Jaden and Grandfather try to talk to him, but he had brushed them both away.

Jarah caught herself nodding off.

I'd better stand up or I'll fall asleep, she thought. With what felt like a great effort, Jarah pushed herself off the ground and went outside to find Shayna. A great sadness flooded into her heart as she saw her father disappearing into the throng of people.

He's going away… again.

ה

It was two weeks after the wedding. Jarah and Tirzah were beating out their sleeping mats. Though the sand in the tent was packed hard at this point, little grains of sand still managed to get everywhere.

"Jarah, when will Moses come back?" Tirzah asked.

"I don't know," Jarah responded, absently. She wasn't really thinking about Moses. She was thinking about how much she missed her father, how tired she was, and how all of her muscles ached from carrying Ximena strapped to her back all day.

"When did he leave?" Tirzah persisted.

"Four weeks ago, I think."

"How many days was he gone last time?"

"Umm…" Jarah thought hard. "Forty days, I think."

Has it really only been just over a month since Mother died? It feels like an eternity. But still… Nothing is getting any better.

"Where's Father?" Tirzah piped up.

"I don't know," Jarah answered. She was starting to get annoyed.

"Well, can't we go look for him?"

"We've tried that," Jarah grumbled. "He keeps slipping away."

"I thought he was supposed to help Uncle Daton and Eitan sharpen the weapons today. Didn't Joshua want the men to be practicing?"

"Yes, he was," Jarah murmured. Her father wasn't meeting his commitments. Everyone in their little circle was upset at him for one reason or another.

"Then where is he?" Tirzah demanded.

"Tirzah!" Jarah whirled around to face her sister. "I don't know, and I need you to stop asking. I know nothing more than you do, all right? Now don't ask any more!"

Tirzah gazed up into her older sister's face. Her lips were quivering. "I'm sorry," she whispered. "I just—I want Father back."

Guilt swept over Jarah. She hadn't meant to yell at Tirzah like that. She wrapped her arms around the crying little girl.

"I want him back, too," she agreed, sorrowfully. "I want him back, too."

ꜝ

Jarah groaned slightly as she filled a clay pitcher with water and set it upright on the bank of a small stream. Her muscles were sore. They were sore almost every day now. With so many new chores and responsibilities and so little rest, Jarah almost felt like she was sleep-walking. It was evening now, and she was so tired that she didn't think she could even carry the two pitchers back into camp. She gazed into the last golden rays of the setting sun as it danced on the warm sand.

"Come on. The day's almost over. You can finish this one last chore," Jarah told herself, though her voice lacked feeling.

"Can I help?" a voice asked directly behind her. Jarah started and whirled around.

"Oh! Ezra. You startled me." Jarah tried to act and sound casual but her cheeks were hot and her heart was racing.

"Sorry," Ezra apologized. "I just happened to see that we both were on the same errand and thought you might need some help." Ezra was also carrying a clay pitcher.

"Well, I'm pretty tired. But I don't want you to go out of your way to—"

"Nonsense. Here, let me get one of those. You've had a lot going on in your life right now and could use some help." Ezra gave Jarah his familiar grin and scooped up the other pitcher before she could protest farther. Jarah returned the smile, remembering how he had helped her carry pitchers back to her house when they had been slaves in Egypt.

"Thanks."

Ezra just nodded. For a moment they both walked in silence. Jarah felt a bit awkward. She didn't exactly know what to say. It had been a long time since they had talked.

"Are you doing all right?" Ezra finally asked. That wasn't really a question Jarah had expected him to ask.

"What do you mean?" she asked with some confusion.

"I mean how are you doing? Your family has gone through a lot with the loss of your mother, and with your father not being around as much. You've had to take on many responsibilities. I just hope you aren't feeling overwhelmed or alone."

It was all Jarah could do to keep her jaw from dropping. That's exactly how she felt. She—well, everyone in the family, really—had taken on so many new roles with Eitan technically acting as the head of the household, Ada still getting used to her role as 'Mother,' and Shayna constantly taking care of Ximena. She hadn't told anyone what she was feeling; they were all going through the same things and didn't need her to complain, she thought. But it felt nice that someone else knew what was going on.

While those thoughts had been whirling inside of her head, she had stopped walking. Ezra paused, too.

"Are you?" he asked. "Feeling alone and overwhelmed, that is?"

"I— I guess I'm feeling a bit overwhelmed and tired. And a little lonely, like you said." Jarah bit her tongue. She hadn't really meant to tell Ezra how much she was struggling. "But I'll be fine," she finished dismissively.

She started to move on and glanced at Ezra, only to find that he was looking hard into her face. Jarah quickly turned away.

"Are you sure?"

"Yes. Really, I'm fine." Jarah was trying to blink back tears. *I'm not going to let Ezra see me cry.* She was glad to see that they were almost back to their tents and she quickly changed the topic.

"Do you miss having Ada around?"

"Well, she's not really gone. I mean, we see her every day. But yes," Ezra grinned again, "it's different. That's why I sometimes come over just to talk to her for a few minutes. It's wonderful that we're so close. I'm sure she's tired of me invading her space all the time."

Jarah giggled. Eitan, starting a fire in front of their tent, looked up and noticed his sister with Ezra. A slight scowl darkened his features. Jarah stopped laughing, wondering what was wrong with Eitan. She and Ezra brought the pitchers into the tent then came back out.

"Thank you, Ezra." Eitan's tone sounded almost cold. "Your family was looking for you. It's almost time for dinner."

"Yes, thank you, Ezra," Jarah tried to say as sweetly as possible to cover up for her brother's seeming disapproval.

"You're welcome. I'll see you both tomorrow." Ezra walked away but cast a curious glance back in his brother-in-law's direction.

"Eitan, what's wrong?" Jarah asked once Ezra was out of ear-shot.

"I just—I want to have a talk with you about something later on," Eitan answered, vaguely.

"Oh. All right. When would you like to talk?" It was obvious that Eitan didn't want to tell her right now.

"How about tomorrow morning, early, when I go check on the flock?"

"I'll be ready," Jarah assented. She ducked into the tent to get some meat, wondering with a small foreboding what Eitan wanted to talk to her about.

ꙮ

The next morning, Eitan was already outside the tent when Jarah awoke.

"Good morning, Jarah. How are you this morning?"

Jarah took a deep breath of the cool, clean air and replied, "I'm well, Eitan."

"Here, let's walk this way."

Eitan took up his staff and headed out towards the open desert. He didn't say anything else. He looked very serious, more serious than usual. Jarah followed alongside, in silence.

"Eitan, what did you want to talk to me about?" Jarah finally prodded after a few minutes.

Eitan still didn't reply. He climbed up on a rock and sat down, his back towards the rising sun. Jarah sat next to him, feeling bewildered. Eitan seemed to be carrying a heavy burden. He let out a long sigh.

"Jarah, I don't know how else to tell you this. I wish Father could talk to you about it, but he's becoming more and more detached from us, so I feel that I need to say it. It may sound a bit blunt, but…" Jarah held her breath. "I think you're getting too attached to Ezra."

Jarah was startled.

"What do you mean?" she asked, slowly.

"I mean you're thinking about him too much and daydreaming about him."

"How can you tell what I'm thinking about him?" Jarah asked, a little defensively.

"Jarah, please. I'm telling you this for your own good. It's something that Father overlooked and I feel like I have to tell you. It'll save you a lot of heart-ache later on."

"But—but what am I supposed to do? We haven't really talked for a long time until yesterday." Jarah felt ruffled and defensive.

"Jarah, I've seen the look in your eyes when you're around him. You're getting too caught up in your emotions and your dreams. In a way, you're giving your heart to him when he hasn't even asked for it," Eitan said simply.

"But he's done so much for us. Think about all the times he's helped me."

"He's done a lot, but he's never talked to Father or me about seeking your hand or winning your heart," Eitan stated, gently.

"But Eitan, doesn't he show partiality towards me?" Jarah persisted.

"Jarah, we're not talking about Ezra right now. We're talking about you. I can tell just from the way you're answering that you like Ezra as more than a friend. Isn't that true?" Eitan's eyes seemed to be boring into her very soul. Jarah looked down at her toes.

"Yes. I'm afraid it is." Though that was the hardest thing Jarah had ever had to admit to anyone, she suddenly felt that a burden had rolled off of her shoulders.

"I thought as much." Eitan exhaled slowly. "Jarah, I'm afraid you're going to have a very hard struggle ahead of you. You need to stop fantasizing about Ezra and getting caught up in your emotions towards him. I want you to reign in your thoughts and your daydreams and instead just treat Ezra as your friend and brother. It'll be a hard thing to do, but you can't give yourself to him when there's been no talk of anything besides friendship. Trust me, it will be much less painful in the future."

Now it was Jarah's turn to sigh. "But Eitan, what if he does really like me? What if he wants to talk about betrothal but just hasn't had the opportunity? He's fifteen and I'm thirteen. People have been married younger."

"That's not the point, Jarah. You're getting carried away with your thoughts and 'what ifs.' You can't assume anything he's done or said to you means that he likes you that way. Ezra is kind to everyone. You can't dwell on that and create something in your dreams. You have to focus on getting ready to have a family, not on who you'll marry or when. You just have to be ready and let Father, Lemuel, and I advise you when a young man does comes along. Do you understand?"

Jarah swallowed hard and nodded. Eitan was right. She knew it.

"Whenever you're really struggling, just turn your attention to Yahweh. He can give you the strength to resist temptation. You must learn to rely on Him before you can rely on anyone else, even me—or Ezra. Can you do that?" Eitan asked, gently.

"I will try very hard, Eitan. But it won't be easy. And what if Ezra seeks me out? I don't want to be unkind."

"No, and you shouldn't be. I don't want you to avoid him or not talk to him. Just make sure your emotions and thoughts are in check when he's around. You'll figure it out. I know you will." Eitan squeezed her hand. "I don't want anyone trying to steal that heart of yours. It's far too precious." Eitan finally smiled for the first time this morning. Jarah giggled.

"Thank you, Eitan. I appreciate that. Really, I do. And thank you for talking to me. It was hard, but I needed to hear it from you."

"I know. That's why I told you." The brother and sister shared a grin and Eitan gave her a hug. "And I just want to tell you that Lemuel and I are always here for you. If you're struggling with something, don't hesitate to let us know."

"Yes, I know. Thank you."

"You're welcome," he said, rising to his feet. "Now, we'd better get back to camp. We have a long day ahead."

Eitan helped Jarah down from the rock and they strolled back into camp. Jarah couldn't exactly describe the way she felt. She was liberated, yet burdened. It would be so hard to stop thinking that way about Ezra, even though she knew she'd been wrong. He was one of the few young men around her that she could imagine being a good husband one day.

But Eitan's right, she assured herself, shaking her head slightly to clear her thoughts. *He's been through this. He knows. I don't want to be silly. And I really do want to devote my heart to Yahweh first.* She looked at Eitan and smiled. Yes, she would rely on Yahweh to be everything that she would ever need and let Him be the One to decide when she should have a husband, and who the young man might be.

ח

After the morning meal, Ezra was outside adjusting the ropes that held up their tent. He looped a leather strap around a tent peg and tied it tightly. He was turning to the next peg when suddenly he saw Eitan coming around the corner of the tent.

"Ezra, do you have a moment?"

"Yes, I do."

"Can you go on a quick walk with me?" Eitan's voice didn't sound right, and he looked upset.

"Of course."

The two young men strode side by side out of the camp, away from the millions of people, and out onto the plain with the animals. Eitan finally sank down in the shade in a boulder.

"Eitan, what's wrong?" Ezra asked, genuinely concerned.

"Ezra," Eitan began slowly, "I've noticed that you seem to be going out of your way to do things for Jarah. I'm your friend but I'm also Jarah's older brother, and I'm concerned about how much time you're spending around her and how much you seek her out. The attention you've been giving her could be interpreted as more than friendship, and I wanted to make you aware of that. I love Jarah a lot, and I don't want you toying with her heart if you really aren't interested in anything more than friendship."

Ezra was taken aback. "Eitan, I don't think of your sister in that way."

Eitan's eyes met his. He was very surprised. "You don't?"

"No. I don't," Ezra asserted. "She's a great friend, very kind and loyal, and she has such a loving spirit. I'll be honest with you and say that for a while, I did wonder if there was a future with us. But that was months ago. I've moved on from that."

"So you're saying you only think of my sister as a friend?" Eitan asked, cautiously.

"Yes. I've tried to be very helpful to her and to your whole family because you all have had such a rough time, but that's it."

Eitan sighed and ran his hands through his hair.

"Ezra, if you don't have any intentions, you might need to be a little more cautious in your friendship with Jarah."

Ezra furrowed his brow.

"What do you mean?"

"I don't want anyone to get the wrong idea," Eitan said. "I mean, yes, you're being very kind. You're thoughtful and considerate, and please, understand that we all appreciate that and don't want you to stop being that kind of man. But you're being so kind to Jarah in particular that all of us older siblings thought you had feelings for her. I'm very grateful that you want to help her and support her and all of us during this time, but as a young man who isn't interested, you're being a little too exclusive in your friendship with her. It might appear that you were singling her out from all the other girls."

Ezra nodded. "I didn't mean to do that, Eitan. I had no idea. I'm so sorry."

"It's all right," Eitan said. "We should've addressed it sooner. In fact, I wish my father was having this conversation with you right now. But please, I'm asking you to do this for your own well-being as much as hers. I know you respect her, and I'm very thankful for the protection and help you've given her. But right now, it might be time to step back a bit, especially if she's only going to be a friend to you and nothing more. That's not saying that you can't be around our family or Jarah any more, but please don't go out of your way to make her feel special. Be a friend by all means! But don't seem to pursue her.

"Do you understand what I'm trying to say?" Eitan concluded.

Ezra realized with relief that Eitan didn't appear accusing or upset. He was just concerned for both of their sakes.

"Of course, Eitan. I'm so sorry. That was not my intent at all. I really feel terrible," Ezra said, as apologetic as he could possibly be.

"No. It's all right. I understand. As I said, it's my fault for not addressing it sooner." Eitan stood up, and Ezra jumped to his feet. Eitan clasped his hand and said, "I appreciate your honesty with me, Ezra. I really do. You've been the best of friends."

"You're welcome, Eitan. And again, I'm so sorry. Do I need to do anything else to make it right?"

"No. Not that I can think of." Eitan clapped Ezra on the shoulder. "Thank you for taking me seriously. You're a great young man, Ezra. Keep growing closer to Yahweh. I'm very proud to have you as my brother and my friend."

Ezra grinned. "Thanks, Eitan."

They both turned off in opposite directions. Ezra blinked several times, still trying to comprehend what had just happened. He felt horrible. Did Jarah really have feelings for him? He hoped not. Eitan had just said "the older siblings" thought he was interested in her as more than a friend.

But if she does have feelings, it's my own fault. Why didn't I think of that? I was just so caught up in trying to help I didn't realize I might hurt her… Or myself.

Ezra knew he was going to miss spending so much time with Jarah. He really valued her friendship, her insight, and her kindness. But he knew that Eitan was right and that he needed to give her a little bit of space.

If I'm going to miss her, does that mean I do have feelings for her? I thought I didn't… But do I?

This thought troubled Ezra. But then he remembered the prayer that he'd prayed months ago about the whole thing.

"No," he said softly. "Yahweh told me that it's not His timing. He didn't make it clear whether it was Jarah or another girl, but Eitan's right. I shouldn't be trying to win anyone's heart until I'm ready to be married, and I'm definitely not ready. I need to be more careful."

ט

Three days later Jarah was trying to occupy the little boys. Ada was cleaning and organizing the tent, and the four little ones kept getting in the way. But Jarah's creativity was wearing thin. They had already done races and played with their cloth balls.

"Why don't you collect stones and build a city?" Jarah suggested.

"We did that yesterday," Raphael whined.

"Well… We could draw designs in the sand. Go find some sticks."

"All right." The boys and Tirzah raced off to find the biggest sticks.

"Jarah?" Ada poked her head out of the tent. "I can't seem to find some things. Have you seen the new length of gray cloth that Shayna just made? Or my clay pots from Mother? I think we're also missing some meat. I thought for sure we had four strings of dry quail meat yesterday, and today I only see two."

"I'm sorry. I don't know what's happened to those," Jarah apologized.

"It's all right," Ada said. She was chewing on her lower lip, looked very puzzled. "Perhaps I've just misplaced them. I'll get everything organized in a few days and I'm sure we'll find them then."

❯

Five days later, when everything was put back into place, all of the items were still missing.

"And there's a blanket missing from this chest, too. This is very strange," Ada said. She was obviously worried.

Lemuel walked into the tent, carrying his shepherd's staff.

"Ada, have you seen Eitan?"

"I believe he just went to talk to Sethur. He should be right back."

"I'm here," Eitan said, presenting himself at the opening of the tent. "What's wrong?"

Lemuel's face was pale. "Eitan, two of our male lambs are missing."

Eitan's jaw dropped open.

"Are you sure?"

"Yes. I'm positive. They were there yesterday. I count the animals every morning and every night. They were there last night, and this morning they're gone. I've checked everywhere. I've asked all of our neighbors. They even allowed me to check their herds. One of the men even said that he was guarding the sheep and goats last night. If an animal had attacked there would've been a disturbance. But there's no blood, no tracks. The animals aren't upset. I don't know what could've happened."

Eitan's brow was furrowed. "Do you think someone could've stolen the animals, Lem?"

"I—I don't know. I would hope that none of our neighbors would do something like that," Lemuel said, quietly.

"Have you asked Father?" Eitan queried.

"I haven't seen him since last night when we all went to bed."

"Have you talked to Ezra or Jaden?"

"No," Lemuel replied. "I just talked to Uncle Daton, and I was going to get them next."

"Jarah," Eitan said, turning to her, "can you go find Jaden and Ezra? I'm going with Lemuel to investigate a little bit more."

"Yes, Eitan," Jarah assented. She tightened the straps that held Ximena on her back and went to go find them. She could see Amissa tending the fire in front of her tent.

"Amissa, where's your father and Ezra?"

"I think they went to see Sethur. Did you hear that Father is becoming a judge in the tribe?" Amissa asked, looking very proud.

"Yes, I did," Jarah answered. *My father would've been asked to be a judge, being Grandfather's son and all, if he hadn't stolen that grain,* she thought bitterly. Out loud she said, "Can you send them over to our tent when they come back?"

"Of course. Is something wrong?" Amissa asked, appearing concerned.

"We're not sure. Some of our animals are missing, and we wanted to talk to your father and Ezra about it to see if they know anything," Jarah explained.

"I'm so sorry," Amissa said, showing genuine feeling. "I hope you find them."

"Me, too," Jarah breathed, turning to head back to her tent.

Jarah was just about to finish airing out the blankets when Ezra came jogging up to her, smiling in a friendly way. Jarah's heart warmed a little and she suddenly realized that she'd missed seeing him. They hadn't talked together in over a week.

But that's all right, she told herself. *You were getting too attached to him, anyway, like Eitan said.*

"Shalom, Jarah!" Ezra greeted, stopping in front of her. "Amissa said that you were looking for me and Father."

"Well actually, Eitan was looking for you. He and Lemuel are out with the animals." Jarah tried to be casual and friendly, but her voice sounded strained.

"Is something wrong?" Ezra asked. His smile disappeared and concern filled his eyes.

"I'm not sure," Jarah began, slowly. "Some animals are missing from our herd. Eitan wanted to talk to you and your father about it and see if you knew anything."

"All right. I'll go see them, then." Ezra spun on his heel, but then paused and turned back to face her, a curious look on his face. "Have you seen your father recently?"

"We saw him last night for dinner and as we all went to bed. He was gone early this morning, though," Jarah responded.

"Hmm... Father hasn't seen him for several days now," Ezra mused. He paused before asking, rather abruptly, "Has my father done anything to offend him?"

Jarah shook her head. "Not that I know of. But he hasn't really told us anything for the past few weeks." There was another awkward pause. "Why do you ask?" she ventured to say.

Ezra shrugged. "On the day of the wedding I thought I heard them arguing. I saw your father walking past our tent. He seemed upset. I never got to talk to my father about it, though. I was just hoping that the matter would resolve itself. But I guess not..."

Jarah shook her head, slowly. "I guess not," she repeated.

"Well," Ezra straightened and grinned at her, "I'd better go see Eitan and see if I need to get Father or not. See you soon."

"Yes, see you soon," Jarah agreed, returning his smile.

She watched him until he was out of sight.

ב

"Eitan?" Ezra called.

"Over here, Ezra!" Eitan and Lemuel were sitting in the shade of a boulder.

"Jarah said you wanted to see me."

"Yes, I did. Did she tell you what happened?"

Ezra nodded. "She said some animals are missing."

Lemuel got to his feet. "Two of our male lambs are gone. I've looked everywhere. I've asked the neighbors, checked the neighboring herds, and looking for signs of wild animals. There's no explanation for it."

"Do you think someone stole them?" Ezra asked in horror.

"That's possible," Eitan said. He was staring at the ground, thinking hard. "Ada told me that several things have also gone missing from our tent. Some food, some cloth, a few pots, and a blanket. I don't know about everything else, but I do know that one of my tunics went missing about a week ago, too. I had three tunics, and now I only have two."

"What should we do?" Ezra questioned.

"That's what I'm thinking about..." Eitan's voice faded away. He looked into the distant sunset.

"Do you want me to get Father? He's just been appointed a leader in the tribe. Maybe he'll have some ideas, but I don't think he would know anything more than I do about what could've happened to your lambs."

Eitan shook his head. "If you don't think he would know anything else, then I don't want to bother him about this just yet, not until I know something definite." He paused, still thinking. "If you would, Ezra, tell your family and Uncle Daton's family about this and have them check their belongings. We want to make sure that nothing is being stolen from everyone else. We all need to set up a careful watch around our tents and watch each others' tents, too. Hopefully we've just misplaced things and nothing is stolen. But if there is a thief, he or she is very crafty. None of us have seen or noticed anything. Whoever it is would have to be very clever to get past all of us."

"All right. I'll tell everyone," Ezra agreed. "Have you checked our herd to make sure they haven't wandered over there?"

A little black and white goat bounded up to Lemuel and rubbed itself against his knee. Lemuel knelt down to scratch it behind the ears. "I already checked, but thanks."

Ezra nodded and headed back into camp, heaviness weighing on his chest. He had the terrible feeling that something was very, very wrong.

ל

The days dragged by ever more slowly and the work felt harder. Jarah was running a dozen different directions: helping take care of the animals, feeding the family, taking care of Ximena, helping Shayna, staying strong for Eitan, helping Ada with the children, and keeping things clean. It seemed like her list of chores was endless and she would never be done. Jarah knew that she couldn't take much more or she would snap.

This realization hit Jarah as she stooped over a bubbling pot of stew. Her shoulders were drooping. She was so exhausted. She didn't think someone could get more tired than she had been last week, but somehow it was possible. She felt ready to drop. She had stayed up even later than usual last night helping Shayna finish up some cloth. Right now she felt so tired and alone. Jarah brushed away a tear.

Don't cry now. You've held up this long. You have to stay strong for Eitan. He asked you to! Jarah commanded herself.

Ada now stepped out of the tent and walked towards Jarah.

"Yanni and Ximena are finally down for their naps," Ada announced sweetly. Jarah could hear weariness behind her sister-in-law's voice.

"I'm glad." Jarah half-grinned up at Ada.

There was a brief pause as Ada's eyes swept over Jarah.

"Jarah, why don't you go rest or take a walk. You've been working very hard recently. You need a break. I'll finish dinner."

"Thank you, Ada. I would like to take a walk right now." Jarah tried to smile but found that she was blinking back tears.

"You go ahead. I'll send someone for you at dinner time." Ada smiled kindly and lightly kissed Jarah's cheek.

Jarah wandered slowly to the outskirts of the camp. She soon found a large rock and sank gratefully into its shade. She could no longer keep back her tears of fear, exhaustion, and sorrow. She burst into tears, thankful for the solitude. She suddenly heard footsteps.

"Oh! Hello, Jarah. I didn't realize you were—"

Jarah looked up into dark, searching, anxious eyes.

"Jarah, what's wrong?"

It was Ezra.

Three thoughts flashed through Jarah's mind.

Oh, how embarrassing for him to see me like this! Then, as she continued to feel his tender gaze, *But it looks like he really cares...* But the last thought ran clear through the others. *Remember Eitan's talk.*

"I—I'm fine, Ezra." She quickly wiped her wet cheeks with her hand. "I just— I want to be alone," she added rather coldly, swallowing a sob.

"Oh. All right." Ezra seemed rather surprised and a bit discouraged. He moved as if to go away and then turned back. "I just want to let you know that we're all praying for you. I know Amissa would love to talk to you, too, if she can help in any way."

"You've all been praying for me? Why?" Jarah didn't even try to hide her astonishment at his previous statement.

"As I've said before, you've gone through a lot these last few months. Your whole family has. The death of a family member is not easy to deal with." Ezra's eyes focused on the distant horizon. "Believe me, I know."

That's when Jarah remembered. Of course Ezra knew. His own brother had died in his arms. She had seen it happen. It gave her great comfort to know that someone outside of their family knew what she was going through—what she was feeling.

"Thank you, Ezra. That—that gives me a lot of comfort. You have no idea how much," Jarah finished in a low whisper.

Ezra didn't say anything, just flashed her a grin.

"We should be getting back to camp," Ezra said after a slight pause. "It's almost dinnertime and we shouldn't be out late, anyway."

Jarah nodded her head and quickly brushed away any traces of tears that lingered on her cheeks. Ezra offered her his hand and helped Jarah to her feet. Jarah hoped that the twilight hid her blush from Ezra's notice as, together, they turned back towards camp.

As they entered the camp again, Ezra suddenly turned to face her. Jarah found that she couldn't look away. The intensity of his eyes was almost unbearable.

"Don't ever stop trusting Yahweh, all right? He cares about you and He won't give you more than you can bear. This season will pass and I know that Yahweh will give you—and everyone else in your family—strength to endure it. Can you believe that?"

Jarah noticed that, behind Ezra, the pillar of cloud stood erect. Yahweh was so close to her, and yet He seemed so far away. But she had seen what had happened when people had stopped trusting Yahweh. They had turned to the golden calf and to themselves, but there was no fulfillment in that. Yahweh had unleashed His fury on the disobedient people, her own mother being one of them. No... She *had* to trust Yahweh. He was the only One with the power. Had she not seen that through the ten plagues in Egypt and all this time in the wilderness? He had provided for all of their immediate needs—food, water, and shelter. And He had given her Eitan, the best big brother in the world, who trusted fully in Yahweh and was seeing their family through this. Yahweh loved them. He was taking care of them. Yes, Yahweh *was* everything she would ever need. She could see that now. And she would trust Him, no matter what.

As Jarah's eyes turned back to Ezra's face, there was a warmth in her heart that had never been there before.

"Yes, Ezra. I will trust Yahweh, no matter what happens. I *will* trust Yahweh."

"I'M A FOLLOWER OF YAHWEH"

Jarah had just finished putting the young ones down for their afternoon nap when she heard a gasp from Ada's portion of the tent. "Ada? Is something wrong?" She hurriedly entered to see Ada staring into a small box, her mouth open.

"My—" Ada gulped back a sob. "Some of the jewels that the queen gave me are gone!"

"What?" Jarah exclaimed. She looked over Ada's shoulder. It was true. The beautiful golden necklace with the emerald in it and the matching bracelets were missing.

"Ada? What's the matter?" Eitan came rushing in, looking alarmed. Ada had tears in her eyes.

"Some of the jewelry that the queen gave me as a farewell present is gone," she sobbed.

"Oh no," Eitan breathed. He took the crying Ada into his arms and held her close. "I'm going to bury your jewelry so that no one finds it. I'm sorry. I don't know why I didn't think of that before."

"It's not your fault, Eitan," Ada sobbed into his chest.

"But I'm supposed to be taking care of you. It *is* my fault," he said, sorrowfully.

"Please don't blame yourself," Ada pleaded, pulling away and gazing into his face. "It's all right. Maybe we'll find them again," she finished, trying to be hopeful.

Eitan kissed her cheek. "I hope so," he whispered, drawing her into another close embrace.

Jarah was worried. Someone was obviously robbing them. But who was it? And why?

א

E zra sat huddled in front of the fire. The afternoon had been blazingly hot, but now that it was dark it was beginning to get a little chilly. The full moon was painting everything silver. The distant roar of the fire on top of Mount Sinai was the only noise to be heard. Ezra was starting to get sleepy. He stood up and paced in an effort to keep himself awake. After Ada's jewels were found to be missing today, Ezra had vowed to stay up that night to watch Eitan's tent. If someone was really stealing things from Eitan's family, Ezra wanted to stop it.

He suddenly stopped pacing. He had heard a noise. It sounded like the bleating of a goat. Ezra melted into the shadows, eyes and ears alert. Asher appeared from behind a tent, pulling with him what appeared to be a small animal. Ezra realized that it was the black and white goat that Lemuel had been petting two days ago.

Where's Asher taking it? he wondered. Asher seemed to be sneaking from shadow to shadow, avoiding his own tent as much as possible. Ezra had the urge to follow him. He waited for a moment, then silently trailed Asher into the camp.

After a few minutes, Asher seemed to relax and become confident in his walk. He moved rapidly in a straight line towards the distant outskirts of the camp. Ezra was hard pressed to keep up with him and still be quiet and unseen.

They moved ahead for what seemed like an hour, maybe a little more. Ezra's concern was growing by the minute. What was he going to find out? What was Asher doing?

Asher was now leaving the camp and heading into the open desert. Several large boulders formed a sort of enclosure in the middle of the plain. A bright fire could be seen flickering from inside the large circle of rocks. Ezra heard coarse laughing and jesting. Asher was heading straight for the rocks. Pulling the little goat along, he disappeared into the hiding place.

Ezra waited, hesitating. Glancing around to make sure he wouldn't be seen, he bolted to the rocks and put his back up against them. He slid around until he reached a small crack between two of the rocks. Here he could observe without much chance of being noticed. Warily, he peeked through the opening.

A large fire burned in one corner, illuminating the square. Fifteen to twenty people were seated in a circle around a crudely built wooden table. The men were spinning a wooden top and cheering and laughing. A flask of wine was being passed around. Gold coins glinted in the firelight. One of the men spun the top and suddenly let out a large whoop.

"I've won!" he hollered.

Jeers, cheers, and exasperated shouts filled the air. The winner scooped up a big pile of coins and dumped them onto his already large pile. Ezra drew in his breath sharply as he realized what was going on.

They're gambling!

Rugs, blankets, jewels, pots, and other household items were tossed around the enclosure. Apparently goods were bartered in exchange for money for those who weren't wealthy enough to pay off their debts with gold or coins.

Why is Asher here? Ezra thought, dreading the answer.

"Ah, Asher!" the winner was proclaiming. "Welcome back! I hope you've come prepared to pay your debts." The men around the winner exploded into laughter, slapping each other on the backs. Asher moved into the firelight, clutching the goat's lead rope.

"The jewels I brought you last night should have cleared up most of my debt, Ennis," he said to the leader. "This goat should make provision for everything."

Ennis stood up and eyed the goat. "Yes. Your jewels were obviously very valuable. I don't know if I've ever seen an emerald so beautiful."

Anger flooded into Ezra's heart. *He's been stealing from Eitan and my sister! He's been taking their goods to pay off his debts and barter to get more money so that he can keep gambling!*

"Very well," Ennis was saying. "The goat will do. But if you lose this time, Asher, you'll have to have something to pay me back."

"Oh, yes! Of course!" Asher sputtered.

"Good. Now, join us! Here, take a share of my coins." Ennis steered Asher to a seat by his side and counted out a pile of coins for him. Handing him a flask of wine and the top, Ennis declared, "Drink up, my friend! And give her a spin!"

The men cheered as Asher spun the top and the game commenced. Ezra felt sick. He knew what was happening. And now he knew what had happened to Eitan and Ada's missing goods, jewels, and animals.

He didn't need to see any more. Ezra crawled into the shadows, and as soon as he was out of reach of the firelight, he raced into the camp. He ran until his breath came hard and fast and he got a stitch in his side. Still he kept running until he felt like he was going to be sick. Then he slumped to the ground, gasping for air, stunned, miserable, and helpless.

What do I do? What do I do? was all he could think. *Yahweh, show me what to do. Show me what to do.*

Slowly his head began to clear. Asher had stolen Ada's jewels and the goat. Had he stolen the rest? It was likely. They couldn't blame him for those things without absolute proof, but it was the only thing that made sense. He had taken food from that man several months ago. It was now obvious that he had never completely repented from that sin and turned from his evil ways.

But how can he steal from his own family? Ezra thought, enraged and accusing. But the anger slowly gave way to this thought:

I've never had grief like he's had. My brother died, but I've never known what it's like to fail my family in so many ways and then to see my wife become sick and die. He must be completely blinded by his grief. He's strayed from Yahweh. And once he strayed, he was susceptible to the attacks of the enemy. He just needs to be pointed back towards Yahweh.

But what do I do?

Yes, that was the question. What should he do? He knew he should tell his father, and possibly Sethur. And—he would have to tell Eitan. That was the last thing he wanted to do. How could he tell one of his best friends that his own father was stealing their provisions and using them to pay off his gambling debts? But he had to do it. Asher couldn't be allowed to take anything else and continue in his sin.

Ezra slowly rose to his feet and plodded back to his tent where he got water and sat next to the burning ashes of his fire. He barely noticed the chill air anymore. All he could think about was the terrible, horrible thing Asher was doing and how he needed to give this bad news to Asher's son tomorrow morning.

ב

Eitan was up early the next morning. It was just starting to become light. He lightly kissed Ada on the forehead before leaving the tent to check on the animals. He did a quick head-count. If his number was right, there was another animal missing. Eitan angrily kicked at a broken branch. He needed Lemuel out here to tell him exactly which animal was missing. He didn't know them like Lemuel did. But this was frustrating. Animals were apparently being stolen right out from under his nose. He and Lemuel were going to have to stay up during the night to guard their animals. He dreaded that.

"Eitan?"

The voice made him jump.

"Sorry. I didn't mean to scare you."

Eitan turned to see Ezra standing behind him. Ezra's face was pale and there were dark circles under his eyes. He looked like he hadn't slept all night.

"Ezra, what's wrong with you? Are you sick?"

"No, not sick," Ezra said weakly.

"Here, sit down," Eitan beckoned. "You look as though you might faint!"

Ezra sat with his back against a low rock and closed his eyes for a moment.

"I'm fine. I'm sorry. It's just—I don't know how to say this."

"Say what?" Eitan pressed. "Ezra, what's wrong?"

Ezra opened his eyes. "Eitan… Last night, after what happened to Ada's jewels, I decided I was going to stay up all night to see if I could figure out what was happening to your animals and your possessions."

Eitan laid a hand on Ezra's shoulder. "Ezra, you're the best of friends. Thank you for doing that, but I wish you hadn't put yourself through such trouble."

"But that's not all, Eitan. Please, just let me finish," Ezra begged.

"All right," Eitan said, slowly. "What happened?"

"I saw…" Ezra took a deep breath. "I saw a man sneaking through camp. He had one of your young goats, the white and black one."

So that's the one that's missing, Eitan thought. Aloud he said, "Go on."

"Eitan, that man was… your father."

Eitan's heart stopped beating. "What—what did he do?"

"He was sneaking off into the camp. So, I followed him at a distance. He walked a very long ways and went to the far outskirts of the camp. There's a kind of hide-out there made of large boulders. Inside the hide-out there were a bunch of men. They were gambling. I don't know their names. I only know that the winner, the one who seemed to be loaning money to others, was named Ennis. He's the one that your father has been spending time with, right?"

"Yes," Eitan replied mechanically.

"I—I heard some of the conversation that took place between your father and Ennis." Ezra stopped and moistened his lips. He was fighting back tears. "Eitan… Your father's been stealing from you to pay off his debts."

A low cry escaped from Eitan's lips.

"I don't know how much he's taken," Ezra hastened to say. "Maybe it's only a few things. But Ennis said that Asher had given him Ada's jewelry. He talked about the gold jewelry with the emerald paying off most of the debt. The goat paid off the rest. I left as they were starting another game. I didn't know what to do."

An emotion was welling up inside of Eitan that he had only experienced twice before. First, when Jarah had been beaten by that Egyptian for such a little fault, and second, when Shayna was being dragged off by that coward, Mayer. But now he was experiencing it again, and he knew what it was. It was rage.

"My father… has been taking food and provisions from our family to pay off his gambling debts?" he yelled, trembling and crying with passion.

Ezra hung his head. Eitan sank to the ground and hid his face in his hands. He vaguely heard Ezra's voice.

"What are you going to do, Eitan? What would you like me to do?"

Eitan raised his head. His face was pale, but his eyes were kindling with a strange, terrifying fire.

"Get my grandfather. If my timing is right, my father will be arriving at our tent any minute. We've got to confront him about this—*now*."

א

J arah stretched and yawned.
Morning came too early, she groaned. She forced herself to sit up. Ximena was whimpering. Jarah crawled over to Ximena and picked her up, holding her close.

Someone came into their tent. It was their father, looking sleepy and dazed. He crashed onto his mat, closing his eyes.

"Good morning, Father," Jarah said, softly. Her father only moaned in reply and rolled over.

Abruptly, the tent flap was thrown open. Eitan stood in the doorway. Jarah gasped. The look on his face was dark, menacing, and angry. He strode up to his father's mat and shook him, violently.

"Get up!" he yelled. Father started and rose to a sitting position, looking stupefied.

"Eitan, what are you doing?" Ada exclaimed, looking alarmed.

Eitan's eyes were boring into their father's. "Don't give me that look," he growled, low and dangerous. "I know what you're up to, Father."

"What are you talking about?" Father questioned, blinking rapidly and trying to shake himself out of his stupor. Shayna grabbed the sleeping Yanni and herded Tirzah and Raphael outside. Lemuel rose to his feet and stood next to Eitan.

"Be sure your sin will find you out! Don't you remember what Grandfather and Jaden told you? Well, your sin has found you out, Father. One of our friends saw you taking our goat and going to meet with a bunch of gamblers. Father, you've been taking our food, our belongings, our animals, and even my clothes and Ada's jewelry to pay for your gambling debts, haven't you?" Father hung his head.

"Haven't you?" Eitan cried, grabbing their father's shoulders.

Father struggled to his feet, his eyes blazing fire. Jarah cringed and cowered into the corner.

"You know nothing Eitan, nothing! You know nothing about how I feel or what I've been doing! I've had a few debts, but soon I'll have more money than we could ever dream about. I'll be able to provide for us again. I'll be able to be happy and be home. Nothing and no one is going to stand in my way. I don't want to hear anything about it, Eitan! If you want me home, then you'll let me be!"

Eitan's lip was quivering. He opened his mouth to say something, then shut it. When he opened it mouth again, he simply said, "Father, you're sinning. You're sinning against my family, your family, and against Yahweh. Don't you remember Yahweh's commands about stealing? While you may own our food and our animals, you've stolen from Ada and myself."

"All right," Father said, shrugging and taking a step away from Eitan. The tension in the tent lessened a little. "I shouldn't have done that, and I'm sorry. I'll make it up to you, I promise."

Jarah saw a tear trailing down Eitan's face. "Father, I can see in your face that you aren't truly repentant. I don't know if I can trust you. You aren't changing. Grandfather and Jaden and I have been trying to help you see your sin for months now. If anything, you're sinning all the more. You've added lying and gambling to your crimes. You've completely deserted Yahweh. And now... You've stolen from your own family, from your own children. We've asked you to repent. We've pleaded with you, and yet you haven't listened."

"Oh, I've listened," Father stated, defensively.

"Then why hasn't anything changed, Father?" Eitan pleaded.

Grandfather and Ezra abruptly came through the doorway. Father's eyes got round as he caught a glimpse of Grandfather's sad and angry face. Grandfather only said one word.

"Asher."

As he heard his name, Father hung his head in guilt and shame. Ezra stepped close to Eitan and Lemuel and put a hand on each of their shoulders in support and encouragement. Jarah heard a tiny sob escape from Ada's lips.

"Asher," Grandfather repeated, "I don't know what's gotten into you or what you're doing, but you continue to sin, continue to harden your heart, and continue to bring Yahweh's wrath upon you. You will have to pay the penalty for your sins."

Father's head jerked up and his eyes were flashing and angry. "What are you going to do? Make me leave? Disown me? Everything I took was my own, Father! I'm guiltless!"

"Not everything," Eitan stated, pointedly. Father's eyes narrowed as he glared at Eitan. Jarah's heartbeat quickened in her chest and she was finding it hard to breathe. She watched Lemuel move closer to their brother as if wanting to protect him.

"What are you talking about?" Father demanded.

"Remember? My clothes and Ada's jewelry? Those things didn't belong to you, Father. They belonged to me and my family," Eitan said in very direct tones, staring his father down. Father looked surprised and a little uncomfortable.

"I'm sorry. I guess I wasn't thinking," Father mumbled.

Grandfather took a step forward and laid a hand on Eitan's shoulder as if to comfort him. Jarah heard him give a small sigh.

"I'm afraid that saying 'I'm sorry' doesn't work in this situation, Asher. You've directly disobeyed Yahweh's commandments when He told us to not steal. You've stolen, not just from Eitan's family, but you've taken things that you and your own children need to use to prosper in the land which Yahweh is giving to us."

"You don't understand, Father," their father interrupted. "As I was telling Eitan before, soon I'll have more money than we ever could've dreamed of having! I can buy all of their things back, and more besides! Can't you just leave me alone and let me sort through this myself? I've got it under control. You'll see. Soon I'll be able to provide again and give these children all that they've ever wanted."

"Father," Eitan began, his voice choking with emotion, "we don't want anything else. We have what we need. We just want you."

"Yes, Father," Lemuel echoed. "We just want you back."

Hope flickered in Jarah's heart as she saw a slight softening in her father's face. But his expression hardened again as he declared, "It's not like I've left, Eitan. I've just—I've just needed my distance to work things through. This place… It carries too many memories and too much pain." Father lowered his head for a moment, seemingly fighting for composure. But in a moment he stood up tall and proud. "Besides, you've said that you wanted me to be providing more and taking care of you more. And this is how I've chosen to go about it. I'm doing what you asked, Eitan."

"No, you're not," Eitan almost yelled. "We've told you to change, to come back to loving Yahweh and leading your family. You're not doing either of those things, Father!"

Father took a step forward, obviously upset. "How dare you raise your voice towards me, Eitan! You're not my father! You're supposed to honor me and respect me, not criticize everything that I do! You've been disrespectful to me throughout this whole conversation and that needs to stop—now!"

Grandfather moved in between Father and Eitan, shielding them from each other. "You're right, Asher. Eitan is not your father. But I am. You're clearly showing an unrepentant heart, and as a leader of this tribe, I'm forced to see that you make restitution for whatever you've stolen. According to Yahweh's laws, you will need to repay four times the value of what you've stolen from Eitan and Ada."

Father's eyes nearly popped out of his head. "Four times?! Father, there's no way that I could possibly do that!"

"If you had listened to Yahweh's laws then you wouldn't be in this situation, Asher," Grandfather responded, quietly yet forcefully.

"I can't possibly pay them back. Those jewels were worth a fortune! Even if I worked for months and years I couldn't pay for those things."

"Then what are you going to do?" Grandfather pressed.

A strange look entered their father's eyes. "If I continue on the path I'm on then I'll win everything back one day," he mused.

"Asher, that's not an option here. Gambling is foolish and stealing is sin. We aren't going to allow or condone that behavior," Grandfather said, bluntly.

"Then how am I supposed to get enough to pay back this ridiculous amount imposed upon me by Yahweh?"

"Maybe you shouldn't have taken them in the first place," Eitan pointed out, bitterness slipping into his voice. Father glared at Eitan again. Grandfather motioned for Eitan to be silent.

"Well if I'm not respected in my own home by my own son then I'm not sure I want to pay him back," Father stated, accusingly.

"Asher, Eitan isn't disrespecting you. He's just upset at his loss and at your actions and your unrepentant heart."

"Of course you would take his side," Father exclaimed. "He's been your favorite for a while now. It's like he's your son instead of me!"

Grandfather was obviously getting flustered now, too.

"Asher, if my son would listen to what I have to say and come to me for advice, then I would treat him the same way."

"So is that it? I have to be perfect and do everything you want me to do in order to get respect around here? I thought I was the leader of this household and that I could do whatever I wanted!" Father yelled.

"Asher, you're living in sin! You're not even trying to do what's right!" Grandfather responded, angrily. "It's not what I say. It's what Yahweh says! And with your angry and unrepentant spirit, it seems like you are willingly forfeiting the right to lead your own family!"

"Well, maybe I don't want to lead anymore if this is the treatment I'm to receive from my own son!" Father bellowed, gesturing at Eitan.

"He's not the problem here, Asher, and you know it!" Grandfather shouted, moving closer to Asher.

"What if I don't think that I'm sinning and that I *can* do whatever I want?" Father asked, crossing his arms across his chest.

"It's not about you and whatever you want, Asher. This is about Yahweh and Yahweh's laws! And you must obey them!"

Father's eyes grew dark as he fixed his gaze on his father's face. He finally turned and looked at Eitan, eying him with contempt.

"Well, Eitan, since you seem to be the perfect man for this job and this family, I suppose I'll just leave it to you." And with that, Father turned towards the door. Jarah gasped as she realized that he had really meant what she said. Lemuel grabbed Father's arm to try to stop him, but Father just shrugged Lemuel's hand away and continued towards the outside.

"Asher, what are you doing?" Grandfather called after him. "You can't do this—just walk out on your children! You have to obey Yahweh's commands, repent, take care of your children, and pay back what you owe!"

Father didn't respond. He simply walked over to the tent flap, opened it, then looked back for a brief moment to say, "Let Eitan figure it out, if he's so good and obedient. I'll be happy to come back when I get the respect I deserve around here."

"Father, no!" Eitan exclaimed. "Please! Forgive me! We still want you here! We still need you! We just want you to repent and turn back to Yahweh!"

A hideous change came over Father's face.

"You just want me to give and give and give some more! You and Yahweh! Well, I can't! I'm done with you—and with Him! He's taken too much from me to deserve my love and respect." He threw one last glance around the room at everyone and then muttered, darkly, "You'll regret this."

And with that, Father left, not even looking back.

For a moment, everyone was frozen, not knowing what to do or what to say. Then there was a mad rush to get outside the tent. Eitan was first and Jarah heard him crying out, "Father!" Clutching Ximena, she darted after him, but looking around, she saw no sign of Father. He had disappeared into the crowd. Ezra, Lemuel, Ada, and Grandfather ran out after them. Jarah heard her grandfather sigh from the depths of his soul. Ada was crying. She heard Lemuel whisper, longingly, "Father."

Eitan looked around at his family. Jarah had a hard time focusing on him because of the tears in her own eyes. All she could see was the look of pain and anguish on her older brother's face.

Eitan slowly whispered, "Everyone meet here at the fire pit in about an hour. Someone please find Shayna and tell her, too. Grandfather, can we talk, please?"

"Of course, son," Grandfather said, tears on his cheeks. The two of them headed out towards the open desert. Jarah, Lemuel, Ezra, and Ada simply stared at each other, too shocked to think or fully grasp what had just happened.

Yahweh, why? Why are you doing this to us? Jarah wailed on the inside. *I don't know if I can take any more of this…*

צ

The little family had gathered around the fire pit. People moved past them, not really paying attention or seeing. No one knew how much Jarah was hurting inside. No one knew what had just happened inside their tent. No one knew that their father had just betrayed their whole family.

Eitan appeared. He didn't look angry anymore. But he did look older. In fact, it almost looked like he had aged ten years in just a matter of hours. His face was pale and grave. He looked worried, burdened, searching for confidence. He sat next to Ada and she took his hand and gave it a gentle squeeze.

"First of all, let me say that I'm sorry for my behavior this morning. I should never have lost control of my temper like that and raised my voice against our father. Please forgive me."

Everyone nodded and murmured that they forgave him.

"Thank you," Eitan said, slowly exhaling. "Now, all of you know that Father is living in sin. He's stolen from us and has chosen direct disobedience to Yahweh's laws and commands. We've asked him to repent, and he hasn't. When we confronted him with his sin this morning, Father became angry and embittered and left. I don't know when or if he's going to come back. Grandfather has sent several men out to look for him. Ezra is trying to take them back to the place where he saw Father last night and see if we can recover Ada's jewels or find Father. But for now... He's gone."

Eitan fixed his gaze on the ground. He was blinking back tears. Ada gently rubbed his back, trying to soothe him. No one knew what else to say.

"I wish it didn't have to be this way," Eitan finally said, vainly trying to keep his voice steady. "I want him back, too, as I know all of you do." Eitan took a deep breath before continuing, "But now, with Grandfather's blessing, I'll be the leader of the home. I'll be the father, so to speak. I don't want it to be like this. I don't want to be the leader, protector, and provider. But I'll take the responsibility and pray every day for Yahweh's help and strength to fulfill it. I want you to be willing to obey me, just as you have done with our father. I want our family to be united and work together to glorify and worship Yahweh."

No one said a word. Jarah's heart was pounding in her chest. Was she really ready to have Eitan be completely in charge of her?

But wait... Hadn't he been already? Jarah's thoughts drifted back to how kind and loving he had been to everyone the last few weeks. She thought of how he'd saved her life a year ago in Egypt. She thought about his love towards Ada; his strong and resolute character. She knew that she didn't want anyone else to lead them, not even Grandfather.

"I think you're ready to be a leader, Eitan," Jarah ventured to say. "I'd rather you be in charge of me than anyone else," she added, firmly.

"Me, too," Shayna agreed.

"Yes," Lemuel added, nodding his head.

"Me, too," Tirzah whispered.

"And me, too!" Raphael announced.

Tears brimmed in Eitan's eyes. "Thank you. To know I have your support means the world to me," he said, gratefully. "But... There's one other thing I want to talk about." He looked seriously into their faces.

"I'm a follower of Yahweh. As long as I'm alive, I'm going to strive to obey all of His laws and be more in love with Him every single day. If I'm the leader of this household, everyone in this household is going to follow Yahweh. We're going to stand firm in what we believe. We're going to strive for holiness. We're going to get rid of sin in ourselves, and help others get rid of their sins. Most importantly, we're going to dwell on Yahweh's words and treasure them. We're going to put Him first in everything we do. And if we do that, then He'll help us through this transition. He'll give us strength. He'll give us joy. He'll become our heavenly Father. We just have to trust Him and love Him even more than we love ourselves, our family, and our lives." There was a long pause.

"Can you do that? Can you willingly submit to my authority and in so doing submit wholly to Yahweh's authority?"

Jarah knew that Eitan was right. Without Yahweh, where would they be right now? They'd still be in Egypt, in slavery. He had brought them out here. He would bring them to the Promised Land. They just needed to trust Him and remember that they weren't alone. Yahweh's presence was right there, right next to them, on the mountain.

"Yes," she stated emphatically. "I'm His follower. I'll follow you as you follow Him."

Eitan turned to look at her. Delight and joy shown in his eyes. That delight and joy seemed to seep into her heart and soul.

Yes, I'm a follower of Yahweh. I'll do whatever He tells me to do.

ה

In the late evening sunlight, Jarah stole out of the tent and into the desert to give vent to her tears and emotions. Her mind was numb. She couldn't believe what had happened today. She knew that she had made a commitment to Yahweh and to Eitan and that she was going to keep that commitment, no matter what the cost. Through a rain of tears, Jarah attempted to sing the words to a song she had been forming in her mind for several days now. It seemed to fit perfectly, but her voice was shaking and trembling so much that it was hard to sing. In vain she choked down her sobs and surrendered her heart and her voice to Yahweh.

"Yahweh, I'm searching for you, looking for the way.
I don't know what You're doing here or what You want to say.

I don't know what You're telling me or what You want me to do.
But I will keep on going, and keep on following You.

"I will not fear the dark;
I will not fear the storm;
I will trust You as you keep me safe and warm.

"Yahweh, please show me what Your plans are for me.
Show me the girl You want me to be.
Yahweh, please guide me in the way that You have planned.
Guide me with Your sovereign, big, strong hand.

"I will walk by faith and not by sight.
Not by power, not by might,
But by Your Spirit I will go,
Until You tell me no.
I will follow You and trust Your holy name,
Until You bring me safely home again,
Bring me safely home again.
Safely home… Again."

Jarah buried her head in her knees, sobbing and praying. She finally made herself look up at the mountain, up at the pillar of cloud, up at the place where Moses was talking to Yahweh. It was Yahweh that she had to look to for answers now.

"Just trust," she whispered to herself. "Walk in faith. Yahweh's right there with you. He'll never leave you or forsake you. Just trust that even when He leads you to places that are rough and hard and you think you're at the end of your strength, there's His light at the other side. He'll see you through anything and everything." And as Jarah looked up at the cloud that had led them and was the constant reminder of Yahweh's presence, she knew that what she said was true. Yahweh was with them… Always.

"I'm following you, Yahweh," Jarah told the cloud, choking back her sobs. "I'm following you. Please accept me as Your child and bring me home—to Your Promised Land."

THE END

RESEARCH

T his research section is going to be very different from the first book. While the last book was based in Ancient Egypt and filled with so much Egyptian culture, we're not in Egypt anymore. We're in the desert! There are not many historical records, at least not yet. So what I'm going to do is go chapter by chapter, give you the Biblical passages and my research on them, and then fill in everything I've learned historically about this time period. I hope that you enjoy learning about it as much as I have and are inspired to go dive more deeply into the Bible and into history!

CHAPTER 1: "THE CLIFFS"
Exodus 12:37-41, Exodus 13:17-22, Exodus 14:1-4

In Exodus 12, we see the Israelites actually leaving Egypt. But it also gives us some of the details for the start of the journey to Mount Sinai and then ultimately to the Promised Land. It says that the Israelites left from Rameses and all met together in Succoth, which is just outside of Goshen and close to the Sinai Peninsula. It says that about 600,000 men, not even counting women and children, met there and headed out from that location. It also says that a "mixed multitude" went out with the Israelites, leading me to believe that many believing Egyptians, and possibly many non-believing Egyptians, left with the Israelites and made their home in the Israelites' midst. I'll expound on this idea later. Exodus 12 also says that on the very day that the Israelites had been in captivity for 430 years, they left Egypt. How amazing is that?

Exodus 13 talks about how God lead the Israelites in a pillar of cloud and a pillar of fire. It also talks about why the Israelites took a longer way through the desert instead of just skirting up the coast to the Promised Land. It says that God knew that the Israelites would be scared and intimidated by battle with the Philistines and that He was going to lead them around the land of Philistia and towards the Red Sea.

Exodus 14 gives us some information about where the Israelites set up camp on the Red Sea. The Bible refers to a place called Pi-hahiroth, between Migdol and the sea. I watched this amazing documentary called "The Exodus Revealed: The Search to find the Red Sea Crossing." Find out more about it at www.acryfromegypt.com/asasinfo

There is a certain beach that is huge, over five miles long, that could have easily held over a million people. It says in Exodus 14 that the Israelites had to turn back to get to that camp, so it was probably off the main road. This supposed beach called Pi-hahiroth is at the end of a long, dry river bed, which would have made a perfect walking path right from the main trading route which the Israelites were probably traveling towards Midian. Moses would have known about this route from Egypt through the Sinai Peninsula to what is now Saudi Arabia, from his experience fleeing Egypt for his life.

In Exodus 14:3, God is giving Moses instructions about where to travel and He says that Pharaoh will say, "The wilderness has shut them in." This supposed beach of Pi-hahiroth is surrounded by massive cliffs on either side, the Red Sea in front of them, and the dry river bed behind them. Since we know that the Egyptians gave chase to the Israelites and were descending down upon them, they would have filled and blocked off the dry river bed, meaning that the Israelites were trapped on this beach with no way of escape.

Chapter 2: "Lost"
Exodus 14:5-20

I quoted many of the exact verses from Exodus 14 as the Israelites are panic-stricken and yelling at Moses to save them. We see that the entire Egyptian army overtook the Israelites, but God moved the pillar of cloud between the Israelites and the Egyptians so that they wouldn't see each other. Moses says that the Lord will fight for them while they keep silent, and that's just what happens as God causes a strong east wind to rise up in the darkness of the night.

CHAPTER 3: "THE RED SEA"
Exodus 14:21-31, Exodus 15:1-21

Most of my research about finding the Red Sea crossing is taken from the DVD "The Exodus Revealed: The Search to find the Red Sea Crossing." In the map that you'll find in the front of this book, you'll notice that I have marked the Israelites' path not going down through Egypt and through the Gulf of Suez, but instead following the trading route across the Sinai Peninsula, to this beach, and across the Gulf of Aqaba. You may wonder why, because in all of the most common and popular maps it shows the Israelites crossing the Gulf of Suez and finding Mount Sinai in the Sinai Peninsula. (We'll go into why I believe that the supposed Mount Sinai in the Sinai Peninsula is not the right Mount Sinai in later chapters.) Well, after extensive research and reading of other people's research, there is no plausible crossing site in the Gulf of Suez. The gulf is very rocky and steep, and plummets down into great canyons. It would be next to impossible to get all of the Israelites, their wagons, and their animals up and down the gorges at the bottom of the gulf. Also, in Exodus 13 is says that the Israelites were brought "out of Egypt." Well, the Gulf of Suez is still in Egypt! So that also doesn't make sense.

Many people think that another possibility is that God dried up the bitter lakes that are right outside of Goshen. However, the lakes aren't so big that the Israelites couldn't have found a way around. They also aren't very deep, usually around 4 feet in depth, which means that the Israelites and Egyptians could really have walked across and it wouldn't have been possible for all of the Egyptian army to be crushed and drowned by the walls of water collapsing on them.

So that leaves us with the Gulf of Aqaba. My research has already explained to you the most likely site for the beach where the Israelites camped according to the Biblical account. But there's also another reason why that beach seems the most likely. The Gulf of Aqaba is much like the Gulf of Suez, very deep and rocky, which would've made it terribly hard to cross. But it just so happens (though we know that nothing that God does is an accident!) that from this beach of Pi-hahiroth all the way across the Gulf of Aqaba that there is a sort of land bridge under the water. It's very flat and sandy, with no rocks to speak of, and gradually goes down and back up again, which would make it easy for wagons, people, and animals to cross right through the Red Sea! There are sharp drop-offs on either side of this land bridge. This is also one of the narrowest points across in the Gulf of Aqaba, about five to ten miles across. How cool is that?

But that's not the only thing. Scientists have discovered very strange and abnormal coral growths that seemed to have just been placed on the sandy floor of this land bridge. There's no huge coral growth on this land bridge, and so these random little dots of coral spread out all over the place don't make much sense. At least, they don't make much sense until you put a metal detector to it and take images and pictures and realize that a lot of these weird coral shapes seem to be encasing chariots, chariot wheels, and chariot shafts! There is even one golden wheel that isn't covered in coral yet! The scientists have found wheels with 4 spokes and wheels with 6 spokes, which point back to the 18th dynasty in Egypt (which matches with many other Biblical dates) when the 4 spoke wheels were slowly being exchanged for 6 spoke wheels. Isn't that amazing?

Can't you tell that I love research?

Chapter 4: "What Happened to Lemuel?"
Exodus 15:22

In this chapter we see the Israelites leaving the Red Sea and heading into the desert. We also see that their water supplies are decreasing.

The Israelites are now in the Arabian Peninsula, which is modern day Saudi Arabia. It is very barren, very warm in summer, and full of mountains, sand, and desert. It's not a fun place to visit. Where the Israelites passed, the land is mountainous and there's little water or food or vegetation. At the season of the story, the temperatures might not be too bad (about 70 to 90 degrees Fahrenheit), but it only gets worse. The mountains, cliffs, and desert scenery are awe-inspiring, but I can understand why the Israelites started complaining.

You can find more history of Saudi Arabia and find out more about the climate and landscape at www.acryfromegypt.com/asasinfo.

Chapter 5: "Marah"
Exodus 15:23-27

Here we see that the Israelites have run out of water a few days into traveling from the Red Sea and God performs the miracle of turning bitter water to sweet when Moses throws a tree into the stream. Continue following the Israelites' path using the map in the book.

Chapter 6: "Celebrations"

In this chapter we learn about two different Jewish traditions, the celebration of a betrothal and a birthday celebration.

The betrothal ceremony is more binding than an engagement. The betrothal means that the young man and the young woman are committed to each other for life. They were still to live in their parents houses and not have any sort of physical relationship, but in all other ways the young woman was to treat the young man as her husband and he was to treat her as his wife. I guess it's best described in our terms as a "pre-wedding." They're basically married, but not quite yet!

Go to www.acryfromegypt.com/asasinfo for a link that talks about the Jewish wedding and betrothal customs, and links them back to the preparation for Christ's return to earth one day. It's really amazing!

There's not a lot of information about celebrating birthdays of Hebrew children. It seems that much of the form of the celebration depends on the time in history or the age that the person is turning. The bar mitzvah or bat mitzvah is the birthday celebration of most importance, because that is when the girl or boy comes of age and is treated like a woman or a man. From different research that I've done, special little things, like gifts or special meals, were used to celebrate a child's birthday, but it was never a huge production like it is for many of us today. Over the years Jewish people have also tried to use their birthday as a day of reflection on what God has done in their lives. Many will use this day to do good for the poor or others in their community. Since Jarah and her family were traveling in the middle of the desert, they didn't have a huge surplus of things to give away to the poor, or lots of gifts to give to Jarah. It was a simple day of fun and celebration for the whole family.

You can read more about Jewish birthday celebrations and customs at www.acryfromegypt.com/asasinfo.

Chapter 7: "What Is It?"
Exodus 16:1-36

In this chapter we see the amazing miracle of God feeding His people with meat and manna. God not only made this food miraculously appear, but everyone had just enough food to eat. There wasn't too much or too little. God always provides for His children! And that includes us, too!

One thing that I've studied is how often the Israelites got meat. In verse 35 it says that the Israelites ate manna for 40 years until they came into the Promised Land, but it sounds like quail was only provided from time to time. The Bible mentions the provision of quail on just two occasions (in Exodus 16 and Numbers 11). I personally think that God didn't provide quail for them every evening, but that He provided meat for them infrequently throughout their time of wandering. While I wouldn't die on that hill, I *would* die on the hill that God provided manna for them every morning, as described in Exodus 16:35.

Chapter 8: "An Unexpected Enemy"
Exodus 17:8-9, Deuteronomy 25:17-19, 1 Samuel 15:2, Exodus 17:1-7

Now you're probably thinking, "Wait! Didn't you just switch the order around of Exodus 17? Mistake!" Actually... It's not a mistake! Let me explain.

You probably noticed in this chapter that there was a lot of ambushing done by the Amalekites. In Exodus 17 it doesn't say anything about that except for this verse:

Exodus 17:8, "Then Amalek came and fought against Israel at Rephidim."

So here it shows that Amalek initiated the battle, or at least started things off, and then Joshua led Israel into battle.

So what about all the ambushes?

In Deuteronomy 25:17-19 (and in a similar passage in 1 Samuel 15:2) we find this revealing information:

> "Remember what Amalek did to you along the way when you came out from Egypt, how he met you along the way and attacked among you all the stragglers at your rear when you were faint and weary; and he did not fear God. Therefore it shall come about when the LORD your God has give you rest from all your surrounding enemies, in the land which the LORD your God gives you as an inheritance to possess, you shall blot out the memory of Amalek from under heaven; you must not forget."

Ah! So there *were* ambushes and attacks by the Amalekites. They were cowardly, cruel, and they attacked the people of the Most High God.

The actual ambush sequences are purely fictional. Knowing a little bit about the Amalekite's character from that passage in Deuteronomy (and other places where the Amalekites are mentioned in the Bible) and how they were very cowardly in their fighting tactics, it seems as though they would attack from the rear frequently, trying to kill off as many as they could and drive the Israelites into confusion.

You can read more about the Amalekites' battles and conflict with the Israelites at www.acryfromegypt.com/asasinfo.

CHAPTER 9: "SORROW"

This chapter takes place in between the day of the ambush and the day of the battle. We show the families grieving for those that they have lost, and also get a little more insight onto the issues of betrothal.

When Rishon tells Shayna that he's not going to go through and have the betrothal, he is not breaking any commands or rules. He and Shayna have not been formally betrothed, though an arrangement did take place. If they were betrothed and Rishon wanted to break it off, it would've been the same as getting a divorce. (See the research in chapter 6.) Since they aren't betrothed, the break-off is clean and there should be no other ramifications if each decides to pursue another relationship.

CHAPTER 10: "THE ISRAELITES' FIRST BATTLE"
Exodus 17:10-16

This battle is purely fictional, but after studying this Biblical account and others this is what I believe *could* have happened. We know that whenever Moses raised his hands God gave victory to the Israelites. We know that Joshua and the Israelites overwhelmed Amalek and fought against him until sunset, sending the Amalekites back to their land. We know that people did die, unlike some of the battles in the book of Joshua where God granted His people supernatural protection. We know that God was protecting and guiding His people, but sometimes bad things were allowed to happen to them in order that they might draw closer to Him.

Very little is known about the Amalekites outside of the Biblical account. It doesn't seem like many records were kept of their ways and of their doings. All we know is that they were a nomadic people. Yes, they had cities and villages and towns, but it seems as though they spent much their time hunting and riding their horses as well as farming.

We know that horses were used often in combat during this time. It's probable that the Amalekites made great use of the composite bow in these battles while they were riding horses and while they were on the ground. (See www.acryfromegypt.com/asasinfo for more.)

On that same page, I'm including a link about the land and the costumes of people in Ancient Mesopotamia. While the Amalekites aren't directly from Mesopotamia (though some of that land was probably included in their domain), this gives great insight into how the Amalekites probably lived and fought. For example, the soldiers with more nobility were the ones with the horses and the bronze armor. The ones with less nobility were archers and slingers and probably wore protective leather instead of bronze. You can read more about my findings there.

CHAPTER 11: "TROUBLE"
Exodus 18

In this chapter, Moses' father-in-law, Jethro, comes to visit Moses while the Israelites are in the territory of Midian. We see that Moses is having a hard time keeping up with the complaints of the people, and Jethro encourages Moses to pick leaders in the tribe to help keep order and peace. Sethur, Jarah's grandfather, is picked as one of the leaders of one thousand families!

I'm going to give a little bit of a spoiler here for my third book. Sethur is actually a Biblical character! From the little information we know of him (Number 13:13) we know that he is a respected leader in the tribe of Asher, and probably a good fighter, too! You'll learn more about him in book 3.

CHAPTER 12: "THE MOUNTAIN OF GOD"
Exodus 19-24

This passage contains the laws given to the Israelites and Moses, including the Ten Commandments. I didn't include every single section from these chapters because there are parts that seem to be directed at Moses alone, or parts that were directed to the elders of the tribes alone, and parts that were directed to all of the Israelite nation. The parts that I believe were directed to the entire nation of Hebrews have been put into this book.

I also tried to bring out the fact that God is the same yesterday, today, and forever! Many people say that the God of the Old Testament is very different from the God of the New Testament. This is not true! God could have killed the Israelites at any time for their disobedience, but He didn't! He loved them and provided for them. Yes, He asked for sacrifices of animals, but those sacrifices told the Israelites and us today that an ultimate sacrifice was needed—the sacrifice of Jesus Christ to pay the punishment for our sins. God never changes. He loves us just as much as He loved the Israelites back then, and He promises to be merciful and gracious to His people.

CHAPTER 13: "COURAGE AND COWARDICE"
Exodus 31:1-5, 6, Exodus 32:1-6

There are many historical and Biblical things to discuss in this chapter. The first one is the incident with the snake. Jarah seems to always be getting into mishaps with snakes, doesn't she? I had a lot of fun looking up the different types of snakes in Saudi Arabia. I picked a Horned Viper as it was very cool and is venomous. I would be scared running into one of these! If you want to know about that and other species of snakes that can be found in Saudi Arabia, go to www.acryfromegypt.com/asasinfo!

In the chapter, we also formerly introduce Hur and Hur's son, Uri, and Hur's grandson, Bezalel. In Exodus 31 God "calls by name" Bezalel, the grandson of Hur, as an incredibly skilled workman to work with wood and metals and make the beautiful articles of service for the tabernacle. It also says in verse 6 that God has given many people skill to do the work for His tabernacle. So I believe that people like Bezalel, Uri, Hur, and others were in charge of many men and women who helped form and create and make the different utensils and cloth used for the tabernacle. This seems very plausible, as there is not much of a chance that just a few men could've completed this monumental task in under a year as the Bible says.

There is a Jewish legend surrounding Hur that he was Miriam's husband, meaning that he was Moses and Aaron's brother-in-law. While there is nothing in scripture that would explicitly say that this is the case, up until the incident with the Golden Calf, we see that Hur is often with Moses and Aaron. He helps hold up Moses' hands with Aaron at the battle of the Amalekites (Exo 17:10-12). Moses also leaves Aaron and Hur in charge of the Israelites while he goes up the mountain for 40 days to receive the Ten Commandments (Exo 24:14). Hur was obviously a great and important man, and he was trusted by Moses and was very close to him. So, it's very likely that the legend is true. Why don't we hear about Hur after the time of the Golden Calf? Well, I'll tell you my findings about that in a moment.

There is a good article about Miriam which includes more evidence and explanation about her relationship to Hur at www.acryfromegypt. com/asasinfo.

And that leads us to the scene where the congregation comes against Aaron and demands that he make them an image of a god to go before them to the Promised Land. This passage has always troubled me and made me upset. It seems that Aaron just gave in to them! Aaron! A man so close to God and so close to Moses and seemingly so strong in his faith! Well, on my research on Hur, I found this Jewish legend.

There is a Jewish legend that says that Hur was an incredibly skilled craftsman in metal and wood. This would make sense, as his grandson was chosen to make the instruments of service in the tabernacle. His whole family probably would have had experience in metal working and so forth, and that experience would have been passed down to Bezalel. That's the way things worked in those days. So that part is probably true. The legend continues that the Israelites went to Hur *before* they went to Aaron and demanded that Hur make them an image of a god to lead them. Doubtlessly they thought that Hur would do a good job making this image. The legend says that Hur refused to make this image and disobey Yahweh's instructions. Because he wouldn't do what the other Israelites asked, the legend says that he was murdered. Then, of course, the Israelites went to Aaron and told him to make them an image. Aaron, scared for his life, agreed to do whatever they asked. Wow.

Now, this is not written in the Biblical account. It's just legend. However, this legend seems to tie a lot of things together and makes more sense to me so I think that it could very possibly be true. First of all, Hur is never mentioned after Moses leaves to go up the mountain (Exodus 24:14). Why? He just kind of disappears. Miriam is mentioned again, but Hur is not. If they were married, why is that the case? It makes sense that he either died or something happened to him. Secondly, it gives us more explanation for Aaron caving under the Israelites' demands and not standing strong. If someone else had been murdered for refusing to do what the Israelites' asked, and Aaron was in charge and was trying to keep the peace, it makes more sense that he would have give in and made the Golden Calf.

Again, since this isn't in the Bible, I didn't state it as fact in my book. I hint at the possibility of Hur's death in some of the dialogue in this section of the chapter, and I show that the crowd was violent, which was probably the case either way. But while I think it's what happened, I didn't want to add things to the Bible that aren't there. You can read more about this Jewish legend at <u>www.acryfromegypt.com/asasinfo</u> and come up with your own conclusions. I tend to agree with Josephus's view that Hur was Miriam's husband, not Miriam's son.

Chapter 14: "A New God"
Exodus 32:19-28

In this chapter we see the terrible sin of the Israelites worshipping the Golden Calf. While in the previous chapter you see Eitan and Jarah and others standing strong, many were swayed by the influence of their friends and went off to pay homage to the Golden Calf. Even Jarah is almost convinced to join in the festivities. The argument that "It's not a different god. It's just an image of Yahweh, the true God," would have been very appealing to most of the Israelites. After all, they came from an Egyptian nation where there were symbols of worship everywhere! And don't all of us find it easier to be connected to things that we can see and feel?

As mentioned earlier, there are several reasons to believe that many Egyptians left Egypt and came with the Israelites. First, Exodus 12:38 says that "a mixed company" left Egypt with the Israelites, as I've already talked about in the research section of Chapter 1. Also, in Leviticus 24:10-16, a young man of half Israelite and half Egyptian descent is mentioned. And this whole section with the Golden Calf shows that there were definitely Egyptian customs that were influencing the Israelites. As we discussed in *A Cry From Egypt*, cattle are sacred to the Egyptians. So it makes sense that there was still a large Egyptian influence that resulted in Aaron making a Golden Calf.

CHAPTER 15: "MERCY MIXED WITH JUSTICE"
Exodus 32:30–35, Exodus 34:28

After the people worshipped the Golden Calf, Exodus 32 says that the Lord smote the people with a plague for their sin. We don't know how many people were killed, but I'm sure many with unrepentant hearts suffered the justifiable wrath of Yahweh.

A few days later, Moses goes back up to receive the Ten Commandments and more of Yahweh's laws. You'll find out what happens to him in Book 3! Or you can read through Exodus, Leviticus, Numbers, and Deuteronomy to see for yourself!

In other research in this chapter, the little lullaby that Jarah sings to Ximena is actually a Jewish lullaby! How cool is that? Find out more at www.acryfromegypt.com/asasinfo.

CHAPTER 16: "I WANT FATHER BACK"

In this chapter we witness the wedding of Eitan and Ada! We see that this is very much like a betrothal ceremony, except for the exchange of rings and the breaking of the glass. You can learn more about Jewish weddings in the research section of Chapter 6.

CHAPTER 17: "A FOLLOWER OF YAHWEH"

This chapter is very sad and was very hard for me to write. But in other ways, it was very fun to research. For a long time I'd been thinking of what Jewish gambling would be like. The first suggestion that came up in my research was the "Dreidel." I was thinking, "What? Dreidel?" I'm sure most of you have heard this little song:

"Dreidel dreidel dreidel,
I made it out of clay!
And when it's dry and ready,
The dreidel I shall play!"

I thought it was just a children's song about playing with tops. And while it is in one sense, people used the dreidel, a four-sided top, to gamble.

Modern dreidels have different letters written on each side, and they each give an instruction for the game. If it lands on one side, the player gets nothing. Another side gives the player everything in the "pot." Another side award the player only half the pot. And the final side means to "stay put," or you don't really get to do anything. There's an article with more information linked at www.acryfrom-egypt.com/asasinfo.

While the dreidel itself wasn't linked to Hanukkah until much later, there is evidence of it being played for quite some time. Maybe not with the exact Hebrew letters that they use today, or in the exact ways, but it is still a game used for gambling.

Also, a big thanks for Tori MacDonald who wrote Jarah's song at the end of this chapter! It matched Jarah's story perfectly and closed out the book in a very profound way. Thank you, Tori!

ACKNOWLEDGEMENTS

There are so many people who have helped put this second book together, even more than for Book One of this series! And this book would not be complete without thanking and giving credit to all the amazing people and friends who have supported me through this journey.

First and foremost, all of the credit goes to my Lord and Savior, Jesus Christ. It is only through His inspiration and blessing that I was able to write this book. My story is based completely on His story, and it would be nothing and worthless without Him.

Secondly, I want to thank my family for all of their help with this book. They eagerly read it, discussed it, listened to my crazy ideas, and critiqued and proof-read it many, many times. My dad spent countless hours reading and re-reading my many drafts and helping me find the themes and channeling my creative energy. My mom helped with my proof-reading, is one of my biggest fans, and helped me along this journey by giving me time to write and food to eat. My brothers gave me inspiration and looked forward to learning all about what happened to certain characters, and were generally great siblings to me through this long journey.

Thirdly, my publishers, Hal and Melanie Young with Great Waters Press. They believed in this book and spent countless hours getting it through the whole publishing process. Their invaluable advice, wisdom, and encouragement to me through this journey is something that I will never be able to thank them for sufficiently. Thank you for believing in me and the message of my book!

Fourthly, my illustrator, Mike Slaton. While this time we gave him a lot more time (and I actually improved in my drawing of my little stick figures!), he still worked so, so hard and was incredibly open and did everything I asked, even when I was really, really picky. His art talent continues to grow, and it's amazing how he can turn my little scribblings into incredible works of art. It was a pleasure working with you, Mike! I can't wait to see how much your art work continues to improve over these next few books! You are so talented, and I know that God is going to use you for great things!

I have so many people to thank that helped in so many various areas, and I'm going to address them personally here.

Lindy Meeker, thank you for putting up with me and being my cheerleader. Your encouragement, love, beautiful serving spirit, accountability, editing skills, and friendship have blessed me in so many ways. Thank you for all the time and effort you put into this book!

Naomi Hinds and Ellie Faggion, I am so thankful for your friendship, love, thoughts about this book, and overall general support. I am so blessed to have you as my friends in my life!

Brandon Hall, you are really and truly an incredible guy and such a talented writer and editor. Thank you so much for helping me with Lemuel's character and providing amazing insights into the different characters' emotions. Thank you for putting up with me, and gladly editing and giving your thoughts on so many random sections and chapters. Our brains are so alike that you were able to explain things to me in ways I could understand, and it was so helpful! I don't think I can say thank you enough. Thank you, Deplorable Person!

Sarah Irish, I know that you are constantly praying for me. There have been many days in our friendship where you have listened to me when I was upset and given me the advice to "give to all to God," which is always a constant reminder of who I'm doing this for. I love you!

Patrick Spain, thank you for "pair-writing" with me in the car on the way to Tryon Palace. Your editing was invaluable, as well as your knowledge of battle scenes and helping me come up with realistic situations and heroic lines. :-) Thank you for all of the time and effort you poured into my book over this past summer making it the best that it can be. Thank you for being such a helpful and faithful friend, kind younger brother, and a gentleman, too.

Crystal Hilton, you are such a great critic. You tell me what needs to change, but are also sweet and tell me the good stuff along with the bad so that I never feel downcast or disappointed. You have been a great friend for many years, and I appreciate all of your knowledge on the English language and on the characters in my book.

Elise Allen, thank you for reading my book and giving me great feedback on where things were confusing and needed more explanation. You were a great help to me!

Darian Horvath, you are a great little (but taller!) bro. Thanks for answering all my random questions about how guys would act in life or death situations and for being my "Masculinity Consultant." Thank you for being genuinely interested in my work and my book, and for being willing to not be macho when you answered questions like, "If three guys with guns were attacking a family in a parking lot, what would you do?" I know the guy characters in my story wouldn't be nearly as realistic without your insight and ideas. And thanks for making me laugh on days when everything was tough. You're amazing!

Caleb Johnson, thank you for critiquing my battle sequences over and over again and giving me valuable knowledge about the Amalekites and the Israelites and their battle tactics. And thank you so much for making the map of the route that the Israelites took. As soon as I realized I needed a map, I knew where to go! It looks so good! Thanks for your friendship, prayers, and encouragement to keep pressing on, as well as being my "walking history textbook."

John and Matt Young, thanks for being my "go to" guys with all questions regarding publishing, my story, battle sequences, random ideas, etc. I don't know where I'd be without your help and answering all my annoying questions over Skype. I'm sure there were days that I drove you both crazy, so thank you for letting me drive you crazy and for not losing your cool. John, thank you for typesetting my book and taking time out of your busy life to do it! Matt, thanks for helping edit and being a great encourager and brother in Christ! I'm so thankful for both of you!

Emmy Slaton, you are a sweet gift from God! Thank you for helping your brother and posing for pictures, helping him with ideas for his artwork, and for reading my story and helping me find typos and other errors. I love being able to talk with you about my book and bounce ideas off of you and to know that you love my story so much. I love you! Thank you! And Jenna Slaton—thank you so much for posing for the cover—you did a great job!

Tori MacDonald and Grace Martin, thank you for taking so much time to give me your thoughts on the book and listen to all of my ideas during our carpools to CYT and back. Your edits and comments have really helped me, and it's wonderful to have people "in the know" that can help me with ideas and keep me energized about the book. You are both sweet gifts from God to me! And Tori, thank you so much for writing Jarah's song at the end of the book. Thank you for letting me use your words and your music in my book!

Zachary Atchinson, thank you so much for giving me another guy's perspective on this book and for your thoughts and suggestions for adding more "happier sequences" that made this book a much more enjoyable read. You've been so helpful! Having you and Brandon as my male editors has been a great and encouraging experience. Thank you for all of the time you spent working on this book!

To all the others who've read it in various stages, thank you!

Christiana DiLorenzo
Mark Faggion
Emily Irish
Jack Irish
Bridget Irish
The Irwin Family
The McClanahan Family
Jake Pendleton
Trillian Skinner
Tristany Massengill
Patience Sleep
Charlotte Talbott
Patti, Joel and Micah Williams

COLOPHON

This book is set in 12-point Adobe Caslon Pro with 15-point leading. William Caslon I (1692-1766) was one of the most influential early English printers and type designers, and his eponymous typeface was so beloved by generations of typesetters that it gave rise to the maxim, "When in doubt, use Caslon." Adobe's 1990 digital revival, by Carol Twombly, is one of the most graceful and versatile typefaces available to the modern digital typesetter.

The display faces are Eccentric Standard, Rockwell, and Bitter, an unusual collection of slab serif fonts, a style known on the Continent as "Egyptian" for their unusual, exotic looks, although they bear little actual connection to Egyptian script or type design.

The main text was laid out in Adobe InDesign CS6 with optical margins and glyph extension algorithms applied. Cover painting and illustrations are by Mike Slaton; map of Sinai by Caleb Johnson. External and internal layouts and typesetting are by John Calvin Young.

More Great Character-Building Resources
from Great Waters Press

A Cry From Egypt – If you haven't read Book One in the *The Promised Land* series, don't miss this tale of adventure and excitement set against the backdrop of the mighty works of God in Egypt. Christian Small Publishers Book of the Year. ACryFromEgypt.com

Hero Tales From American History – Written by Theodore Roosevelt to teach character through the stories of America's heroes, we loved it so much we turned it into an audiobook series. We added sound effects because history is way better with cannon fire! RaisingRealMen.com/herotales

Pollyanna – When we first picked up the classic children's book Pollyanna, I just assumed it would be boring and didactic, but I couldn't have been more wrong. We loved it! All of us – boys, girls, young men, mom and dad. We laughed out loud at Pollyanna's antics – and the reactions of the people around her. We became more grateful people. RaisingRealMen.com/pollyanna

Books by Hal & Melanie Young

Raising Real Men, Christian Small Publishers 2011 Book of the Year. RaisingRealMen.com

My Beloved and My Friend: How To Be Married To Your Best Friend Without Changing Spouses. MyBelovedandMyFriend.com

Need a Speaker?

Great Waters Press has national level speakers available on Biblical family life, raising sons, homeschooling, parenting, teens and young adults, and writing and publishing. Write speakers@greatwaterspress.com to receive access to our private event coordinators site.

Social Media

Read Hope's blog ACryFromEgypt.com,
Join her on Facebook facebook.com/hopeauerbooks,
See her on Pinterest pinterest.com/hopefulstories,
And follow her on Twitter! twitter.com/hopefulstories

Made in the USA
Monee, IL
22 October 2020